Angel's Mask

The Phantom Saga

Jessica Mason

Published by Murmuration Books, 2023.

Table of Contents

To my own angel, Heidi.

Foreword

The Phantom of the Opera already existed. He was not, as many may believe, the product of a filmmaker's imagination or a ludicrous fantasy concocted by a love-struck composer. His story has been told again and again for over a hundred years, yet it still captivates all who learn it. The Phantom is an icon that excites our imaginations and stirs our hearts. Perhaps that's because we can all see something of ourselves in the story of an outcast, or because we are thrilled by the mystery and beauty of the dark, or perhaps we are simply helpless to resist a ghost story full of love songs.

So why tell his story again? For the same reason we read the same book until its binding breaks or sing a beloved song until we hear it in our dreams: love. And hope. We never stop looking for something new to discover in the familiar, searching for a mystery yet to be unmasked. And hoping that maybe, this time, it might be different.

Perhaps you know some version of Opera Ghost's love story. Perhaps not. Either way, the story you know will not be the one you read here. Though the melody is the same, we have changed the key, adjusted the harmony, and expanded the orchestration. This is the story as discovered by the author over many years in the Phantom's labyrinth. And while much is different, the spirit remains, if you will pardon the pun.

Yes, the tale of the Opera Ghost already existed, but a new ghost story always waits to be told. The search for Erik and his angel haunts us all and demands reconsideration, like a persistent specter; that is to say...a Phantom.

Prelude

Paris, 1880

No one wanted to go below the third cellar, especially after dark. Not that the hour made a difference, down there. It was easy enough for firemen like Papin to avoid the duty most days; there were no doors or gaslights to check that far below. Besides, who needed to worry about fires with a damn lake beneath? Tonight though, there had been reports again from the furnace attendants of *something* in the shadows. Papin had earned this unenviable job by daring to say that they all should ignore the nonsense. There were always strange things moving in the dark below the Paris Opera. Everyone knew the stories.

The flare of Papin's match in the cold quiet of the underground did little to drive back the gloom. As he lit his lantern with a shaking hand, he cursed each shadow – and his fool mouth for good measure. He shivered as he walked deeper into the maze of silent, gray stone. Less than twenty years these walls had stood, and yet it felt ancient. Lonely. And quiet as the grave, save for the echo of his boots and the rasp of his own breath as he counted his steps. God forbid he lose his way. No one, even the firemen, really knew the deep cellars. There were maps of course, which he had taken care to examine before making his descent, but they were useless when every corridor and stairwell looked the same, like some dungeon out of a fairy tale.

Papin slowed every time he heard something move beyond the protective circle of his lantern's light. Even the scratch of a rat's claws in the black. A sound from a few feet ahead made his heart begin to pound. Rhythmic. Cold. Oh – nothing to be scared of. Simply the drip of water. He relaxed as he came to the alcove cut in the rock, where a small fountain trickled down the wall and through a grate to the black below. A petite statue of the Madonna had been placed, there long ago. This had been on the maps, though he had not thought he was so far. The workers had prayed here when they laid the foundations of the Opera. After that, the communards and their prisoners had knelt here and prayed for their souls. Or so the stories went.

He bent before the virgin as he drew a candle stub from his pocket and lit it from his lantern flame. Funny thing, he thought, crossing himself as he rose, for a fireman to leave an open flame unattended. But it was comforting to look back and see the flickering light – the glow of faith pushing back ever so slightly against the dark of the place that so close to hell. Of course, you didn't need to get to hell to find the dead waiting here, they said.

Papin continued to follow the corridor, glancing back before he turned a corner to see that the light was still there. It was, though not as far off as he had expected. It was so hard to tell distance down here. He descended a flight of steps and swallowed his fear. He was surely close in the fifth cellar now – as deep below the Opera as one could go.

Each step echoed the with stories; stories of fools like him who had gone below and were never seen again, of dark water, flaming skulls floating in the black, and the suffering of men whose bones remained lost in the foundations. He glanced over his shoulder once more, wishing he could still see the light at the virgin's feet, and his heart stopped cold when he did.

The flame was still there, exactly as far behind him as before. Papin turned slowly as he watched the little candle flicker and the shadows around it shudder and dance. The shadows continued to move, drawing closer to the light as Papin's heart began to beat again, harder than ever before in his life. The shadow, for it was *one* shadow that had coalesced out of the blackness, lifted the candle. Papin followed the light with his eyes as it rose, unable to look away. He saw a flash of white in the dark before the flame extinguished.

He opened his mouth to scream when he saw the other lights that remained, but no sound came as he stared in horror at what had to be eyes, glittering like yellow stars. The only sound in the darkness was cold laughter. Perhaps he was going mad, because he could only think that the sound was as beautiful as it was terrifying. It was only a second's thought though. Soon the crash of his footsteps fleeing filled the dark as he ran.

The shadow was too fast. In a heartbeat, it had Papin in its grip. Frozen hands locked around his throat, as the lantern crashed to the ground. The flame flared before guttering into nothing and Papin saw the mask of white around those terrible eyes again. The sound of laughter echoed in Papin's ears as the world washed away and the light of the Phantom's eyes faded into black.

1. Shadows

She had thought the so-called *Palais Garnier* would be more beautiful. Or at least, that the building of her dreams would look more like a palace than a train station. But contrary to her fantasies, the edifice squatting at the end of the *Avenue De L'Opéra* was less like a palace and more like an ornate stone wedding cake, glowering at the carriages, and bustling foot traffic below. She was an Empress in a country that had done away with the title, Christine Daaé mused.

The great copper dome, flanked by winged horses, was a dowager's crown. Filigree and busts adorned her all over, like too many jewels. She wore layers of crests and cherubim, masks of comedy and tragedy, and busts and names of the great and not-so-great composers. Christine was pleased to see her beloved Mozart there, but she wondered if Meyerbeer truly deserved the honor of inclusion. On the top corners above the grand loggia, crowded with columns, stood twin angels, and far above Apollo thrust his lyre to the heavens. Perhaps in the summer sun he would have glittered gold, but against the cold gray of the October sky, he looked dull and distant to Christine's eyes.

"So, there you are," she whispered to herself, stepping into the shadow of the great building. It had been a long journey to get here. The *Gare du Nord* train station was miles from the Opera, and Christine had found herself terribly lost at first among all the streets filled with identical cream-colored buildings. Everyone had been able to point in the right direction though. That was the point of the new Paris that Baron Haussmann had birthed a decade before:

relentless order, sameness, all roads leading to one modern world. Christine did not like it, but at least it was easy to understand. Now she stood among the noise and bustle at the very crossroad of the world.

Christine walked slowly to what she hoped was the main entry. There were so many arches and doors, flanked by frolicking nymphs whose bare stone breasts seemed even more scandalous and ill-considered with the clouds above threatening rain. There had to be a way in, past the iron gates. Despite her weariness and doubt, Christine could not help but feel a thrill.

There were days when Christine thought of her spirit like a garden. It was abandoned long ago and now grew thin and wild, but hope sprang up like a weed, no matter what she did to stop it. Even now filthy from days of traveling and carrying all she owned in a threadbare satchel, she could not help it. The single open gate came into view and Christine stepped through to see the main doors. A man with sallow skin and spectacles sat at a podium beside the door, sniffling.

"Excuse me, Monsieur—"

"Not open," the attendant snapped. Christine glanced to the open door beside him, ornate tile just visible on the floor inside.

"Is the National Academy of Music not a public building?"

The man looked at her like a stray animal that had somehow gained the power of speech. "Not open *to beggars*."

At least blushing made her warmer. Christine swallowed and pushed on. "I wished to enquire about auditions."

"You think you can just walk into the premiere opera house in the world and *audition*?" His laugh was not promising.

"Are they not looking for choristers? Even just people to fill the stage?" Christine stammered even as the man's frown soured. "I need work and—"

"Try in the *Pigalle*. I'm sure you'll find openings there." Christine's blush deepened. She knew of Paris's infamous red-light district.

"Monsieur, I'm not—"

"Then go around and see if they want help shoveling shit in the stables," the man snapped just as thunder rumbled and the rain began to fall. "And get out of here before I call a gendarme."

Christine hurried away, determined to at least spare herself the embarrassment of being removed by force. Cheeks burning, the deluge that soaked her was the final indignity. A different girl would have started to cry. But for her, disappointment was so familiar that it was comforting. The joke about the stables had been the worst, she thought, adjusting her soggy shawl. Even the enormous Paris Opera didn't have *stables*.

Christine followed the perimeter of the massive building, the stone slick and dark from the storm. At the least she might find a dry place to wait out the rain. She sighed again at the thought. What would she do when the storm passed? Try again? What was her plan when they turned her away a second time or a third? Where else could she possibly go in this sprawling, indifferent city full of strangers?

The few others she saw braving the storm scurried from building to building, tucked under umbrellas or papers, trying in vain to outrun the drops. She was the only one just walking.

The Opera Ghost enjoyed the scent of rain. It mixed with the earthier smell of the stables into something that reminded him of distant, wild places far from the chaos of the city or the murky dark beneath it. César liked it too, if the way the white gelding snorted and shook his mane was any indication.

"Easy, my friend, just an autumn storm," the Ghost whispered, petting the animal's flank before guiding him back into his stall. César's neighbor, a bay mare, whinnied in greeting as the shade retreated back into the shadows. It wouldn't be too long before others would notice the Andalusian's return.

On cue, the head groom of the Opera rushed to César, breathing exactly as hard as a man who had been passed out drunk in a bale of hay until three minutes ago might. Indeed, Jean-Paul Lachenal's affection for wine and sleep, and general distaste for work, was what made borrowing César so easy.

"Damn it all, there you are!" Lachenal exclaimed as he examined his prize steed. His face was ruddy around his grey moustache, but his hands were steady as he made his inspection. "It's nearly noon! I have told you: no more excursions during the day! What if someone important had happened by? What would I have told them? That you were off with some phantom?"

The phantom in question smiled in the shadows. Half the fun of taking César for a ride was Lachenal's fits when he was returned. Today he appeared primed for a truly amusing performance.

"Maybe that would have been the best," Lachenal went on. "If that cursed *thing* keeps making off with you, maybe the management should know. They can get me some damn locks for my stable doors!" he bellowed into the shadows.

"Now, where would the fun be in that?" the Phantom spoke, smooth as night. The color fled from Lachenal's face, and the man crossed himself.

"Ah, Monsieur! I didn't know you were still here!" the groom yelped.

"I'm always here," the Ghost replied, his voice right at Lachenal's ear, making the man turn as if he expected to see someone standing behind him. César whinnied in agreement. "I'm sure you would never mean to insult or question me. Would you, Jean-Paul?"

"Of course, Monsieur! Didn't mean a word!" Lachenal croaked, spinning like a lethargic top.

"You called me a *thing*." It was far from the worst insult the Ghost had endured, but he couldn't let such disrespect stand.

"Oh, Monsieur, you know I would never insult *you*," Lachenal said, gulping. The Ghost knew something bold and foolish was coming next. "It – it's just that you keep taking my damn horses without warning!" Lachenal finally stood still and focused on a point far from where the shade he was addressing actually lurked.

"Perhaps you would prefer to work elsewhere?" the Phantom taunted, and his prey began to shake. The Phantom laughed.

"Oh no!" Lachenal blubbered. "You, Monsieur, keep this work so – so exciting! I would never want to leave your employ. I'll do anything to show you—"

"Hello?"

It was a woman's voice that startled Lachenal out of his begging. It surprised the Ghost as well. They both turned their gaze to the soaking vagrant shivering in the cover of the stable doors, wide eyes attempting to make out the shadows and the idiot within them.

"Mademoiselle?" Lachenal asked.

"I'm sorry, I was just looking for a place to wait out the storm," the girl replied.

"Oh, well. Hm." Lachenal stared at the girl. So did the Ghost. She looked small and sad with the pouring rain behind her, little more than a leaf blown in by the storm.

"Invite her in, you buffoon," the Phantom ordered, and Lachenal jumped.

"Yes, of course, come in!" Lachenal said, too loudly. The girl stepped into the stables with understandable apprehension in her face.

"I didn't mean to interrupt." The girl looked around, past Lachenal to the horses and empty space around him. "Oh. Weren't you talking to someone?"

"Just to the horses." The girl blinked. "They get lonely," Lachenal added. The Ghost restrained a chuckle.

"I can't believe there's really a stable here," the girl muttered after a pause.

"Where else would we keep the Opera's brightest stars?" Lachenal puffed with pride, giving a slight bow, and gesturing to the half-dozen stalls.

"They perform?" The girl came closer, and the Ghost could see her better. Her clothes were old and dirty, and overall, she was wholly unremarkable. Dark hair, perhaps slightly taller than most if she didn't slouch. She appeared to be in her twenties, but her eyes were sad and made her look older. She wasn't ugly, not at all; she might even have been pretty, past the grime. But something prevented her from being beautiful, like looking at a stained-glass window at night.

"César here gets a louder ovation than the tenor when he appears in *Le Prophète*," Lachenal explained with a grin. He gave the girl a nod as approached the white horse, indicating it was alright to touch him. The girl presented her hand to be sniffed before receiving César's approving huff and then caressed the animal's snout.

"It's nice to know you, César," she said. "I've never met so famous a performer before. I hope I can see you on stage someday."

"There's a performance tomorrow," Lachenal piped up. "Alas, *Faust* has no horses, despite my suggestions for where they could be included."

"The man at the front made it quite clear I wasn't welcome during the day, so I doubt I'd be allowed in for a performance. Even if I could afford a ticket." She said it with a dry, brittle tone.

"Why were you trying to get in front?" The Ghost was glad Lachenal asked on his own.

"Oh. I was hoping that…I mean, I was looking for…" She obviously didn't want to sound like a beggar, which was useless, since she certainly looked like one. "I need work," she managed with a defeated sigh.

"Well, there are all sorts of places around that need a hand, the hotel across the *Place De L'Opéra* might need maids." Lachenal truly was trying to be kind, but the Ghost saw the way the girl's face fell. Perhaps even the glimmer of a tear in her eye.

"She wants to work here, you moron," the Ghost whispered.

"Why would she want—" Lachenal stopped himself at the girl's fresh look of confusion. "Why, uh, why do *you* want to work here of all places?"

"I love music," she said with a shrug. "I've dreamed about coming here for a long time." It wasn't the whole truth, the Ghost could tell that, but it wasn't a lie either. She said it with the tired sort of affection one has for the only thing left in your life that brings you joy.

"Take her to Grelot, you imbecile." The Ghost surprised himself with the order. Perhaps the rain had him feeling charitable. And he did have a certain affection for lost and abandoned things. "Earn my goodwill this way. Don't let her leave without a job."

"In costumes?" Lachenal said, and the girl once again stared at him as if his hair was on fire. "I mean yes! The costumers! Louise always needs warm bodies!" Lachenal exclaimed too enthusiastically. "Come on."

"What?" the girl asked.

"Follow me, I *promise* I'll get you set up nicely." He said it too loudly, to make sure the Ghost heard.

"I – *what*?" The girl was rightfully suspicious and moved slowly to follow Lachenal as he fetched his keys. "You're too kind, Monsieur. I don't even know your name and I—"

"Jean-Paul Lachenal," he grinned. "And you are?"

"Christine. Christine Daaé."

"Come on, Christine, it's your lucky day," Lachenal grinned and led her out of the stable.

The Ghost remained, considering his own actions. He wondered whether (if by some miracle Lachenal could convince Louise to take in the girl) the miserable creature would even survive a day in the *Palais Garnier*. Another wounded stray, looking for a place to belong. The Opera was already full of them, including the very ghost that had saved her on a whim. It was easy to pity her, with her dirty clothes and eyes that might have been gentle in another life.

The stories about him were usually so dark, it made things interesting if he mixed in some charity once in a while. It kept his subjects on their toes and earned loyalty where he needed it. Not that a damp vagabond could be of much use. But still, sometimes it was...pleasant to indulge in human kindness. Though it had been a while since he'd counted himself human. Well, just like the rain, it would pass. But perhaps the girl would remain.

"Good luck, Christine Daaé," the Ghost whispered into the dark. "Don't disappoint me."

Christine hurried after the mad groom, ready to wake from the dream at any moment. But it was real because she was dry and warm and finally inside the Paris Opera House. It had been a long while since she had felt anything akin to wonder, but it edged into her heart as Jean-Paul escorted her through the dim halls. The walls were painted with the lower half a deep maroon and the top a pinkish yellow; the lighter color reflected the smoky gaslight while the deep red magnified the ever-present shadows. The air was ripe with the musty, wonderful smell only theaters had.

Somewhere deep in the theater, they entered a large chamber. Bright gaslights illuminated the huge, glittering room stuffed with every color Christine had ever dreamed of and even some she hadn't. Exquisite tutus, sparkling gowns, dark robes, and monsters' faces hung to the rafters, and the workshop buzzed with female voices gossiping and laughing as they worked at long tables. In her drab, wet clothes Christine was just a smudge on the otherwise beautiful scene. She shrank when she noticed the imposing, middle-aged woman stalking towards them, her stern face as red as her russet hair.

"What in God's name are you doing here, Jean-Paul! You'll get your muck all over my workroom!" the woman barked.

"Hello, Louise, my darling," Jean-Paul sputtered. "You look lovely today!"

"I am *not* refitting another costume for a horse, you – what is this?" Louise turned her blistering gaze to Christine, who withered more.

"This is, uh, a new friend, and she's looking for work and I thought that you might be in the market for a new, uh, what's the word again? With the mending and cutting and—"

"I wouldn't take on a new girl off the street on the word of a stable hand."

"Chief groom!"

"Especially not one that looks like she just rolled out of the workhouse."

"It was a train, actually," Christine muttered.

Louise's eyebrows rose high. "Or one without manners." She began to turn away and Christine sighed. At least she could say she had been inside the Opera.

"Louise, please!" Jean-Paul called out, oddly urgent as he caught Louise by the elbow. "Think of this as a favor, not for me but in honor our...mutual departed friend," Jean-Paul said slowly, looking directly into Louise's eyes. It had to mean something because Louise's face went pale. "Besides, woman, she's got nothing in the world but some dream of working here. You can't deny her that."

Christine tried not to squirm as Louise looked her over down with a critical eye. "Can you sew?"

"I know the general theory." Louise did not seem convinced. "I work hard and I'm willing to learn."

"Do you scare easy?"

Christine squinted, lost again. "Excuse me?"

"Are you easily frightened? Superstitious?"

"No, I don't. I mean, I'm not."

Louise gave Jean-Paul a long, meaningful look and finally heaved a sigh. "Fine, *fine*. We'll set you to launder and mend," she said. "I suppose you can't do too much harm there." Jean-Paul gave a laugh of triumph. "And *you* can leave."

"Excellent! Thank you, darling Louise, thank you!" Jean-Paul gave Christine a grin and a wink then sauntered away, a new spring in his step.

"Come on then, girl," Louise grumbled. Christine turned back to the older woman, who was gesturing for her to follow. She walked with sure, deliberate strides as Christine scurried after her to a small side room filled with decidedly unglamorous coats and shawls. "Leave your things here. What did you say your name was?"

"Christine."

"Good, we don't have any Christines. There was one a few months back but, well, she *was* superstitious." The overwhelmed new employee dropped her bag and shawl and followed Louise back into the main room. "You can work the laundry for the rest of the afternoon, won't hurt since you're already wet and you look like you could use some warming up. Patrice! Take our new girl back to help with the wash. Follow her. Good luck."

Christine was suddenly following a ruddy-faced woman towards a door from which steam was spewing.

"Dig in," Patrice ordered cheerfully as they entered. Christine was confronted by a heap of clothes as tall as her, piled on one side of the room and a huge copper tub filled with steaming, soapy water on the other. Two other older women were moving back and forth from the clothes to the water, their faces shining from the heat. Christine tentatively began to pull garments from a pile. Louise had been right: it was nice to be warm again.

The day passed quickly. No one paid Christine much mind. She sensed eyes watching her on and off, but anytime she looked up, the women skillfully hid their stares. In a few hours, she felt she had mastered the finer points of laundering the extravagant costumes of ballerinas and divas. She had been given her orders or instructions only when she did something blatantly wrong, so she had not been obligated to speak much, which was a relief. She always preferred to stay quiet as long as possible, delaying the inevitable moment she would be exposed as "odd" or "curious" or some other polite expression for "strange."

In time the room began to empty, the other workers prompted by some cue Christine had missed, until Christine was the last one left, scrubbing the delicate tule of a white tutu. Just as she was wondering what to do now, a crash startled her. She rushed to the hall to find the source. A woman about her age was there, swearing quietly over a basket of ballet slippers. She had skin the color of strong coffee with milk and jet hair thick with tight curls. Another woman walked directly past her and the mess, sending the girl a sneer.

"Let me help," Christine said, bending to gather the slippers back into the basket.

"It was a damn rat that spooked me! Ran right past my foot and I thought it was—" the other woman looked up, her deep chestnut eyes catching Christine's. "You're new."

"I started this afternoon," Christine confirmed, placing a final slipper in the girl's basket.

"Welcome to the Paris Opera then. Julianne Bonet." She held out her hand, which Christine shook timidly.

"Christine Daaé. I'm sorry, my hands are all wet and…shriveled." At least the hours in the laundry had left them clean.

"You get used to it," Julianne shrugged. "The rats, less so."

"I'll take your word for it."

"Thank you, by the way, for helping," Julianne nodded towards the slippers, and stood straight. "Everyone else gets in such a hurry to leave before dark. I guess I can't blame them."

Christine didn't know what to make of that comment, even though Julianne looked like she was waiting to be asked about it, dark eyes sparkling as they looked over Christine. "Could you tell me, when do we get paid?"

It was obviously not the question Julianne was expecting. "Oh, not until the end of the month."

Christine's stomach would have fallen had it not been so empty. "That's almost two weeks."

"You do get extra in cash if you stay late after the performances, and there's one tomorrow."

Christine braced herself. She hated begging but she had to ask. "Is there any way to get an advance?" Now Julianne looked like she might laugh. "I just need something to pay for a room for a few nights. All my money went to the train ticket to get to Paris and—"

"Let me guess, you don't have anything for food either?"

"Not much."

Julianne looked at her with a mix of curiosity and pity. "Follow me," she sighed, leading Christine to the now-empty cloakroom. "I can't spare money, but – here." Julianne pulled a package from her own bag and handed it to Christine. Christine pushed away the oily brown paper to reveal a baguette.

"Thank you, thank you so much," Christine breathed, staring lovingly at the freshest meal she'd seen in days.

"As for a place to stay..." Julianne glanced around the dim room. "Do you scare easy?"

"You're the second person that's asked me that today." Christine was used to the particular type of madness of musicians and theater folk, but the denizens of the Opera were clearly a peculiar breed. "But the answer is no, I'm not afraid of much."

"We'll see." Julianne strode out of the costume room with Christine trailing her, entirely confused again. She led them up several flights of stairs and then down another dark, two-toned hall that looked suspiciously like all the other poorly-lit halls Christine had seen that day, and finally to a door. The room Julianne revealed was illuminated only by the dim orange glow of the gaslights being lit outside the window as the last traces of day faded.

"No one comes here much, it's too far from the workshops and the salons, but not close to the stage. If you stay put, you should be fine for the night."

Christine looked around the cluttered room: it was full of broken and disassembled musical instruments, mostly old, dusty pianos, and furniture covered with sheets. "I can sleep here?"

"You can try," Julianne replied. "Just don't wander about."

"Will I get caught?" Christine didn't relish the thought of losing this job or trading in a storeroom for a jail cell.

"Oh, no. Like I said, no one stays here past dark when there's no performance. They, uh..." Julianne bit her lip as Christine's curiosity flared again. What on earth were people so afraid of here? "If you make it through the night, I'll tell you then."

"*If?*"

"Oh, you'll be fine. Just stay in the light." Julianne handed her a candle and matches then looked around the room, giving Christine the impression that she expected to find someone else there. "Good night and good luck."

And in with a final wink, Julianne was gone back down the hall.

Christine clutched the candle in her hand, telling herself she was as brave as she'd claimed. She didn't fear the dark, but even so, a shiver ran up her spine. The building around her was eerily silent now that it was empty. And yet Christine still felt the prickle on the back of her neck of being watched.

Steadfastly ignoring the feeling, Christine stepped into the room, taking her place among the other abandoned things hidden in the dark of the Opera. It was exactly where she belonged: among the instruments that, like her, would never make music again and the other silent shadows.

The girl was still in his opera. The Ghost had expected Louise to take her in (the costume mistress had a soft heart despite her bravado, after all) but he had not expected the urchin to repay his kindness by trespassing in his realm after dark. Yes, he knew he shouldn't blame her *per se*. It had been the dresser, Bonet, who had decided to test the limits of the Phantom's charity. This *Christine* didn't know her crime. But, alas, that didn't mean she would survive without punishment. He did have a reputation to uphold.

The Ghost waited, tucked away in the deepest shadows, silent and still as the grave in the old storeroom, until the girl returned from washing. As he had throughout much of the day, he watched her. She was fascinating for some reason – perhaps the quiet sadness she carried. It was almost enough to make him pity her for the fright she would soon endure. Almost.

The girl sat on the floor next to the window, in a small patch of orange light from the gaslights below. There was no way she could see the moon or stars, but even so, her face turned to the sky, and once again, unbidden, the Ghost considered how almost-beautiful she was. He took a soundless step closer to her, his long black cape sweeping around him, flexing his thin, pale hands.

"I know you're there," Christine spoke, calm as could be, and the Ghost froze. How could she? But her eyes were not on him, they were focused on the floor. As the Ghost kept still, not even breathing, he watched the same spot as her. And heard it. The scratch of tiny claws. "Come on out, I won't hurt you."

The Ghost watched as the girl pulled some bread from her bag and broke off a small piece. She set it on the floor a safe distance from herself before taking her own bite. Sure enough, the rat scurried out and grabbed the prize. For the first time, he watched Christine smile.

"Now, my friend, I'll make you a deal," Christine said to the rat as she finished her own bite. "I'll give you a bit more if you promise not to scurry over my feet while I'm sleeping, alright? I'm nervous enough here as it is."

The rat did not respond but regarded the girl thoughtfully as they both chewed.

"Thank you," Christine said, tired and amused. "Everyone else here has been surprisingly kind, I'm glad you are too. Well, except for that doorman but...I honestly never expected all that's happened today."

The rat remained silent as Christine threw it another crumb and the Ghost found himself hoping this strange, kind girl would go on.

"Would you believe I've been dreaming about coming here for years? All my life it feels, and now I'm here." Christine sighed deeply. "Begging for charity, sleeping on the floor, and talking...to a rat." She gave a hollow laugh. "It's almost like a fairy tale, don't you think? The part where the heroine is all alone, and some spirit comes to help her. But I guess I've had enough help for the day, I can't really complain."

The Ghost smirked. She had no idea how right she was.

"Have you heard the story of Vasilisa the Beautiful? She would feed her little doll and tell it her sorrows and it saved her from the Baba Yaga." The Ghost smiled, genuinely this time. He did know that story, but how did she? "I always liked that one. My friend and I, when we were children, we would collect stories from anyone who would tell us and bring them back to..."

Christine stopped, a shadow passing over her face. Her eyes closed and the Ghost considered taking his chance. But as he moved, he saw the tears on her cheek. Her eyes were shining when she opened them again.

"God, I wish I had a little doll like Vasilisa, carrying a blessing. Just so she could tell me what to do," she told the rat, her voice thick. "I'm here and I'm so grateful but...what do I do now?" She drew her knees close to her chest, wrapping her arms around them. She looked incredibly small and broken. "What do I do now?" she repeated, barely a whisper.

The rat responded by scurrying away and Christine let out a pained laugh. "Well, good night then, it was nice to meet you. I'm Christine, by the way."

And I am Erik. He almost said it aloud, imagining her terror as he emerged from the dark, eyes ablaze and mask shining in the shadows. But he didn't. Erik stayed frozen, the name he had not spoken in years caught in his throat and echoing in his mind.

"I wish you could hear me," Christine whispered and when Erik looked, he saw her eyes were once again on the sky. She wasn't speaking to him, or to the rat. It was another, unknown ghost who haunted her.

He drew closer, fascinated by this girl who was odd, kind, and so very sad. He wished she would speak again, but she remained silent as she finished her bread and curled up to sleep, her bag serving as a pillow and her tattered shawl her only blanket. It would have been the perfect moment to spring on her, but Erik no longer had any intention of taking his revenge tonight.

He waited in the dark, as still as a statue, listening to the sound of her breath as it slowed. When she was asleep, he would go and leave her in peace to whatever sad dreams she could manage. It was already a mercy. But he didn't leave. He found himself drawing closer, inch by inch, until he stood a foot away from her, at the edge of the light. A looming, masked figure waiting beside her, like a nightmare.

He didn't want to be a terror for this girl though. Not tonight. She was lost and hurt enough and didn't deserve more pain or fear. He had been lost when he came here, wounded and alone when these stones had become his shelter. When he had come to the Opera, only the ghosts had helped him as well.

As his feet, Christine shivered in the deepening chill. Or maybe some part of her sensed a phantom lurking close. How little did she care for herself that she hadn't even bothered to pull a sheet off one of the old pianos? It was a reflex for Erik to grab the nearest covering and placed it over her. At least she could be warm for tonight.

The gaslights below illuminated her sleeping face with an eerie light as Erik knelt beside her. Close enough to touch her.

"There is a ghost watching you, Christine," he whispered, oddly compelled by the memory of her words and tears. "I can't tell you what to do now. But I..." he what? Would be happy to help when she did? What would be the point in that?

Erik stood abruptly, appalled by his weakness. He had become the monster he was so as to never feel such foolish longing ever again. He was the darkness now. There was no use for sympathy or yearning, not for someone like him. And this girl – she was nobody. There was nothing in her worth even a second thought from the Phantom of the Opera.

He stalked soundlessly to the door. The damn girl had caused him enough trouble already. He had learned to forget hope before and he would forget her just the same.

2. Haunted

Christine woke automatically before dawn. The stiffness in her body was worse than usual, but that was to be expected after a night on a hard floor. At least she was warm. Christine sat up, bewildered. *Why* was she warm?

She pushed herself from the floor, blinking in the washed-out light. Nothing in the dusty storeroom had changed except that some sort of drop cloth was covering her. When had she moved it? She chewed the last of her half-stale bread as the room brightened, hoping to remember when she had pulled the cloth over her or what that voice in her dream had said.

In the pale light of morning, the Opera was empty and unnerving, like a sleeping giant. All the strangeness of the previous day was even more disconcerting when Christine thought back on it now, as she made her way through silent halls. Jean-Paul talking to no one, his remark to Louise about a departed friend, everyone asking if she was easily scared. What was wrong with this place?

She tried to put it out of her mind as she made her way back to the costumers. It took her several tries and detours, but she found the workroom just as the other women arrived. Louise sent Christine to table far in the back of the workshop beside a massive pile of costumes and tutus with the simple instructions to find any holes or tears and mend them.

Within an hour Christine's shoulders ached from hunching over her sewing, and she had pricked her fingers a dozen times. No one noticed her, even the women doing the same work, and all the better since Christine's sewing was only slightly better than terrible.

It wasn't the worst job. The costume shop was warm and smelled pleasantly of dust, sweat, and cloth. Christine's work was mindless enough that she could let her mind wander. Once in a while, her attention returned to the torn peasant's costume in her hand and the hope she wouldn't bleed on it, or the unending stream of conversation among the women who barely noticed Christine's presence.

The only person with more than a passing interest in her arrived much later in the day. Julianne swept into the workshop and immediately plopped herself across from the table, grinning at Christine. A few other costumers gave the dark-skinned girl a look that Christine wagered wasn't just to do with her manners.

"You made it! I can't say I'm not surprised."

Christine rolled her eyes and smirked. "Well, there was a rat that gave me a hard time, but I survived." Julianne looked over Christine as if she were surveying for damage.

"Well, I did warn you about the rats. But you do seem to be in one piece."

"I am. Now, will you tell me why you thought I wouldn't be?"

A mysterious smile spread across Julianne's sharp features. "Well, I guess you've earned it." She leaned in close to Christine, who found herself holding her breath. "The Opera is haunted."

"Haunted?" Christine exclaimed, then laughed loudly. Perhaps she was out of practice and had done it wrong because a handful of other women turned at the sound. She shut her mouth, trying to school her face into something more somber. "You aren't serious. Are you?"

"She's dead serious," an older woman at a worktable next to them replied, scowling at Christine over her embroidery. "And you should be too when it comes to *him*." The way she said 'him' could have made someone want to cross themselves.

"You *all* believe the Opera's haunted," Christine asked the gaggle of women now staring at her, including Louise who had come to investigate the pause in work.

"Of course we do," Louise said, grim and careful. "As long as the Opera Garnier has stood, he has been here. The Phantom."

"Everyone knows about the Opera Ghost," Julianne added with relish. "He walks the halls dressed like he's on his way to a performance, but he always wears a white mask. They say if you see beneath it, you're never heard from again."

Christine fought back a scoff at the theatrics of it all, just as the older woman who had spoken before chimed back in: "His mask is black, you foolish girl."

"No, Maxine, it's *white*!" A small girl at another station squeaked. "You see it floating in the dark like the moon. Or his eyes – his eyes *burn*!"

"He lives near the lake, they say," Louise added, her voice dark. "Deep in the fifth cellar. No one goes down there for fear of him."

"Oh so there's also a lake?" Christine snorted.

The white-haired woman, Maxine, glared at Christine. "The Ghost is the soul of the Opera," the matron declared. "It's he who really holds the power here, not the managers or the stars. Without his approval, everything would be cursed."

"As if it's not cursed already," Julianne snapped back, and Maxine sneered like Julianne had blasphemed. She turned back to Christine. "He makes all sorts of accidents happen. Especially when he's unhappy."

"He's certainly made more costumes disappear than I can count. Carlotta's especially," Louise added.

"Lord in heaven, he *hates* her," Maxine muttered before Christine could ask who in the world they were talking about.

"Can you blame him?" Julianne replied.

"And then there was the fireman, just the other day, the one who they found half-dead! A mile from where he was supposed to be," the young woman added, visibly pale. Christine's head was swimming.

"But ghosts aren't *real*," Christine countered, hearing uncharacteristic coldness in her voice. There were few things left in this world that could inspire her ire, but this was one. The women looked at her with a combination of pity and derision. "I mean, these stories are amusing, but I just don't think—"

"It doesn't matter what you think, girl," Maxine cut her off. "The Opera Ghost is real. As real as you or me."

"I don't think you understand," Julianne added to Christine, gentler. "We've seen what he does, people hear his voice and see him. I've heard he has a private box and a concierge who takes messages to the managers for him."

Christine opened her mouth to say that sounded completely insane, then shut it. She knew better than to debate matters like this with believers. She'd tried it too many times and paid the price.

"Don't let them scare you away," Louise said, looking between Christine and Julianne. "Especially Julianne, she just likes the ghost stories because they're good for frightening the ballet rats."

"Christine doesn't need to be scared, I don't think," Julianne said with a secret smile. Louise shook her head and left the two alone. The rest of the room returned to ignoring Christine as well, which was a relief.

"What did you mean by that?" Christine asked, fiddling with her mending.

"Well, he let you sleep here last night, he must like you," Julianne said.

Christine tamped down the impulse to laugh again. "*Or* I survived the night because ghosts aren't real."

Julianne shrugged. "You'll believe soon enough. He has a way of making himself known." Christine shivered at the promise in Julianne's voice, thinking back on the night before. Not just the sheet that had moved itself, but the eerie feeling of the Opera; that sense of being watched from somewhere in the dark. Julianne's eyes widened. "Or he already did..."

"No," Christine said it for herself as much as Julianne.

"Did you see something?"

"No. Just shadows and rats," Christine pushed back. "I don't believe in ghosts." Julianne could not possibly know how deeply it hurt Christine just to say it.

"We'll see, my friend, we will see," Julianne said. Christine held her tongue. She very much doubted that.

Erik was bored. And a bored ghost was a dangerous thing. Nothing had held his attention, even music, so he was wandering his kingdom, considering the excitement of yesterday and the monotony of today in contrast. He found himself beneath the stage, among the pulleys and wheels taller than him that moved the scenery above.

It was calming to walk in this secret, mechanical corner of the world, where it smelled of wood, hemp, oil, and shadow. Soon the theater above would be bustling with activity ahead of the performance and it would not be safe for him in the warren of ropes and machines. He would have to find some other distraction to keep him from thinking of the girl he'd decided to forget.

The first sound of a stagehand's heavy footfall and a wheezing cough echoed through the stillness. It was time to leave. Erik pushed through a trap door onto the empty stage and stole away. He passed the billowing black curtains in the wings and crept towards the dressing rooms. It was possible that some other fool might catch sight of him here, but they would just scream and run, and the Opera would have another story.

Erik found himself at the door of dressing room three, by far the largest and most highly desired of all the dressing rooms. Of course it was Carlotta's and despite years of efforts, he had been unable to evict her from it.

Erik slipped into the room without a sound. He left the door ajar, allowing a sliver of gold gaslight to penetrate the empty gloom. A box on the diva's vanity practically overflowed with jewels, all gaudy and charmless. He broke a string of ugly beads, scattering them. But he'd stolen enough of Carlotta's baubles that even that was boring. She had so many that she barely even noticed when they were gone.

He turned to the costume the woman would wear in a few hours and raised his hand to the pink satin gown. Now, a tear would be such a terrible inconvenience...Erik stopped, his hand hovering in the air. That girl – that *Christine* – was at work in the costume shop right now, likely mending tears like the one he was ready to inflict. His hand fell, unwilling to add to the pathetic creature's work.

He grabbed the diva's shoes. Those would have to do, and Marguerite didn't need bejeweled slippers anyway. He stood with his prize, laughing darkly. But he moved to the wrong place. The light from the door reflected in the vanity mirror and onto his mask. And for a second, Erik saw his own masked face.

He froze, loathing and panic overcoming him before he smashed the mirror. The glass shattered under Carlotta's heels; cracks blooming to obscure his hated reflection. The shoes had the benefit of protecting his hands, which was a blessing. It would never do for a ghost to bleed.

Christine had found a pleasant stairwell to rest and eat her supper. Said supper was just an apple that she assumed Julianne or Louise had left in her bag in a fit of pity, but it was something to fill her starving stomach, so she was content. She stared at the plaster on the walls as she chewed, slow as possible to make it last. The wall would be white in daylight, she guessed, but here it took on the warm, orange glow of the gaslight. There was a small crack running down a few inches from the brass fixture. This building had only been open five years. How quickly things fell apart.

"There you are." Christine looked up at Louise's stern face. "You staying for the performance?"

Christine gulped down her final bite and nodded. "I heard there's extra money if we do."

"Were you planning on lurking here 'til then or were you going to go up?"

Christine stood too quickly, stumbling over herself. "I can listen?"

Louise chuckled. "Of course, just stay out of the way. Julianne seems to like you, see if she needs help with the *petit rats*." Christine's heart beat harder than it had in days as she straightened her dress and rushed out the door. "The stage is the other way!" Louise yelled after her and she corrected course.

It wasn't hard to find her way to the stage. She just followed the people in costume. At last, she heard the sound of the orchestra tuning from above, one pitch flowering into dozens of echoes and variations. The sound, so familiar and magical, filled her with both joy and aching regret, like notes in harmony. More performers passed by, sweeping past her without a thought. She didn't care. Jean-Paul had said they were presenting *Faust* tonight.

Finally, she spotted it: the great stage of the Opera Garnier with its subtle slope so each seat saw every inch of grandeur. The fire curtain blocked the view of the audience as the stagehands completed their work arranging Faust's study. Behind the flat meant to be the doomed Doctor's wall were layers of painted backdrops, creating the illusion of expansive countryside in the distance. Off to the sides in the wings were ropes and winches and pulleys and sandbags, all manned by burly stagehands. Christine followed the miles of rope with her eyes, up and up, to where it disappeared into the flies. The heaven of ropes and catwalks above was alive with movement and the sheer height and expanse of it made her mouth fall open in awe.

Someone pushed past Christine – she guessed it was a chorus member by their peasant's dress. The chorus was already assembling in the wings to sing the idyllic air that would inspire Faust's bargain with Méphistophélès. Christine backed away from the crowd, ducking behind a set piece. She didn't want to be reprimanded for being where she so very obviously didn't belong.

She had meant to find this stage in a very different way, and she wasn't worthy of being so close to it. There was still time to leave, she thought with regret, but where would she go? Just as it had been for years, she had followed music to another dead end. She didn't leave though. She couldn't.

Christine wedged herself into a hidden corner, closing her eyes as the overture began. Slowly, Gounod's marvelous, ominous music welled up from the unseen orchestra. It made her heart race as it rose and crested, like waves on a mysterious sea. She let it sweep her away as the dark chords warmed into something more like a dream, a promise of heaven and hope, despite the devils awaiting.

Christine smiled in the dark as she listened. She didn't believe in ghosts, she wouldn't let herself; but she believed in *this*.

Everyone had routines for performances. The chorus with their vocal exercises and teas, the stagehands with their shouts and barked orders. The directors fretted and the violinists tightened their bows. Erik watched all of them, making sure to keep to his own routine as well. The *petit rats*, the youngest members of the ballet, had a new tradition this year of leaving "gifts for the Ghost," so he wouldn't take anything important at an inconvenient time. They placed pins and pennies and beads in a porcelain dish outside their dressing rooms in the dark hall. It was only polite for Erik to accept and give the dancers a thrill.

The treasure sat safe in his pocket as he moved through his secret paths in the dark, listening to the beginning of Faust's lament. He had seen the production enough times that he didn't mind not being in his box. Especially because he had another tribute to collect.

Carlotta had to be fuming at the chaos he'd left for her. He knew just the place to wait for the uproar. In the twilight area between the stage and the dressing rooms there were many places to hide. The one he had in mind would be perfect...were it not occupied.

Of all the places Erik had expected to find *her*, this was the last one. Yet there Christine Daaé was: tucked into the shadows like another ghost, eyes closed as she listened to the opening scene. Below the stage, beneath a trap door, Robert Rameau awaited his entrance as Méphistophélès, but here in the dark, the devil had already arrived and was ready to finally show this girl exactly why she should be afraid. Erik readied himself.

"Fucking hell, she's going to kill someone for this!" Erik darted back at the voice, just as Christine's eyes shot open, curious. A pair of women were whispering close together. He knew them. The one who had spoken was a dresser for Carlotta, poor thing, and the other dark-skinned one usually kept to the dancers, though she had helped Christine last night.

"Calm down, Anette, we'll find them," Bonet said.

"Julianne?" The women turned to see Christine emerging from her hiding place. "What's going on?"

"Carlotta's goddamn *shoes* have gone missing and she's about to fire me for it!" Anette snapped. "Who the hell are you by the way?"

"I'm no one," Christine answered quickly. "But I can help you look for them if you like."

"That's very sweet, but…" Julianne looked over her shoulder as if she could feel Erik near. "I doubt you'll find them if *someone* doesn't want them found."

To Erik and Anette's surprise, Christine laughed. It was a small, sad laugh and not at all what the Ghost expected upon mention of his power. "Because your ghost has taken them?" Christine asked.

"Don't talk like that, you fool," Anette snapped, and Erik bristled at the way it made Christine wince.

"Christine's not a believer yet," Julianne said, much kinder. This made Erik smile. There was little he relished more than inspiring new faith in a skeptic.

"Maybe you should…ask for them back? Does that work?" Christine said. The other women stared at her, which Erik found offensive. If more people were as polite as Christine suggested, perhaps *he* would be more generous. "Just say '*Monsieur Fantôme,* please give back—' what was it again?"

"Carlotta's shoes," Anette answered. "And good luck with that. If you'd like to actually be useful you can help us look." Christine shrugged and the three started searching, as Méphistophélès popped up on stage with a slash of smoke. Soon Marguerite would need to make her first entrance and it *would* be funny if she had to do it shoeless as Erik had intended.

But that would mean Anette would be out of a job and that Christine's kindness would go unrewarded. And Erik didn't like the second idea.

He moved fast, first slipping into the secret passage to where he'd hidden the shoes, then placing them in Christine's path, stealthy as a shadow. He watched her see, then examine them, and rush back to the other women. He wondered if this would be enough to make her believe, and why he cared so much that she did. He watched from the dark as Christine returned with her prize.

"Are these the ones?" Christine asked, presenting the shoes to Anette as Julianne joined them.

"Oh, thank Christ, they are!" Anette's earlier sourness was gone, and she grabbed Christine for an embrace and a kiss on the cheek before running off, leaving Julianne laughing quietly and Christine bewildered.

"Well, I guess asking politely does work," Julianne commented, making Christine scowl. "Told you: he must like you."

It was Erik's turn to bristle. He didn't *like* anyone, or at least he told himself that most days. The girl was simply kind and lost and deserved help. That was all.

"Do you need any more help?" Christine asked.

"Not right now," Julianne replied. "You can go back to whatever it is you were doing."

"Listening," Christine murmured. Julianne made an interested face. Erik assumed that she, like so many of the employees of the Opera, had tuned out the actual music they were all here to support. Too few people took the time to show any reverence for the art created in these walls.

"Well, enjoy. I have my own adventures to keep up," Julianne gave Christine a wink and disappeared into the halls. Christine herself didn't leave, she moved back towards the shadows. Closer to Erik. And as she had done before the commotion, she closed her eyes...and listened.

In the darkness, her face barely illuminated by the lights of the stage, Christine listened and before Erik's eyes, the girl who was so sad and lost came alive. Until now she had been like a starless sky, but as she listened, light returned. As Faust finished his devil's bargain, she mouthed the words, surprising Erik further. She *knew* this opera.

What had she said before? She had dreamed of this place. She had come to his Opera for the unquestioning beauty of music. And that, like her loneliness, he could understand.

As voices filtered through the darkness, Erik watched the girl lose herself in music. It was the most active thing he had seen her do. Her face expressed and perceived every nuance of the music. Her eyes stayed closed as he strayed closer to her to better savor the play of her features. It was ridiculous, yet he could not move from the shadows until the act ended and the girl scurried away to avoid discovery.

He should leave too. He had a box after all, that he had taken great pains to secure. There would be comfort there, but it was comfort born of boredom, the same ennui that had nagged him all day until this moment. He would wait out the mediocre performance, fuming at how the bored chatter of the audience beneath the blazing chandelier would barely decrease when the curtain rose. He would survey the patrons in their satin vests and black coats, next to their wives and mistresses, all of them more interested in who was attending with who and sitting where than the performance on the stage, and he would try to forget how he hated them. There wouldn't be a single face in that audience that would betray as much passion for Gounod's melodies as this girl's.

And so, act two began with Erik still hidden, his haunted gaze fixed on Christine, watching her live the music in a way he hadn't in a very long time. There was some commotion when Carlotta made her entrance, with her swatting at attendants and the musical director as well. Her antics made Christine grimace, and when Carlotta tore into the "Ballad of the King of Thule," ornamenting it until it was unrecognizable, Christine pulled a face that made Erik laugh quietly to himself. At least the young lady had taste.

He watched her breath quicken at Faust and Marguerite's passionate duet, watched her shiver at the demons of

Walpurgisnacht, and even saw her smile and mouth along when Marguerite called to the angels. He hid, still and silent until his feet were sore and his back ached and he enjoyed that too. It was a reminder that he had a body, which was easy to forget as a phantom. Watching this girl through the dark, hearing the music as she might be hearing it...by some strange magic, it made him feel just a little bit alive. And he knew he should run from that and hate her for it, but he didn't. Or he couldn't.

How strange.

"So, how was it?" Julianne asked the moment she found Christine in the halls, unceremoniously dumping a pile of petticoats into her arms.

"Wonderful," Christine replied with a smile before considering. "Well, mostly. Marguerite was not what I hoped. Who sang the role?"

"Carlotta Zambelli," Julianne pronounced the name like a curse. "*La* Carlotta. The one whose performance you saved. Or shoes at least."

"Well, now I regret helping," Christine muttered, and Julianne gave a dark laugh.

"Put those in the bin over there, and come help me with the rats," Julianne ordered, grabbing a pile of cloaks from another dresser, and heaving it into a large laundry cart.

It amused Christine that everyone called the young ballerinas "rats" but after a performance watching them scurry about, she understood the name. As she and Julianne made their way through the maze of corridors, finely dressed women Christine recognized from the chorus jostled past them in the other direction.

"They're going to meet their patrons in the *Salon du Danse* behind the stage" Julianne explained. "Prettiest brothel you'll ever see."

"Excuse me?" Christine knew performers weren't renowned for their virtue, but she hadn't expected it to be commented upon so blatantly.

"Do you know how to tell a courtesan from a chorus girl, Christine?" Julianne asked with a wicked twinkle in her eye.

"No?"

"Neither do I," Julianne laughed at the joke, if it was one, and pushed her way into a dressing room crowded with ballerinas still in their costumes.

"Where have you been, Julianne!" a petit ginger exclaimed immediately as they entered. "I can't get out of this thing without you!" The dancer gestured to the laces at the back of her costume.

"There are three other people here, Marie," Julianne countered with a laugh.

"None of them as are good with laces as you," another dancer, a blonde with her hair half up, muttered in a truly scandalous tone. Behind her, a third dancer, older than the others, smirked.

"Oh, don't get her started," the elder muttered. The redhead blushed to her freckles but still rushed to Julianne for help. "Who's this?" It took Christine a moment to realize she was the subject of the question.

"This is Christine, she's a new costumer, fresh from – well, actually I don't know," Julianne said, but it wasn't a question. "Christine this is Marie," she nodded to the girl before her. "That's Cécile, call her Jammes, and that's Blanche Carcaux, don't call her anything, she's a terrible gossip," she said, indicating the blonde in front of her then the oldest dancer, who stuck her tongue out at Julianne in response. "And that's Meg Giry." The final dancer was in the corner, taking in the scene with wide eyes. She looked to be the youngest

"Nice to meet you," Christine muttered.

"Meg's new too, at least to this part of the Opera. The Ghost just had her promoted," Jammes said, her tone conspiratorial.

"Oh, did he now?" Julianne asked, giving Christine a pointed look. Christine couldn't help but roll her eyes.

"Does she not believe yet?" Marie asked.

"Not yet, even after he gave Carlotta's shoes back to her," Julianne said.

"Well, it sounds like no one likes this Carlotta, maybe someone else moved them," Christine tried. She was beginning to wonder if there was any topic of conversation at the Opera other than *the Ghost*.

"Oh, no, it was *him*," Julianne said, and Marie nodded as she was finally released from her costume. She rushed to a wardrobe, her thin chemise barely concealing her pert breasts from the others.

"He's locked her in her dressing room ahead of performances so many times they had to take the lock off her door," Blanche said, her voice and face deadly serious.

"That could have been anyone." Christine didn't mean to argue, but it rankled her she wasn't allowed to not believe in peace.

"No, it's him. He's real," it was little Meg who had popped in. "My mother, she hears his voice in box five." The room grew still as the women turned their attention to the small dancer with brass blonde hair. "She says...she says his voice is beautiful. Too beautiful to be human."

Christine didn't know what to say without telling this girl her mother was mad.

"People all over talk to ghosts," Marie said, emerging from behind the wardrobe in a blue silk dress still needing to be fastened.

"There are mediums holding seances in fancy flats on the *Boulevard des Italiens* every day."

"Most of those people are charlatans," Christine said. "Trust me."

"Victor Hugo went to see them!" Marie snapped back and Christine sighed powerfully.

"Let me take these," Christine grumbled, grabbing the discarded costumes from the floor, and pushing out the door in annoyance.

The hall was quiet and dark, as she'd already become used to. Like so many dark corridors she'd already explored, it was completely empty yet felt like there was someone waiting and watching. Christine huffed as she deposited the costumes in their bin. The thought was as insane and stupid as the ghost stories she'd been hearing all day.

The absurdity of it all and the emptiness within her compared to the faith of the foolish girls in that dressing room suddenly pierced her heart like a knife. She'd come here chasing her own ghosts only to be reminded again and again what a ridiculous fantasy her whole life had been. She could barely breathe, tears stinging her eyes.

"Are you alright?" It was Julianne in the hall behind her.

"No. I'm not," Christine replied, trying to compose herself, not daring to look at Julianne and show her tears. "I don't like ghost stories."

"Why? What makes you so sure he can't be real?"

"Because no ghost or spirit can be real," Christine said as firmly as she could manage.

"But you've heard the stories—"

"Let me tell you a story, then," Christine growled, rounding on Julianne. "Once upon a time there was a violinist who had a daughter. He taught her to love music and stories. He told her tales her whole life of spirits and magic, but her favorite was the story of the angels of music, who blessed musicians with marvelous gifts, protected them and guided them." It sounded so absurd said aloud, and it was more shameful how much she still wished she could believe it.

"But that violinist, he got sick," Christine went on. "He grew worse for years, and he knew he was going to die, but he promised his daughter that it would be alright. When he was in heaven, he would send an angel of music to protect her."

"Christine..." Julianne's face was full of pity and Christine hated that too.

"Can you already guess what happened when he died?" she barreled on, her voice angrier and harder with each word. "*Nothing.* Less than nothing. No angel appeared to that girl. And every time she tried to sing, the notes dried in her throat. She kept trying though, kept looking for something. For three goddamn years. But the money he left her to attend the conservatoire ran out, and they wouldn't keep her. So, she ended up destitute, sleeping in storerooms and eating scraps. *Alone.*"

Julianne opened her mouth to speak again, but Christine didn't stop.

"So, that's how I know it's all rubbish. Because if ghosts and spirits and angels were real, *I* would know," Christine said, voice breaking and fighting back more tears. "And don't tell me that maybe they are, and I've just been unlucky. Because it's either all lies or it's not and he abandoned me *twice.*"

Christine's shoulders shook as she tried to breathe. Her chest was tight and a dark part of her wondered what even the point in was breathing in this senseless, cruel world where she was forgotten and forsaken.

"So that's why I won't believe, Julianne," Christine said softly, wiping her cheek with the tattered cuff of her dress.

"I'm so sorry, Christine, I am, but—"

"Please, stop," Christine cut her off. "If my lack of faith so offends your damn ghost, then let him tell me so himself."

Christine started walking. She didn't even know where she was going, just that she had to get away. She strode into the corridor and turned as soon as she could, whipping around a corner into a darkened hall that should have been empty.

But it wasn't. It wasn't empty, because just as she had dared him to be, the Opera Ghost was there.

The Phantom himself stood before Christine, exactly as the stories had described him, from the black opera cape to the white mask covering all of his face except the mouth set in a grim frown. He was tall, cold, and real as the darkness, his glowing eyes ablaze with unnamable menace. The rest of the world stopped, frozen, as the Ghost stared her down and drew closer without making a sound.

Christine could not breathe. She could not think. All she could do was stare, her heart beating so hard it hurt. His eyes locked with hers, searing into her soul, and somehow the danger and menace within them began to fade into something deeper, and infinitely sadder as she stared.

His eyes were gold, like the sea at sunset, and Christine was drowning in them. Fresh tears stung her own eyes as looked at the Ghost. She took a deep, shaking breath; something inside her breaking, while something else surged back to glorious, aching life.

"Christine!" Julianne yelled from miles away.

Christine spun around, reality rushing back like a tidal wave. Julianne looked terrified and why wouldn't she? Christine spun back to the Ghost, only to find him gone. She didn't think she could move, but Julianne grabbed her and dragged her back to the rats' dressing room.

"What in God's name?"

"Is she alright?"

The girls swarmed and chattered but Christine could barely hear them. It didn't matter. Nothing mattered except the Phantom of the Opera and his shining eyes.

3. Miracles

Erik didn't like this hiding place. It was too small and close for his tastes, and he had little use for listening in on the dancers' dressing rooms besides hearing stories about himself. Moreover the view through a crack in the wall rarely revealed anything exceptional. But how he wished it would right now so that he could better see Christine Daaé's face as the dancers and costumer chattered around her.

"This bloody fool thought she'd issue a challenge to the Ghost and, well, he answered," Julianne was saying.

"What?" Little Marie gasped, kneeling next to Christine to take her hand like an old friend. "Are you alright?"

"I'm fine," Christine murmured. "I—"

"You don't look fine!" Blanche exclaimed.

"Are *you* alright?" The question was asked by Jammes of Julianne. The dancer had the costumer nearly in her arms, holding her with an intimacy Erik might have found intriguing any other day.

"I'm fine," Julianne said, though her voice shook. "I'm not the one who had to stay *staring* at him for God knows how long!"

"You what?" Marie asked in horror. Erik shut his eyes, waiting for Christine to answer. Remembering.

It had been such a simple thing, to let her see him after such a blatant challenge and knowing that she needed so desperately to *believe* in something. But he hadn't been prepared for her reaction. She had not screamed, or run, or fainted. Instead, she had...come alive. The starless sky of her face had blazed into dawn, and it had been incredible. How had he not seen her eyes before, how that they were the color of a forest? How had he not known that they were so beautiful? He had wanted to turn away, but her eyes would not stop staring even when they filled with tears.

"What was it like?" someone asked, and Erik shook the image of Christine's face from his mind, even as he strained to hear her quiet voice.

"It...*he* was just like your stories. Tall, in his cape and hat, like he was going to the opera," Christine said, her voice weak. "He was wearing a mask. A white mask. And his eyes..." Erik's heart jumped as he strained to see her expression.

"Did they burn and glow?" his box keeper's daughter asked in a hushed tone.

"They were...sad," Christine whispered as if waking from a dream.

"What?" Julianne asked in shock.

"His eyes were frightening at first, but then they were so sad. And lonely." Christine shook her head like she couldn't find the words. Erik desperately wished that she would. "There was so much pain."

"You sound like you feel sorry for him," Jammes said, finding it as unbelievable as Erik did. People in the Opera feared him, some ever respected him or honored him, but no one, not even the maddest, had ever *pitied* him.

"Wouldn't you?" Christine replied – like it was so simple. "To bear that sort of pain, even in death, it must be awful."

Erik watched little Marie draw back from the girl and saw young Giry shudder. And they were right to be repulsed. This girl was foolish but kind, and he'd shown himself to her as a reward for that. But that did not make him less of a monster. Christine would not pity him if she ever *really* saw him. This stupid game was over and if he ever encountered her again, he would show her how ridiculous her sympathy was.

"You didn't tell us she was mad, Julianne," Blanche hissed. And even though she was right, anger rose in Erik's gut at the insult. And that too felt strange and insane.

"We should go," Julianne said, drawing away from Jammes and taking Christine by the wrist. "I certainly won't be letting you walk alone for a while." Christine nodded and they made their goodbyes.

Erik watched them go and told himself not to follow. He'd done more than enough damage today and he didn't need the pity of some girl off the street who he had helped for no reason at all.

He didn't need her.

It took Christine a while to finish her work in the costumers and even longer to find her way back to the stables. It didn't matter, time and words and work swirled around her like a storm she wasn't part of. She could focus on nothing but the thought of the ghost who had seen fit to save her faith and perhaps even her soul.

It didn't make sense. None of it made sense. But she had seen him. Julianne had been there too. He had appeared because she asked. For some reason, he had favored *her*, and not for the first time. But why her? Why now? Why this?

And so Christine found herself with the scent of straw and horses in her nose as a fresh autumn rain fell beyond the gates, looking for the man who had helped her in the first place. She found him passed out at a table in the back, an empty bottle of wine rolling beside his hands as he snored.

"Monsieur Lachenal?" Christine tried. The groom snorted in response. "Jean-Paul!"

"What!?" The man sprang up, brandishing his bottle like a weapon. "I won't let you take me – Oh, it's you." Jean-Paul deflated as he blinked at Christine. "Wait, who are you?"

"Christine, you helped me get a job with Louise yesterday." The man rubbed his stubbled face and nodded, only the dimmest recognition in his eyes.

"You leaving already?" Jean-Paul asked, his words still thick with the wine.

"No. I had to ask you something." Jean-Paul nodded and looked as if he might fall asleep again right there. "Why did you help me? I heard you talking to someone. And since I've been here, I've heard stories about the—"

"Oh. Yes. It was him," Jean-Paul cut in with a pleasant grin. "The Ghost. He told me to help you."

Christine's blood jumped. Somehow, the moment she'd seen the Phantom in that hall, she'd known. "But why? I'm nothing. Why would he do that?"

Jean-Paul shrugged, his whole body drunkenly leaning to the left as he did. "Who knows! He's like that sometimes. Folks don't talk about it as much as the frightening bits but...he helps people. The ones he thinks are good enough."

"Why would he help me?" Christine said, more to herself than Jean-Paul. "Who – what is he?"

"No one knows," Jean-Paul replied through a yawn. "There are a dozen stories about how the place opened with a ghost already there. None of us know what he is: Communard prisoner, violinist who killed himself, a builder buried in the foundations, or something else." Jean-Paul shrugged, hiccupped, closed his eyes, and keeled over onto the table again.

"Something else," Christine whispered, shivering.

She walked back into the Opera proper. It was very late, and the building was silent and dark, but Christine had the candle Julianne had given her the night before. The quivering light did little to dispel the shadows down every hall, and at any other time, the stillness and the dark would have made Christine afraid. But not tonight. She didn't feel the sense of being watched as she had on and off since her arrival, but she still felt welcome. This was *his* opera they said. So, she hoped he would not mind where she was headed. She had a promise to keep.

The auditorium of the Opera was never fully dark. It simply was not allowed. Once the chandelier was extinguished and the footlights doused, a single oil lamp always remained on the stage, burning low in a wrought-iron cage meant to keep the fire in check. It was called a ghost light. Every theater had one, and Erik could not help but think that if it was meant to keep ghosts away, it was extremely ineffective.

The ghost light cast the great chamber in a hundred shades of shadow. The golden gilding on the boxes and statues shone ever so dimly, and the red velvet of the seats and curtains looked almost black. High above, a few of the great chandelier's crystals shimmered like fairy wisps in the dark, leading travelers astray.

Perhaps the lights had led him here, Erik thought, as he gazed about the empty theater, pushing his lank hair carefully out of his eyes, and realizing for the first time he had forgotten his hat somewhere in his distraction. He'd wandered for hours, far below the Opera, to his home and back, unable to escape the thought of Christine Daaé and her shining eyes. The cold and the utter quiet of the theater were a welcome relief.

A noise broke through the stillness. Footsteps. Erik hid in the shadows of the orchestra pit, alarmed that anyone would be on stage at this dark and dangerous hour. Whoever it was, they would never dare to intrude upon his nighttime kingdom again after what he would do now. He steeled himself as the steps grew closer, preparing to strike...and swore in consternation under his breath. It was her. Of all the places he could have been, fate had led him to this ridiculous, astonishing girl *again*.

Erik watched dumbstruck as Christine came to the very center of the immense stage and set her candle down. Her hands were shaking, and she looked more nervous and scared than he had ever seen her. She knelt, as if to pray, and stared into the dark.

"I know you can hear me, ghost."

Erik tensed at the tremulous, extraordinary words.

"I don't know how, but I can feel it. I can feel you here. And I just needed to tell you...thank you." Erik recoiled deeper into the gloom. "You heard me. You made me believe. I tried not to for so long, but you saw me, somehow, and helped. So, thank you."

He looked away, the strangeness of the sentiment twisting in his brain. Pity *and* gratitude in one day were too much.

"I believe. I can't deny that now. So, with your leave, there is someone else I must talk to." Erik's eyes flew back to her. Was she holding back tears? She looked up, towards the chandelier; no, towards heaven. He knew before she spoke which ghost she sought now.

"Father...I promised you I would sing on the stage of the Paris Opera one day. And you promised me that you would send me an angel to guide me so that I could." She bit her lip, a tear escaping down her cheek. Erik knew he was intruding on a terribly intimate moment, but he could not turn away. He had barely thought about how showing himself to her in that hall would bring back someone long lost to her. Such a deception might have filled a good man with guilt.

"I'm so sorry, Papa. I don't know what I did to make you break your promise. And I know this isn't the way you wanted me to keep mine, but it's the best I can do."

Erik tilted his head as Christine rose, closed her eyes, and took a quavering breath before the first soft notes of Susanna's garden aria from *The Marriage of Figaro* quivered unsteadily from her lips.

"*It is at last the moment, when I can rejoice without care,*" she sang in Italian. Erik flinched at the breathy, broken notes, and turned away. He already knew too much about this girl's heartbreaking dreams. He didn't want to hear a voice that was just as pathetic and miserable. "*In the arms of my beloved...*" He stopped. In the lower register, her voice gained strength and depth. And beauty.

"*Timid scruples, leave my heart...*" Something in the thin, shaking sound was changing, growing in strength and confidence. No, her voice was not terrible, far from it. This was the girl who has listened, rapt, to *Faust* from the shadows and now she sang Mozart with the deepest love in her voice. "*Oh, how it comes, the fire of love, to this place.*"

Erik turned back slowly to watch her, fascinated, and fighting back mounting amazement as the recitative continued. Note by note, her song transformed, growing rich with longing and astounding light. "*The earth and the sky respond! How the night furthers my deceptions...*"

Erik could not deny it anymore. Her voice was like her eyes in that dark corridor: completely unexpected and utterly beautiful.

"*Please come, do not tarry, oh beautiful joy.*" He relaxed into wonder as she began the aria proper. Not only was her voice beautiful – shining and warm, like a summer sky full of stars – he could hear her heart as she sang. "*Come to where love calls for your delight.*" Behind Mozart's idyllic melody was such yearning, such beautiful loneliness, and he felt each note in the depth of his own forgotten soul.

"*Here the river murmurs and the light plays, and restores the heart with sweet ripples,*" she sang. The song was a call to another world, begging heaven to hear her. Erik tried to focus on the many deficiencies in her technique – her shallow breaths and wavering pitch in the tessitura – but the untamed beauty of her voice was too intoxicating. Her song swept him up in ecstasy even as her eyes gazed out into the dark, the ghost light making her tears shine like gold.

"*Come, my love, into this hidden garden. Come, come...*" The phrase grew slowly, flowing, ardent, and full of longing that took Erik's breath away. He had never heard a voice with such raw potential or true feeling in his theater. "*And I will see your brow crowned with roses.*" The perfect, flowering notes filled Erik with an aching as strong as the one he heard in her voice. He had to *do* something. How could he let her prayer go unanswered when she had looked at him and pitied him? How could he dream of forgetting her? This girl didn't deserve only a ghost's charity. She deserved everything she ever had been or could be promised.

"*Crowned with roses...*" The last notes faded into silence and Christine closed her eyes and shivered, as tears streamed down her face. Even weeping, she had stopped being *almost* beautiful. To Erik, in that moment, she was radiant.

"I'm so sorry, Papa, please forgive me," she whispered, again looking to heaven. "I know you wanted more from me than this. But I can't. I can't make that dream come true. Not alone." She gave a defeated sigh as the darkness answered with silence, as it always would, unless...

Erik shook his head. No. It was insane. He couldn't. Even though it would be so easy, so perfect. As if heaven itself had set the path before him.

She began singing again, her voice weak and sad once more, just a snippet of another phrase from *Figaro*: "*Perhaps you will pardon another.*"

Erik knew it well: it was the Contessa's line, and if there had been a chorus on stage, they would be singing in subdued but lively awe at the sight of the noble lady, suddenly arriving to confront her husband's infidelity. Then the Count would come forward and reply in a perfect melody of supplication, begging for her mercy...

"*Contessa, forgive me...*"

Erik didn't even realize he was singing until he saw Christine gasp, her eyes widening the same way they had hours ago. She trembled, shrinking into herself in shock as his voice encircled her, as plaintive and beautiful as he could make it.

"*Forgive me,*" he sang, praying to heaven and hell and this girl might forgive him for the sin he committed with each note. "*Forgive me,*" he sang, and the notes lingered in the dark air like smoke. "Go on, Christine, finish it," Erik encouraged in a whisper, desperate to hear her voice again. "Sing for me."

"*I am kinder than you,*" Christine sang back, her voice tremulous, yet as the phrase grew into an exquisite melody of forgiveness, the sound blossomed, echoing with a wonder and beauty Erik hardly believed possible. "*I will say yes,*" she sang like a promise and a prayer. "*I will say yes.*"

"*Ah, all are happy,*" Erik joined her in the final chorus. "*And ever shall be...And ever shall be.*" Their voices joined together perfectly, effortlessly, and Erik watched Christine's eyes close in pure ecstasy, even as she sank to her knees. Erik didn't even dare to name the feelings that threatened to overcome him as he sang with her. To name them might make him stop.

As the silence fell again, Erik waited, unsure of what madness awaited next. Christine's eyes opened, staring anxiously into the dark. "Am I dreaming?" she whispered. "Or have I gone mad?"

"No, Christine, this is not a dream or madness," Erik replied before any rational thought could stop him. "This is real, I promise you. I heard you and I am here."

"Who are you?" she asked, reverent and urgent.

"You know who I am." Erik knew the power of his voice, how it could entrance people as much as his cursed face repelled them. And he put that power into every word. "I've watched you and helped you from the first moment you came here."

"But you can't be a ghost! You have the voice of..." She froze in fresh wonder and Erik felt the briefest stab of guilt as she gasped. "*An angel*?" Her hands flew to her mouth in awe and Erik pushed away all lingering remorse or caution. "My Angel of Music? You were here all along?" she asked, her voice small and completely overcome.

"I've been waiting for you, Christine," he answered, telling himself *that* wasn't a lie. He had been waiting for a voice like hers for his stage for a very long time. And what was the guise of an angel but another mask?

"I'm so sorry it took me so long to get here." There was such pain in her voice, and Erik had no idea how to soothe it, but he wanted to.

"You had to live the life you did to bring you here, to this moment. You needn't regret it, nor ask my forgiveness." That seemed to help, and Erik's heart jumped at the hope in her face. "And now that you are here, we can begin."

"Begin?"

"Your voice is a great gift, Christine," he said, savoring the taste of her name and the pure joy in her eyes. "If you let me, I will teach you to use it. I will make you into the greatest singer the Paris Opera has ever heard."

"How?" she asked, and he couldn't blame her, since he had no idea what that promise meant. All he knew was he intended to keep it.

"Have I not already proven myself to you?"

"You have. I will never doubt again," she replied, smiling.

"Then give me your voice and your trust, and I will give you my opera. I'll give you the world," he continued madly, his voice gentle as temptation. "No one has ever known what I truly am but you. I will be your angel, Christine; if you will have me."

"Yes, please, yes," she replied, passion in her voice and her face as ecstatic as a saint's. Again, it stirred something in him ferocious and hungry, lonely and entranced. He knew this was madness, but he didn't care. "Thank you," she added and for the first time since she had come into his opera, she truly smiled. Erik was completely unprepared for how beautiful the sight was. New, unnamable longing struck him like a blow, pushing the air from his lungs. It was terrifying.

"We will start tomorrow. For now, you need your rest."

"Oh, yes, I..." she hesitated and immediately Erik realized the reason: She had no bed to go home to. That wouldn't do.

"You don't think I'd let you sleep on the floor again, do you?" He would have to be fast, but he knew the perfect place to lead her. "Go to stage left and follow the light."

Christine stepped into the darkness that should have made her shiver as wax from her candle dripped onto her hand in a way that should have hurt. But there was no pain, no fear. There was just *him*. Her heart had not stopped racing from the moment she heard his voice, more beautiful and perfect than any sound she could ever dream. An *angel* had found her and now he was leading her to a safe place in *his* opera.

She gasped at the light in the hall ahead of her, the flicker of a flame just around a corner. She rushed after it, following it as he had said and trying not to trip over her own feet. He led her down flights of stairs into a part of the Opera she could barely describe. It was storage of some kind, with flats stacked against walls in some places and painted backdrops hiding in others. But the light led her past those relics, under something meant to look like the arched gate of a distant castle, and to a smaller area full of old furniture. It wasn't normal furniture, Christine realized, as she examined a flimsy chair; but the stuff made and used for the stage above.

Christine looked to see that the light had stopped moving, just around a corner. She followed it to a hidden enclave and could not help but laugh when she saw it. It was a bed – or part of one. A marriage bed maybe, adorned in dusty silk flowers. It wasn't quite the right scale for a real bedroom, but it would more than serve for her. As would the lantern burning next to it. There was no sign of the Ghost, but she knew he was close. She could feel him in the air.

"Another miracle," Christine whispered to herself. She had no idea how she could be worthy of the wonders she had been gifted that day, but her whole soul was grateful.

"You'll be safe here, as long as you need it," his voice replied. As before, it seemed to come from all around her, from the shadows and the walls. As if the air itself was whispering just to her. "Sleep now, you will need your rest for tomorrow."

Christine obeyed without question, setting her tattered bag to the side on a gilded statue of an elephant. Tomorrow. The promise in the word made her shiver and kept her heart pounding. She settled into the bed. It was the softest place she'd lain in weeks. She breathed deep, trying to calm herself, ready to weep again at the sheer madness and magic of it all. How could her entire world and life have changed so much in a few hours? How could she have awoken only that morning not believing in anything?

"How am I supposed to sleep, after all this?" she asked the darkness around her. It wasn't frightening. It never could be. He was in it: the ghost that had restored her faith, the angel that had saved her life.

"You must be tired. It's very late," he said, gentle and soft. The world was suddenly so fantastic, now that he filled it, so alive, magical, and stunning, yet nothing was as beautiful as his voice. She could listen to that voice until she faded to dust.

"Will you sing to me? Please, just until I fall asleep…" It was greedy, really, to ask it of him after all he had given her. But his song had been like the first drop of rain after a drought, and she was thirsty for a storm.

"Until you are sleeping," he replied, nearly reverent. He waited for a breath and then began to sing.

He sang to her in a language she had never heard, a low, plaintive song that was part-lullaby, part-lament. It was sad and beautiful, carrying the sound of distant shores and ancient, aching love. It was like nothing she had ever heard before. Her eyes closed as she drifted in his sublime song.

"Siúil, siúil, siúil a ruin. Siúil go socar agus siúil go ciúin."

There were no more thoughts, and slowly she forgot her body, her bed, and her fatigue. The voice of her miraculous angel wrapped around her, and she began to fall asleep but fought it. She wanted to listen to his song forever. It carried the sadness she had seen in his eyes and more. So much more. The drops of rain on her parched soul grew to a torrent, and she happily let herself drown.

It was hours before Erik finally turned away from where Christine slept and retreated into the cellars. He'd covered her in a blanket again and left the few coins in his pocket from the dancers in her bag. It was all so sentimental and foolish, but just like becoming an angel, it was so easy and felt so right. She was intoxicating, but Erik knew had to leave her light. He knew the way home in the dark and once he was there perhaps he might sleep. If the ghosts were quiet. He had barely rested the night before and he needed it. He was only human after all.

The thought hit Erik like a slap, the force of reality slamming into him so hard he gasped for air, clawing against a cold stone wall.

"What have I done?" he asked aloud.

You took a girl's faith and made it another mask for your hideous face and rotten soul, the shadows laughed in reply. Erik wanted to tell them to shut up, but the sick, terrible truth of it couldn't be ignored. He had never been a good man, he knew that very well, but he had never done anything this *cruel.* Nor had he ever done anything that so stupidly risked exposure.

She'll find out and lead them to your door, the dark declared, as Erik rushed deeper into his private underworld. *And when she finds out the monster you are, it will kill her.*

"No..." he sighed as he sank down at the edge of the lake, bowing his head. He had told her he was a bloody *angel* and for what? A voice? To give the poor deluded creature *hope*? He pounded a fist softly against the stones, trying not to think of Christine's joy at the sound of his voice or his own delight at the sight of her smile. He had damned them both.

4. Breath

Christine woke in darkness, but in her soul it was the brightest dawn she had seen in years. She woke in a world with angels. There was a blanket over her, and this time she knew where it had come from. Joy bubbled inside her and out in a laugh. He was *real*.

She sat up in the bed he had found for her, looking at the lamp he had left to save her from the dark, and laughed again. She sounded mad, but she didn't care. If this was madness, she wanted it to last forever. She stretched, filling her lungs with a yawn, and surveyed her new bedroom. It wasn't strictly a *room*, just a hidden place protected by old backdrops and piles of abandoned prop furniture. It reminded her of a cave or a burrow; a strange refuge for sure, but she could certainly see herself staying here for a while until she found somewhere else. Though she didn't like the idea of being any place where *he* wasn't there in every shadow.

The thought stopped her. Yesterday and even the day before she had sensed him watching so clearly, his presence hanging in the air like fog. But she couldn't feel it now. What if he was gone? What if he didn't return? What if she never heard his voice again?

Seeing him had been like a resurrection, but that voice – it was Pentecost. The vow hadn't been forgotten; the angel her father had promised had only been waiting for her to find him. He had made such the promises to her, surely the Angel would keep them.

Christine tried to keep her rising anxiety in check as she left the prop room. It was still quiet in the Opera, and only in a few places did the light of day manage to pierce the gloom. But there were more gaslights on now, which helped as she made her way to the costume workshop. And found it completely empty. There was no one mending; no one washing. Christine searched the halls and other workshops and found them similarly vacant. Of course it was empty; it was Sunday. Everyone was at worship and the Opera was closed. She considered finding a church to join them but dismissed the idea immediately. This place – this was her church.

Christine took advantage of the vacant building, taking longer to wash, and laundering the clothes she had worn for far too many days in a row while changing into her only other set. She managed to brush her hair as well and felt almost like a new woman by the time she was done.

She still couldn't feel him when she returned to the empty halls, but perhaps he didn't like the daylight world? She told herself he would find her. He would begin teaching her when it was time. For now, she stole through the maze of passages and chambers, wondering when she might start to feel like an interloper, but no guilt came. If this was his opera, it would welcome her. Even the parts where a simple seamstress would not be allowed.

It took her a while to find the entrance to the subscribers' foyer. Stepping from the wood, plaster, rope, and curtains behind the scenes to the marble and gilding of the audience's half of the theater was like entering another world.

There was not a surface that wasn't covered in gold, marble, filigree, or delicate mosaic. Even without the candles and lamps lit, it was overwhelming. The marble in a half-dozen shades of pink and gold made the cold space warm to the eyes. At the bottom of the double horse-shoe grand staircase, sensuous nymphs raised unlit candelabra to the murals above. In the salons where the rich and mighty met before performances, mirrors and golden pillars gave the impression of something more like a palace than a theater. Christine had never been to Versailles, but she imagined it couldn't be far from this.

Christine explored every salon and foyer to her heart's content, trailing her fingers over the details. Her favorites were the twin salons dedicated to the sun and moon on each side of the *Grand Foyer;* like miniature temples to Artemis and Apollo. Those, and the massive staircase that made her feel so small, an insignificant speck of dirt among boundless beauty.

It was all stunning and sumptuous. But it was also hollow. In her drab clothes, Christine couldn't help but feel like a rat who had snuck into a palace; built with riches she could never imagine, for people who would never give her a second glance. She thought of the beggars she had seen outside the train station just days before and wondered how many meals the gold from one room here might buy.

And it was empty in another way. Just like the halls and cellars and stage. Where was he? He hadn't even told her where to go or what to do. Was she supposed to find him? How? With some difficulty, Christine retreated backstage again, now exploring the dance salons and dressing rooms, then the practice rooms for the chorus, and more. By now, her heart was racing.

What if he decided she was unworthy and didn't come? What if he realized what a mistake he had made? What if it had all been a dream? Fear began to choke her as she walked faster.

It was then that she heard it: the sound of a piano far down the hall. She knew instantly that it was him by the perfection of the music. And it was Mozart. The *Fantasia in D minor,* if she was not mistaken.

She followed the dark sound, entranced, and came at last to an open door. As she stepped inside, unsure of what she would find, the music stopped. Christine frowned. The meager light of a single candle on a small table by the door showed a practice room, almost completely submerged in thick shadow. The upright piano was angled and half-hidden behind a screen so that she could see nothing on the keyboard side.

"I was wondering when you'd find your way back to me," the Angel said gently and a thrill like lightning went down Christine's spine. He was here. He was real. And he was hers.

"You didn't tell me where to come. Or when."

"I shall be more precise next time."

She could not see much beyond the small pool of light. Perhaps if she strained, she could make out a shadow seated at the piano, somewhere in the dark. She swore she saw the glint of his eyes but was not sure. Christine didn't care. She would take any glimmer of him to hear his voice.

"Tell me of your studies," the Angel commanded.

"I was at the conservatoire in Rouen for two and a half years," Christine answered with a scowl, looking at her tattered shoes.

"And before that only your father taught you." It wasn't a question. Of course, he knew. She nodded anyway, with pang of sadness at the memory. "The conservatoire: they sent you away before you came to Paris. But you didn't thrive there anyway."

"I never fit in. I just got by as long as I could. They were happy to be rid of me and I must say I didn't disagree." She didn't try to keep the bitterness from her voice. "My teachers didn't like me. They didn't think I had – what was it? Oh yes: 'the voice, the technique or the heart' for a career."

"Is that all?" There was something warm and encouraging in his voice that spurned Christine on, as if he was already on her side against the teachers with sour faces and brittle fingers that had harangued her for so long.

"According to them, my lower register was too heavy, my upper register was harsh, and my middle register lacked clarity. Oh, and my voice had no character or strength. I was too dark to be a soprano but too weak to be a mezzo, so they gave up on both."

"They were fools." He said it with such certainty it struck Christine cold. With three words from him, the past was erased. "I can understand why they thought you might be a mezzo, your lower range *is* more robust than most sopranos, and we can work with that. But you're not Cherubino, my dear, you're Susanna. You're Juliette and Gilda. And, of course, Marguerite." The praise made her smile and blush. "And one day you will be the Contessa and Violetta."

"If someone had said that yesterday, I would have told them it was impossible, but...I believe it when you say it."

"As you should." Once again, his voice took on the commanding timbre that made her shiver. "Technique can be learned. And you certainly do have the voice to learn it. Now, let us see what you can do," he commanded, and Christine straightened her posture, ready to sing at last. "Breathe."

"Breathe?"

"Breathe in like you're singing, but don't sing yet."

Christine took a deep, nervous breath, her chest expanding and her shoulders rising.

"No," the Angel snapped. "Breathe from below, don't let anything above your lowest ribs move." She tried again, better this time, but still tense. "Relax. Breathe into the base of your back and your stomach. Feel it down to the floor, like you're a tree breathing all the way through the roots. Imagine how it should feel and do it."

Again, she took a breath. This time she could feel it was right.

"Again. Good. Now let it out the breath slowly and maintain the support." Christine obeyed and let the breath hiss past her lips. She could feel him watching her critically from the shadow. "Support lower and relax." Again, she tried the deceptively simple exercise, focusing her entire will on her muscles.

"Better. Again."

She relaxed the muscles framing her ribs and belly, automatically she took a deep, correct breath. Again, she let the air fill her then pushed it back out from below. This repeated many times until he was content. At long last, a single middle C sounded from the piano.

"Single notes, on the main vowels, beginning on *ee*. Breathe."

Christine took a breath and sang the first note, hoping more than concentrating.

"No, Christine," he stopped her before she continued. "Support it. Know what you're going to sing *before* the sound comes."

Christine concentrated, imagining herself doing what he asked and doing it perfectly. She inhaled, feeling the breath in her back as she formed her mouth in the shape that would produce the desired vowel. She felt her vocal cords engage, felt the inside of her mouth expand, and felt herself making the perfect space for on the note. Finally, a single pulse of sound emerged.

"Next vowel, *eh*," he commanded, and there was the same eternity of preparation then the satisfaction of the sound at last flowing from her. Again and again, through all the pure vowel sounds – *ee, eh, ah, oh, oo* – slowly and carefully. Over and over up the scale. Small moments of accomplishment were lost in exchange for more imagination, preparation, and at last, fleeting moments of music.

"You don't need to force the sounds out, let them float right behind your eyes. Let them happen. Singing should always be a pleasure," her teacher explained before he finally played a scale from C to G. "Just sing; technique is preparation and maintenance of a space for the sound to thrive. The real beauty comes from the soul of the singer. Stand up straight and open everything *from the inside*, don't be afraid." As if he sensed the doubt still nagging at her, he added: "I am with you."

Her voice rose through the scale, and indeed, it was a pleasure, and it was perfect. They moved through her range, and she was merely a piece of raw material under a master's hands as he meticulously whittled and smoothed her rough edges, found where she was strong, and nurtured it.

Joy rushed through her as she sang. She hadn't taken this much pleasure from her own voice in years, but she had not worked this hard in years either. There were no words, just vowels and scales. It was just sound and breath, and it was amazing. The most exquisite moments however were when the Angel's voice rose in song to guide her. Sometimes it was just for a second to let her hear how the note should sound, but it made Christine's heart race each time.

Once her middle range was warm and ready, he plumbed her depths, testing the lower extension of her chest voice with a hint of wonder as the deep notes tingled to her toes. And then it was up to the heavens with staccato runs to the upper limit of her range to an E flat peak she had not touched in years. It was a wonder. And when he let her truly soar to sustained high Bs and Cs, it was like flying.

"That's enough for today," the Angel pronounced far too soon, as Christine was still catching her breath from the giddy delight of song, her cheeks flush and her skin warm from the effort.

"But we didn't get to any songs," she protested. She could feel his glare from the darkened half of the room.

"Nor will we for at least a week, we are focused on your technique alone and building the strength of your voice for now. And that lovely voice needs to rest."

"Can I come back later then, after I've rested?"

From beyond the light, she heard a new, wonderful sound: her angel's laughter. The sound was warm and dark, like wind through the trees on a summer night.

"We will recommence *tomorrow*, my eager student," he chided. "At ten, here. No sooner."

"I'm sorry," Christine said with a shy smile. "I just didn't think it could feel so good to sing, ever again. I missed it. And I'll miss you."

"You have the greatest city in the world to amuse you until then," the Angel replied. "And you do need to eat. And sleep."

"Oh, I forgot about that, I...don't know if I have the money for much to eat."

"Check your pockets," he said simply. Christine was certain her pockets were very empty but obeyed. She was quite sure there was no order he could give her that she would not follow immediately and joyfully. As promised, her pocket jingled with coins. Enough for a simple meal.

"How?"

"Magic."

She opened her mouth again, unsatisfied. There were a hundred questions she wanted to ask him about himself and heaven and ghosts and the Opera and why his eyes carried such pain, but she sensed there would be no answers for a mere mortal like her.

"Will you be here? If I come back tonight?" she asked instead.

"Of course, and the doors will be open to you. My home is your home. Eat. Rest. Explore. We've just begun our work." Christine nodded and turned to the door. "Christine." She paused, her heart jumping at the sound of her name in that perfect voice. "You did very well today."

"Thank you, my angel," she whispered back then rushed away. It had just slipped out, but the endearment was real. He was *hers*, her angel. He had rescued her and already he had changed her whole life. She dashed through the halls, her cheeks on fire and laughter bubbling past her lips. She had to laugh. It was all too wondrous and mad and perfect.

After so long alone, she had found him, and he was an amazing teacher who believed in her and her voice. He would protect her. Had anyone ever been so blessed? They were just beginning, and she could not wait to hear him again.

Erik stalked through the Opera's halls and wondered if he had ever been so specifically and utterly *fucked*. He had drunk himself to sleep in the wee hours of the morning and avoided leaving home as long as he could after. He had hoped that distance and then the structure of a lesson would ease his madness when it came to this girl. He had been absolutely wrong.

Hours later he couldn't expel the image of Christine from his mind or the sound of her voice from his ears. The progress she had made in one lesson was astounding, as remarkable as she was. When she sang, she was on fire, and Erik wanted to bask forever in the warmth.

He had meant to be cold, distant. He had meant to regard her voice as an instrument and the lesson as an obligation he had trapped himself in via a moment of insanity. God, he'd deluded himself. Now he was wandering the halls of his empty opera, mourning that she had left his walls even though he had encouraged it.

But the halls weren't so empty, Erik realized, as footsteps sounded ahead of him. They were slow and careful. Heavier. A man, but one who was trying not to be heard or detected. Erik smiled. The perfect distraction had arrived.

Unlike his prey, Erik was able to move without making a sound. He kept his distance at first, following the footsteps, until the intruder paused. Erik advanced, smug that he had been right as he watched the man in the Astrakhan hat trace his fingers along the paneling of a corridor wall, his concentration complete.

"They'll really let anyone in the Opera these days," Erik said, casual and calm. The Persian jumped and spun to face Erik, fumbling in his vest for a pistol. "Oh, put that away, Daroga, I'm just saying hello."

"Like hell you are," the Daroga spat back (but did indeed retract his hand from his weapon). "And I made it in because *you* left your damn door unlocked."

Erik leaned against the wall, crossing his arms beneath his cloak, and smiling. "Perhaps I missed you," he lied. "What were you doing assaulting that wall? Still trying to find my secret ways and failing?"

"Biding the time until you found me to posture and threaten," the Daroga shot back. Erik smirked again. The years they had known one another had not been kind to his adversary. (Though to be fair, they had not been kind to Erik either.) The Persian's olive skin had grown ashen in the years away from his home and in the gaslight, Erik could make out a few grey hairs in his neatly trimmed beard and by his temples. But Shaya Motlagh's brown eyes were still as sharp and precise as ever.

"I'm flattered. I was beginning to think you had forgotten me."

"What did you do to that fireman?" Shaya demanded. To the point, as always.

"Oh, so that's why you seem more constipated than usual."

Shaya scowled. "What did you *do*?"

Erik let his eyes go cold, thinking back to the incident. "I merely gave the young man a good scare. He wasn't where he was supposed to be."

"He says he was strangled," the Daroga snapped back, voice dire. "Did you use your hands or the lasso?"

"Did he not say?" Erik countered and Shaya's frown deepened. "Oh, I see, you only read a report or heard a rumor. He wouldn't speak to *you*."

"Answer the question, Erik." His name always sounded like a profanity in Shaya's righteous mouth.

"My hands, if you must know," Erik relented with a sigh. "The lasso would have been unfair. These fools don't even know to keep their hand at the level of their eye." He put meaning behind the words and watched Shaya shiver, his own hand twitching to raise in defense. "Don't worry, Daroga, I won't be punishing you for forgetting. Today at least."

"Posturing and threats; just as I expected."

"As if you're any different," Erik replied. "You came to harass me about that stupid fireman, but for what? So you can feel superior?"

"So that I can remind you I'm watching."

"Oh yes, because that is the crusade you have set for yourself. To watch me and do nothing," Erik mocked. "Honestly, after – what has it been, three years now? – I'm starting to think there's no endgame here."

"I won't let you destroy any more lives," Shaya replied, hatred and grief flaring in his eyes. "If I hear about another assault like that—"

"You'll what? Hunt me down and kill me yourself?" Erik sneered. "You've been trying to find your way to me for years and you've failed, and you have neither the skill nor the heart to end my life. Would you go to the authorities then? The management or the police? They wouldn't believe a Frenchman if he came with such a mad story, they certainly won't believe a foreigner with no evidence." Shaya clenched his fists and his impotent fury made Erik laugh. "It's a stalemate, Daroga, always has been."

"I will find a way," Shaya protested, and Erik waved a thin hand in the air.

"You're so unfair to me, you know," Erik drawled. "You never compliment any of the charitable things I do. Or the work I put in maintaining the artistic integrity of my opera."

Shaya scoffed. "Spare me your artistic sensibilities. You only care about what happens on that stage because it's the same old game for you. You think if you had something to do with it you win your little war against them – the audience, the nobles, whoever you deem your enemy that day. But there's not a soul here that wouldn't rejoice to be rid of the Phantom."

"I'm not so sure of that," Erik said, unable to repress a smile. In fact, he was certain one person would be quite heartbroken if the

Opera Ghost were lost. Or revealed. "But you do make a good point. Sometimes I forget it *is* all a game."

"What are you talking about?" Shaya asked in new alarm.

"I get complacent too, Daroga," Erik went on, singsong and thoughtful as his mind raced. "I forget my duty here. My own dreams and ambitions."

"Erik, I swear—" Erik cut him off with a long, low laugh.

"You needn't worry, Daroga. This chess match isn't between me and you. You're just a rook who gets in the way." He declined to say whose piece Shaya was, knowing that mystery would infuriate him. "I'll see you again soon, I'm sure."

"We're not done," Shaya said, but Erik had already turned, gliding around the corner and instantly out of sight. He laughed at the sound of Shaya banging on the wall.

"And I wouldn't look for my doors, Daroga," Erik called, making his voice echo through the empty hall. "You wouldn't like what's on the other side."

"Damn you, Erik," the Persian hissed, and Erik gave one more laugh before he descended to the floor below.

Seeing the Daroga had been a good reminder: of what he was, and what he wanted. He had become so comfortable at the Opera and in his routines, he had forgotten the game. But it was still there. And he had a new pawn to convert to a queen.

What a queen she would be too, Erik mused as he crept deeper through his theater. She would sweep away Carlotta and shine brighter than anyone who had ever taken that stage. The spineless nobles with their bloody hands would fawn and bow to her...and they would be bowing to him. Yes. This is why he had found her. It had to be. This growing obsession wasn't about her beauty or her faith or her smile. It was her voice as a tool. He could cope with that. Allow it.

It was a perfect falsehood, good enough to convince a prince of lies like himself. Or at least he hoped it was.

Christine smiled up at the Greek Temple set in the heart of Paris. If she was honest, she preferred the façade of The Madeleine to the Opera, it was simpler, if no less grand, and if she squinted, she could pretend she was some ancient maiden, come to pray to the old Gods.

She didn't enter, of course. Rather she made her way to the small plaza on the side and took a seat on a bench to enjoy her dinner under the orange leaves of the sparse trees and watch Paris go by. It was so much louder here than in the Opera, she thought as she chewed her tart of cheese, onion, and egg. Pairs of sturdy horses hauled omnibuses past her, men in tall black hats walked with canes next to demure ladies wearing bonnets decorated with silken flowers. Christine had sold her last hat for a few sous in Rouen. Maybe when she was paid, she could buy a new one. In fact, there were still a few coins jangling in her pocket. Perhaps it would be enough.

Christine cast her eyes to the shops around the Madeleine, finishing her last bites as she let herself dream just a bit of the life of a diva that the Angel promised her. She was sure that being a lady in fine satin with a carriage and twenty pretty hats would never make her as happy as hearing his voice.

"Monsieur, can you spare a few coins?" The female voice was accented, and when Christine looked, she saw that indeed the woman who had made the entreaty of a finely dressed man striding across the plaza had the dusky skin and features that marked her as one with no land. Romani.

"Get out of my way, you filth," the man sneered, swatting at the woman with his cane. She ducked away quickly and made eye contact with Christine as she did.

"Here," Christine said automatically, pulling her remaining money from her pocket. "It's not much, but I hope it helps."

The woman was hesitant, clearly wary of taking money from someone who looked nearly as destitute as herself. "Are you sure?"

"I'm sure your family needs it more than I," Christine replied, holding out her hand with the coins. Carefully, the woman took them, nodding as she did.

"Thank you, Mademoiselle," the Roma woman said, then turned quickly and disappeared down the busy street.

Christine picked up her remaining food from the bench and pulled her shawl tighter around her shoulders. She had wandered for so many years, just like that woman. She had been a nomad just days before. And now by a miracle, she had a place to return to that felt like home. She looked to the great church one more time and smiled to herself, nodding in thanks. She did not know how her angel fit into the ranks of heaven or the halls of Olympus, but she would not question it. She would not spoil this miracle.

Erik made it a few hours at home before he found himself ascending from the depths and through a hidden door in an old set from *Le Roi de Lahore*. It was very easy to find her from here. She was wrapped in an old wool blanket, reading a book by the light of the lamp. The light made her profile even lovelier, as did the soft smile that spread over her face as he watched her. How did she know he was there?

"You came," Christine said softly, looking into the darkness around her. "I've been waiting."

"What are you reading?" Erik asked, helpless in the face of her warmth and trust. There were two more books beside her, and just like the one she held, they looked very old and well-loved.

"Fairy tales. I've carried these with me for a long time, but it's been a while since I've been able to read them." She traced the edge of one volume. "I guess I've started believing in magic again. Since you found me."

Erik had no idea how to respond. It was frightening: being the reason for an innocent girl's faith.

"Did you eat?"

She nodded and held up a paper package in the lantern light. "And I have enough for tomorrow."

"Good. I can't have you starving." She smiled again and he ignored the thrill it gave him. "I'm glad you found your way back."

"It did take me a while, without a guide," she said, her eyes unfocused as she spoke to the dark. "It's lonely here when you're not close."

"Most people are scared when I'm close," he replied without thinking. "But not you, my brave girl." It made his skin tingle just to say it, not that she was brave. But that she was his.

"I never considered myself brave before," Christine murmured, playing with the hem of her dress. "I've been afraid of everything for so long. These last few years...I didn't feel very brave."

"You survived alone in a cruel world for three years, don't you think that's brave?" Erik prodded. There was a part of his mind screaming at him to stop this conversation. If she was just a tool, then knowing her didn't matter. But it did. And so did comforting her as sadness edged her expression. "You kept going, you didn't give up."

"No, Papa was the brave one. But when he...left..." New tears were visible in the corners of her eyes, sparkling in the light of the oil lamp. "I did give up."

"I know you miss him." What did she expect her angel to know about her father, he wondered? Did she picture them talking about her in heaven? What in Hades had he tangled himself into? "Tell me about him."

"He was a great musician," Christine began with visible difficulty. "And he loved stories. I grew up with the sound of his violin and all those stories; of trolls and old gods, the *nissa* and the *tomte*, Vasilisa and Little Lotte, and stories...about the Angel of Music, about you." Erik cringed at the look of joy in her eyes. "It was just the two of us nearly my whole life, from the time I was six; when we left Sweden."

Sweden. The name Daaé made more sense now, though not entirely. Her features and hair were darker than those he would expect from the North.

"After we came to France, we tried to stay in one place, but Papa couldn't live that way. We went everywhere, singing and doing any odd jobs that would feed us. Sometimes Papa would find work in an orchestra or symphony, but he hated staying anywhere for too long. Sometimes we worked as servants, or we joined in with fairs, and even entertained wealthy families." The words and memories were coming easier now. Erik wondered exactly what kind of rootless travelers Christine and her father had been.

"There were places we'd return to each year, especially near the sea. We both loved the ocean. Those were the only places where I really had any acquaintances that came close to friends. Well, just one actually. I'm sure he's forgotten me now." She smiled at the thought; a secret, sweet smile that for some reason made Erik's gut twist unpleasantly.

"You haven't talked about your mother," Erik stated. He already guessed why.

"She died when I was six."

"The year you left Sweden."

"That was why we left. They gave up so much to be together and the home we made in Sweden reminded him so much of her. And yet we went to back to her homeland, to France and the family she left to be with him. Our time with them didn't last very long." Christine's expression darkened. "I look like her, and that made him sad too.

Papa wouldn't speak about her for years. He told me other stories. He kept telling me stories long after most girls outgrow such things, and he told me that he would never lie to me, that all his stories were true." She paused, more unnoticed tears staining her pale skin. "He was my world. When I lost him, I wasn't brave. I stopped believing and living. I was just...empty."

There it was. Erik was a liar and there were no angels, but oh how this girl needed them just to live.

"You think part of you died with him," Erik guessed softly, reading the story from her beautiful face. "Not just the part of you that was brave, but the part that could feel. And believe. And you wanted to let it die, because if you were dead to the world, it could not hurt you again. If you weren't even alive, you would not have to miss him."

Replace a father with an entire world and he might as well be telling his own story. That was why he'd helped her, wasn't it? He saw in her pain and loneliness like his own. He could admit that, here in the dark with her.

"But you didn't die, Christine. You survived. And you cannot be dead when you sing. This is what I want to teach you. Singing is breathing. And breathing is life, the conscious act of living. Somewhere deep within when you choose to breathe, you choose to live. Some un-surrendering part of you chooses to continue," he whispered, surprised at his own words even as a new light began to glow in Christine's eyes. "When you sing, you are living. You are transforming the very force of your life into something beautiful, even when it hurts so terribly. So, I know you're brave, Christine, because even after all the pain, you keep breathing."

She breathed deep, as if on command, closing her eyes as her tears fell. Some of them were tears of joy, he hoped. And Erik breathed too, the need for air so deep and sudden it made him ache. Silently he breathed, moved by the girl before him. And he was reminded, terribly and unavoidably, that he too was alive and no matter how many lies he told himself and her, no matter how many masks he wore, he couldn't change that.

"Thank you," Christine whispered. "I know I keep saying it but...I cannot thank you enough for what you've given me. I don't know how these stories of you as a terror can be true, because you truly are an angel."

"Only for you, Christine," he said and meant it.

"Angel..." her voice was small and soft and supplicant. "Will you sing for me again? Sing me to sleep?"

"Of course," he sighed. He knew already that it was going to be quite impossible to refuse her.

He began to sing, his own breath and life transforming into a lullaby thick with longing. He chose a different song tonight, a Romani tune that echoed with windswept roads and yearning for something unreachable. And it made her smile as if she had just seen an old friend. Like so many of her smiles, it made his heart swell and ache.

When he had entered the room, smug with the idea of her as his pawn, this would have been easy. He could have pretended, the way he had pretended to be a ghost and now played at being an angel. But he was a man, and he was alive. He had felt more alive close to her in the last few days than he had in years. She had tempted him from the dark, and with each step he took closer to her, the illusions he had so built so carefully were falling away.

Before her, he had been content, not happy (someone like him would never truly be happy) but he had been pleased with the life he had created for himself far from the cruel, cold light of day. He had learned, finally and so painfully, that the world of the living wanted nothing from him, and he wanted nothing from it, but she made him forget all that. She made him realize that he had never stopped breathing.

He could lie to the world, to Christine, but his breath would not let him lie to himself. He was alive. And the girl before him who leaned back on her bed, her eyes closed in ecstasy at the sound of his voice, her breasts heaving with her breath, and a blissful smile on her face...this damn girl made him *want* to be.

5. Patronage

Christine closed her eyes and let the weak autumn sunlight warm her face as she sat on the front steps of the Opera, just out of view of the horrible doorman, enjoying her lunch. Halfway through November she'd take any light she could get, and right now, it made her humble day perfect. She had a warm pastry in her hand and a lesson with her angel to look forward to tonight. What more did she need?

Being near him was like the sun in the winter, she thought, taking another slow bite. And just like leaving the light, leaving him and the Opera always left her feeling cold. She was glad to explore Paris' avenues and shops (or at least their windows), but it was always a relief to be home. Funny how in under a month she'd come to think of her little hidden bed among the old sets as her home. And in that time several additions had appeared to make it more like a real room: a small clock had shown up after Louise and the Angel had complained about her tardiness on the same day. A new brush also had materialized, as had a vase of silken flowers.

But the best gifts were the books. She had felt him watching her re-read the volumes of myths and fairy tales she had carried with her for years. And so, it was not a surprise when the first book had appeared. It was a translation of Goethe's *Faust*. More had followed.

Last night she'd listened to another performance of Gounod's version, after a performance of *Le Prophète*, the week before. Although she preferred Gounod to Meyerbeer, she had been delighted to see César take the stage. He and the mezzo singing lead were both preferable to Carlotta. Thinking of the woman's success made Christine frown. Not because of the lack of musicality the woman exalted in, but because it reminded her of the progress she was and was not making. Carlotta had a thin, crystal voice like a demonic choir boy, yet used it to sing with the gusto of an angry cat. But at least she was allowed to *sing*.

After more than three weeks of astonishing lessons, Christine knew her voice was stronger and clearer than she ever could have imagined. But was it the voice of a diva as he promised? She had no idea. How could she when he still would not let her sing actual music? Everything had been scales and breathing and single tones and trills and breathing and long notes spinning out the sound and still more breathing. She was ready to truly sing. Why was he not letting her?

"What is this garbage doing on the steps?"

Christine jumped at the shrill voice. The woman who had spoken loomed above her, her angular, slight frame wrapped in cream furs and satin ruffles, a feathered hat perched precariously atop her perfectly coifed blonde curls. She was flanked by a small man with a thin moustache and spectacles and a more robust man, also well-dressed, who looked bored. If Christine stood, she would be taller than her, but the woman sneered down at her in a way designed to make her feel small and useless. Christine knew the look well and she hated it.

"LeDoux, Herbert – remove this thing from my way," the woman commanded her male followers. Her voice carried a strange accent.

"There's room to go around," Christine retorted. "I promise you won't exhaust your pretty feet with a few more steps."

"The steps of my opera are not a place for beggars or vagrants," the woman snarled. "Get out."

"It's not your opera," Christine snapped back. She let her offence at this woman's ignorance of who the Opera truly belonged to buoy her past her shame.

"I said *remove her*," the woman trilled to the men, and it was the little one that nervously moved towards Christine.

"Don't make us call a gendarme, Mademoiselle," he stammered as he reached for her.

"Don't touch me," Christine snarled, jumping up, even though it meant surrendering to these bourgeois boars. Her heart raced, and she felt as if her very bones were trembling as she rushed to the employee's entrance. As soon as she was inside the shaking stopped and she was solid, calmer. She waited for the hairs on the back of her neck to stand up as she made her way back to the costume workshop.

She didn't feel *him* at all times in the Opera, which made sense. He wasn't just her angel. He was the guardian and spirit of the entire place. (How an angel had come to be a ghost was a mystery to her, and she was afraid to ask). The fact he chose to watch her, to linger close outside of lessons, was a gift and she treasured it each time it was given. She walked deeper into the Opera and grinned when she sensed *him*.

It was only for a moment, but it made her entire body tingle. It was like walking by a room with a warm fire on a winter's day, a brief reminder of heat and comfort. She sighed as the sensation disappeared, thinking not on her lessons but on the time after, when he would sing to her and sweep her away with his voice. Sometimes he would sing old songs she knew, other times he would weave ballads in languages that sounded like they came from a dream.

And sometimes he would sing music that she simply could not define that took her breath away with its beauty. Those songs made her dizzy, like the strongest wine. They made her skin tingle and her pulse quicken in the strangest way, as his voice enticed her body to come alive at the same time as it lifted her into heaven.

She tried not to think of the emptiness she felt upon waking, the longing for him to be there in the dark. Sometimes she would dream of his shadow close to her. Most mornings she would wake aching for him – for something she couldn't name.

The workshop was buzzing when Christine returned and took her place in the back corner amongst the mending. While her vocal skills had grown incredibly over the last few weeks, her sewing had only improved from terrible to almost passable, but no one seemed to mind. Other than Julianne, she hadn't made any friends. Perhaps that was why, since the majority of the costumers sent dirty looks at Julianne too often. Rumors about "the girl who summoned the Ghost" had traveled fast and the other women in the shop treated her with a certain wariness too. They made a good pair then. Two outsiders.

Christine caught a glance towards her over someone's shoulder as a conversation recommenced in quiet tones.

"He died at a masquerade," Maxine was telling her small tablemate, Camille. "And that's why he has a mask."

Christine pretended not to listen. She took great interest in the ghost stories but never participated in telling them, knowing the truth as she did. But she too had thought about his mask, and what it meant. Her own theory was that the face of an angel was too glorious for mortals to behold, but she couldn't say that.

"Well, I heard he's hideous underneath, rotting away like a corpse," Camille sniped back, and Christine bristled, privately. They didn't know.

"Well, speaking of hideous," Maxine sighed, and it took a beat for Christine to understand that she had turned her attention to the entrance of the workshop. As it swung open, an extremely familiar woman sauntered in.

"Oh no," Christine sighed. It was the woman from outside, with a slightly altered retinue. The robust man was gone, replaced by a terrified maid, but the sniveling man with the spectacles was still there.

"Ah, she's here," Julianne muttered as she came to stand by Christine in the corner. "The diva herself."

"Wait are you telling me—" Christine surveyed the woman again: her ostentatious gown and fur, her entitled air. It matched the voice she had begun to detest. "That's *Carlotta*?"

"I forgot, you haven't met her in person," Julianne said. "I guess your luck has run out."

"I think it ran out when I met her by the front entrance and nearly told her to fuck herself," Christine replied, and Julianne raised a delighted eyebrow. "I didn't. But I wasn't polite."

"Maybe stay out of view then," Juliane offered, and Christine attempted to shrink even more. Carlotta strode through the workshop, giving bored glances to the work going on as she headed to Louise.

"Shall we get this over with?" Carlotta drawled, her accent curiously muddled.

Louise for her part looked as annoyed as could be politely managed. "As I told your maid and your...whatever he is," she gestured at the man beside Carlotta. "I am not ready for your fitting today, nor do we have room here to do it at the moment."

"Well, there is no room in my dressing room any longer," Carlotta retorted.

"Because she had a copper *bath* installed this week," Julianne whispered to Christine. "Demanded it of the management after someone broke her mirror or something."

"And I'd like to have more input on the new gowns," Carlotta went on. "Especially for *Faust*. They're far too drab."

"Again, Signora, there has been no order from the directors for new costumes for *Faust*. These will just be for *Rigoletto*."

Christine shuddered. She couldn't stand this woman as innocent Marguerite; she could hardly imagine her as Gilda.

"The Signora would like a new dress for the prison scene," the little man said. "In the Spanish style, as a tribute to her."

"The Signora doesn't sound Spanish at all," Christine whispered to Julianne under her breath and the other girl repressed a snort of amusement.

"Don't speak for me, LeDoux," Carlotta snapped, smacking him with the end of her fur. "But he's right. I cannot abide that sack they make me wear. The bodice isn't even boned!"

"It is a prison dress, Signora," Louise replied through her teeth. "And I can have it refitted *another day*."

"I'll expect you to be ready with something suitable at my next fitting. Which I will be doing here, but I'd rather not have –" she gestured at the workers around her "– the unwashed masses about." Carlotta's eyes surveyed the room and Christine's stomach dropped as they fell on her. "Some of them are so dirty I don't know why you even let them touch anything for the stage. I wouldn't want to get fleas. What's next, Gypsy tinkerers building our sets? The disgrace." With a flourish of her fur stole Carlotta spun and exited the room.

"Bitch," Julianne muttered.

Christine sank into her seat, a well of emotions bubbling inside her: shame, fear, rage, doubt. She knew she was more than that woman saw, or at least that her angel saw more. But she couldn't help but feel like Carlotta had also seen the truth: that she didn't belong among the gilded finery of the Opera and its callous, cruel denizens.

Most days there was only one place she wanted to be and yet it would be hours before she could retreat there. She had waited for so much of her life, she thought as she sighed and returned to her stitching. She could wait a few hours more, but sometimes that need to be close to him was so deep she didn't know if anything could fill it.

Erik knew Christine's voice very well by now. He could tell when she needed more sleep or water, knew the difference between a lesson in the morning or in the evening. But tonight, there was something else causing imperfection in the sound.

"Are you alright?" he asked as she finished an octave run. He knew he'd hit on something as she looked at her hands with a frown. "You sound...sad."

"I'm sorry," Christine stuttered, shame and disappointment written clearly on her face.

"Don't be sorry, just tell me what's going on."

"I met *La* Carlotta."

"Well, I can see how that would be upsetting for anyone," he said. She smiled weakly at the joke. "Was she cruel to you?"

"Yes, but that's not what I can't get out of my mind," Christine replied. He was silent, inviting her to continue. "She was so elegant and sure of her greatness. It just made me feel like I don't belong in the same world as her."

"Carlotta's jewels and airs only serve to hide that her heart and voice are rotten garbage," Erik tried to console her.

"She said as much about me," Christine sighed. "And I can't blame her. I mean, look at me. I'm just a ragamuffin off the street. And I know you can see me on that stage one day, but I can't and..." Christine sniffled. "And I still haven't even sung any proper music! And—"

"*Christine.*" She gasped and her mouth snapped shut at his tone. "Do you dare doubt me?"

"Never!" she answered instantly and to Erik's shock, she fell to her knees. "I'm sorry, I didn't mean to question you!"

Erik's heart jumped to his throat, panic, and something else gripping him as his student prostrated herself before him, her face a perfect picture of devotion and desire for his approval and faith.

"Then believe me when I say that you belong on my stage more than any singer who has ever walked these halls. And also believe me when I tell you that you are more beautiful and captivating than Carlotta in every single way."

He meant it. For weeks he'd sung to her, watched her, and come to know her. And every day and every lesson convinced him even more that she was incredible. Her strength and kindness and voice were all he could think about lately. His growing obsession was on the verge of becoming a serious problem and it was only the idea that this girl was a means to something greater that kept him sane. At least, when he was apart from her.

When he was close to her, he forgot all that. Singing to her in the dark, drifting closer to her each night. He forgot everything. Right now, in fact, nothing else mattered but the pure awe on Christine's face.

"That woman – she's shattered glass, Christine. You are a diamond," he whispered, and Christine took a shaking breath.

"How is she still here? She's horrible to everyone and she can't even sing! There're probably a dozen singers just in the chorus better than her!" Christine stood, much to Erik's relief. "Why do you—"

"Allow her to stay?" Erik finished for her with a laugh. "Oh, I don't. If being a star were about talent, most of the divas in the world would be out of a job. People like Carlotta thrive because of who they know and the power they hold. And she has the most terrible power on her side: money."

"Money?" Christine echoed and Erik deeply envied her naivete. "Is she that rich?"

"Not her, the patrons. They give money to the Opera, in exchange for prestige and some feeling of power. Some give quite a lot. Carlotta has her claws in enough of them that if she goes, they will too. Or at least she likes to remind the managers of that."

"Why though? They can't like her voice," Christine balked, and Erik had to laugh.

"Some of them prefer her private performances." Christine gave a quizzical look and he laughed again. "She fucks them, my dear."

"Oh!" Christine exclaimed and even in the darkened room, Erik could see how deeply she blushed. "More than one?"

"A few at least, and sometimes a manager or director when it's convenient," Erik explained. An angel shouldn't speak this way, but he was a different sort of angel, and she knew that. "Other patrons have their own concubines among the chorus or corps de ballet, and Carlotta makes sure to remind them that she'll introduce those women to their wives if they step out of line."

"God, that's awful," Christine sighed. "I mean – not the lovers; the control."

"The Paris Opera runs on money, much to my own dismay," Erik told her. "The nobles, the patrons – they don't care about the music. The art. They defile it with people like Carlotta, but when you sing, my dear Christine, they'll have no choice but to listen and change their minds."

Christine looked down, blushing again. "I trust you."

"Good," Erik said. "Because today I think we will try an aria. You've earned it." He could have laughed at the way her face brightened at the words. "It will be Mozart, and only Mozart for at least a week, perhaps two."

"I'm more than happy with that," Christine grinned.

"We'll start with your *Deh Vieni*, since I know you have it memorized. From the recitative."

As ever, he wasn't prepared for how her voice affected him as it rose in song, and she sang of longing and love. Even as he stopped her to correct her vowels and support, he could not help but think of the way she had blushed. He dwelt on the thoughts of her kneeling and then of her, rapt by his voice in her secret bed. The memories sent a long-forgotten thrill through his body, and again, in the dark near her, he felt alive.

"What are you humming?" Julianne snapped at Christine as they carried overflowing baskets of toe shoes to the *Salon du Danse*. "Usually you hum *Faust*, but that's not what you're on today."

"It's Mozart," Christine smiled. "Do I hum that often?"

Julianne scoffed. "If you stopped, I'd worry you'd died."

Christine smiled back at her friend. "What can I say, I love the opera."

"Must be why *he* likes you so much," Julianne said with a wink. "Maybe he'll let you pick the next show."

"If only," Christine said as they entered the packed salon and were instantly set upon by dancers, flocking to the them like the pigeons in the Tuileries when Christine offered them bread.

"Calm down, girls, there's enough for all of you," Julianne laughed.

Christine watched in fascination as the girls sorted through the slippers, looking for the right size and style. The rats scurried away with their prizes and almost immediately began tearing and beating at the new gear, each with their own little rituals and quirks to make the shoes their own. Jammes was the last to approach. The blonde dancer smiled as Julianne produced a hidden pair of slippers for her with a sly grin.

"Just as you like them," Julianne purred.

"Thank you," Jammes smiled, locking eyes with Julianne like Christine wasn't even there. She was used to it.

"Everyone seems on edge," Julianne commented over the sound of ripping and chatter.

"Rehearsal is open to patrons later today," Jammes said with a sigh.

"Ah, the meat market," said Julianne.

Christine swallowed. It had been a week since her angel had given her Mozart, called her beautiful, and educated her on the real ways of the Opera. *She fucks them, my dear.* The words rang in her head over and over, especially at night. She looked around to the women stretching and preparing throughout the salon. They were almost all younger than her.

"They're hoping to snag a...patron?" Christine asked innocently. God, she couldn't even say the word 'lover' for fear of offending someone, and yet here they were.

"A few of the stupider ones," Jammes replied. "They think that will make them the next Sorelli. As if any of them could get the attention of a count." Christine's brows rose high. She had seen La Sorelli, the prima ballerina, a few times. A cliche as it was, the woman did look very much like a swan, with pale skin and black hair. She was as sour as a swan too, which is why Christine avoided her. She hadn't heard that she too had a powerful lover, but it made sense.

"Luckily, you're not stupid," Julianne remarked, giving Jammes a pointed look.

"Oh yes, why would I need a patron to bring me flowers and gifts when I have you to bring me shoes," Jammes replied with a cool smile.

"I didn't realize more was expected," Julianne said in a tone Christine couldn't place – something between offended and sad. "Come on, Christine, we'll be missed, unless you want to get a patron who'll pay the managers to put your humming on stage."

"As if *she* needs that," Jammes scoffed. "Of all people, to think a *seamstress* has the only patron that matters."

It took a moment for Christine to realize what Jammes meant: the Ghost. The rumors about her had faded, due to not being very interesting, but Jammes remembered. "Let's go," Julianne said and pulled Christine away from the mirrored splendor of the salon. "Don't worry about her, she's in a pique," Julianne grumbled as they made their way through the halls.

"I guess she's not wrong." Christine shrugged and Julianne gave her a look. "I mean, he's let me keep sleeping here."

"Quite the patron indeed," Julianne replied. "I've heard some of the richest ones keep their mistresses in lovely flats on the boulevards, but I'm sure wherever you run off to is just as nice." Julianne laughed to herself. "Then again, you aren't spreading your legs for him so—"

"Julianne!" Christine gasped. She wasn't sure why. It was an outrageous thing to say of course, and Julianne burst into giggles at Christine's scandalized look. But there was more to it than that. It brought things to mind that only ever skirted her thoughts when she woke in the dark, sure his shadow was close enough to touch.

"Oh, dear you'll need to get used to jokes like that if you're to survive here," Julianne chuckled.

"I'll try to toughen up." Christine wanted to say something smarter but at that moment they both caught sight of a veritable hurricane of furs, satin, and jewels barreling down the hall at them. "Oh no."

"Out of my way, you little scabs," Carlotta hissed as Julianne and Christine flattened themselves against the wall.

"Pardon us, Madame," Christine said and drew a glare, a spark of recognition in Carlotta's eyes. "I'm sure you don't want to be late to your fitting."

"It's *Signora*," Carlotta spat, then stopped. "I thought that was tomorrow," she said with a frown. Her little secretary began to scramble through his valise.

"Did the note not reach you? Valerie was told to get it to you directly," Christine continued. Out of the corner of her eye she could see the curiosity and horror in Julianne's expression, since she knew there was no fitting, nor anyone working in costumes named Valerie.

"What note? When is this?" Carlotta demanded, agitation growing.

"It was meant to inform you that – since Madame Grelot knows you need privacy and that you are accustomed to a certain standard – she has arranged to have the fitting done at your dressmaker's salon. What was his name?" she muttered looking to Julianne for help.

"Monsieur, uh, Grenier?" Julianne stammered.

"Did you mean Monsieur Gauthier?!" Carlotta squawked. "That's on the *Boulevard des Italiens*! When is this? Never mind! LeDoux! Run and tell that idiot Gabriel I don't need to rehearse the trio again anyway. I'll have someone summon the carriage." Carlotta continued muttering as she raced the other way down the hall. It was not until she had fully disappeared that both Christine and Julianne burst out laughing.

"You are mad!" Julianne exclaimed between guffaws. "She'll kill you when she finds out you lied. Or at least fire you."

"She doesn't even know my name," Christine replied with a shrug. "And, like Jammes said, I do have the only patron that matters." Christine smiled at the thought. It made something warm and brazen dance within her. A she waited for Julianne to make another bawdy comment.

Her friend remained silent and dubious, leaving Christine to the train of thought: of what the mortal patrons demanded in exchange for their aid and protection. And how the thought of bestowing such gifts on her own protector filled her not with fear or shame, but with simmering, breathless...curiosity.

“*E se, non ho chi m'oda, e se non ho chi m'oda...Parlo d'amor con me, con me...Parlo d'amor con me!*" Erik wanted to rise to applaud as

Christine finished Cherubino's sparkling aria of youthful infatuation. She was in the finest form he'd heard from her yet, and the ease with which she took on the mezzo piece, after sparkling earlier in the lesson in her highest range, was astounding.

"Wonderful," he told her, trying to keep his praise contained. "You're in a very good mood."

"Well, it was a very exciting day," she said with a mischievous smirk.

"What have you been up to?"

"I...may have tricked Carlotta into missing rehearsal?" Christine confessed, barely pretending at shame. "And sent her off to a fake fitting at some dress salon instead?"

"Did you really?" Erik asked, ready once more to applaud her.

"Well, she did call me a scab," Christine shrugged. "And I'm sure the rehearsal was easier."

"I'm sure it was. And you weren't afraid of her retaliating?"

"Not with you on my side," she said with a truly genuine smile and faith that took his breath away. The extent to which his girl trusted him was only comparable to the lengths he would go to keep that trust. "Shall I go through the aria again?" she asked brightly.

"Rest now, you've sung enough, and it's getting late," Erik said and knew she could hear the regret in his voice. He wanted to stay too. "There will be more Mozart tomorrow."

"Here at least," Christine sighed. "I do wish they would perform more of it in Paris."

"As do I, but the managers are set in their ways," Erik replied, as sad as her. "They want opera in French, so no one has to think too much, and they want their ballets and bombastic spectacles like Meyerbeer. At least Massenet and Gounod have some merit."

"And Verdi doesn't mind his work being translated. Still...it would be nice if *this* opera honored the greatest composer in history with more than a bust for pigeons to perch on."

Erik smiled in the shadow. "Why is it you love Mozart so?"

"Well, it's perfect," Christine smiled. "I think it's because there's so much *light* in his music. I can't quite explain it."

"Many composers know how to write music with the sound of tears and death, but Mozart..." Erik mused. "He could also write laughter. And desire and joy. His music sparkles like no one else's."

Christine smiled again, and gods above, Erik could savor that smile forever. "And no one dies in his operas," she added, wistful. "Every woman in every opera written in the last half-century dies. Violetta, Gilda, Juliette, Lucia, Carmen, even Marguerite...all dead by the end."

Erik felt a pang of guilt he'd never thought of it that way. "Don Giovanni dies."

"Yes, but everyone wants that; it's a good thing when he dies," Christine countered with a playful scowl. Erik bristled.

"Is it? I always found it ambiguous. He dies defiant to the end, refusing propriety, opposing men in power...a libertine unrepentant," he mused, his thoughts turning to a very different tale of Don Juan, hidden deep beneath the Opera, meant for a much darker end.

Christine's expression was suspicious and confused. "He's a seducer," she said carefully.

"But he's dragged to hell for murder and defiance, not that." Again, he could not read her face. "Quite the opposite of Marguerite lifted to heaven, I guess. But still dead."

"Still, if I could choose, I'd rather the Contessa, singing of love and hope, living on, than Marguerite blazing for a moment, only to be taken by death."

Erik smiled at that. "I should like that for you too, my dear. But you may have to die, just a little, until we can convince our managers to mount *Figaro*."

"As long as I can sing for you and with you," Christine said, her voice warm and gentle. "I would die a hundred times."

The way she said it made a thrill rush through his body. He clenched his hands into fists above the piano keys, willing himself not to feel it. He had to do that often lately, with her. Each night he drifted closer to her when he sang for her, and even closer when she slept. Each day she became more of an *idée fixe*, intruding on his thoughts at all times. Every composition had begun to sound like her voice, each machination for the management only mattered because of her career. He was barely in control as it was, but when she said things like that...that thin cord binding him to some semblance of sanity frayed a little more.

"Good," was all he could say to that. "But as I said, it is getting late."

"But I'm not tired," she whined, faux-petulant.

"You need your rest if you're to continue our little war on Carlotta tomorrow," he said and savored the way she tilted back her head as she laughed, baring her pale neck in the candlelight.

"You mean there's nothing we can do to vex her right now?" she asked, running a hand over her hair to realign the many locks that had escaped her chignon. It gave Erik a mad idea.

"Now that you mention it, didn't you say recently you wished you could have a nice hot bath?"

"What does that have to do with—" Christine stopped as she realized what he meant.

"I can assure you, the lock on Carlotta's dressing room hasn't worked for a long time."

Christine laughed again, giddy at the suggestion. "I can't!"

"Of course you can. Go. No one's here to stop you." She laughed again as she raced out of their little practice room and her absence struck him like a cold wind.

He rose from his place in the shadow, where he remained forever hidden from her eyes, and stretched. Erik ignored his body most of the time. It was easier to be a ghost when one didn't dwell too much on the aches and pains of living. But lately, he couldn't even do that.

She kept him awake, kept him tense, and because of that, he ached more and more each night. And of course, there were the *other* responses a beautiful body could inspire in a man. He hadn't thought about those things, or more correctly, *let* himself think of such things for a long time. There was simply no point. But she reminded him that those feelings and desires – so long forgotten and pushed away – were still there, like warm embers beneath the banked ash of a fire.

Erik did not mean to follow her. The same part of him that constantly argued against the madness of this whole endeavor tried to steer his feet home. But the passage to take him there went past the dressing rooms. Even if he went slowly, trying to control himself, he would pass by Carlotta's opulent room. Like so many of the salons and rooms of the Opera, the mirrors there provided Erik with a window into a private space. He rarely used the view to Carlotta's chamber for obvious reasons, and the glass was actually far smaller than others, especially the grand mirror in the farthest dressing room that could also become a door.

And so he found himself drawn by the lamplight from the prima donna's dressing room. Through the mirror that was his window he could see steaming water filling the ridiculous copper tub she had installed. The object of Erik's obsession perched at Carlotta's vanity, admiring the diva's costume jewels and perfumes. And she was already half-undressed.

Erik caught his breath at the sight. Christine was in just a white chemise and drawers, and the sheer, thin linen clung to each curve of her body beneath. She was humming to herself but stopped for a moment when his eyes lit upon her bare shoulders and back. She had to sense his eyes, as she always did. That strange power was why he had so far avoided looking at her in such intimate, exposed moments. She would know. Which meant he had to leave. This was an intrusion too far. But she had begun to hum again, and as she raised a gaudy necklace to her throat, she began to fully sing.

"*Ah, I laugh to see myself so beautiful in this mirror.*" Of course it was Marguerite's Jewel Song. She repeated the phrase, setting the aria lower than the original key, intoning the melody to Carlotta's mirror with a husky, gentle lilt. "*Is it you? Marguerite? Tell me, tell me, tell me quickly.*"

"I don't believe I authorized Gounod," Erik said, unable to help himself.

"I knew you were there," Christine said with a sly smile.

"You always do."

She rose from the vanity, turning to check the water of the bath and add splashes of soap and perfume to the steaming tub. Erik could see the outline of her breasts beneath the flimsy fabric of her chemise and the sight made his mouth go dry.

"I should leave you to your private enjoyment," he forced himself to say, tearing his eyes away before he could ogle her further.

"You don't have to." Erik's eyes flew back to her at the soft words. Her face was hesitant but somehow determined as she looked to the empty air around her. "Don't you know there's nothing I would hide from you?"

"*Christine.*" He meant the name to come out as an admonishment, a dismissal of a foolish girl saying things she didn't understand. But instead, he spoke it like a prayer, and she smiled. Somehow encouraged, she lifted her hands and slowly pushed the chemise off her shoulders, exposing her bare breasts to the cold air and her angel's rapt eyes.

She was so beautiful. That was Erik's first, breathless thought; beautiful and perfect. Her breasts were plump and alert, and he could see goosebumps on the pale flesh. Her taut, pink nipples held his eyes for a fantastic moment until her hands continued to move, pushing the chemise down to her hips, until it, along with the drawers, fell to the ground.

Erik could barely breathe or think, his heart pounding in his ears as Christine stood exposed to the gaze of a false angel that was anything but heavenly. He took in the curve of her waist and hips, the gentle softness of her belly, and finally, the thatch of dark hair above the juncture of her thighs. At the sight of her, naked and trusting in view of her teacher, the embers of lust he had ignore for so long suddenly burst into a raging flame. His blood flowed so fast to his cock it made him dizzy, and in moments he was harder than he had been in his entire, cursed life.

He was doomed.

"Am I allowed to sing, if it's Mozart?" Christine asked, her eyes downcast as she loosed her hair and let the dark tresses cascade free over her back. Finally, she turned to enter the tub, the view of her round, lovely ass giving Erik no respite.

"If it's Mozart," he echoed, hoping she would not hear the strain of lust in his voice.

Christine smiled again and sank into the tub, moaning in unabashed pleasure as she did. Erik bit back his own groan, grabbing the wall next to the mirror for support. If he could just calm himself, he could get through this. Get away. He could escape and spend the rest of the night telling himself this hadn't happened. Whatever game she had decided to play or boundary she wanted to test wouldn't matter.

He couldn't stop looking though. He drank in the sight of her wet, shining skin, flushed from the heat, and the roundness of her breasts peeking from the water. His cock throbbed at the spectacle, straining against his trousers. He wouldn't give in to this, he couldn't. He didn't know what she wanted or why she had made this display but...he couldn't give in, even as desire twisted in him like a knife.

Then, she began to sing.

"You will see, my dear, if you are good, the cure I can give you," she began, once again dropping the formal technique he had so painstakingly taught her for something rougher, darker, and incredibly tempting. It was Zerlina's aria from *Don Giovanni,* consoling the wounded Masetto. It was teasing, flirtatious, and absolutely maddening. But in the soft, seductive notes there was more than temptation. There was permission.

His eyes never straying from her, Erik let his hand find his cock at last.

"It is natural, not filthy, and no apothecary can carry it," she sang, and Erik bit his lips to hold back a moan at the pleasure that engulfed him as he listened and palmed himself through his clothes. It was obscene and felt so incredible, and he knew he was damned.

"There is a certain balm I carry within me, I can show it to you, if you desire," Christine sang and through the fog of yearning, Erik saw her own hands moving, touching her exposed skin with delicate curiosity. *"Do you want to know where I keep it?"* Her hands slipped below the line of the water, out of Erik's view and he dug his fingers so hard into the wall that he was sure it would leave marks. The hand on his cock moved rough and fast and a patch of moisture soaked through his trousers at the sensitive tip.

"Feel the beat of my heart," she sang, her head falling back as somewhere beneath the water, her hand moved. *"Touch me here."*

Erik obeyed, finally loosing his member from the stifling confines of his trousers and taking himself fully in hand. What was she thinking? What was she feeling? Was she imagining angelic hands upon her as touched herself?

"Feel the beat of my heart, touch me here...here..." The phrase repeated again and again. *"Touch me here,"* she sang, her voice reaching a peak as her back arched and Erik's hand sped over his shaft. At the urging of her song, he came. It was a climax the likes of which he hadn't experienced in forever, whiting out his vision,

making the world sing and spin as he poured his seed against the rough wall. He could barely catch his breath as he came down, the image of his Christine once again filling his eyes.

Had she come? She was blushing, biting her lip, but her hands were visible again for a moment before she dunked herself entirely under the water, then rose back up, gasping. Would she even know if she had? She had to be a virgin. What fumbling first exploration had he just been witness to? What sort of corruption had he somehow inspired?

What more could he achieve?

The idea would have made him hard again, had he the capacity. He wanted her. Desperately. He had wanted her for a long while, and he could no longer deny it. There was no use for this lust because there was no way to ever, ever be with her. But he wanted her, nonetheless. More than that, he knew if given the chance he would take any opportunity to be closer to her and feel that ecstasy again. Like Giovanni, he was already damned. Why not do his worst?

"Oh come to the window, my beloved," his own voice rose in Don Giovanni's plaintive love song. *"Come and dispel my sorrow, if not I will surely die."* He watched as she smiled, watched as her bare breasts rose and fell in the water, her eyes half shut in her own bliss. Her hands remained on the edge of the tub, even as her legs writhed in the water. Maybe she was afraid or having second thoughts...but that would change, the next time they allowed a moment like this. He was sure of it.

He had filled her world with angels, but he felt far more like the devil. A snake in the garden, regarding Eve in her nakedness and bent in his defiant heart on sharing the apple's taste.

6. Sin

It was the between time. That's what Christine had taken to calling it in her head. The twilight hours between when work and rehearsals stopped, and a performance began. At these times the Opera wasn't empty, but it wasn't bustling either. It made it hard for Christine to wander and explore, for there was always someone hiding around a corner, gossiping, resting, or eating. She wished they were all gone so she could be alone with her ghost and her thoughts...and yet she had also begun to dread such solitude.

Christine walked past the empty singers' dressing rooms and her face heated. It had been three days and four nights since she'd borrowed Carlotta's bath. Sometimes when she thought about how she had *displayed* herself she wanted to crawl out of her skin in shame and embarrassment, and other times she chastised her foolishness for not doing *more*.

What had she been thinking? Heaven knows. But she had ignited something in herself that she had no idea how to control or tame. Or understand. Every night since then she'd been beset by vague dreams of his shadow solidifying into something solid and real that could touch her. In the dreams, her angel's vague form would be the one to push apart her legs and caress her as she had barely dared to explore herself in that bath. She'd see his sad eyes and call out to him. Then she would wake, gasping, that treacherous, sinful place between her thighs throbbing. And her clumsy, curious hands could do nothing to relieve the ache.

There was no way to question it, because they had not spoken of or acknowledged anything that had happened. Her lessons continued and her teacher remained strict and focused on the music – though he had added Gounod to their repertoire. What would they even *say*? She had no words for what she had done anyway, but the question of what he made her feel twisted inside her constantly.

Therefore, her feet wandered like her restless thoughts. Julianne had mentioned looking for Jammes, and so Christine found herself crossing the stage to the dancer's side, her footsteps echoing in the auditorium beneath the unlit chandelier. She still couldn't believe that one day she'd sing on this stage. The thought sent a different kind of thrill through her than remembering his gaze upon her bare skin.

The wings were quiet as Christine left the stage, the kind of quiet that made it so easy to believe in ghosts. The curtains swayed, perhaps from Christine's passing, or perhaps from some unseen spirit. High above in the flies, she could see movement, a stagehand maybe. Or something else. She paused, trying to feel if her own ghost was close but there was no familiar prickle on her skin. Alas.

A soft cry startled Christine from her reverie. Not a scream, more like a whimper, but it was clearly coming from the dancers' dressing rooms. Christine walked quickly down the hall and the sound came again. It wasn't quite a cry of pain or grief, but it also seemed urgent and strangled. To her shock, when she arrived at the door of Jammes' dressing room, the sound came from inside. Worried, she turned the knob carefully and the door opened just as the woman inside whimpered once more. Christine was not prepared for what she saw.

It was Jammes, sprawled on a chaise, her clothes in disarray around her. Her head was thrown back, her mouth agape as soft sounds and cries escaped between her rapid breaths. Her breasts were bare, and her skin flushed. At her hips, her skirts were gathered high, giving the woman between her legs complete access to her sex. And

Christine knew the other woman too. She knew Julianne's jet curls. It was her friend who knelt with her head buried between Cécile Jammes' thighs, doing something to the dancer that made her moan and gasp.

Christine stood frozen. She didn't understand what she was seeing but she knew without question it was not meant for her eyes. Still, she couldn't move. Her heart was pounding, and she could feel each beat between her own legs, aching in the place that her angel ignited.

"Fuck! There!" Jammes cried and Christine jumped. She retreated down the hall, her mind swimming, unable to find solid ground. She should be shocked. Scandalized. But all she could think of was the glimpse of another world of pleasure and surrender. She tried to walk away but found herself leaning against a wall in the shadows, straining to hear more. "Yes! Oh, God, yes!" Jammes exclaimed, the words dissolving into a gasp. And then: footsteps.

Christine started, turning to see a new figure approaching down the dim hall. It was a man, a stagehand she guessed from his dress. And his attention was intent on the dressing room where Christine had left the door ajar.

Shit, she swore in her head as the burly, unkempt man peered carefully into the room and grinned as Jammes exclamations reached a peak. Was he going to accost them? Accuse them? Christine's blood froze as she watched the man start to fumble at his belt. No, he meant to do much worse.

"Get away from there!" Christine yelled. The stagehand jumped as a crash sounded in the dressing room, and instantly Christine regretted the outburst. The man's attention was on her now and there was something terrifying in his eyes as he strode towards her.

"You know what those whores were doing in there, girl?" the man hissed. "You out here keeping watch so they can be an affront to the good Lord?"

"You didn't seem like you were concerned for their souls," Christine snapped back, bracing herself even as terror filled her. She had never wanted her angel beside her more.

"I'd be concerned for yours; I don't like getting interrupted," the man was close enough for Christine to smell his stink and sweat.

"Get away from her, Buquet, you animal!" It was Julianne who screamed it, rushing to Christine's side and past Buquet. Christine knew the name: he was the master of the flies, one of the chief stagehands. And his reputation was repugnant enough that she'd been warned to avoid the flies because of him.

"Oh, the little *fricatrice* has something to say now?" Buquet laughed. "Glad you can talk at all, hope that jaw isn't—" Julianne's swift kick to Buquet's nether-regions cut off the insult. Buquet doubled over, gasping in pain. "You little mulatto *bitch*!"

"Get back to the flies, you degenerate," Julianne growled. Christine had never seen her so furious.

"Oh, I'm the degenerate? Wait until the whole Opera hears what you and your rat whore were doing!" Buquet sneered, still breathless.

"Don't say a word about them!" Christine was shocked to hear the words come from her own mouth but not by the fire behind them. "I swear, you'll regret it if you do."

"Who the fuck are you to threaten me!" Buquet spat, just as Julianne froze next to Christine, her hand a vise on Christine's arm. Christine understood the reaction to the sight they both saw, but she could only smile.

"I'm no one," Christine said calmly, looking past Buquet, to the man's confusion. "But I have a friend in management."

The scream the man gave when he turned to see the Opera Ghost looming like a dark god behind him was truly satisfying. He tripped and scrambled as the Phantom stared him down, moving without a sound.

"No! Get back, devil!" Buquet shouted as he pushed past Christine and Julianne, the scent of sweat and cheap brandy wafting after him. "Fucking witch!" Christine heard Buquet exclaim as she watched him disappeared from sight. Of course, when she and Julianne turned to the hall, the Ghost was gone.

"Jesus Christ," Julianne sighed and finally Christine had a moment to look at her friend. She was tousled and ruddy-faced, her hair half undone, and she looked horrified and miserable.

"I'm sorry, I didn't mean to—" Christine began, but Julianne wasn't listening. Her attention was on Jammes' door, which now was shut tight.

"Jammes, please, he's gone and I –" Julianne pleaded at the door, trying the knob, and finding it locked. "Cécile!"

"Go away!" Jammes yelled from inside. Julianne winced; her fist clenched against the door.

"Let her have a minute," Christine said. "We need to get back to work anyway." They didn't, but Christine sensed Julianne needed a distraction and space of her own. "Come on."

Julianne didn't complain as Christine guided her by the elbow, down the halls and stairs to their part of the theater. Her expression remained dark and drained.

"What's wrong with her?" Louise asked immediately as they entered the workshop. Luckily, they were the only ones there aside from her.

"We had a scare," Christine offered.

"Oh yes. Yes, we…ran into Christine's good friend," Julianne said, and Louise raised an eyebrow.

"Just for a moment," Christine said. "I'm sure he was just on his way somewhere more important. Maybe to rile up Carlotta. Again."

"Hm, I wouldn't mind that," Louise said, still scowling. "She's still in a tizzy about *someone* sending her to a fitting that didn't exist and keeps trying to fire every dresser that comes near her. I don't even know who I'll assign tonight."

"I'll take her," Julianne said instantly.

"What about your rats?" Louise asked. She was suspicious again.

"Give them to Anette," Julianne snapped. "Christine can take what's her name – Valerius' bitch understudy in thirteen."

"Giving her the haunted room now too?" Louise scoffed. "Fine. Go."

Julianne grabbed Carlotta's costume from the rack and Louise helpfully shoved another into Christine's hands. Without another word, Julianne rushed off and Louise sighed. "Is everything alright with her? She certainly wasn't herself."

"I think she'll be fine," Christine said, hoping it was true.

Erik had stayed close, he told himself, to make sure Christine was fine. But now he took to his secret passages, rushing ahead to meet her. It was foolish, perhaps, but he too needed an assurance that his student was alright after Buquet and whatever she'd seen of Jammes and her lover.

As if the week hadn't already left him in a crisis. Now this. There was one thing he had been sure he could do for Christine in the Opera: keep her safe. And he'd nearly failed. (Of course, there was always the pernicious voice in his head reminding him that she was far from safe when it came to the most dangerous person in the Opera: him).

Arriving behind the mirror of dressing room thirteen reminded him of his own sins all over again. He'd been a wreck of lust since their strange dalliance in Carlotta's room. He had tried to remain cold and stern in lessons to compensate for his desires, but it didn't help. Each evening he found himself near her bed, each night his songs to her were full of longing and he knew she heard it. He'd retreat just in time, exiling himself back into the darkness to eke out a shameful climax as his thoughts swam with *her*.

It was easy to assure that the door to dressing room thirteen was unlocked before taking a place behind the glass. The singer currently assigned this chamber was Nicole Duval, who Erik knew hated the room, as most singers over the years had. Not only was the dressing room far removed from the elite corridors near the stage, but the great mirror that filled nearly half the wall to the left of the door tended to unsettle people. It was as if they heard voices come from it.

Christine did not seem troubled at all when she entered with Duval's costume. She turned up the low-burning gaslights and surveyed the mirror, a smile playing on her lips. The fact she always knew he was there remained one of the few things that kept Erik in check, and he was both grateful for and hated that her strange power kept him from seeing her, all of her, again...

"I wonder why Carlotta doesn't take this room," Christine mused aloud. "Surely she'd love such a grand mirror to see herself in."

"Well, it's quite haunted you see," Erik replied easily, and Christine's smile spread into a grin. "Truly, are you alright?"

"I'm fine," Christine replied, not entirely convincing, but he didn't pry. "I'm worried about Julianne though. She's still upset."

"People knowing about her and the dancer is dangerous," Erik said. "I'm sure they're worried."

Christine's brows drew high in interest. "Did you know? About them?"

"I suspected," he answered, honest for once. He liked to know most of what was going on in his opera, but he could never know everything. And some things he didn't need to know. On the other side of the mirror, Christine frowned, a flurry of different emotions flashing over her face. "What's wrong?"

"I – I know I can't ask questions – big questions – of you, or at least I shouldn't ask about heaven or God or secrets I can't know," she burst out, much to Erik's surprise. "But Julianne and Jammes – what they did or are – are they damned? I know the Bible says—"

"The Bible is nothing but another book written by dead men," Erik cut her off and her face fell in shock. "And most of it is a tool to keep people afraid and obedient. There's very little in it that's correct when it comes to, well, anything."

"If you were anyone else, one might call that blasphemy," Christine said quietly. Panic seized Erik; the fear that she'd know from his sacrilegious words that he was the farthest thing from an angel. But she just smiled, subtly, the faith in her eyes still shining. "So, what they did is not a sin?"

"Love is never a sin," Erik told her, thinking back to similar words he had heard in another life. He'd laughed at them then, as any monster such as he would laugh at talk of love. Now, though, he understood better.

"Thank you," Christine said, her eyes still on the mirror but not on her own reflection. "For saying that. And for stepping in when you did."

"Buquet is a brute," Erik said, cringing at the thought of what the chief of the flies might have done to her. It made his blood boil. "He deserved far worse."

"Is he that bad?"

Erik had no chance to answer, as the dressing room door flew open. Nicole Duval strode in, her angular face irate.

"Who are you? How the hell did you get in here?" Duval demanded, looking suspiciously around the room then at Christine.

"I'm your dresser for tonight," Christine stammered. "I'm sorry, the door was unlocked. I just came in to get things ready."

"Dressers wait *outside*," Duval snapped, making Christine flinch. Again, rage rose within Erik.

"I'm sorry, Mademoiselle," Christine replied, placating.

"And who were you *talking* to?"

Christine gulped and Erik wondered how much Duval had heard. That could be a problem. "No one, Mademoiselle," Christine answered.

Duval did not seem convinced, still scowling. "Well, come on then, do your job," she ordered.

Christine rushed to obey as Duval stepped behind a silk screen to remove her street clothes. Erik was thankful for the display of modesty, though it made his mind once again return to Christine's pointed lack of such compunctions...

"You, over here, tighten this corset before you get that monstrosity on me," Duval barked. "I'm not just regular chorus you know, I'm Adèle Valerius' understudy. The lead! I shouldn't have the same costume as all the other peasants."

Erik wondered how much time this woman spent around Carlotta since she clearly had learned how to be a terror from the diva. It said far too much about the standards Carlotta had set that even a second-rate understudy treated people so poorly.

"I don't know, Mademoiselle," Christine said nervously as she approached Duval. "Are you sure? About the corset?"

"What? Of course I am."

"It's just, it looks quite tight already and if you cinch your waist anymore, how will you be able to maintain proper support for—"

"Are you giving me advice on *music*?"

"I just thought—"

"You're a damn dresser. You're less than a servant. You don't *think*," Duval said, and Erik clenched his fist. "Your job is to be invisible and silent and obey. So do your job and get out."

"Yes, Mademoiselle," Christine whispered, glancing at the mirror just long enough for Erik to see the tears in her eyes. It was absolutely unacceptable.

"Alas, if it were only your job to be silent, the chorus might be better in tune," Erik said, letting his voice waft softly through the room. Duval jumped at the words, clutching her half-fastened costume to her chest.

"What did you say?!" Duval demanded and Erik nearly laughed at the naive, confused look Christine gave her.

"I didn't say anything, Mademoiselle. You made it quite clear I was to be silent," Christine said, her face perfectly innocent as she finished her work on the costume. "Good luck with the performance." Christine gave the mirror one last smirk before exiting and Erik's heart leapt. Not that he needed permission or encouragement. It had been too long since he'd given someone a real fright. Duval kept looking around as the door shut, her face pale.

"Tsk, tsk, tsk," Erik whispered, low and dangerous. "Doesn't she know it's bad luck to say something like that?"

"Who's there!" Duval yelled into the empty room.

"Someone who doesn't appreciate rudeness to hardworking employees of *my* opera," Erik replied, fully truthful. "Especially from someone so easily replaced."

"What? No! I didn't mean any disrespect!" Duval protested. It was a pity she could not see the Ghost shrug.

"I would be careful tonight, Mademoiselle," Erik continued. "So many accidents can happen in a theater. Even invisible things can hurt you if you're not careful."

That was all the woman had to hear to rush from the dressing room. Erik let his laughter echo through the stillness and follow her through the dark.

It took Christine half of act one to find Julianne, though her search was delayed when she stopped to wish César a good performance and feed him a few sugar cubes. The idea to look for Julianne in a place she'd shown Christine came to her late. But when Christine opened to door to the storeroom where she'd spent her first night at the Opera, there Julianne was, curled by a piano. She looked up at the creak of the door when Christine entered. She was disappointed.

"I thought you might be…" Julianne sighed. Christine knew who she had been hoping for. "We meet here, sometimes."

"Jammes will come around, just give her time," Christine said. She picked her way through the detritus and sat on the floor next to Julianne. "You'll have to do with me until then."

Julianne laughed hollowly and continued to pick at a bent nail in the floorboard. "You're not appalled? Or afraid to be alone with me?"

"Why would I be?" Christine knew why, and Julianne gave her a dubious look in turn. "I don't think of you any differently if that's what you're worried about."

"But you'll pray for my immortal soul?" Julianne said the phrase as if she was quoting it, and the pain in the words made Christine wince.

"I don't think you're a sinner or damned," Christine told her friend. Julianne squinted back, cautious. "Someone I trust very much told me that…love is never a sin. And I believe that." Julianne's expression thawed, something like gratitude and relief washing over her face. Christine was glad of it, and the weak smile that followed.

"Thank you," Julianne said. "Good to know you're not too scandalized."

"Well, this is the Paris Opera, not a convent."

The sparkle rekindled in Julianne's eyes. "You don't think they get up to the same thing in convents? All those women all alone together…nothing else to do…"

"Julianne!" Christine gasped as the other woman burst out laughing.

"You know it's true! I bet that's half the reason some women join!" Julianne continued to cackle, and Christine shook her head.

Her cheeks were hot already but if they were joking about it, perhaps...

"I know I shouldn't, but I have to ask..." Christine stammered, her pulse increasing as she spoke. "How do – I mean – two women – what do – oh God, never mind."

"I thought you got a good look," Julianne snickered, and Christine wanted to sink into the floor.

"I'm sorry! For all of it. But I mean..." She wasn't even sure what she was asking, but she so desperately wanted to understand what lovers felt and if it was close to what she desired. "I just don't understand *how*—"

"How a woman can make another woman come?" Julianne offered far too easily. "Much better than a man can, usually." Christine stared at her friend, utterly lost. "Good Lord, you can't think fucking is just all cocks and cunts. There's a lot you can do with all sorts of parts." Julianne laughed again at Christine's blank expression. "A hand, a tongue, a thigh. They can all get you to that special place."

Again, Christine found herself staring while also wanting nothing more than to crawl out of her skin and disappear. "I don't know what that *means*," she whispered.

"Coming?" Julianne waited a beat, maybe expecting Christine to laugh or understand. "For most folk, it's the whole point of fucking! For fun at least. Wait, have you never...?"

Christine buried her face in her hands, her cheeks on fire. "I've never been *with* anyone. That way," she said, voice muffled.

"Well, the good news is you don't strictly need another person to get there," Julianne replied, casual and easy, and Christine's gaze shot back to her. "Jesus, girl, I'm going to assume you've maybe...explored?"

Christine gave a small nod, thinking back to Carlotta's copper bath and so many moments in the dark, longing for something unknown.

"Christ in heaven, I can't believe I have to be the one to educate you on this, but...when you're enjoying yourself, let's say. It's like you're trying to get somewhere, right? That's what I'm talking about. People call it the little death sometimes, and that's not wrong. It's this moment, at the end, where everything is perfect and wild and quiet and..." Julianne let out a breath and Christine's head continued to spin. Was that what she'd been fumbling for and unable to find?

"How do you know if you have...arrived?" Christine asked, sheepishly.

"Believe me, you'll know," Julianne replied with another husky laugh. "And like I said, don't let anyone tell you that you need a man for that. Get there however you like with whoever you like. Or with your own hands!"

Christine didn't think it was possible to blush more at this point, but she kept surprising herself. At least Julianne's laughter was kind as Christine hid her face again. For too long she'd refused to name the things her angel's voice made her feel, but she couldn't ignore it, not now. The desire, the ecstasy, the hunger for a pleasure she hadn't even known was possible.

"How did I end up friends with one of the last virgins in the Paris Opera," Julianne sighed, and Christine looked up enough to glare.

"Come on, the rats aren't all corrupted," she said.

"Oh, give me time," Julianne winked. Christine couldn't help but laugh, pushing her friend playfully. The merriment only lasted for a few seconds before Julianne's face darkened once again. Christine knew she was thinking about Jammes.

"I won't tell anyone," Christine offered, hoping it would help. "I'd never do that to either of you."

"It's not you I'm worried about," Julianne sighed. "Buquet likes to gossip. Some of it he spreads for fun and some he sells. I just hope that we don't matter enough to be a topic."

"I hope so too," Christine said. She also hoped that the Ghost had put enough fear into him to stay quiet, but she wasn't sure. A chill ran through her, recalling some of the darker stories about her phantom and she wondered if Buquet knew them.

"You have to get back to work," Julianne said, nodding to the door.

"What about you?"

"I think I'll go home. Carlotta dismissed me after I poked her with pins for the fourth time. And she didn't even know I was doing it on purpose." Christine snickered at the image.

"Be careful," Christine said.

"I'm going home to eat my mother's cooking and sleep in my own room in a real flat, I'm not the one who needs to be careful," Julianne replied pointedly.

"I'm fine, don't worry about me."

"Don't you ever get scared though, wandering around here in the dark alone?" Julianne asked, and for once it was sincere.

Christine shrugged as she stood and walked to the door. "Who said I'm ever alone?"

Erik did not linger long in his box. *Le Prophète* was no one's favorite opera and he found himself yawning nearly as much as the audience. It was a shame that the only production that didn't feature Carlotta as lead was so underwhelming, but he did laugh when César received an ovation. He liked the horse better than the soprano too.

He left the box before curtain, and he wasn't the only one. He noticed the managers doing the same, matching sour looks on their faces.

It was easy to follow the men since Erik knew exactly where they were headed. The gilded *Salon du Danse* behind the stage was the regular meeting point for artists and patrons after performances, and it was there that Guillaume Poligny and Herbert Debienne were huddled in a corner, glasses of brandy already in their hands. Luckily, it was a corner where Erik could listen well and see them through yet another two-way mirror.

"Half the loge was empty, we can't afford another performance like this," Debienne sighed. "We need to rush the new production. Maybe we can have it ready before Lent."

"Is that you talking or her?" Poligny replied with a scowl. "I can't think of another reason you'd be pushing for an Italian work now."

"*Rigoletto* suits her," Debienne bristled. "*And* Fontana and Rameau."

Erik's mind raced as he listened. He had known *Rigoletto* was on the horizon, just not so soon. He hated the idea of Carlotta as Gilda, a role so perfectly suited for Christine.

"What about the New Year's gala? You haven't done anything to prepare," Poligny continued. He looked tired and worn, more so than Erik had ever noticed before. As the manager in charge of the financial side of operations, he had a far more boring job than Debienne. Not that Erik had made either task easy in the last few years. "Or are you waiting for the Ghost to tell you what to do, as usual?"

"He hasn't had anything to say lately," Debienne said with a shrug.

"So, Carlotta's doing your job instead?" Poligny scoffed and Erik's hackles rose.

He had been so caught up with Christine in the last month, he'd barely given the managers a thought beyond collecting his salary and leaving a few notes on the orchestra. He scowled, once again furious at how he'd allowed this girl to overtake his life. The entire *point* of teaching her was to elevate the Opera and give him the victory he'd desired and designed for years. At least that's what he kept telling himself. Lingering near her at night, sick with unquenchable lust, all his excuses evaporated. Perhaps focusing back on her career and her voice would somehow help.

"The demon has been quiet, and I'm glad of it. Let's leave it at that," Debienne replied and wiped his brow. "I don't think I could take any more notes from the dead on my work." The manager shuddered. His face was wan, making his oily black hair and moustache stand out.

"You think it's easier on my end?" Poligny huffed. "The minister of fine arts keeps asking questions about our books and I'm half ready to tell him it's a patron or a singer swindling us."

"Tell him the truth!" Debienne replied. "I heard he's been going to seances with some American medium for the last year. He's convinced he'd had a conversation with Beethoven."

"Maybe we should hire him," Poligny said with a scoff and Debienne raised an eyebrow. "The medium. Not the minister. See if he can do an exorcism. Or maybe we can just have a séance and tell our dear ghost to go fuck himself."

Erik couldn't be expected to stay silent at that, could he? He let his voice drift right to Poligny's ear, a cold whisper. "Don't be so coarse, Guillaume, you never know who's listening." It was glorious, truly, watching all the blood leave the taller man's face.

"I hate this place," Debienne whispered, downing the rest of his brandy, and walking away without another word.

"I-I apologize, Monsieur," Poligny said to the walls and rushed away in another direction. Erik's amusement faded as soon as they were out of sight, his mood souring again.

He was losing sight of everything, all because of *her*. She was always there, at the back of his mind but it was when she was near him that he truly lost all reason. Erik could hear the applause in the distance and wondered if such ovations for Christine would end this madness. Somehow, he doubted it.

But if it wouldn't...what was the point? He was only torturing himself. And he was mad to think any naïve desires she harbored would ever allow him to be closer to her. Maybe he should end it now. Ignore her calls and cast her out. What was the point of wanting her like this when there was nothing he could give her and nothing he could take?

Christine's little sanctuary in the cellars was much warmer than one might expect. And over the weeks she had added bits to her bed and bower to make the space hers. A blanket there, a dried flower here. It was a perfect nest and she'd filled it with little treasures like a magpie, she thought to herself. But despite all that, as she undressed to sleep, she shivered.

She slept in her clothes more often than not. Usually, it was because *he* would be there when she went to sleep and until recently, she had thought it wrong to disrobe under an angel's gaze. But she didn't feel him yet. Her mind buzzing with the possibilities Julianne had planted there, Christine carefully undid her buttons, pulled off her dress, and stripped to just her chemise and pantalettes. She brushed her hair and let it fall free down her back. And she waited.

She closed her eyes and curled her arms around her knees. She waited and let her mind wander. Christine thought of the way he'd sung Don Giovanni's love song to her. She thought of Jammes, her head thrown back in pleasure. She thought of Julianne's assurance that a person needed only their hands and no shame to feel that same ecstasy. But Christine wanted something more than that and it made her tremble to consider such a sin. And yet at the same time, the very idea made that ache between her legs flare. She whimpered. She wanted desperately to touch that forbidden place, but it still felt so wicked, so wrong.

Then at last she sensed it. The magical prickle on her skin as heavenly eyes alit upon her. Unbidden, she gasped at the thrill of being *seen* by him. She thought of his shining eyes, of how bright they had been when she'd glimpsed them today, and her entire body came alive. She pulled her legs closer to her chest to stop herself trembling.

"Christine," her angel whispered in the dark. "Are you alright?"

Did she look distressed? She raised her head, trying hard to just breathe. "I'm scared." Her voice quavered as she said it.

"Why? What is wrong?" There was such tenderness in that beautiful, impossible voice. How could she find the words to explain that the same beauty and affection was driving her mad? That it made her desire things that damned her?

"I – I can't..." she stammered. God, what if she ruined everything?

"Christine." He said her name in the tone of unquestionable command that made goosebumps ripple over her body. "Tell me why you are scared." She had no choice but to obey that mesmerizing, intoxicating voice.

"I'm scared of what I feel – of what I cannot stop myself feeling – when I am with you," she confessed, voice and body tremulous, as she dug her nails into her bare legs. "I know you said love is never a sin but – the things I want – they must be wrong. You are holy and a gift. It has to be a sin to want...more."

For an agonizing moment, her angel was silent, and Christine felt as if she might die right there.

"I have told you once today that what mortals think they know of things like me is often wrong. There is no wickedness in you, I know it. Now tell me, what more do you wish from me, Christine?" he asked at last, each word careful and powerful. A new shiver passed through her as she stared into the dark, imagining she could see the glint of his eyes. Carefully, she unfurled herself, her nipples tightening beneath the worn fabric of her chemise as she rose on her knees, kneeling in supplication.

"I want to give myself to you in every way," she whispered. "Ways I can't even imagine or understand. I want to be yours, entirely. My voice. My soul...and my body. I don't know how that can be, but I want that more than anything."

There it was: the confession that would either damn her or finally set her free.

"And do you know what I want?" the Angel asked, voice low.

She froze, terrified of giving the wrong answer. "I can't presume—"

"I would delight in your pleasure, Christine, and I treasure your desire. And what I want is simply your surrender to me alone." Christine bit back a moan, her body once again igniting at his words. "Do you think it is a sin, to surrender to me?"

"No," she breathed, "never." She could barely contain her joy at his confession. It was unthinkable and insane, but it was real. He was offering her the very thing she had so feared to ask from him. "My angel, what I wish to give you...Perhaps it is not a sin if you command it."

"Then let me command you." Each word made her skin feel hotter and tighter, and the arousal between her thighs even more desperate. "First, let me see you, my Christine. All of you."

She obeyed without hesitation, pulling off her chemise too quickly and then taking more time as she released herself from her drawers. She savored the weight of his gaze over the entirety of her bare body and just that made her swoon.

"Lie back and close your eyes," her angel ordered and again, she instantly complied. It was like falling back and out of herself into someplace warm and welcoming, and her mind stilled into the perfect calm of surrender. "Spread your legs."

She whimpered and obeyed, her body shuddering at the obscenity of it. Even in the bath before, she hadn't shown him *this*. But now her thighs parted without question or resistance, and she let him see. Entirely and absolutely.

"You're so beautiful, my Christine," he said, and his voice was ecstatic. "You have no idea."

She grasped at the sheets below her, her breath coming fast and shallow as her body screamed in need. "Angel..." she begged. "Tell me what to do. Please, let me be yours."

"Touch yourself, your breasts first," he commanded, soft and urgent. She needed no more prompting. Her hands flew her aching breasts, catching her stiff nipples between her fingers as she kneaded and let out a moan. "Let your hands be my hands. Give yourself to me."

Her hands were hot as they moved over her skin, chasing pleasure that continued to scamper just out of reach. She writhed on the bed as they drifted lower, to her ribs and then her stomach. To the utter edge.

"Lower," her teacher instructed. "Don't be afraid. Give me everything."

And then her angel began to sing.

"Yes..." she sighed as the song swept over her. It was another love song in an unknown language, but there was unquestionable desire and danger in the lilting melody. It encircled her like a snake, driving the last shreds of shame and rationality from her mind. His voice seeped into her ears and under her skin, and she let her hand move without thought, as if he truly was moving it for her. Her fingers raked through hair that was both silken and coarse. Then at last, she touched her sex without fear. The pleasure that flew through her was almost too much to bear.

Christine gasped at the feeling, her hips moving of their own accord. As she explored, each note of his song enticed her to more. She was wet, slick with arousal between the hot folds and every movement of her fingers brought new sensation and pleasure. The melody became more urgent as she moved her hand faster, focusing on a spot above her opening that sent lightning bolts of delight through her as she rubbed, thrusting her hips to meet her hand.

"*Oh my god, my angel*," the obscene prayer hissed from her lips, the only words adequate for this moment, and the last ones she could manage before her voice broke into a series of gasps and cries, rising in counterpoint to her angel's ecstatic song. Her breath raced and her muscles stiffened as she continued to chase that unknown thing. But now it wasn't unknown. It was music. It was all *music*, and she was a chord unresolved, a melody trying to find home. His song and her hands that were also his hands were the whole world. She was helpless to the pleasure cascading through her by her angel's power.

His voice rose to a peak, compelling her, calling her. She didn't know what the words meant, and yet, she understood their command: to trust him and be his. That was all that mattered. And she did. She was. And suddenly, the world stopped. There was only her body and the sound of his voice and a glimpse of heaven. She convulsed, her back flying off the bed as the little death took her, ecstasy pulsing through her from her very core.

After what felt like forever and yet not long enough, Christine fell back onto the bed, breathless and giddy. She knew what Julianne meant now, that she'd know it when she arrived at that special place.

She wanted to laugh, but more than that, she wanted to listen to his voice and linger. The song was gentler now, not urgent, and she let it overtake her. She pulled a blanket over her bare skin and let herself drift, awash in love and wonder. His.

Erik had no idea where to run, just that he *had* to run. He had meant to be strong for once and instead he had obliterated every remaining shred of decency in his depraved soul. But, gods above and below, he could not even bring himself to regret it. Watching Christine bring herself to orgasm with the help of his voice – at his *command* – had been the most sensual moment of his entire cursed life. He'd barely needed to graze his cock to come himself as he watched her sleep, peaceful and sated.

The moments after his own climax, panting in the dark, had been blissful. For a few seconds, he had forgotten who he was and why he needed to hide in the shadows to even be close to someone like her. The return to reality had been brutal. So here he was: running.

He couldn't go home, not yet. He didn't want to be locked in a tomb with his music and distractions because every note would sound like her, and nothing could distract him from the truth: that she wanted him, or at least a false version of him. That she had practically begged to be his. It was incredible and terrible.

And so instead of descending below, he climbed, high into the flies where painted clouds and castle walls hung among catwalks and endless miles of rope. It was there that he finally stopped to breathe, like the foolish, earthly man he was. Christine had given herself body and soul to a false angel and that knowledge thrilled and disgusted him in turn.

Was it so bad? To have her like this? It was more than he ever could have imagined, and it hurt no one. Why shouldn't he bring her pleasure and take some himself? It's not like he had actually touched her or violated her. Just the thought of crossing that line made his skin and heart scream in panic. But perhaps...perhaps by some means she would allow that too...somehow.

He sighed and let his head fall into his hands. It was a simple gesture, normal for anyone but him. But the moment his fingers touched the mask he remembered exactly why no one, least of all a kind, beautiful wonder like Christine would ever let him close. He gripped the edge of the mask, his hate for the thing and the face it concealed flaring like gunpowder meeting a spark. Erik tore the mask off, letting the cool air brush his face as he stifled a scream.

What would she say if she saw this?

The mask clasped in his left hand; he raised the right to do something he had avoided for years. He touched the scarred, shriveled flesh of his cheek then the edge of the hole where a nose should be, just to remember. Did it make what he had done worse, knowing this face kept him from ever doing more? Did it justify his crimes?

"Dear God..."

Erik spun at the voice, another simple reflex, and another terrible mistake. Below him on another catwalk none other than Joseph Buquet stood, staring at Erik's unmasked face in abject dread.

"Dear Lord in heaven! You are a demon!" Buquet screamed, stumbling backwards. For the second time that night, Erik acted without another thought and jumped.

Mask still in hand, he advanced on Buquet, letting the wretch take in the full horror of the Opera Ghost's face. This was the man that had nearly hurt Christine. He deserved to suffer. Buquet turned and ran, rushing down from the catwalks via a ladder then another rope. But as soon as he tried to cross again, Erik was right there, and he knew the fire in his eyes was burning bright.

"Please! Oh God! Get away!" Buquet screamed. His face was red, and his hair was wild, and he smelled like a sewer of wine. "Let me go! Please!"

Erik saw no reason to do so. He had already done one monstrous thing this night, why not keep going? He pounced on Buquet, locking his hands around the man's neck. He couldn't touch Christine, so why not feel this flesh beneath his fingers and remember that he was a monster?

"I should have made it clear earlier," Erik growled as Buquet pawed uselessly at him, gurgling for breath. "You're no longer welcome in my theater, Joseph. Do you understand?" He pushed Buquet away and the man gasped for breath. Erik expected him to nod and run, but instead, the brute looked up. Something cruel and stupid kindled in his drunken face.

"You want to drive me out, monster? Now that I know what's under that mask of yours?" Buquet spat. "You'll have to do more than threaten if you want to get rid of me, devil!"

Erik carefully replaced the mask as Buquet stood defiant, fists half raised. Erik had taken off the mask to remember who he was, hadn't he? Now he wouldn't forget.

"As you wish, Monsieur," Erik said.

He wondered who else was left in the Opera right now. Surely Christine was too far away to hear the scream.

7. Adoration

The Opera was livelier than usual as Christine made her way to the costume workshop. The very fact that she noticed was impressive, given how full her head still was with the wonders of the night before. It was the sort of nervous energy and activity that usually only preceded a performance. When she reached the workshops, no one was working. Instead, costumers, carpenters, firemen, and stagehands were all gossiping in the halls.

Christine easily found Julianne in the crowd, next to Maxine, and Alonzo, a huge stagehand with close shorn hair and olive skin who Christine had met only in passing.

"Well, speak of the—" Maxine began, sneering at Christine before Julianne kicked her in the shin. Both the vitriol and the fact she'd been a topic of conversation stunned Christine.

"What's going on?" Christine asked, trying to gauge Julianne's expression. Her dark eyes held uncharacteristic worry.

"Joseph Buquet," Julianne answered, and Christine's stomach dropped. "He was attacked."

"The idiot fell is all," Alonzo cut in. "He was drunk somewhere he shouldn't have been, and he fell."

"Is he alright?" Christine asked, her heart not beating right as the blood drained from her face.

"Broke his damn leg, probably won't work for a month or two," Alonzo rumbled. Christine's eyes met Julianne's, and she finally understood the conflict in her friend's face.

"They found him on the stage this morning, raving," Julianne said. "He probably was delirious. And still drunk."

"Doesn't mean he was lying," Maxine snapped, glaring at Julianne and Alonzo before turning her eyes to Christine. "He said it was the Ghost."

"Buquet says a lot of foolish things," Julianne hissed back.

"I was there, he was out of his mind, talking nonsense," Alonzo said.

"So, you heard what he said! What he saw!" Maxine shot back, again glancing at Christine.

"What did he say?" Christine almost didn't want to know.

"Well, he kept going on about a witch," Maxine sneered. "Said she called the Ghost down on him."

"He was saying that before he fell," Alonzo corrected, which did not make Christine feel any better. "This morning he – he said the Ghost came for him because he saw his face."

"That proves he's lying to cover up that he fell like an idiot," Julianne said. "No one has ever seen the Ghost's face."

"Someone has now! And he nearly died for it!" Maxine exclaimed.

"Bad business," Maxine said, shaking her head and still looking at Christine like a leper.

"Did he say what he looked like?" Christine asked. She often imagined her angel, but anytime she tried to think what his true face might be, the fantasy evaporated. What had Buquet seen?

"Death," Julianne answered quietly, eyes locked on Christine. "He said the Ghost's face was death."

Erik disliked the hiding place beneath the manager's office. It was darker and more cramped than most other passages throughout the Opera. And it was always disconcerting to be below people's feet.

But in his spot beneath Debienne's desk, he could hear every bit of conversation. And today there was much to listen to.

Above him, a door slammed, and agitated footfalls shook the floor.

"We've lost four more stagehands!" Poligny exclaimed. "That's on top of the two from this morning and seven firemen. Seven!"

"Can you blame them?" Debienne replied. The boards above him creaked and Erik imagined the man sinking dejectedly into his chair. "They want to live."

"You're not still blaming me for this, are you?" Poligny said.

"*You* provoked him and the next morning a man is found broken on our stage, so, yes I'm blaming you," Debienne spat. "And I'm tired of this, Guillaume. So goddamned tired."

At that moment Erik heard a distant knock on the office door. He recognized the precise steps of Rémy, the managers' secretary, as the door opened above. "Messieurs," Rémy said nervously. "Monsieur Gabriel and Monsieur Mercier are both outside."

Finally. Erik had been waiting all morning for the directors. "Let them in," Poligny sighed. A flurry of footsteps above Erik's head released another cloud of dust, reminding Erik exactly why he wore his hat even in places like this.

"Gerard, Henri," Debienne sighed. "What now?"

"I'm down three singers, probably more by the end of the day," Gabriel snapped back.

"I'm sure the chorus will survive," Poligny replied, unmoved.

"We're not worried about the chorus," Mercier said and paused. Erik imagined that Gabriel, the director of said chorus had given him quite the look. "We lost Nicole Duval and, damn, what even was her name—"

"I don't know who the first one was, get to the point," Debienne drawled. Erik heard a thump and wondered if it was an empty brandy glass being set on the desk.

"They were both understudies!" Gabriel shouted. "Now if something happens to Adèle or Carlotta, we're fucked!"

"Nothing ever happens to Carlotta," Poligny said with a laugh. "You'd have to poison that woman to keep her from her spotlight."

Erik smiled to himself in the dark. Not a bad idea.

"We still need understudies and no one in the chorus now can take it on," Mercier lamented.

"Why are you complaining about this to me? Poach some warm bodies from the *Comique* or hold damn auditions!"

"There's no time!" Gabriel protested, which the managers ignored.

"And that foreign fellow is lurking around the offices, badgering people about Buquet," Mercier added. Erik perked up as the floor creaked above him.

"Then call the gendarmes and have him thrown out! I don't need that Persian trespasser causing trouble today!" Debienne roared. "Now get *out*!'

Poligny began to speak but Erik didn't bother to listen. If he was fast enough, he might be able to kill two birds with one stone. He moved carefully through the Opera corridors, keeping to shadows and hidden places for now. He'd already caused quite enough commotion in the last 24 hours; he didn't need to be seen again. At least not by the wrong people.

The one person he wanted to see was, as always, too easy to find. The Daroga was lurking near the offices of the directors as promised, making notes in the little book he always carried. Ever the detective.

"One day I'm going to steal that, see what you really think of me," Erik declared, and Shaya nearly jumped out of his skin. Erik stayed mostly in shadow, smirking just enough that it would drive Shaya mad.

"What did you do?" Shaya demanded. "Or shall I simply ask: why did you do it?"

"You mean Buquet?" Erik asked back. "I think you'll find I've done the Opera a favor."

"Everyone thinks you're sending a message," the Daroga went on. "The managers, half the singers, including Zambelli."

"Why would Carlotta care about that brute?"

"Because you *nearly killed him*!" Shaya growled. "I warned you. If I heard about another assault—"

"You'd be extremely cross with me, I recall," Erik sighed. "God, you're boring."

"I know why you did it," Shaya went on. "It wasn't about anyone but you. You went after him because he saw your face." Erik shrugged in reply. "What I don't understand is why you let him see."

"I didn't *let him*," Erik snapped. "He chanced on me when my guard was down."

At that, the Daroga laughed. "*You* let your guard down? You're getting old. Or sloppy. I like it."

Erik rolled his eyes, but Shaya wasn't wrong. He'd made a dozen more mistakes that the detective didn't even know about, the most glaring of which he would continue to make at a lesson this evening. The dread of seeing Christine again made him cold. How could he teach her after he had incited her to *that*? Surely, she had heard about Buquet by now. How would she look at him? Not that she ever actually looked at him or ever could. Again, Erik thought back to his mask and why he had made the mistake of removing it.

"It's not really so bad, is it?" he asked, gesturing to his face with a long, pale hand. "Someone once told me it was almost tolerable; if I recall."

"Don't you dare speak of him to me," Shaya hissed, all traces of humor leaving his face. Not that there had been much. "He's dead. Just like all the rest who dared to look at you in those *rosy hours of Mazenderan*."

"You're alive, aren't you?" Erik said, quietly. He'd been avoiding the thought all day, after drinking himself to sleep last night. The woman he wanted, who he'd corrupted and claimed in body and soul...she'd die if she saw his face. Just like the one whose name he dared not even think in Shaya's presence.

"What I have isn't a life," Shaya replied, with the same sadness in his voice. "You've seen to that."

The sound of footsteps saved them. Shaya turned to see who was coming up the hall, but Erik spotted him first. Gerard Gabriel, with Henri Mercier behind him. Exactly as Erik had hoped. He stepped from the shadows just long enough for the men to realize exactly who the Persian had been with before disappearing to his own path. And it all happened too quickly for Shaya to understand.

"You! Persian!" Erik heard Mercier cry. "You're not supposed to be here! We're calling the police!"

Shaya didn't bother to protest, at least not that Erik heard. His attention was on Gabriel anyway. If he was going to solve everyone's problems, (most of which he had caused) he would need a word with the chorus master.

Christine shivered as she entered their practice room. Just as the slate clouds had overtaken the bright morning sun, fear and confusion had blotted out each bit of joy she'd awoken with. All day the stories and rumors had swirled around her, and each time she remembered her wanton display for her teacher, her shame grew. What if he didn't even come for their lesson...and what if that was a blessing?

"You look upset," his voice came from all around her, warm and kind, and her relief was instant.

"I've been so worried. They've been saying such things about you."

"Joseph Buquet has always been a liar and teller of tales," the Angel replied, reading her mind, as he often did. Another wave of relief washed over Christine. So, it was all lies from a terrible man. Good. "What else troubles you, my dear?" It made her giddy each time he called her that. And it made her brave.

"Last night, was...astonishing. I've never done anything..." She found herself blushing, which was honestly absurd at this point. "I've never felt anything like what you made me feel."

"And never have I been given such an exquisite gift of trust," he replied, and Christine's heart soared.

"I would give you anything you asked," she replied. She did not even know what more he could ask of her, but, God, to feel that way again, she would give it.

"Right now, I want you to give me your voice," he said, firm yet warm. "Sing for me."

And sing she did. It was as if the night before had unlocked an even deeper well of music than the one he had already found within her. Every bit of hesitation was gone as he ran her through their scales and exercises. She trusted him completely, letting her voice flow free and yet entirely at his command. It was ecstatic and remarkable, and only grew more so when he allowed her to sing her arias.

First was Cherubino again, as giddy with lust as Christine, then Juliette's Waltz. Christine was a comet in the firmament as she sang of wanting to live forever in a blissful dream. She reached the final high C and felt just as she had spread out for him on that bed, soaring to an ecstatic climax at her angel's command. She was flushed and breathless as she finished, dizzy with joy.

"That's enough for now," the Angel told her unexpectedly, his voice softer than usual. "Get some food and rest."

"But..." Christine protested.

"I have my own gifts to give you, don't question me," he replied, and something in the authoritative tone in his voice made her smile and shiver.

"Yes, Maestro," she replied with a nod. The thought of any sort of gift from him made her heart race.

"Who on earth are you?" a voice asked the second Christine stepped into the hall and she leapt in shock. "I'm sorry! I didn't mean to startle you!" the man who had spoken added, apologetically. He was a slightly short, with caramel hair and moustache, and looked vaguely familiar.

"No, I'm so sorry. I didn't mean to disturb anyone," Christine said, panic vibrating through her.

"Oh, you mistake me, Mademoiselle," the man said. "I want to know who you are because if that was you singing in there…it was remarkable. More than."

Christine blinked. "It was me, yes."

"But you're not in the company! You don't look like a student either. What are you doing here? How did you get in?"

Christine swallowed a wave of embarrassment. "I'm not trespassing, I promise! I come here to practice, but I do work here. You see I came from the conservatoire in Rouen to sing here, but there were no auditions, but I still wanted to be at the Opera, so I took the first job here I could, it just happened to be in…the costumers."

"The costumers?!" The man echoed in disbelief. "A voice like that and you spend your days sewing and laundering?"

Christine gaped at the man. "I…"

"Well, not anymore you don't."

"Please, don't fire me, sir!" Christine's panic returned full force, but the man smiled at her with a warm laugh.

"I'm not firing you, young lady," the man said. "I'm hiring you. To the chorus."

"What?" Christine was surely dreaming.

"Do you know who I am, girl?" The man appeared insulted as she shook her head. "My name is Gerard Gabriel. I am the director of the chorus. That's why I know everyone's voice and didn't know yours. Now tell me, you were singing mezzo and soprano in there, can you manage either?"

"I can," Christine was proud she could speak because she felt as if she might faint.

"And do you know any of the chorus parts already?" Again, she nodded, and Gabriel's grin widened. "And, well, I'll just ask it to see if this truly is a miracle...how well do you know the role of Siébel?"

"Siébel? In *Faust*?" Christine echoed in shock. She'd never given the mezzo part too much thought, though she liked it. "Quite well, not perfectly. But..."

"Miraculous," Gabriel breathed and clapped his hands together. "We'll have you with the second sopranos and you'll be replacing Nicole Duval as the understudy for Siébel. You can have her dressing room too, just tell the stage manager. I'm rehearsing with Adèle Valerius tomorrow morning. In the small rehearsal hall at nine. Can you be there?"

"Uh, yes, Monsieur," Christine stammered.

"The library will have a score for you, get one for *Rigoletto* too, we're beginning rehearsals for that as well next week. I'll get you sorted out with all the boring bits tomorrow."

"Alright..." Christine stammered, still blinking in wonder.

"Very well then. Oh dear, what did you say your name was?"

"Christine. Daaé." Gabriel nodded, satisfied, and looked her over one more time.

"I shall certainly be interested to see what other surprises you have in store for us, Mademoiselle Daaé." With a final nod, the chorus master turned on his heel and continued down the yellow and red hall, obviously pleased with himself.

Christine collapsed against the wall, covering her mouth as she broke into laughter that was close to sobs.

"Do you like your gift, my dear?" a ghostly voice whispered in her ear. "Get some food and daylight, and then meet me in your new dressing room when you are done."

"Yes, my angel," Christine whispered with a grin.

Erik waited behind the mirror, trying to simply breathe. He'd done it. It was almost as if he'd planned everything to get to this moment. He hadn't, of course, but he liked to think that he was still as adept at riding the shifting winds of chaos as he'd been in his youth. How he'd come to this point didn't matter. Christine's career had begun in earnest. It would take time to get Carlotta off the stage, of course, and Christine was not quite ready but...it was all so much closer now.

And oh, how she had sung today. It was as if her absolute surrender to her angel the night before had released something incredible. Or perhaps it was simpler. He'd heard more than one singer boasting that a good fuck was the best thing for the voice and while he had little experience of his own to judge by, the same could certainly be true of whatever it was they had done. He still couldn't find a word for it, in any of the many languages he knew. But here he stood, determined to do it again if she would allow it.

The door creaked as it opened, and Erik's heart jumped. Christine was radiant, her cheeks still red from the December wind, her shawl clutched tight around her shoulders.

"You know, Mademoiselle Duval was so quick to leave, she left a few dresses and other things," he said, hating the thought of his pupil in the cold.

Christine smiled, bright and reverent. "I do think she and I are close to the same size. I shall have to see what she left." She looked around the dressing room, awe in her eyes. "I can't believe this is mine now."

"It will serve us well for some lessons too," Erik replied, and Christine raised an eyebrow. "You'll certainly have better light to read your scores."

"What about accompaniment?" He could tell already that she was entranced, under a spell only her angel could cast. In the dark, he raised the instrument he had brought to answer that same question.

Christine's breath hitched as the first note from Erik's violin vibrated through the dressing room and blossomed into an intricate phrase. She drifted to the mirror and, to Erik's shock, knelt before it in wonder as he finished.

"The way you play, you sound..." Christine's face was overcome. "It reminds me so much of him." Erik had known the violin would remind her of her lost father, but not that it would affect her so deeply so soon.

"What was your favorite thing he played?" Erik asked, perhaps stupidly.

"*The Resurrection of Lazarus*; it's an old folk tune, no one knows it..."

"I know it," Erik replied, fascinated. It wasn't just a folk tune; it was a Romani piece passed down through their masters of the fiddle. Erik had learned it from them decades ago. How had the elder Daaé come by it?

The mystery was unimportant. All that mattered was the utter emotion on Christine's face as he played the sweeping, swooning tune for her. His violin was Christ calling on the dead to arise, just as he had brought his student back to radiant life a month and a half before when he appeared to her the first time.

Christine looked as moved now as she had then, her hands clasped to her chest as an angel's music played just for her. Tears streamed down her face, and Erik understood why. In this one moment, he was giving her back her father in a more profound way than ever before. As the air at last came to a close, Christine heaved a sob.

"Thank you," she whispered through her tears, and to Erik's shock, he felt tears below his mask as well. "*Thank you.* You've given me so much. I can't ever repay you. I can't ever thank you enough."

"You repay me with each note you sing for me, my Christine," he replied, entranced by her. She was so close to him on the other side of the mirror. And yet so very far. "When you give me your song – when you give me your trust and your surrender – it is I who cannot repay."

Something darkened in her eyes at the mention of surrender, and Erik watched as her breath grew deliberate and slow.

"Will you let me give you that again? Please?" She was on her knees before him, Erik realized; like a penitent at the feet of a saint, begging him to bless her. To command her pleasure again. How could he say no?

"I could never refuse such a gift," Erik whispered and brought his violin to his chin once more.

He wondered if Christine recognized the piece, a caprice by Paganini that only the most daring of performers would tackle. Rumors abounded that the devil himself taught the notes to the late master. Erik watched Christine as he played, the melody dancing like a fire and an answering flame igniting in her face. She was breathing raggedly already, her breasts rising and falling in time with the music as she fell under his spell.

"Show me how you are mine, Christine," he said over the cascading notes, adoring that he could give her music and instruction this way. "Lie down."

She obeyed instantly, rushing to the chaise across from the great mirror, her head tipped back in ecstasy already. He watched as one hand drifted to her neckline while the other clawed at the fabric of her skirt, her body writhing subtly. But she did nothing more. She was waiting for his command. "Please," she murmured. "*Please.*"

"Touch. Don't be afraid," he replied, and immediately, one hand was at her breast, fumbling at the buttons of her blouse, and the other was between her legs. He played, imagining his fingers on her body as they raced over the violin strings. The thrill of the spectacle and his power over her rushed through him. He was achingly hard, but he didn't care, this was about her. She freed a breast, toying with a taut nipple, but the music enticed her towards more. Erik willed her to more.

"Touch where my music touches you. Give into it. Give yourself to me," he commanded, and she did. She abandoned her breast and raked her skirts high, exposing that she had chosen to wear no pantalettes or drawers today. It made Erik bite back a moan to think of her walking his opera, so secretly exposed and ready for him. She spread her legs further, showing him everything as her delicate hand began its work.

The sight was obscene, or would have been to a decent, god-fearing man. To Erik, it was perfection. The notes burned through the air, desperate as a storm as she bucked into her hand, whimpering and squirming in pleasure.

"Inside," he ordered, breathless. "Feel me inside." She nodded fervently as she complied, and he watched in salacious awe as she sank one curious finger into her slick opening. She added another with ease and soon enough he was watching his perfect student fuck three fingers into herself as he played the devil's music for her alone.

"Oh God...oh yes..." she moaned; her brows knit as she rode the crests of pleasure that her angel's violin propelled. Erik was right with her, imagining what it would feel like to be touched by her, to let his cock do the work of her clever fingers. The music swelled to a dizzying peak, her hand on her cunt moving as fast and wild as his on the violin.

"Now, my Christine," he nearly moaned as the crescendo hit. And she came. She cried out and spasmed, nearly doubling over in abject pleasure. And so did he. He came untouched at the sight of her ecstasy. His cock spilled and twitched, and he fell to his knees from the shock and force of it.

There was nothing but her breath to fill the silence now. He had to keep his own raged breathing under control, unheard by her, because angels did not breathe.

Angels did not do anything he had just done. (Or perhaps they did, who was he to speak for the unknown powers of heaven?) Still, he felt entirely like a man now, amazed and intoxicated by the woman separated from him by a pane of glass and a hundred lies. This was the only way he could have her, and he accepted that. It brought both of them pleasure and joy, and there was no more to it than that.

Despite himself, he recalled Buquet again: the feel of his clammy skin, the sound of his scream. And the memory became a hundred other screams, and the skin grew cold and dead in his recollection. He could never share more with Christine than this. And why would he ever need or want more? What he had was already a marvel. A miracle.

Her voice and her body and her soul were his. What more could he even dream of?

Christine was nervous. There was nothing for it. She was itchy and anxious and terrified in Nicole Duval's old dress, new scores heavy in her arms. *I'll be with you, don't worry*, he had whispered as she left the dressing room, but how could she not worry on her first day as an actual part of the chorus.

The small rehearsal room was already occupied when she entered, and it did nothing to calm her nerves. The lone woman sitting by the piano was unquestionably beautiful and refined too. Christine had only ever seen Adèle Valerius from a distance on stage, but she recognized the woman she was now meant to understudy.

She was at least a decade older than Christine, maybe more, with auburn hair and ample curves, and Christine wondered what sort of corsets and bindings she had to endure to play a young man like Siébel. Listening to her sing, Christine had always admired her voice, though she'd found it too mature and dark for Siébel. Indeed, Madame Valerius (no one called her Mademoiselle) was far better suited for one of Verdi's mezzo heroines, a perfect Amneris or Eboli. Perhaps Carlotta wanted it that way; to only share the stage with a true mezzo and not someone who would take *her* roles. Someone like Christine.

"Now, that's Nicole's dress but you aren't Nicole," Valerius said before Christine could speak.

"Oh. Well." Christine gulped. "I was given her old dressing room and it was there and—"

"It looks better on you," Valerius said. Her smile was thoughtful, and her eyes discerning. "Let's hope you're just as well suited to her job."

"Did Monsieur Gabriel tell you I was coming?" Christine asked, and Adèle nodded slowly, picking up a cup of tea and taking a long sip as she continued to survey Christine. "I hope I can be as good as Mademoiselle Duval."

"Nicole was a bitch who didn't like that I don't get sick," Adèle said. "And she had no appreciation for good music. She thought Meyerbeer was the height of art."

"Oh," Christine said, not sure what she was supposed to say. It did not satisfy Valerius.

"Name me a composer from the last decade who has achieved *real art*," Valerius demanded. "And don't say Wagner. Or Verdi," she snapped before the names could make it past Christine's lips. "Who do you know in France?"

"Bizet," Christine finally said and to her surprise, Valerius smiled at the answer. "Unless you wanted someone alive. In which case, Delibes."

Before Christine could speak further, the door opened again and Gabriel entered with another man, both carrying scores. "Oh good, you're here," Gabriel exclaimed, his smile bright. "We have about an hour, that should give us enough time to catch you up. Adèle, we'll start with your aria."

"Why me?" Valerius replied, cool and calm. "If this is her rehearsal, shouldn't she begin?"

Christine's heart jumped to her throat. This was a test and a challenge, judging from the older woman's discerning expression. Perhaps she had assumed she might catch a new rival unprepared or not warmed up. But this was exactly why her angel had prepared her this morning. And she could feel him watching even now, waiting for her to sing for him.

"If you'd like," Christine said, remembering how he had also told her she was brave. Gabriel shrugged and nodded to the other man, an accompanist apparently, who took his place at the piano and opened his score to Siébel's one aria.

Christine prepared herself as the first notes sounded, concentrating only on her voice and the thought of the one who had given it to her. "*Confess to her for me, give her my wishes, flowers who bloomed at her side*," Christine sang and even though she was trying to ignore the others, she saw Valerius' expression change from interest to grudging respect. The part of Siébel was simple, compared to Marguerite, but still innocent. She felt less than innocent herself, but if women like Carlotta and Adèle could pretend, so could she.

The aria was finished quickly, and Christine turned to Gabriel for a critique, but it was Valerius who spoke. "My lord, Gerard, where on earth did you find this one?"

"You wouldn't believe me," Gabriel replied. "Now, Christine, that was quite lovely, but watch the return from the bridge, the tempo has to catch back up, especially with an orchestra. Adèle, can you go over it now?"

Adèle complied, standing, and delivering the phrase, her voice smooth and powerful in a different way than Christine's. She liked it. She smiled, which Adèle caught, and in her eyes, something warmer had finally taken over.

The rehearsal passed quickly, with Adèle and Christine trading phrases and notes. When the session was done, Gabriel took a moment to speak to the pianist and Adèle took the opportunity to step close to Christine, leaning in conspiratorially.

"You're much better than Nicole," Adèle began, and Christine smiled. But Adèle raised a hand. "And let me warn you now, you can't sing like that if Carlotta is in a room with you."

Christine blinked. "What?"

"She's not wrong," Gabriel said with a sigh, joining them. "You have a great light and if you're anywhere that Carlotta might hear you, you'll need to hide it under a bushel."

"Or five," Adèle added. "Otherwise, she'll have you out the door in a second."

"And I don't think you're ready to go back to the costumers!" Gabriel said with a laugh and Adèle looked between them, incredulous.

"I was just there to bide time..." Christine muttered, then winced. "Damn, I haven't even told them yet!"

"You better go do that, we won't reconvene until afternoon, all principals and understudies," Gabriel said. "And then you'll join the chorus rehearsal tomorrow morning. Won't be too hard for you, I think, we'll have you ready for the performance next Friday."

Christine's heart soared at the idea of finally being part of a performance, rather than just listening from the shadows. "I'll try not to disappoint."

Adèle smiled and shook her head, amused again. "You might as well tell them to fit you for your costumes while you're there."

Christine nodded and rushed out of the rehearsal room, pausing in the halls to catch her breath as the air grew cool and electric around her. He was close. "Did I do alright?" she asked the shadows.

"You were amazing," the Angel's voice replied, and Christine felt like she could fly. She rushed towards the costume workshop, a simmering question in the back of her mind of how he might reward her tonight.

The workshop was as lively as ever when Christine reached it, but not so much that Louise and Julianne didn't pounce the moment she entered.

"Where have you been, girl!" Louise demanded, striding to Christine with fire in her eyes.

Julianne rushed between Louise and Christine, taking her friend by the arm protectively. "You had us worried."

"I'm fine," Christine answered automatically.

"I'd fire anyone else for being this late," Louise admonished and then frowned as a smile broke over Christine's face. "God, have you gone even more mad?"

"No, it's just...you can fire me if you like," Christine said, and Julianne joined Louise in looking shocked. "I found a new job."

"Where?!" Louise balked and Julianne's mouth fell open. "No one in Paris would be daft enough to hire you as a seamstress."

"Here," Christine answered. "In the chorus."

"What!?" Louise yelped. "How desperate are they?"

"She can sing?" The three women turn to look who had spoken. It was Maxine looking as incensed as ever.

"Well, she never stops humming," Julianne snapped back. "And she's trained! She only ended up here because she needed work!" Christine smiled; she had not counted on Julianne remembering her history. "I'm so happy for you. But damn, I'll miss you!"

"Who says you have to miss me?" Christine countered. "I'll need a dresser. And who better than a best friend for the job."

"You only say that because I'm your only friend," Julianne laughed. "But I accept. Louise, I think this one will need some chorus fittings soon."

"I guess so," Louise muttered. She was trying to look dubious, Christine could tell, but there was pride and happiness in the matron's eyes too.

"And for Siébel too, at least, the understudy costumes," Christine added, and Julianne's mouth fell agape.

"How on *earth*?" Julianne demanded.

Christine gave a small, mischievous shrug. "You wouldn't believe me if I told you.

Erik had meant to do something more with his day than just watch his protégé, but somehow, once again he found himself entranced by her. He told himself it was his duty, as her teacher and protector, to make sure her first rehearsal went well, which it did. Christine managed admirably among the principals, though Erik bristled with jealousy when she was introduced to Robert Rameau and the rakish bass pressed a kiss to her hand. If Erik had not known the kind of company Rameau preferred to keep in private, the man would have been in great danger.

There was no danger for Christine though, as Carlotta did not even bother to attend the rehearsal, much to the relief of all. When

Gabriel and Mercier brought things to a close without having rehearsed some of the most complicated ensembles, the singers grumbled but endured it. They all knew that no rehearsal at all was be better than a session with the great diva.

Erik's pulse quickened as Christine gathered her things. Soon he would have her to himself again. Soon he could speak to her and sing to her and...

"Are you done for the day, oh great prima donna?" Erik recognized Julianne Bonet's voice, and from his hiding place, he saw Christine smile towards the door.

"I am. What are you doing here?" Christine asked with a bright smile. "Do you miss me already?"

"Of course, we also need to celebrate," Julianne replied. "Come on, I borrowed a few things from the kitchen, let's find somewhere to enjoy them."

Christine made a faint protest that Erik couldn't hear as Julianne pulled her away. His sudden solitude left him cold. It struck him, painfully, how alone he was. How separate he was from the real world, where anyone could take Christine's hand and smile at her in the light.

He took his time finding them, the reminder weighing heavy on his mind as he walked the halls, haunting the shadows. He often told himself that he had chosen this life, this role as a phantom. But just like his face, it too was a prison, even if he had built it himself.

He heard their laughter before he found them, coming from a storeroom; the exact one where Christine had stayed the night when he had first seen her kindness and her strength. He leaned on the wall beside the door, straining to listen. He could only see a glimpse of them, enough to know Julianne's bounty included a bottle of wine passed between them, and a few cakes from the Opera kitchen, the kind they made for patrons to enjoy between acts.

"So, all this time you've been practicing your singing?" Julianne was saying through a mouthful as Christine took another sip. "And Gabriel just happened to hear you?"

"Something like that," Christine muttered. Through the half-open door and in the dark, Erik could see her cheeks were rosy from the wine and her eyes were sparkling and bright.

"*He* had something to do with it, didn't he?" Julianne demanded and Christine choked. Erik tensed.

"I have no idea who you're referring to," Christine replied, faux-offended. Julianne must have made a face Erik could not see, because Christine laughed. "Enough about me. How are you?"

"How am *I*?" Julianne laughed. "I've had no such adventures."

"What about Jammes? Have you spoken to her?"

He heard Julianne sigh deeply, and Erik saw Christine frown in compassion. No then. "I wonder if she'll ever speak to me again," Julianne said.

"Do you love her?" There was no fear or judgment in Christine's words. Erik hadn't expected the question and wondered himself at the answer.

"What is love anyway?" Julianne replied, voice sad and resigned. "How would I know if I did?"

"You just know," Christine replied and something nervous stirred in Erik. She sounded as if she was speaking from experience.

"Have you been in love?" Julianne asked in disbelief. Christine took a deep swig from the wine bottle and Julianne laughed. "You have! When? How?!"

Something like terror overtook Erik, turning his blood to needles. Was she talking about...him? That was impossible. Wasn't it? She couldn't...

"It was a long time ago, I was just a girl," Christine answered sheepishly, and something grim and hurt immediately replaced Erik's fear. Of course, she didn't mean *him*. She didn't even know him.

"I'll need more than that," Julianne was saying. Erik hated her for asking but he too needed the answer.

"When I was young, my father and I traveled constantly, but there was a village in Britany – Perros-Guirec – where we'd return every summer. It's beautiful. There's a lighthouse that looks out over the rocks and the sea. And there was a rich family, noble, who had a summer home there."

Erik could hear the love in her voice: love for the memory of happier days, for things lost, for the warmth of the sun. It made something inside him ache.

"I was thirteen when I met him, the youngest son of that family," Christine went on, voice still warm and soft. "My favorite red scarf had blown into the sea, and he rushed in to save it. From then on, we were best friends. We'd cavort all over the village together, collect stories, listen to father play. His family didn't mind then. We were both young and they liked the music we brought to the house."

"Go back; you said he was nobility?" Julianne interjected and Christine nodded. Listening from the shadows, Erik's hate rose higher. Of course, she had been used like a plaything by one of *them*.

"His father was a count, of all things, but that didn't matter then. He was my best friend each summer until I was seventeen, then suddenly he was more. I don't know what changed but I knew that I loved him. And he loved me, I think. And that was too much for his family."

Erik seethed at the words. He didn't even know this boy's name and he had never hated anyone more.

"Oh God, I can just imagine you two little fools," Julianne groaned, "star-crossed lovers kept apart by cruel fate. Did you ever—"

"We kissed, a few times, but it was all quite chaste," Christine cut her off. "We had plans though. The kind of grand, stupid plans you make when you're young. We were going to get married, and he'd leave his fortune to travel the world with me as I sang." Christine laughed at the absurdity of it, which soothed Erik somewhat. "But our fathers would have none of that. At the end of that summer his father died, his brother inherited the title, and...well, he never came back to Perros."

"How tragic," Julianne remarked, and Christine gave her a glare.

"That was six years ago. He's probably forgotten me, but...I'll never forget him. And how all I wanted every second that summer was to be with him or see him again," Christine sighed.

"I doubt he's forgotten you, if he felt the same," Julianne replied and took a sip of wine. "And so that's love? Wanting to see someone all the time? Sounds too simple."

"Maybe," Christine shrugged. "But I think that's what being in love is, at first, this...ache whenever you're away from them. And when you're with them, it doesn't stop, you just want more. You can't breathe without them."

Erik closed his eyes, the air in his lungs turning to ice and his heart crying out. He knew that ache. He'd known it for weeks.

"Does it hurt not to be with her, right now?" Christine asked gently. She meant Jammes, but Erik's own answer was undeniable.

He loved her. He knew it with a horrible certainty, and worse, he had loved her a very long time. The idea had been so fantastic and terrifying that it had never even occurred to him. How could a phantom – a monster – feel love after so long in the dark? Yet somehow, she had found her way past every mask and defense until each empty aching place in his heart had become filled entirely with her. He could never be with her, never even touch her without destroying everything she believed in, but he loved her, nonetheless. Foolishly and terribly, with every breath of life in him, he loved her.

"I should probably go look for her," Julianne said quietly. Erik's heart jumped. That meant Christine would finally be alone...and what would he say to her? How would a faceless angel compare to the memory of her first love? How could he even look at her knowing that she could never speak that way about him?

Footsteps in the hall startled Erik from his brooding and he withdrew into the shadows just in time to see Adèle Valerius of all people stride to the storeroom and fully open the door.

"Grelot said you'd be here, glad she was right," Valerius declared. "Daaé, you're coming to supper with me. I've decided I want to know you better."

"I – what?" Christine sputtered. "I have to—"

"You sleep here, you don't have to get anywhere!" Julianne burst out and Erik could only imagine the looks of fascination and annoyance she received from both singers. "Sorry."

"I'm just waiting to find a place I can afford," Christine grumbled.

"That's perfect then because I also happen to have a room that's begging for a lodger. Come along, my dove, I have all sorts of plans for you."

"But..." Christine protested. Erik watched as Valerius tugged Christine into the hall with Julianne tailing behind, bottle still in hand. Christine froze, perhaps finally sensing him there, and looked over her shoulder. Just the sight of her *hurt* like a vise on his heart. Erik suddenly wanted nothing more than to escape from her.

"Just go. You don't need to bother with me when you have *so many* earthly delights to distract you," Erik whispered, throwing his voice to her ear. He had not meant it to sound so cold, but it did. Christine's face fell as Valerius pulled her close, interlocking their arms. Erik closed his eyes so he didn't have to watch her leave.

The sound of footsteps faded, and Erik was left alone in the darkness once again. The pain, he considered, didn't come immediately. It was very much like a knife wound: it took a few moments for the agony to break past the shock. But when it did it was like nothing he had ever experienced. He sank to the ground, struggling to breathe, his mind swimming and his stupid, useless heart breaking over and over.

He loved Christine, utterly and entirely. He loved her and he felt as if it would kill him. He loved her and he had sent her away. Just as it always would be, she was beyond his reach, and he was the one who had put her there.

8. Illumination

Christine had not eaten so much in months. The café Adèle had taken them to had not been particularly elegant, but the food had been magnificent. The chef had even come out personally to greet Adèle and offer her a sampling of duck right out of the oven. The wine had been good too, and it, along with the noise of the great *Avenue de L'Opéra* – streetcars, carriages, horses, and endless people – made Christine's head spin as she followed Adèle now. She could barely breathe in such chaos, and as Adèle made a left turn onto the *Rue des Petits Champs*, Christine's gut twisted. She couldn't see the Opera if she looked back now, and it made her feel more lost and alone.

She was imagining things, she told herself again. The Angel wasn't upset with her, no matter how strange he'd sounded. He'd told her to go. He allowed her to leave the Opera all the time. She'd sung enough for the day and he...he didn't need her there.

"I've had this flat for a few years. I was tired of men paying for my rooms and thinking they owned me," Adèle said, casual, grabbing back Christine's attention. "But it does get lonely, so I take on girls from the chorus that need the help once in a while. Not that I was able to save my last girl." Adèle gave a huff of disappointment.

"What happened to her?"

"The poor idiot fell in love," Adèle scoffed as they turned left again on the *Rue des Petits Peres,* avoiding the large *Place des Victoires* further down the street. In a moment they had turned again, to the

Rue Notre Dame des Victoires, the basilica bearing the same name looming on one side.

"That doesn't sound too terrible," Christine offered.

"She fell in love with a *musician*! From the orchestra no less. A *flautist*!"

Christine couldn't help but laugh. "That sounds like how my parents met."

"Oh Lord, please don't tell me you're a romantic," Adèle laughed as they walked beside the Basilica. Christine looked at the cobblestones and pulled her shawl tighter against the winter chill. She didn't know the answer. Talking about love with Julianne had made her remember so many things and long for so many more. "Now, the real question is, are you really a slut and a boy, or are you actually a virgin martyr?"

Christine nearly tripped over herself in the street. "Excuse me?"

"You're understudying me, you sing mezzo, and most mezzos part are either sluts or men," Adèle explained, not faltering in her confident steps. "But I heard your upper range. You weren't even worried. So, are you hiding that you're secretly a soprano, and thus a virgin martyr?"

"I..." Christine had no idea what she was, on stage or off. She had never been touched by another in that way, and yet she felt as if she had a secret lover who knew her most wanton desires. "I'm not sure yet."

"Hm," Adèle said, looking at Christine over her shoulder. "Neither am I. I'm sure that you'll need help, whatever path you pick."

"I won't argue there," Christine sighed. "And I do...appreciate your help. Truly."

Adèle's face was tender for only a moment, but it was enough to confirm that whatever bravado and brazenness the woman wore on the outside, there was more to her than that.

"Here we are," Adèle declared as they came to a large red door with brass fixtures. It wasn't a glamourous building, but it wasn't a hovel either. Adèle let them in and ascended the stairs. Christine glimpsed a courtyard, though it was empty of life in this season. Adèle's flat occupied the left side of the top floor. When the mezzo guided her in, Christine could not help but think how well it suited the older woman.

The flat was warm and welcoming, with inviting furnishings and a cozy fire, but it was also just slightly opulent, with a piano and gilded bird cage by the window, and vases full of dried flowers set about. The finely-papered walls were adorned with framed posters and circulars, where Christine could see Adèle's name and even a few depictions of her. On the mantle above the fire was a framed photograph of a younger Adèle next to a handsome man in a uniform.

"This is lovely," Christine said. She wondered if she would ever afford a place like this, or if she would want to. Would she ever want to stay anywhere her angel could not follow? Would she be able to rest here without him singing her to sleep? Adèle's posters were in different languages, from theaters around Europe, but how could Christine sing at any theater where *he* couldn't guide her?

"You're in there," Adèle pointed to an innocuous door and Christine followed. The room was much plainer, save for the dark red and black wallpaper. The bed was sturdy, and the vanity was clean and neat. A month ago, Christine would have been delighted by it. She didn't know what to think now.

"I do have visitors, once in a while," Adèle said. "Whatever you hear, you didn't. I'll pay you the same courtesy. And if you ever don't come home, I won't ask questions." Christine blinked, shocked by the frankness.

"I – that may happen," she muttered.

Adèle smiled wickedly. "Well then, maybe mezzo does suit you."

"It's complicated, I'm not..." Christine tried, and Adèle clucked her tongue.

"Don't worry little one, it always is," Adèle said. "Just listen to me and don't be like that other fool, don't fall in love. If you find a man or a patron or a lover, whoever it is: fuck them, use them, enjoy them. But *never* love them."

Christine stared at Adèle, shocked in a different way now. She'd heard similar words before. *Never love what you can lose, my dear,* her father's voice whispered from the past, thick with despair. And despite herself, she thought of Raoul de Chagny. She had loved him so much as a girl and remembering him today had warmed her heart...but then her angel had sent her way. Was it because of love?

"You've never been in love?" Christine asked timidly, following Adèle back into the drawing room.

"Oh, no, I have been, far too many times. Which is why I don't recommend it," Adèle said with a certain heaviness and a glance to the photograph on the mantle. "It's good for your art but bad for your career if you know what I mean."

Christine nodded.

"May I look at these?" Christine asked, indicating the scores piled on the piano. The one open on the stand showed an aria Christine didn't recognize, but the lyrics intrigued her. "*My heart opens to your voice?*"

"It's Saint-Saëns," Adèle explained. "*Samson and Delila.* I keep hoping that if I can get Bosarge or Gabriel to let me perform an aria somewhere, the patrons will like it enough to demand a staging. But it hasn't happened yet."

Christine sat at the piano, gently testing the keys as she read the music. "May I?" Adèle nodded and Christine began to play. The music was gorgeous, and when Adèle began to sing with such longing and depth that it nearly took her breath away, Christine knew with certainty that Adèle had been in love. Listening to her made Christine wonder if her feelings of long ago could even compare to what Adèle and Delila sang of.

Hours later, the melody and words resonated in Christine's head as she tried to sleep. She'd read and reread it, playing long after Adèle had shuffled off to bed. Now, her own bed made strange noises. The sheets were cold against her skin, and she was empty and agitated. She missed the Opera, but more than that she missed *him.* She ached. She thought back again to what she'd told Julianne, of how she could have sworn she felt her angel's disappointment with her foolish mortal heart and desires the moment she stepped into the hall. She fell asleep at last, trying not to weep.

Erik had not slept until he returned to the mirror. He had wandered all night, to all the places that belonged to her and were so empty. Their practice room, the costume workshop, the storeroom where she had spoken of loving that nameless boy and where Erik had first begun to love her, so many weeks ago.

Somehow it was better to be in her absence, to linger in her memory than to be anywhere else, especially across the lake with the whispers of ghosts in his ear. He'd haunted her makeshift room, caressing her beloved books of fairy tales and myths, and for the first time, he'd dared to touch her bed. The blankets had been coarse and cold under his fingertips. Perhaps he had dreamed it, but he had thought he could smell her in the dark air, like rain.

He had come to the mirror in the murky hours before dawn and sunk to the ground, then finally slept with the unyielding stone against his back. Now, he woke again in darkness, empty and cold, a terrible contrast to the warmth of her smile in his dreams.

He didn't move, just stared at the blank glass. This was hell, it had to be. To want her was one thing. He knew lust and understood it. Lust was an animal instinct; one he had always (until lately) been able to deal with like any other inconvenient need of his mortal flesh. But love...that was different. Love had only ever hurt him, in his terrible and limited experience. Love had left a trail of corpses and broken dreams through his horrible life. And those infatuations were distant and dim compared to what he felt now.

The door of the dressing room burst open without warning, and Erik jumped, concerned immediately by the pale cast of Christine's face and her worried expression as she rushed in. Gods, he'd sent her away to save them both and it had failed so completely.

"Angel? Are you—?

"I'm here, Christine," he replied immediately, instinctively. "Are you alright?"

She fell to her knees before the mirror in reply, tears filling her eyes as she shook her head. "No. I've been so worried. I missed you so much last night and I-I'm afraid I displeased you or upset you to make you to tell me to leave."

"Oh, Christine, no..." He wasn't talking like an angel. He sounded as desperate and dejected as she did, but her face still brightened at the words. "It was not anger. It was...regret. To know your heart might be elsewhere, either now or some other day."

"Because I talked about my..." Christine looked down in shame. "My first love?"

Something terrible coiled inside him at the reminder. He hated the boy, without even knowing his name or face. Hated him and anyone that would ever take Christine from him. Even if she could never truly be his, he would die before he let her be someone else's.

"I hated hearing you speak of another. I hate the thought of you with one who can give you things I cannot," he confessed, his voice soft and sincere. He moved carefully towards the mirror, on his knees like her, and traced the outline of her beautiful face with his fingertip against the glass. A shadow on a perfect rose. Her eyes closed for a moment, as if she could feel the phantom touch. "I don't wish to share you, even with a memory. I love you too dearly."

Christine's eyes opened, brimming with fresh tears, but they were not tears of sadness. Her face was a mosaic of joy and devotion as she pressed her hand to the mirror, inches from Erik and yet a world away. Had she not already guessed how he loved her? It didn't matter, she knew now.

"My Angel, what we had was nothing. It was a candle, but you...you are the dawn," she breathed as Erik pressed his hand against hers, dreaming he could feel her warmth through the glass. "That fancy was nothing compared to my love for you."

Erik froze, unable to comprehend what she meant. How could she? But after all that he had given her and all she had shown him...how could she not? "You love me?"

"Do you not know?" she asked, breathing deep. "As you are mine, I am yours." And then, to his further amazement, she began to sing.

"*My heart opens to your voice, as ever do the flowers to the kisses of the dawn,*" she sang to the mirror. It was Saint-Saëns, a melody so passionate, seductive, and modern that it would scandalize the patrons of the Opera. It was perfect. "*But oh, my beloved, to quench my tears, let your voice speak again. Tell me, to Dalila, you will return forever. To my open heart, speak oaths; respond to my tender love and fill me with ecstasy!*"

He had never heard her sing with such unbridled passion. It echoed through the dark, surrounding him with the love and desire in each note. It was sublime, and his soul sang back to her in return. To think, he had awoken in hell and now...her voice lifted him to heaven.

"*My heart trembles like wheat in the wind, awaiting the consolation of your voice, which is so dear to me. The arrow is not as fast as the death I find in your arms,*" she sang on, and Erik's blood sang with desire in turn. Her face was as full of adoration and yearning as he had ever seen, and somehow this song was as intimate as any moment they had yet shared.

"*Ah, respond to my tender longing, fill me with ecstasy,*" she called out to him, and he let himself imagine it. He imagined taking her into his arms, sinking into her warm, welcoming body. Feeling her kiss. "*My angel,*" she sang, shocking him from the reverie by replacing "Samson" with his title in the final, rapturous call and untold ecstasy engulfed him. "*My angel, I love you.*"

He had never loved or wanted anyone like this. And he would do anything in his power to keep her.

Christine felt like she had spent the whole week trembling. In rehearsals she had shaken in anxiety avoiding Carlotta's eyes, then in helpless anger to hear the thin, heartless way the woman sang. She'd shivered in anticipation on the nights when she had snuck to her hidden room rather than back to Adèle's flat. And there she had quivered and writhed when her angel had gifted her with his voice and allowed her pleasure that left her quaking and breathless on her bed.

And now she was shuddering like a leaf as she walked to her dressing room ahead of her first real performance. She still felt like an imposter, like she didn't even belong in the chorus. Tonight, she was meant to sing for him on the stage she'd dreamed of her whole life, and she was convinced someone would find her out beforehand and turn her back out on the street.

She paused, taking a deep breath at her dressing room door. She could already feel him close, waiting for her inside.

"Don't tell me you're nervous," a familiar voice said, and Christine jumped. Julianne strode towards her, grinning over the costume in her arms. "The luckiest girl in the Paris Opera can't possibly be *nervous*."

"You'd be surprised," Christine muttered. She was happy to have Julianne there, but disappointed to be denied a moment alone with her guardian.

"I can't wait to see you in this," Julianne said as they entered the dressing room. Her friend looked to the mirror just as Christine did, but Julianne shuddered. "Lord, that mirror gives me chills. But of course *you* don't mind the haunted room."

"The whole Opera is haunted," Christine said with a shrug.

"Remember when you didn't believe?" Christine stepped behind the dressing screen and began to undress, the first time she'd bothered with such modesty. "How things change."

"This place has a way of doing that. Changing you."

"Are you still angry?" Julianne asked and Christine looked over the screen at her in confusion. "When you told me – about why you didn't want to believe – you were mad that you'd never been visited by your angel of music. But you don't seem disappointed anymore."

Christine glanced at the mirror, then hid her face. "Who's to say I haven't been?" Christine took the costume from Julianne and ducked into the shift, then stepped into the skirt. Julianne helped her into the red velvet bodice and cinched it tightly from behind. Christine gasped.

In her time with Adèle, Christine had been gifted a few new pieces of clothing, outer and under, by her mentor. Adèle had been appalled that Christine didn't own a proper boned corset or bustled dress. She still wasn't used to it, but this costume had a much lower neckline than any dress she owned, and the bodice pushed her breasts up in a way she'd never seen. She knew he could see it when she stepped out from the screen, and it made her more breathless than the tight laces.

Julianne pulled her to the vanity and began on her face, much to Christine's surprise. "Most of you divas do this yourself, but I help Jammes and her rats. And I'm guessing you have no experience with stage makeup." Christine shook her head then tried to stay still as Julianne lined her eyes, rouged her cheeks, and painted her lips. When she finally saw herself in the mirror, she blushed again.

"Like a fair lady, he would find me beautiful," she whispered to the mirror.

"Don't forget: Marguerite's pretty jewels were from the devil," Julianne said, and Christine gave her a glare. "Sorry, it just always struck me as sad how she sings such a sweet song while being tricked. I guess that's the tragedy."

"Well, I'm not Marguerite tonight," Christine muttered. "Not yet."

Julianne gave her a suspicious look. "You'll be wonderful, no matter what. I'll be watching." Julianne gave the mirror another suspicious look. "I guess he will be too. They say he sits in box five on the grand tier. Meg Giry's mother is the concierge."

"So I've heard," Christine smiled.

"They also say he can control the rats. The real ones, not the dancers, so maybe they'll watch too. I'm not sure how that works." Julianne gave a shrug and Christine scowled.

"Thank you, I'll see you later."

She didn't mean to herd Julianne out, but the stage managers were already yelling through the halls that it was almost curtain time. She had thought she'd have more time alone with him before...

"I will be watching," the Angel said as if reading her thoughts. "The only one I'll see is you."

"I don't know why I'm nervous," Christine replied. "I've wanted to be on that stage for so long and I know you've prepared me. But I'm scared."

"I would be more worried if you weren't nervous," her teacher replied, his perfect voice encircling her like loving arms. "You love this music, you love this art, and so it is natural to fear not doing it justice. But know that you can, and you will."

"And I love you," she added, closing her eyes, and wishing she could speak those words to *him*, not her reflection. To the Angel beyond the mask.

"And you could never disappoint me," he replied. "Sing your love to me tonight and know that it is returned."

"Always," Christine whispered, the thought of him filling her with strength and adoration.

"Two minutes! Places!" a stagehand yelled through the hall, making Christine jump.

"Go. Sing for me," the Angel ordered, and Christine obeyed.

She made her way to the stage, caught up with the rest of the chorus. Together they waited in the shadows of the wings, listening to the audience murmuring. The overture was over in a heartbeat and soon it was time to sing, taunting Faust. It was so different from the first time she had been backstage, only watching and listening. This time she was part of the music, and it thrilled her. But the true excitement only came in act two, when she finally stepped into the bright lights of the Paris Opera stage.

The chorus had a great deal to do in act two, as soldiers sang, and the devil tempted the villagers with the tale of the golden calf. Christine sang with all her soul, but in the moments of silence, she could not help but look out at the audience in awe.

She'd never seen the theater with the glorious chandelier alight before. Her angel had mentioned more than once that he disapproved of keeping the great mass of brass and crystal illuminated during performances. He was a proponent of the modern, German idea that a theater should be dark to bring the focus to the stage and not to the audience. But this way, Christine could finally see the glittering world of the upper crust, just on the other side of the blazing footlights.

The auditorium that had always been a dim sea of red velvet and gold before now sparkled like a trove of jewels. What was it like, Christine wondered, to live such a life among such riches? She could see women in satin gowns and white gloves and even make out their jewels and silken fans. She couldn't see their faces well, but some looked bored, as if they were only at the Opera to be there, and not for the great spectacle before them. Every seat and box was full, she noted. All but one.

Erik had chosen box five for its awkward location: almost on top of the stage, only two premier boxes separating it from the proscenium, on the grand tier, one level above the orchestra. The hollow column he had constructed that allowed him to enter and leave the box was quite useful and almost eliminated the need for a concierge, but Estelle Giry had proved extremely useful in other ways.

Quite the opposite of the other box-holders, he did not come to the Opera to be seen and instead kept to the shadows at the back of the box. He was grateful for those shadows tonight. He hoped their soft chill would dim the memory of Christine on the other side of the mirror, so utterly stunning. And now, there she was, on his stage at last, a vision of loveliness with a voice so perfect he could hear it through all the din. And it sang for him.

Erik could not take his eyes off her in the crowd scenes of act two. Carlos Fontana and Robert Rameau did their level best as Faust and Méphistophélès, while Simon Fayard brought some bombastic verve to Valentin, but it was Christine who shone for him. Enough so that he had no desire to stay for act three, where the chorus did not appear. He slipped out of the box and made his way to the dressing rooms, taking his time to listen to the gossip.

Fontana held room one, and as always, was using the interval to sip tea and reapply his makeup. Rameau was across the hall in a room Erik usually could not look into, but it sounded like he was entertaining a male visitor whom he knew well.

"I don't know. I think I'm too young for it," the unknown man was saying.

"If the minister is looking for new blood, you should seize on it," Rameau replied, still sounding like a tempting devil even off stage. "And I'd certainly be happy about it."

"As if I could even do the job with you around," the man protested, and Erik raised an eyebrow.

"I've spent years here watching sopranos be such *distractions*, don't you think it's my turn?" Rameau laughed. Erik wondered what position Rameau's paramour was being considered for.

"It's different with us, you know that," the man said quietly.

"Maybe you're right, you're far too demure for the Opera," Rameau laughed. "And too superstitious."

"More ghost stories now?" the man asked back. Erik did love to hear himself talked about, but movement in the corridor forced him to retreat, back into the dark confines of the walls. And behind Carlotta's mirror now.

Like Fontana, Carlotta was seated at her vanity, applying more rouge to her lips and decolletage, while LeDoux simpered behind her, scribbling notes in a little book, the night's program also clutched under his arm.

"Is there anyone new tonight?" Carlotta asked, her attention intent on her own reflection and her regular mélange of an accent completely absent. "I'm getting tired of the Marquis and his crooked prick."

"Yes, Signora, I was getting to that," LeDoux stammered, flipping through his little notepad as Carlotta rolled her eyes in impatience. "Tonight, Comte Philippe has been joined by his younger brother, just out of the navy. Uh," LeDoux flipped the page. "Raoul. He's quite handsome I'm told."

"Why would I care about the younger brother of someone Sorelli already has under her skirts?" Carlotta seethed. "And yes, I know Philippe de Chagny has no heirs or wife, that doesn't mean I want to bother trying to fuck his baby brother."

LeDoux gulped and nodded, flipping to another page as a faint sweat gathered on his moustache. "There's a rumor Léo Delibes may be here..."

Erik turned away, shuddering, and wishing he could use Carlotta's copper bath for himself. It was repugnant, the way she spoke of and used people. Not that the so-called nobles with their empty titles and useless gold didn't deserve to be used, but it was the way she did it that disgusted Erik.

He ignored the rest of the dressing rooms, finally giving into the real reason he was backstage, and found himself once again behind the mirror of room thirteen. Christine was already there, sitting on the floor of all places, with her eyes closed. It looked like she was praying, and perhaps she was.

"There you are," Christine whispered before Erik could even take a moment to appreciate her beauty in her act four costume; his angel dressed in a red velvet cloak to join a choir of devils. Beneath that she wore the dark bodice and skirt of a witch, who would join Méphistophélès in his dastardly spectacle while the ballerinas danced the *Walpurgisnacht* sabbath. Erik loved that an opera so concerned with the soul and salvation made hell and damnation so entertaining.

"I'm sorry to have kept you waiting," Erik replied. He still didn't know how she always knew he was there. Perhaps she was a witch, he thought as she opened her forest-colored eyes. She certainly had bewitched him.

"Did I—"

"You were perfect," he answered before she was finished. She smiled, bright and kind as always, but there was sadness in her eyes.

"Do you think he—" she stopped, her voice breaking. "My father told me I'd sing on this stage one day and now I have. And I just wish I knew if he was proud."

Erik's blood froze in his veins. There had always been an unspoken agreement between them that Christine was not to ask too much. She did not question her angel's divinity or nature and had never asked about *the other side*. Erik often wondered if she had already tried to reach her father, judging by the scornful way she spoke of mediums and spiritualist science. But now she was asking her angel, whom she believed her father had personally sent, for a message.

If he told her this lie, there was no turning back. To reveal himself would shatter her faith and her soul completely. There would never be a chance to touch her, be part of her life as a real man.

"Angel?" she asked, apprehension in her voice as the silence stretched between them.

Erik took a deep breath. There had never been a chance.

"He's proud, Christine, so proud," Erik intoned carefully, and tears blossomed in Christine's eyes. Erik looked away. He couldn't look at her face as he lied; the light in her eyes was too beautiful and terrible to bear. "He cannot speak to you as I can, but he hears you. He has always heard you and he is always with you." Perhaps it was not all a lie in some sense. "When you love someone, you carry them in your heart. They can never truly leave you."

"Thank you," Christine whispered. Erik dared to look at her again. She was as overcome as he had expected and so beautiful. He could not stop himself from smiling weakly. "I don't know what to say."

"When you cannot speak, you must sing," he reminded her simply. "Sing for him tonight. And sing for me."

Christine nodded in resolve, wiping a stray tear from her cheek. He could see the strength inside her rising. She stood from the floor and straightened her red cloak, face resolute. She opened her mouth to speak again just as a knock sounded at the door.

"Are you decent in there, Daaé?" Valerius called from the other side of the door.

"I – yes," Christine said, glancing to the mirror as she unlocked the door. Valerius walked in without ceremony, wearing her blue doublet and hose for her part as Siébel.

"I always hated this room, glad you have the stomach for it," the mezzo declared, giving the mirror where Erik hid the same suspicious look everyone but Christine did. "Everything going well so far?"

"Yes, it's wonderful to be on stage, finally," Christine replied, distracted. Erik understood why a second later, as Gerard Gabriel followed Valerius inside.

"Gerard has finally started putting together the program for the New Year's gala," Valerius declared. "And someone gave him the fantastic idea that you and I should perform a duet for the festivities."

Erik smiled in the dark, glad his note to Gabriel had hit home. It was completely useless lately to bother with the managers.

"Yes, well, I wanted to be the one to share that news," Gabriel said with a gentle glare at Valerius. "It was suggested that you two sing the letter duet from *Figaro*."

Christine's face lit up in a grin. "I would love to!"

"It's rather old-fashioned for my taste, but it will get you the right kind of attention as we expand your reach," Valerius said. There was no hiding the warmth in her face when she looked at Christine. "As would coming to the reception tonight."

Instantly, Erik's respect for the mezzo evaporated. Gabriel as well looked green at the prospect, as Christine glanced between the mezzo, the director, and the mirror.

"As I told you, I don't think that would suit me," Christine said carefully. Valerius sighed and Erik let out his own breath in relief.

"Fine, be that way," Valerius said. "Come on, Gerard. I haven't harassed you about Bizet yet this week. Christine, I'll see you...eventually."

He loved the way Christine blushed as Valerius closed the door. He wondered what the elder singer thought of Christine. Since she'd taken the room with Valerius, she'd only spent a few nights there. Did Valerius think Christine already had a lover? Perhaps that was for the best.

"I hope you will stay here tonight," Erik whispered through the glass when they were alone. "Your first performance deserves a great reward." He loved the way he could make her shiver with such words.

"I could never refuse you," his pupil replied, her eyes darkening as she placed a hand on the mirror.

"Good."

Her voice and her soul belonged to the Angel of Music, and none but that angel would ever own her ecstasy or her heart. Erik clung to that. She was his and she loved a part of him in a way no one ever had or would again, and he loved her desperately in return. Yes, one day he would place her in the spotlight on his grand stage and all of Paris would bow before her. But he would know she was his, his alone. And no other would ever touch her.

9. Dreams

Julianne's mother was an incredible cook, Christine had been happy to learn. When Julianne had told her, just yesterday, that Christine was *expected* for Christmas dinner, Julianne had made her sound far more formidable. But Élodie Bonet had welcomed Christine into the home she shared with her daughter with open arms and good humor. Her chestnut skin was darker than Julianne's, and her features were rounder, but her eyes had the same mischievous sparkle, and her laugh was just as warm. She had insisted Christine lead them in carols, before stuffing both girls to the brim with food.

Sitting next to the crackling fire in the little flat, topping off her stomach full of croquembouche with sips of mulled wine, Christine struggled to think of the last time she had felt so content. She certainly remembered the last Christmas she had spent with people, but she had known then it would be Papa's last and had hidden her tears whenever she looked at him too long.

There had to have been some point, deep in the past, before Papa's illness, when all the world had been full of dreams and magic and potential, when she had been this blissful. But even that paled in comparison now. Truly, she had never been as happy, day-to-day, as she had been in the past weeks. Her days were full of music, her nights were full of pleasure. And it was all thanks to him.

Christine was glad to be with Julianne for the holiday meal, but she also couldn't wait to be back in the Opera. She would have to go back to Adèle's tonight, to not raise suspicion. Thanks to that, guilt gnawed at the edges of her contentment. Even more so when she noticed Julianne glancing at the door more and more as the evening wore on.

"She may still come," Christine said after the tenth such look. "She didn't say no when you asked."

"She didn't say yes either," Julianne muttered. And as if the world was listening, a knock sounded at the door. Julianne jumped to answer, rushing past her mother as she re-entered the drawing room. When Christine saw Jammes on the other side of the threshold, and Julianne's grin at the sight, her heart warmed immeasurably.

"I hope I'm not too late," Jammes said, looking bashful.

"Not at all, my dear," Élodie replied. She supplied Jammes with a plate of food in a blink, and wine too, and soon they were all seated by the fire.

"You missed the carols," Julianne said. "It turns out Christine is indeed a better singer than a seamstress."

"Didn't you tell me she had the worst sewing you'd ever seen?" Jammes remarked over a sip of wine.

"It wouldn't have been a lie," Christine shrugged. "What else do you do for Christmas?"

"Ghost stories of course," Élodie declared. "And I demand some. Julianne refuses to tell me about your Opera Ghost most days. Says she gets enough at work."

"Oh, well, Christine is the one with the stories," Jammes said. "She's met him."

"So I have heard," Élodie said, as sly as her daughter when she looked at Christine.

"I've...only seen him a few times," Christine stammered. She hoped they couldn't see her blush.

"Well, I've changed my opinion on him," Jammes declared. "If he did push Joseph Buquet off that catwalk, or strangle him or whatever the story is now, God bless him. He did the Opera a service."

"Here, here," Julianne said as she raised her cup.

"How can a ghost strangle someone?" Élodie asked, chuckling. "Sounds more like a revenant, if you ask me."

"Did you hear what that fireman saw just the other day?" Jammes asked, perking up more. "Scared him to death!"

"The fireman?" Julianne asked. Christine had not heard either.

"What could be so terrible as to scare a fireman? They're brave fellows, aren't they?" Élodie said.

"Well, he claims he was on his rounds and saw a head floating in the dark in the cellars!" Jammes said breathlessly.

"A...head?" Christine echoed.

"*On fire,*" Jammes went on. Christine scrunched her face. She'd seen her ghost in his mask, and glimpsed his shining eyes more than once, but a head on fire was quite another thing. "And when he approached, the dark around it came alive and attacked him. Scratched him all over!"

"That's ridiculous," Christine found herself saying aloud.

"I didn't mean to offend the expert," Jammes snickered. "A head of fire is better than a death's head like Buquet claims he saw, I think."

"A ghost would look dead though, wouldn't he?" Julianne added. "Or a revenant. Whatever that is."

"But maybe he's not a dead person," Christine again said without thinking and Julianne gave her a curious look.

"You believe the ones who say he's a demon?" Jammes shot back and Christine was suddenly less happy she had joined them.

"Or something else," Christine muttered, casting her eyes back to her nearly-drained cup. "Who is to say?"

"I heard from Sorelli, who heard it from her favorite lover, that the management send the Ghost ten thousand francs a month *as a salary*!" Jammes went on, ignoring Christine again. And again, Christine rolled her eyes.

"What would a ghost need that much money for?" Élodie laughed. "And do you think he can spare any?"

"Who is it Sorelli is sleeping with again?" Julianne asked. Christine had barely met the prima ballerina, given how separate the worlds of the ballet and the singers were, but she had a better reputation than Carlotta in terms of her character at least. Christine could envision the elegant woman with any manner of well-off patrons at her service.

"Philippe de Chagny," Jammes drawled, unimpressed. But Christine's heart jumped to her throat. "He claims some title, I forget what."

"Count," Christine said, and all the women looked at her. "He's Comte de Chagny."

"How would you know?" Jammes said, but next to her, Julianne had gone wide-eyed.

"Wait, is that...is that *him*?" Julianne asked with glee. "No, you said that was the brother! Jammes, does Sorelli's man have a brother?"

"I have no damn idea," Jammes scowled. "Sorelli keeps him to herself. Why do you care?"

"I don't," Christine said flatly. She didn't. She couldn't. "It doesn't matter. I don't want any part of the patrons."

"You're right there," Élodie declared, more serious than Christine had heard her all night. "Men like that aren't worth chasing. They don't see people like us as, well, *people*."

"Mama, they can't all be that bad," Julianne argued. Christine wanted to do the same but Élodie shook her head.

"The men at your opera, the ones that trade and buy ballerinas and divas like the latest fashion, they're the same kind that thought my mother was a thing they could own and sell," Élodie said grimly. "You're safer keeping away. You too, Cécile."

"Oh, I think I've quite given up on any man at all." Jammes muttered, then chuckled to herself. "I was about to say you'd have better luck being in love with a ghost but, well, some of us are."

Christine scowled and looked into the fire. She knew it was a joke, but she also knew it was true. Or at least close enough to the secret she held. If any of them really knew...they would call her mad. Or a whore or a witch. Something wicked and damned. They didn't understand that the ghost they feared was an angel and that the girl they teased lived for him entirely.

Erik usually didn't bother with anything other than his opera cape and a good wide-brimmed hat in the Opera, but tonight, he had ventured into the waking world. And that meant more precautions. He wore a long, black velvet cloak with a deep hood, and a scarf wrapped around his face. It was over-dramatic perhaps, but no one had ever accused him of subtlety. The disguise meant that no passerby would see his mask, and he could blend into the shadows in alleys and catacombs when needed.

He was at the edge of one such alley now, right off the little *Rue Feydeau*, watching the building that Christine had entered hours before. It was rash, to have followed her, he knew that. But he hadn't seen her since the day before, and she had to walk home alone from Bonet's in the dark.

It had been an hour since Jammes had arrived, to Erik's slight surprise. The love lives of the company were not his business, but there was a small part of him that was relieved to know Bonet and her lover had reconciled. He had never seen a moment of anything but friendship between Christine and Julianne that would have ignited his jealousy. But he also knew better than to assume the kinds of people others might desire. Still, he had no animosity towards the dresser. There was a world of difference between someone like

Bonet – poor, female, with African blood and unconventional taste in lovers – and a patron. While noble titles had meant nothing since the latest revolution, the rich still wielded them like swords.

Finally, the front door of the building opened, and Christine stepped into the snowy night. She had a heavy shawl on, and a new hat, to keep the snow at bay, but she still had to be cold. Indeed, he watched from the shadows as she shivered and pulled her shawl tight, her breath forming a cloud before her in the flickering gaslight.

Erik stayed well behind her as she made her way home. Down the *Rue Feydeau* to the *Rue Vivienne*, she walked with a shadow behind her. Erik, like so many Parisians, both hated and respected the modern streets. Paris was orderly, clean, and bright; a beacon of progress. But he preferred the older parts of the metropolis, where the buildings leaned and listed, and once in a while you could see remnants of the city that had stood for centuries peeking through. Places like that were easier to find on the roads Erik would take home.

That city beneath was the Paris Victor Hugo had known and written about, Erik thought to himself; the *real* Paris full of thieves and rebels and monsters, not the tidy, fussy version presented to others in grand spaces like the *Place De L'Opéra*. But even in this Paris there remained dangerous things and people. Erik was certainly one of them. But his concern was with the others, like the new shadow that emerged from a dark doorway when Christine cut through the alley between the *Rue Vivienne* and the *Rue de la Banque*.

Erik sneered. This was why he had come. It wasn't safe for a young, beautiful woman to walk alone, no matter how holy the day. The man moved like a predator, quiet behind Christine as he readied a knife.

The Punjab Lasso made no sound in the winter night, but the man did gasp as the length of catgut trapped his throat. He struggled, slipping in the snow as Erik reeled him in like a floundering fish, pulling the ruffian into the shadows just as Christine turned to look behind her.

Erik kept his hand over his prey's mouth as he watched Christine. She hadn't seen, but she did look curiously at the path behind her in the snow. She paused a moment longer, then continued. Erik returned his attention to the criminal in his clutches, sputtering for air as Erik kept the lasso tight around his neck.

"Were you going to rob her or rape her?" Erik asked calmly as the fool clawed at his throat. "Or both? I guess it doesn't matter. Is hanging still the sentence for both? It's been a while since I've checked the laws."

"Please!" The plea was hard to make out, but Erik understood it. What was it about him that made men beg so pathetically when he had them like this? He could not possibly give the impression of a monster with mercy. Maybe it was instinct.

"Don't worry, you're going to live. I don't want to bother with your body. But I do hope this experience serves as a reminder to you, of—" The man didn't even have the decency to stay conscious for the lesson, his eyes rolling back before he went limp. Erik sighed, letting the oaf fall to the ground in a heap. He did still have a pulse, which would please the Daroga if no one else.

Erik left the man where he dropped him. He carefully re-coiled the lasso and returned it to the hidden pocket of his coat. He had stopped carrying regularly when he was in the Opera years ago (again, a fact only the Daroga would appreciate), but it was always with him in the outside world. He'd had it on hand rather often lately.

He never strayed too close to the flat on the *Rue Notre Dame des Victoires*. He would usually lurk beside the great *Notre Dame des Victoires* basilica, looking across the road at the window where once in a while he would catch a glimpse of the face he loved. It was strangely peaceful, to watch her that way, a false angel in the shadow of a true house of the Lord. He especially liked it when he could hear the choir.

Tonight, the vespers were especially joyful, celebrating the birth of their god. *Gloria in excelsis deo.* Erik smiled, but not for the song, instead he had found his own light in the darkest nights of winter. High above, the light glowed in Christine's room and for a second, he saw her looking out to the night. He wondered if she missed him. If she longed for her angel tonight as he longed for her. He wondered if she knew he was watching, even now.

Very rarely was the Angel with Christine when she woke, but this morning was special. It was the last day of 1880, and tonight was the gala celebration. Perhaps that was why he had been there when Christine had passed from dreams into wakefulness with her whole body burning with need for him. She had called out and he had answered.

Christine had started slowly, just as his song had, exploring herself with her fingers and paying special attention to the sweet, secret spot that made her ignite like dry kindling. But now she was frantic, riding her hand as she tried desperately to touch as deeply as his glorious song. Her breasts were bare to the cold air of the cellar as she pawed at one, writhing on her bed and whimpering.

"More, I want more," Christine panted, her hips rising off the mattress as she chased her pleasure. Her whole hand was slick with her own wetness, but it was still hers. She wanted his hands. The thought of it made her shudder, pushing her closer to that dizzying peak.

What would an angel's hands feel like upon her? He had a form, she'd seen it. He moved things, touched people. He had to be able to do it – to *touch* her.

"Please, Angel, I want more," she begged the darkness as it sang around her. "I want you to touch me. Please, please touch me!" she keened, as the very thought of it pushed her over the edge. Her body convulsed, stealing her breath with an explosion of pleasure. And then...silence.

Terrifying, dead silence.

"Angel?" she asked, her voice shaking as she pulled her sheet around her exposed body.

"Do not ask that," the Angel's voice came, as stern and furious as he had ever sounded. "You must *never* ask that."

Christine felt like she'd been thrown into a freezing ocean in a storm. "I...I'm so sorry. I didn't know."

"You're going to be late," he admonished, his tone unchanging. And then like the air from her lungs, he was gone.

Christine dressed quickly, trying to keep calm. What had she been *thinking*? She hadn't been thinking was the entire problem. She'd crossed a line and incurred the wrath of the one being she cared for the most in the world. She was an idiot and found herself burning with regret and shame.

Her newest dress was mostly white, with black trim at the hem, neck, and cuffs. Adèle had helped her buy it and it made her feel like a real artist rather than a poor girl pretending to be a diva. But even that armor didn't settle her. She tried, as usual, to wrangle her hair into something approximating the fashionable chignon of a proper lady, but a few strands flew free as always. Julianne and Adèle had promised to help her look the part for the gala tonight and she had no idea what that would mean. Christine could tell by Adèle's amused look when entered the stage for rehearsal that she didn't quite look the part today either.

"And where have you been, my little dove?" Adèle purred, looking Christine over.

"I was here, like always," Christine grumbled back. There was nothing she could do to convince Adèle she didn't have a lover, especially given that in a strange, unbelievable way, she did. "I was...practicing."

"Oh yes, you look very *practiced* this morning," Adèle laughed. "I had an excellent practice myself with Antoine last night anyway, I didn't mind your absence."

Christine was glad of it too. She was never offended by the sounds she would hear through the thin walls when Adèle had company, but rather it made her long for things herself. Things she couldn't have, as she had learned this morning upon asking. Another wave of guilt washed over her as she remembered.

"Is she here?" Christine asked, changing the subject. She and Adèle had been lucky in avoiding Carlotta in any rehearsal so far. All they had to do was make it through a final practice with the full orchestra this morning and the performance tonight.

"No, late as usual. We'll be on after the ballet, so there's time."

She followed Adèle into the auditorium to take a seat, walking on a ramp over the orchestra pit that was set up for rehearsals. Usually, it was more difficult to cross the line between the observed and observers.

The seats of the auditorium were comfortable enough, but Christine remained distracted as Claude Bosarge conducted the orchestra through the ballet's rehearsal of scenes from Delibes *Coppelia*. The theater was full of movement, from workers adjusting and cleaning the massive chandelier, to singers and artists meandering through the aisles and boxes, waiting for their turn on the great stage. Charles LaRoche, master of the dance, watched his troupe like a general commanding an army.

Christine's eyes drifted to the chandelier itself, thinking back to less than a week before when she'd found her way above it to the gaping space beneath Garnier's great copper dome. There were windows there, and the vast space had glowed with bright winter sun. She'd sung, her voice echoing in the emptiness and her angel's voice had answered, bright as the light that had surrounded her. What if she had done something to lose that voice?

"Adèle," Christine whispered to her companion. "I'm not saying I do have...anyone. But if I did and if I had, say, upset them saying something stupid." Christine bit her lip. She sounded just as foolish now but there was nothing for it. "How would I make it up to them?"

"That's easy, give him something he wants or likes," Adèle replied with a shrug. "If a man is ever stupid enough to get cross with me, I give him my best performance on the silent flute and he's mine again immediately."

Christine blinked, trying to parse what Adèle could mean. "Oh! Dear God, I didn't mean like that!"

"It's the principle, you silly girl," Adèle said, grinning at Christine's mortification. "And we will need to have a talk about that one day too. Just remind him why he cares for you."

"Remind him," Christine muttered to herself.

"It's us," Adèle said, bringing Christine back to the bustling real world. She swallowed down her worry about the morning, and her nervousness. She had sung for Adèle and Gabriel many times, and they had assured her that the duet would be a welcome addition to the gala, but she had never sung alone with the orchestra. Indeed, she had never sung solo at all on the stage with other people present...

As she and Adèle took their places, she breathed deep and remembered. She remembered everything he had taught her. How to breathe and why. How to turn all that was in her heart into glorious song for him. She looked towards box five and felt that familiar tingle. He was there, despite her failure this morning, he was there watching and waiting. And she would do as Adèle suggested and give him the only gift that mattered: her soul through her song.

The orchestra started, simple, steady. Then as Susanna to Adèle's Countess, she began in Italian, "*On the wind...*"

"*With a sweet little breeze,*" Adèle answered.

"*A little breeze,*" Christine echoed in return as the Contessa continued to dictate the letter that would bring her indiscrete husband to the garden that night. The words were so simple. It was the melody, lilting and longing, which carried the true entreaty of love.

"*A little breeze will sigh this evening, under the pines of grove....*" they went on. "*And the rest he will understand, certainly, he will understand.*"

Christine sang and let the world fall away; everything but the music. She sang out her adoration, her love and devotion, and her hope. She sang to him, her voice blending with Adèle's in a gentle dance. The chaos of the theater stilled around them, as dancers and workers paused in their stretches and repairs, taking a moment to let Mozart's gentle melody of love entrance them as well. They all floated on the song, free, for the barest moment of perfect harmony and grace.

The orchestra finished, gentle as a bird landing on a reed. And then, to Christine's shock, applause.

She hadn't been dreaming. Somewhere along the way every eye and ear in the auditorium had turned to her and now people she didn't even know were clapping and smiling brightly. Even Bosarge, with his keen blue eyes and perfectly trimmed white hair and beard, was beaming.

"Where have you been hiding?" the conductor asked Christine, eyes bright.

"I did not know we would be offering our patrons antiques, Maestro Bosarge," a shrill, horribly familiar voice asked from the wings before Christine could reply.

"Oh fuck," Adèle hissed as Christine turned to see Carlotta, in all her bony, blonde glory, striding towards center stage. Her little weasel LeDoux scurried after her, and behind them, the managers themselves. Christine gulped. She had never so much as spoken to Debienne or Poligny and now they were looking at her with a combination of interest and annoyance.

"Signora, I did not think you would be here so soon," Bosarge said, utterly unbothered by the diva's clear ire. "Señor Fontana has not yet arrived to rehearse the prison scene."

"I saw our dear managers on the way to observe and thought I would join them. Thank heavens I did, or we would be stuck with this dull trifle on the program," Carlotta declared, her accent as ridiculous as always, surveying Christine with withering disgust.

"What are you talking about? It's too late to change the program," Adèle protested before Christine's heart could fall deeper into her feet. "This was approved weeks ago. Monsieur Debienne agreed to it personally." In that moment Adèle reminded Christine of some sort of fierce creature, a lioness maybe, defending her young.

"How did you manage that?" Carlotta sneered. "A private performance for Gabriel as usual? Why waste such capital on...this?" Christine clenched her fists as Carlotta glared at her again. "Dear God, don't I know you from the costumers? Is that how desperate these directors are?"

"You can't just come in here and bully people," Christine said at last, voice quavering only slightly. "You aren't in charge." It was the wrong thing to say, she knew it immediately.

"Aren't I? Herbert!" Carlotta shrieked so loud that Debienne jumped before he dashed to her side. The man looked absolutely exhausted with all of it. "Madame Valerius' duet with this...creature is out of the gala. And keep whatever dreck she's dragged over from the Opera Comique at the top of the program as well so it's out of the way early."

"Of course, Signora, an excellent suggestion," Debienne agreed with a sigh.

"You utter bitch," Adèle said flatly.

"Oh, don't act like this matters. It's a glorified dinner party for New Year, no one actually *cares* what's being sung," Carlotta shot back. "And you," she said to Christine with a fresh sneer, "you should thank me for keeping you safe. Imagine what the patrons would think of such a ripe little worm dangling on a hook before them. You'd be chewed up and spit out before the midnight toasts."

Christine had never in her life wanted to slap someone as much as she did right now. Her hands were clenched so hard her nails dug into her palms and she was worried they might start bleeding. At least she hadn't been fired yet.

She turned and walked off stage without waiting for Adèle, and Carlotta's laugh echoed behind her. God, she'd been such a fool to think it would be this easy to start a career with that harpy ruling the Opera. She had thought having the Ghost himself as her protector would matter, but maybe she had lost that too. Maybe that was why this was happening. He'd forsaken her because of what she had asked.

"No, please," she whispered aloud to the empty air of her dressing room the moment she was inside. She fell to her knees and shut her eyes, trying to hold back the hot tears that filled them. "Please, please don't be gone. I'm so sorry...I'm..."

"Christine, I'm here." His voice was like the sun after a storm, warm and loving and miraculous. Christine let out a sob of relief. "You could never lose me."

"I was so scared after..."

"Shhh," he whispered. "I'm not angry. How could I be after you sang for me like that?"

Christine smiled at the mirror, pushing down the desperate wish she could see him rather than her own reflection. "I thought I would be singing for you again tonight. I'm sorry."

"No, my darling girl, do not be sorry. You *will* sing tonight, and all of Paris will hear you. I promise." There was something dangerous in his voice, a darkness that reminded her of every terrifying story about the Ghost that she tried to ignore.

"What's going to happen?" she asked, breathless.

"Carlotta Zambelli and her useless toadies are finally going to learn how foolish it is to defy the Phantom."

E rik knew, logically, that simply killing Carlotta would not improve anyone's situation. It would send the Opera into chaos, bring the Daroga banging at his door with gendarmes in tow, and in the end, it would do nothing to actually help Christine. But how he wanted to watch the life drain from that hateful woman's face with his hands around her neck for the way she'd made Christine cry. Alas, it was not to be. For now.

Before he dealt with her though, he had other business that he had neglected for far too long. He had a choice of who to enquire upon first. Debienne was Carlotta's creature through and through, but he was also barely doing his job at the moment. Poligny was far more superstitious and easier to manipulate. Yes, Poligny would have to do.

It was surprisingly hard to find the man. He'd taken to avoiding the managers' office lately, just as both men had taken to ignoring Erik's correspondence. Instead, he'd secreted himself in one of the empty dance studios to drink. It was a lovely room, usually, with its high ceiling and round windows. The painter in residence had captured them so well in his most recent exhibition, but the great scandal had been thanks to his statute of little Marie. Poligny, slouched in a chair too small for him, emptying a bottle of rusty liquor down his throat, was a marked contrast to any such art.

"You look tired, Guillaume," Erik said without ceremony from the door. He made no attempt to conceal himself now. He wanted this fool to truly see him.

"You," Poligny whispered, dropping his bottle so that it smashed on the smooth wood floor. "What do you want now?"

"Nothing. I want *nothing* more from you or your partner, ever again," Erik replied, damnation in his voice.

"What?"

"You're done here, both of you," Erik said, advancing into the room. Poligny struggled to stand, the chair falling behind him as he backed away from the approaching wraith.

"What are you going to do to us?!" Poligny asked, sweat coating his balding head.

"I will do nothing, if you follow this last command," Erik replied. Poligny startled as his back hit the wall, but Erik didn't stop, slowly coming closer. "And that command is this: retire. Announce tonight at the gala that you and Debienne are leaving effective immediately." It was a risk, he knew it, but the only chance he could see to truly change this theater was with a fresh start. "Retire with your dignity and your good health," he hissed and Poligny nodded, screwing his eyes closed as Erik leaned closer.

He could have made his point with more pain, but he didn't. Instead, he took the moment to vanish, or more accurately, retreat from the room without a sound. Back into the halls and then to the cellars. He needed one specific thing from home before he paid his next visit. He had many options among his stores for Carlotta, but he had to be thoughtful. It had to be something natural, just to be safe...

Erik smiled to himself, coming to the idea just as he entered the house. There was no garden here, or anywhere close to the Opera. But he did keep his store of herbs and roots fresh and there was one plant that would be the perfect flower for Carlotta tonight: The Narcissus, of course.

Christine had stayed in her dressing room most of the day, even after the Angel had gone. It was safe here, far from the chaos ahead of the gala. It wasn't the same as a regular performance. No costumes, fewer sets. In truth, it was as Carlotta had so cruelly said: a musical prelude to a larger party for the patrons in the *Grand Foyer*. They would toast in a new year to laughter and music. Or so she assumed. She wasn't sure if she was welcome at the party or if she would want to go if she was. Despite her worries, Christine began her warmups without her angel there.

"Delivery." Julianne's voice at her door startled her from her scales.

"What on earth?" Christine muttered, unlocking the door, and finding that not only was Julianne there but Adèle as well. And Julianne's arms were overflowing with violet satin. "What is that?!"

"Your dress for tonight," Julianne replied with a sparkling grin. "Surprise. Your friend here bought it, and I altered it since I have your measurements."

"I was just going to wear this," Christine protested, and both her friends gave her withering looks. "And I'm not supposed to sing aside from the chorus parts in the prison scene anyway."

"I've decided I might be sick and need my understudy," Adèle declared. "And you need an actual evening dress no matter what." Adèle herself was already dressed in a rust-red gown trimmed with golden ruffles. It hugged her waist, and the low neckline exposed her ample, sensuous curves perfectly. She was a goddess.

"Adèle, you don't need to do that, and you didn't need to do this," Christine muttered. The dress was beautiful from what she could tell, the color of a crocus in spring.

"It's too late now," Adèle said. "To send the dress back that is. Come on."

The two hustled Christine behind her dressing screen and before she knew it, she was cinched into the loveliest thing she'd ever worn. It barely had sleeves, as was the popular style, only lace and frills that barely covered her shoulders. The skirts were full, with cascading folds gathered in the back over the bustle. Adèle produced long white gloves out of nowhere and Julianne added a black silk ribbon around Christine's throat to complete the ensemble. Christine had developed some skill with her makeup in the month she'd been on stage, but Adèle still darkened her lips and eyes even more.

She sensed him watching when she finally looked at the mirror. Seeing herself as he might see her made her catch her breath. She knew it was vain to think herself beautiful, but she truly looked like she belonged in a fine salon or on the grandest stage.

"You'll charm all of them," Adèle declared, and Christine spun to her in confusion.

"All of whom?" Christine balked.

"She doesn't want to be a patron's pet," Julianne scowled, and Christine was glad of it.

"Oh, not just them, there are artists coming tonight too!" Adèle cried. "Cravalho from the *Comique* will be here. As long as Carlotta's here you'll be stuck in the background, but he could put you in something exciting. They're doing works there that are so modern! Bizet and Delibes! Things that won't make it on this stodgy stage for a decade!"

"Oh, Adèle," Christine sighed. "I don't want to sing anywhere but here." Indeed, Christine didn't want to even think of joining another company or ever leaving this place. The Opera was her home in every sense.

"Well, I approve of that," Julianne said, gruff. "She belongs here. Where else would she have a ghost as her greatest admirer?"

Christine blushed at that, avoiding Adèle's look of suspicion and confusion. "We should get to our places," she muttered, casting one last glance to the mirror as she pushed her friends out the door.

"You're ready, my Christine, just know that you are prepared for what is to come," his voice whispered softly in her ear. She had to believe that was true, and yet part of her refused to even think that what he promised would happen tonight. It was impossible.

The choristers were chattering louder than the audience when Adèle and Christine joined them. (Julianne, to Christine's surprise, lingered in the wings to watch as well, just as Christine had done months before).

"What's everyone so agitated about?" Adèle demanded of Robert Rameau, who looked as dapper and devilish as usual in his tails and white tie.

"Oh nothing, just that her highness the diva has not seen fit to arrive at the theater yet," Rameau replied with a dark laugh.

"What!?" Adèle demanded, but there was no time for answers. The orchestra had already begun, starting the night with Saint-Saëns' delightful *Danse Macabre*. The music reminded Christine of the ghost stories about her angel, and she wondered again which of them were true. If he had hands to strangle a stagehand, why couldn't he have hands to touch her?

Before she could worry more, the company was on stage, to perform the chorus from *Rigoletto*. It was meant to whet the audience's appetite for the new production, as was Fontana's performance of the duke's great aria on the fickleness of women.

Then it was Adèle's turn, with an aria from *Le Prophète*. All the while, the whispers backstage grew more frantic. Christine watched messengers rushing back and forth to Gabriel and Mercier, whose faces were pale as they came back and forth from the dressing rooms. Curious, Christine inched closer to the pair.

"What are we supposed to do?" Gabriel was demanding. "Do Debienne and Poligny not even care?"

"I told him and Poligny said to do whatever we liked," Mercier cried. "Then he just walked away. The man was drunk! And talking like a sleepwalker!"

"Where is she!" Christine jumped as Carlos Fontana accosted the directors, whispering furiously.

"Too sick to leave her flat! Or even get a yard away from a chamber pot!" Gabriel hissed back. On stage, Adèle had completed her aria, and the sets were changing for the ballet. In Christine's gut, suspicion, excitement, nervousness, and faith were all fighting like birds in a cage.

"What do we do? She's half the program!" Mercier moaned, running his hand through his greying hair, and sending it into chaos.

"What's going on?" Adèle asked, joining the conclave. Christine gave up her pretense of not listening and joined as well, standing behind her. "Is Carlotta still not here?"

"No, she's ill," Gabriel groaned, just as another messenger appeared with a note that he handed to Gabriel. He read it and immediately looked to Christine, his face unreadable.

"Daaé and Valerius will do the duet, that will buy us time," Gabriel declared.

"What?" Christine had been prepared for this, but it was still wondrous to actually hear it come true.

"That's all fine and good, but the audience is expecting Juliette's Waltz after that!" Mercier growled. Gabriel's eyes remained locked on Christine, the note still in his hand.

"Tell Bosarge to play it, Daaé will sing it," Gabriel said, and the explosion of questions had to be loud enough for the audience to hear. Christine said nothing though. This was just as the Angel had foreseen it. No, not foreseen. Promised. She hoped she would not disappoint him.

Erik had to keep reminding himself to breathe. This was the moment he'd hoped and planned for. His glorious creation would take the stage tonight and with it, her place as a star – if things went right. There was still a chance of course that Gabriel would ignore him, or that Bosarge would use his veto and refuse to conduct numbers added so suddenly, but Erik couldn't think about that.

The crowd murmured when Gabriel emerged in front of the curtain as the ballet was cleared behind it. Hidden in the shadows of box five, Erik grinned. It was happening.

"Mesdames and Messieurs, a surprise addition to the program," Gabriel began, his voice only shaking slightly. "We are happy to introduce to you a new talent. Singing the Letter duet from *The Marriage of Figaro* with our esteemed Adèle Valerius: Christine Daaé."

Erik watched the audience in their boxes. Some ladies fiddled with their fans, while a few husbands checked their pocket watches. Only a smattering of spectators were paying attention, most notably a young man in one of the premiere boxes right next to the stage, across the auditorium from box five; he was nearly leaning out of it in intense interest.

Erik's attention left the boy the moment Christine took the stage with Valerius. The music began and just as it had during rehearsal, magic happened. It started slowly, like Mozart's steady build of melody on melody through the duet. First, the audience grew quiet, then still...then enraptured.

"*Certainly, he will understand,*" the women sang. But only Erik truly understood. Only he knew that the exquisite invitation in Christine's voice was for him alone. His heart ached, recalling the morning. He should have expected that she would ask for more from him; finally demand a gift that her angel could not give.

"*And the rest he will understand*," Christine's voice rose like a prayer and Erik let himself imagine it, for just a moment. Touching her. The feel of her skin, warm and soft. Surely the second she felt the touch of his hands, rough and cold as the grave, she would understand that it was not an angel that loved her, but a corpse. And what if she wanted to put her hands on *him*? The terror of such a thing stopped his heart so completely that only the audience's ovation brought him back to reality.

He shook off the thought. The audience was entranced, yes, but now was the real test. It was Valerius who stepped to the footlights and gestured for quiet. She smiled, broad and proud.

"Most cherished patrons, I am sure you came here tonight expecting to enjoy the special gifts of our beloved La Carlotta, however, to all of our dismay, the great lady has fallen ill. But in her place, our newest rising talent, Mademoiselle Daaé shall present Juliette's Waltz for you."

A new murmur went up, and once again, Erik held his breath. He wondered what this crowd thought of his pupil. Christine looked apprehensive, as was natural. She was radiant in her lavender dress, like royalty, but also demure. She looked up, first to heaven, and then directly to box five as Gounod's sparkling orchestration began.

"Sing for me, my angel," Erik whispered and somehow, he knew she felt him with her.

She entered, first with a trill, then a run, unaccompanied, her voice clear and perfect as it swooped through the difficult notes and confirmed what the duet had only hinted at: that this was a voice like no other.

"*I want to live in this dream that intoxicates me*," Christine sang as the waltz truly began. She smiled as she sang, losing herself to the music as Juliette did. "*Sweet flame, I will guard you in my soul like a treasure,*" the aria went on. It was brilliantly written, bouncing and dancing like the young Capulet, full of life and potential, but also doomed.

"It does not last, alas, more than a day," Christine sang on, the threat of tragedy edging onto the music like the first frost. *"The heart gives way to love, and happiness flees without return."*

Love was doom. Shakespeare knew it. Gounod knew it. Erik knew it as well. This moment was perfection, but it would not last. The audience watched in rapt attention as she sang, and they thought it was for them. Christine was no longer just his alone, his secret treasure. The audience would love her now too and what if that love would doom them as well?

"I want to live in this dream." Christine returned to the first melody, more impassioned now having considered the fate she could not avoid. *"Let me smell the rose before it is gone,"* Juliette sighed. Erik's pulse quickened. He was with the entire audience on the edge of their seats as Christine launched into the climax.

"Sweet flame, stay in my heart, like a beautiful treasure, for as long as can be." And then, the run. Christine's voice sparkled, pure and dark at the same time, like moonlight on a mountain stream, sweeping away any remaining doubt that she was an artist of the highest caliber. A voice like the Palais Garnier had not heard since it opened its gaudy doors. She flew at last to the high C, the note shining out like a true angel come to earth.

The crowd was on their feet before the orchestra had even finished, and Erik wanted to join. He wanted to stand and clap until he couldn't feel his palms, throw roses at her feet, and bow to her from the edge of his box, as so many men were doing right now...but it was too great a risk. And he did not want to distract from her triumph with rumors of a ghost joining in the ovation.

Christine was radiant, her smile beaming as she bowed and placed a modest hand over her heart. Rameau and Fontana rushed onto the stage, bowing to her, and pressing kisses to Christine's gloved hands. How Erik hated them for those few seconds, envy at such a simple gesture taking his breath away again.

They led Christine off stage as the orchestra moved onto more Gounod, now his playful *Funeral March for a Marionette*. Erik did not care, nor did the audience it seemed, as they whispered about the new diva who they all thought they had just discovered. They were all in love with her, he could feel it, see it in their faces.

Erik had dreamed of this moment for so long. In his fantasies, he had imagined himself drunk on the power of it, thrilled to know that all of Paris bowed to his creation. And somewhere in the back of his mind, that thrill was there. Yes, they loved a part of him, hidden in plain sight on the stage. And he should have felt that love as a triumph. That had been the plan. But he didn't. They wanted her and thus they might want to take her as their own. And that terrified the Phantom.

10. Bound

This was a dream. That's all Christine could think as people surrounded her backstage. And just like Juliette, she wanted to stay in it forever. She could feel her angel's love all around her, and even something more than that. Something like pride from far beyond that made tears sting at her eyes. Singers who had never given her even a passing glance were clamoring for her attention, Carlos Fontana himself was by her side, his arm locked with hers as he placed himself between her and the onslaught. Rameau was on the other side of her, and it took Christine a moment too long to realize he was asking her a question.

"What?" she asked back, trying to anchor herself back in reality.

"We're supposed to sing the prison trio next, my dear girl, do you know it?" Rameau (apparently) repeated. At some point Gabriel had arrived as well, and his look was expectant.

"I do, yes," Christine replied, perhaps too shakily for Fontana's comfort.

"If you botch this, that crowd out there will turn on you as fast as they fell for you," Fontana said. "Don't do this if you're going to make us all look like fools."

Her fear and doubt turned instantly to defiant steel through her spine, and Christine looked Fontana dead in the eyes. "I promise I know the piece, and I hope you'll give it your best effort as well, unlike the last performance where you were a quarter tone flat on the finale."

Rameau burst into laughter as Fontana's face went from offended to resigned in a few beats. "I like you," Rameau declared.

"Christine!" She turned to see Julianne trying to get to her through the crowd. She reached for her and found herself pulled into a hug as her friend laughed. "You *can* sing!"

Christine laughed, withdrawing from the others as Julianne held onto her. "Did you think I couldn't?"

"Not like *that*!" Julianne crowed, then her face softened. "I think your father truly did send that angel of music to bless you."

Christine couldn't help the tears that returned to her eyes. She looked away, wishing she could feel her angel now and hating that she couldn't tell her friend how true her words were. "I hope he's proud."

"I know he is," Julianne whispered. Christine didn't know if she meant her father or the Angel. Perhaps both.

"Daaé! Places for the trio!" Gabriel called. Christine gave Julianne's hands one more squeeze. She looked around for Adèle as well and made eye contact long enough for the mezzo to blow her a grinning kiss. Rameau and Fontana led her back to the stage and instantly she felt her angel's gaze upon her again. She didn't want to disappoint any of them.

"Don't think about if you might fail," the memory of her angel's voice just hours before echoed in her mind. *"You've already lost that way. Think about how happy it makes you to sing. Think about the music and the love you put into it. Sing for that. Sing for me and you will astonish them all."*

The start of the scene was abrupt, like being thrown into the ocean. Méphistophélès was trying to win Marguerite's soul on top of Faust's, to have her come with them and escape prison. But she refused, finally seeing the devil and her lover for what they were.

"Come let us save her, we may still have time!" Rameau sang.

Christine stole herself and sang to heaven. *"Dear God, protect me!"* The way the duet swept in out of nowhere had always thrilled her the many times she had listened to this moment from the dark backstage. Even Carlotta couldn't ruin it entirely. But now it was her turn, and she gave herself to it completely.

"Angels pure, angels radiant! Carry my soul up to heaven!" she sang, a beseeching anthem that rose over the chaos of Faust and the devil. She sang and felt as she only ever had in the most sublime moments alone with her own radiant angel. She sang out her soul, the crescendo rising to the sparkling chandelier.

Then suddenly it was over. She shrieked at the blood on her lover's hand and fell into Fontana's arms. Had it been a real staging, a baritone dressed as either the holy spirit or an angel (she was never sure) would have lifted her from the floor and placed her on the complex heavenly machinery to be carried to heaven as the chorus sang of her salvation. In this case, Fontana just held her through it.

"Well, that was a pleasant surprise," Fontana whispered, and Christine cracked open one eye to see him smile. He helped her up as the audience began to applaud, not even waiting for the final chords. The people in front were the first to rise from their seats, then more. The noise of the ovation swept over Christine like a wave as she gave a shaky curtsey. She thought she was imagining it at first, but no, she could hear the word so many of them were repeating: "encore."

"They want more," Rameau said from beside her.

"Am I allowed?" Christine had no idea why she thought Rameau had any authority, but the man still grinned. He rushed from her side to consult with Bosarge, then back to her.

"It seems the orchestra is prepared for the Jewel Song if you are, my dear lady," Rameau said. Fontana gave Christine an encouraging nod as the applause continued.

"Alright," she said. There would never be another moment quite like this, she knew it. So, she had to seize it. It was what she had dreamed of and trained for. She was ready. She gave Bosarge a confident nod and the elder man smiled back, blue eyes bright.

The orchestra came in at the moment Marguerite opened the casket of jewels, gifts from the devil so Faust could win her and steal her honor.

"*Oh God, what beautiful jewels!*" she sang, and the audience fell silent, most of them returning to their seats. However, a few remained standing and to Christine's shock, one man in the front row tossed her the bracelet off his wife's wrist as she sang. "*If only I dared to adorn myself for a moment!*" she sang, her heart racing, laughing as she put on the pearl bracelet. Another man threw her another bracelet. Another, a necklace. Heavens, she hoped no one intended to throw earrings at her.

There was no mirror at the bottom of the casket to admire herself with, but she remembered how she looked earlier. Adorned and decorated, a true lady to the eyes of all. "*Why not be coquettish?*" Bosarge led the orchestra into the dancing, laughing melody of the aria proper and Christine let it carry her as well.

"*Ah! I laugh to see myself so beautiful in this mirror,*" she sang and indeed her whole soul was laughing. This was madness. Less than three months hence she had stood on this stage in rags and sung to heaven in hope. And now here she was, sparkling like a jewel herself, with the nobles of Paris throwing treasure at her feet. "*Is it you, Marguerite?*"

Was she still herself now? Did it matter? The Angel of Music loved her. He had loved the girl in rags and come to her. Now the lady in satin sang for him on his stage. "*No, it is not you anymore, it is not your face. It is the daughter of a king, whom all salute as she passes by.*"

She looked out into the audience, first to the ghost's box, imagining she could see his shadow, and then to the rapt faces across the loge and to the premiere boxes. And out of nowhere, like a dream, she swore she saw a familiar face. Her own noble suitor from so long ago. It had to be a dream...

"Oh, if he were here, he would see me and find me beautiful, like a true lady," she sang, her heart straying for a moment to the memory of Raoul. And for that second, her voice faltered. No. She could not dream of that. If she did, just like Marguerite, she would lose her soul and all she cherished.

"Ah, I laugh to see myself," she sang again, returning to the main refrain, turning her heart entirely to her protector and thinking wickedly to how he saw her with no adornments, with nothing. And how he commanded her, how he adored her with his voice and music. She wanted to be his entirely. Forever.

"Marguerite, it is no longer you, it is no longer your face," she sang, her ribs pushing against her corset as she flew into the final phrases, her heart soaring with the notes. *"No! It is the daughter of a king! Whom all salute as she passes by!"* The high C rang out to the chandelier, and again the audience was on their feet before she even finished.

Christine laughed, throwing her borrowed jewels back into the crowd. They had done it. For this one glorious moment, Paris was hers as her angel watched. She didn't feel like a princess. She felt like a queen.

The standing ovation went on and on. Flowers were thrust into her arms. She curtsied and tried to leave, but Rameau, Fontana, and Adèle all pushed her back on stage. Joining her to bow with and then *to* her. She laughed even as a few tears slipped down her cheeks. It was too much, and yet, the sight – and she knew it was real this time – of a shadow in box five joining the applause made her heart truly soar. She had pleased him.

At last, Christine escaped the stage, but there was no less commotion behind the curtain. Adèle was beside her, leading her away from the dressing rooms.

"Where are we going?" Christine asked, trying to stop but unable. She was like a leaf carried by a river's current as everyone headed the same direction.

"To the party, you silly girl!" Adèle cried. "Every patron will be lining up to kiss your hand!"

"Oh, no, please," Christine protested, her joy turning instantly to terror. "I don't think I'm ready for that."

"We'll be with you." It was Robert Rameau who had said it and Christine had not even noticed he was beside them. "Don't worry, my dear. This is just how it's done."

The transition from the dark world of wood and plaster backstage to the bright marble climes of the public sections of the Opera would always shock Christine, but stepping out of the stage door tonight was like the first blast of dawn when curtains were pulled back. Every light was on, fully illuminating the mosaics and fountains and baroque adornments on every column and arch. Like everything right now, it was beautiful but completely overwhelming.

On either side of her, Adèle and Robert kept talking, pointing people out to Christine in the throng as they climbed the grand staircase to the loge level and made their way to the *Grand Foyer*. Christine had never seen it alight in all its glory, the gaslights and the candles reflecting in the mirrors and gold, illuminating the murals on the ceiling. It was all so ostentatious and fantastic, packed to the gills with men in black opera jackets and women in luxurious dresses. It made Christine nearly swoon. This was too much. Too much finery. Too many people. Too far from him.

People introduced themselves, praised her, kissed her hand, and flattered her. She barely could thank them before someone else accosted her in an endless line. At last, they made to the fireplace near the end of the salon, where a large group was gathered.

"Mademoiselle Daaé!" someone called, and Christine was sure she didn't know the man. "Our new Marguerite!" a cheer went up and people turned to her, raising shallow glasses of champagne in a toast. A glass appeared in her own hand, and she sipped as a reflex. A terrible decision because the bubbles went right to her already-spinning head.

"And to think, I thought you would be the new Siébel," Adèle purred beside her. "I was so excited for my retirement."

"Oh no. You can't leave me now," Christine replied, trying to catch her breath.

"I guess not," Adèle smiled. Christine did need her, if this was to be her life now, she needed all the friends she could manage. Including new ones, she thought, as Robert took the champagne from her.

"Thank you," she said to him.

"I'm only the devil part of the time," Robert replied. "Now, where are our esteemed managers? I heard they were meant to make a speech. Ah, there we are!"

Christine could barely see the men at the center of the room as they clinked their glasses with knives to get the attention of the crowd. From what she could see though, Debienne and Poligny looked horrible.

"God, you'd think someone had died," Robert whispered.

"Maybe we've been blessed and it was Carlotta," Adèle said on the other side of Christine.

"Mesdames and Messieurs," Debienne began tiredly. "Thank you for your patronage this past year and for all the years of our service to this opera."

"It is fitting that it is with such a glorious gala that my esteemed partner and I..." Poligny continued, his voice shaking and slurred. "Announce our retirement."

Christine could hear nothing more over the uproar that followed. Adèle's mouth was slack in shock, but Robert grinned.

"I'm sorry, my dear ladies, I need to find a friend and celebrate the good news." In a heartbeat, Robert was gone.

"Jesus Christ in heaven, this will be a mess," Adèle muttered. "The whole point of having two managers is for continuity. I guess the Ghost finally got to them."

"I guess..." Christine murmured. Had this been her angel's doing as well? The thought made her shiver.

"Are you cold without your red scarf, Christine?"

She spun at the voice behind her, her heart leaping to her throat. It couldn't be. And yet, there was the familiar face she had dreamed she saw in the audience, smiling at her. In the years since she had known him, Raoul de Chagny had become a man; sturdy and tawny as if he's spent months in the sun, with lush golden-brown hair, gentle brows, and broad shoulders. But his eyes were still the same: sky blue and full of joy.

Christine could not help but grin back in delight.

"I nearly drowned rescuing that scarf, I should be quite sad if you lost it," Raoul continued, his handsome face as open and sincere as it had been when they were teenagers. "Here, take this one if you have need."

Christine and the crowd around her gaped as Raoul removed his white silk scarf from around his neck and presented it to Christine with a bow. She took it without thinking, her jaw slack.

"Christine, do you know the young Vicomte?" Adèle asked in clear amazement.

Before she could answer, a new murmur rippled through the crowd. Christine looked up, following the commotion, and feeling her blood freeze as she heard someone whisper: "*The Ghost.*"

She saw him. Standing there as real as anything, his white mask standing out in the sea of black and gold, his eyes full of rage and heartbreak. He stared at Christine only for a second, before vanishing into the crowd as the patrons gasped.

"What on earth was that?" An older man beside Raoul asked. Christine recognized him too: though he had not worn such an elegant moustache when she knew him, Comte Philippe de Chagny still cut a charming figure.

"It doesn't matter," Raoul said, drawing back Christine's attention. Her previous joy she was replaced with sick terror. "Christine has not answered my question."

Christine swallowed, clutching the scarf in her hand, her mind racing. Laughing was the easiest and so she did. It was a cold, cruel laugh she didn't recognize coming from her throat, and the way it caused Raoul's to face fall made it taste all the more bitter on her tongue. But that was the point. "I'm sure I have no idea what you are speaking of, Monsieur," she said formally.

"Christine..." Raoul said as his brother sighed in annoyance beside him.

"I need to go," Christine declared to no one in particular. She peripherally noticed Adèle's shock and the curious looks of the crowd as she turned and walked out of the salon. She rushed as fast as she could away from the party, feeling her angel's rage following her like a cloud. She had to get back to him. She could not let this night end in such ruin. She couldn't lose him now.

Erik beat her to the dressing room. He knew it was where she was going but it was empty when he arrived and for that, he was grateful. His head was spinning, and his heart was ready to break.

How had this happened? Less than an hour ago he had been on his feet, clapping for her. He had never applauded before. It was unseemly and he never had been moved enough to break character to do it. But oh, how he had clapped for his angel tonight. His hands had stung.

And then they had taken her. All of them had swept her away to their bourgeois bacchanal and he hadn't been able to follow fast enough. There were so many dark halls and trap doors backstage, but such secret roads were in much rarer supply in the foyers and salons. And so, he'd done something mad and simply walked out into the crowd. It would cause a stir; he knew that, and he meant for it. What better assurance that Debienne and Poligny were gone because of his displeasure than for the Ghost to arrive for their retirement speech? But in truth he had been there for Christine. Only Christine. Then he'd found her, in some cruel joke of fate, just as *that boy* had accosted her. And she had smiled, that beautiful pure smile he loved more than light.

He looked through the mirror as the dressing room door flew open. Christine slammed it and locked it behind her as she fell to her knees before the mirror, her face awash in fear and regret.

"Who was he?" Erik demanded, heart breaking again. "*Who* was that boy? He knew you and you knew him. Don't lie to me."

"His name is Raoul," Christine whispered, shutting her eyes in shame. "He..."

"Was that him?" Erik wanted to hear it from her. He looked at the silk scarf still clutched in Christine's hands and a new wave of hate overcame him. "The boy who saved your scarf. The one you loved."

"Yes..." Christine breathed, then looked up to the mirror again. "But I didn't say anything to him! I laughed at him, and I left. He means *nothing* to me." She dropped the scarf and stood, leaning against the mirror with her forehead against the glass. She was crying.

"I have made it very clear: if you wish to serve me, there can be *no distractions*," he admonished, hating her tears, and hating himself for his part in causing them. "You cannot be part of that world."

"I don't want to be," she pled. "I love *you*."

How many times in one day could this girl shatter his heart? He placed his palm against the glass, wanting nothing more than to hold her and tell her how much he loved her in return. "Oh Christine, I know you do."

"All I want is you," she whispered to the glass and looked up, her expression darkening as she stepped back, and though Erik knew she only saw her reflection, it was as if she was looking right at him. Without taking her gaze away from the mirror, she removed her long gloves, then the ribbon at her throat. Then the pins from her hair.

"I want you," she repeated, and Erik caught his breath as her hands rose to the buttons of her pretty satin dress and began to loosen it from her body. Her voice was deep with desire and devotion. If he did not know better, he would have called this a seduction. "I want your music. Your blessing. To serve *you*."

With that, the dress fell to her feet. But she continued, undoing her corset, and casting it away as well. Erik was breathless again as she doffed her final underthings, removing her chemise, pantalettes, stockings, and shoes so that she stood entirely exposed before the mirror. Before her angel.

"I'm yours, I swear," she entreated, her voice breathless and shaking. Her nipples were tight and erect in the cool air, gooseflesh rising all over her body. Would her skin be cold to the touch? Or would she be warm and alive? "Only yours," she whispered and waited.

She stood, bare and expectant, like a virgin sacrifice before an ancient god. She trusted him and wanted him. She had begged him this morning to touch her, and tonight she had sung for him like an angel herself. She deserved an answer to her prayer.

In the dark behind the mirror, Erik surrendered. He tore off his gloves, hat, and cape. They would only get in the way.

"Turn down the light," he commanded, soft and unquestionable. She obeyed instantly, springing to the gas key by the door. In the second the light dimmed to almost nothing, he opened the mirror and stepped through without a sound, coming just inches behind her, and at last...he touched her.

She gasped at the shock of the cold hand at her throat, perhaps in fear. Erik had touched others like this, in his long years alone, and it had meant violence and death to have his hand at someone's neck. Her fear was natural.

"Close your eyes," he whispered in her ear as he caressed her, gentle and loving. Her skin was soft and warm, warmer than he'd ever dreamed. He had no way of knowing if she had obeyed him, he couldn't see her eyes. So, he traced his fingers up her neck, feeling her shiver as he found the line of her jaw, her cheek, and then her eyes. They were indeed obediently closed.

Still, bodies in passion often disobeyed their owners, hers might do the same. He could not risk it. One hand barely touching her cheek, he loosed his cravat with the other, then brought it to her face. Christine shuddered as her angel placed the silken blindfold over her eyes. He was safe now. Perhaps.

He let his hands wander over her shoulders, down her arms, barely grazing her skin. He could feel the hairs all standing on end as he did, and her breath was shallow and quick. He found her fingertips and stepped aside, guiding her to turn and follow him.

"Lie down, my darling," he ordered and guided her to the chaise. The light was not entirely out; the dim golden glow and a lifetime in the dark meant Erik could see her just well enough. Lust and love swelled inside him. He would give her this, but he could not risk her touch in return, not on his hands or body, and especially not on his mask.

He knelt beside her, noting how she was breathing hard with her legs parting slightly for him already. He began to sing, and she gave a soft moan. It was a song he had sung to her many times; a primitive ley of love and need, composed just for her. He had sung it to her the first time she had given herself to him and it affected her the same way now.

Erik quietly took the boy's scarf from the floor, dragging it from Christine's hip all the way over her breast and up her arm as he guided it above her head. She moaned again as he did the same to her other arm, the sound going straight to his hard cock. There would be time for him after, he told himself, as he bound her wrists above her with the length of white silk, then anchored that to the chaise with the only other rope he had: his own deadly lasso.

"Please," Christine whispered as she writhed on the chaise, delicately testing her bonds. "Please touch me again." She was the most beautiful, debauched thing Erik had ever seen. How could he refuse her?

His hands slid from her bound wrists back down her body and he finally let himself explore her fully without fear. She was wondrous, every inch of her responding to his gentle touch as he found her. From the softness of her belly to the muscles of her back when she arched towards him, from the curve of her ass to the hot length of her thigh. She groaned and twisted beneath him when he at last reached her breasts, savoring their round heft as they filled his hands.

"Shh, my love, we can't let anyone hear," he whispered, pausing his song, and she nodded fervently. He began again, keeping his melody close to her ear as he tested and savored her. He swept one hand between her breasts, feeling her pounding heart. His own pulse matched hers in fervency as he moved lower, ever so carefully. Her hips rose and she spread her legs, her body entreating him as her breath came in quick, quivering sighs.

His long fingers combed through the silken hair of her ruff, and at long last, he found her. She bit her lips to stem a cry as her angel began to explore her most intimate anatomy. She was hot, wet, and as yielding as velvet beneath his fingertips. Erik had never experienced anything like it, and he was dizzy with wonder as he pressed and pet her in turn, each touch provoking a new buck of her hips or strangled whimper of pleasure.

"My angel," she sighed, her voice broken as her hips found a rhythm against his hand. He had studied her in moments like these from afar, watching and noting where she touched herself and what made her lose all control and restraint. He tested the swollen mound above her opening, and she bit back something like a scream. Again and again, he paid care to that spot, his fingers slipping between her wet folds and then, almost without thinking, sliding home inside her.

She was everything, Erik thought, his mind suddenly distant from his body as he watched her fall apart under his careful ministrations. He could feel her whole body respond as he thrust two long fingers inside her while his thumb attended to the spot above. His song rose to a crescendo as he touched her more deeply than anyone ever had. Or ever would if he had any say in it. She was his. His alone. His entirely and it was at his will and command that her pleasure would sing.

Her whole body grew stiff for a prolonged moment as his voice brought her to the precipice. And then with a gasp like a song, she came around his fingers, undone and shaking. He tamped down his own body's response, forcing himself to feel just this as her cunt tightened and pulsed around him. She strained against the bindings as the little death claimed her, and Erik was glad of the precaution.

He kept singing as he carefully withdrew, watching as her breath slowed and her body relaxed. With a thief's deftness, he untied the scarf, lasso, and cravat and kept them in hand as he retreated behind the mirror and let his melody come to an end.

He kept his eyes on her as the glass slid back between them. She moved languidly, barely visible in the dark. But the memory of her skin and her sex beneath his hand was still fresh. Erik freed his cock, stroking himself feverishly with the hand still wet with Christine's slick. He came in mere seconds, biting his lip so hard he tasted blood. He poured his hot spend into the silk scarf, the act of defiling it so intoxicating it drew another spurt just as Christine opened her eyes.

She smiled broadly then hid her face with her arm, laughing and blushing. "I don't suppose it would be proper to just sleep here like this?"

"Alas, I do think you will need to make an appearance in your flat," Erik replied with a sigh. "I don't want Valerius getting too many ideas."

Christine nodded and rose carefully, affording Erik another view of the perfect body he had just claimed as she turned the gaslight back up. She began to gather her clothes and smiled as she donned her chemise. He hated making her leave, but he hated the thought of anyone assuming she had absconded with some patron even more.

"Return tomorrow at nine o'clock for your lesson. We have much to discuss," he added as she fastened her corset as loosely as possible.

"Oh God, I don't even know if the performance pleased you," Christine said, and Erik laughed warmly.

"You were astonishing, my dear."

She tugged on her dress, bashful again. "It was for you, all of it. I sang only for you," she said tenderly, looking towards the mirror again. "Could you hear that?"

"I could," he told her, his heart filling with adoration. "Such a tribute. I think, Christine, you must love me."

"With all I am," she whispered, drifting closer to the glass yet again, then, to Erik's amusement, she stifled a yawn.

"Are you very tired?" he asked, wishing he could sing her to sleep here.

"I gave you my soul tonight, and now I am spent," she replied with such devotion and tenderness, it pierced his heart. He *had* taken her soul tonight, first on stage and then with his hands. She was his and he loved her for it, and he hated himself for the crimes he continued to commit against her. He was a liar and monster for having taken her this way, but he would be damned if he would give it up.

"Your soul is a beautiful thing, my dear girl, no king or emperor has ever received so fine a gift," he told her, and he felt moisture beneath his mask. He had not wept when she had looked at that boy, but he did now, tears falling in awe of her love and in shame and anger for the fact that she loved a lie. "The angels wept tonight."

Her face was perfect as she pressed a hand to the mirror. "Are you sure I have to go?"

"It's for the best," Erik replied. Indeed, he suddenly needed distance from her. He needed to consider his sins if he could manage sanity for long enough.

"Goodnight then," she murmured. He closed his eyes as she left. He never liked watching her go, but tonight it hurt even more. The silence and emptiness she left behind in the darkened room were suffocating. He knew he should leave too, but he lingered, remembering what it had been like to touch her. Just as she had shone like a comet on that stage tonight, so too had those brief moments of contact blazed then faded. All that was left was the memory, and the longing for more. A longing he would never be able to satisfy...

Erik started at the sound of the door. Had she come back so soon, defiant of his commands just to be close to him? But the person making their way into the dressing room was not Christine.

"Who's there? Show yourself, I know you're here." It was a man's voice and before he even struck his match, Erik knew who it would be. The boy.

The little noble who had stolen Christine's heart in another life had now come to steal it again. Had he been listening at the door? What could he have heard if he had? The thought was both alarming and incredibly amusing to Erik. This handsome fool might already think Christine had a lover; one she had chosen over him tonight. It was quite perfect.

"What on earth?" the boy muttered as the match burned down to his fingers and sputtered.

Yes, what on earth indeed, Erik thought with a laugh as he turned away. Let the boy think that Christine's secret paramour had disappeared into thin air. Let the questions torment him. Erik continued to grin as he made his way lower, deep into the cellars. He made one stop though, at the furnaces. They never stopped burning, these miniature infernos, though the fires were low at this late hour. Still, the boy's scarf burned nicely on the coals.

Christine woke still in bliss. The memory of the night before had echoed into her dreams, from the deafening applause to the ecstasy of her angel's touch. Even the New Year's frost over her window could not chill the warmth in her heart. Or the fire still in her blood. Already she ached for him again, thinking back to the heavenly thrill of that first brush of his ghostly fingers on her body.

She stretched and nestled deeper into her lonely bed. She could almost still feel the tightness of silk around her wrists, or the cold air of her dressing room as he laid her out for his inspection. How wanton she must have looked, bound and bare; it made her blush at just the thought. But the image of herself, and the delicious memory of his ministrations, also stoked the heat inside her.

Her hand found its way to her throbbing cunt, almost unbidden, and she was unsurprised to find herself wet and open. She heard his voice in her head and tried to move her fingers like he had. He'd known exactly how to touch her, drawing ecstasy from her like a virtuoso pulling a melody from an instrument. Her own hand was clumsy in comparison, but even so, just the memory had her soaring to a peak of pleasure in no time. She moved frantically, turning over so that her hand was trapped between the mattress and her body, allowing her hips to grind and squirm. But it wasn't enough. She stifled a moan in her pillow, her body begging for release as the tension in her grew and grew. But the crescendo eluded her.

"Damnit," Christine sighed and relented, falling back to stare at the ceiling. It wasn't the first time she'd tried to pleasure herself here, but it was certainly the most aroused she'd ever been. Even so, she knew in her heart that without his voice to enflame her or his gaze upon her, satisfaction would be impossible. Her passion was his and his alone.

She rose from bed at last and the shock of the cold morning air was almost enough to bring her back to reality. The fact that the water in the pitcher in the washing basin had a layer of ice on the top sobered her entirely.

By the time she emerged from her room she was swearing to herself and blowing on her hands. Adèle did employ a maid, but she came rarely and lived on her own. Thus, it was up to Adèle and Christine to keep the fires stoked in the flat and they were both terrible at it. Christine set to the task of relighting the fashionable stove, covered in white enamel, and within half an hour there was a pleasant blaze going to welcome Adèle home.

"Oh, you beat me back," Adèle purred when she saw Christine. She looked a mess, but in a pleasant way. Like Christine, she hadn't bothered with all the fussy buttons of her dress, and her hair was loose.

"I was home before the New Year, if you care to know," Christine rebuked her playfully. Adèle did not look convinced.

"The only thing I'd forgive you leaving your own party for would be a good fuck," Adèle said, coming to sit by the fire and looking Christine over critically. "And given your talk yesterday about a lover's quarrel *and* the fact you're practically glowing now, I'd say that I do forgive you."

"You're terrible," Christine muttered, blushing.

"No, Antoine is terrible," Adèle sighed, rubbing her neck. "He wasted an hour of my time last night, trying to find his little count for late supper, and when he did, he had the audacity to tell me he was *tired*."

Christine laughed. "Who did you see instead?"

"Oh, Gerard turned out to be in quite the celebratory mood, so I joined him," Adèle replied with a devilish wink.

"Gabriel? I thought you said – what was it? That he 'fucks like metronome?'"

"Oh, he does," Adèle sighed. "But at least he lets me relax. Antoine fancies himself such an athlete. The night before he had me on my knees and kept pulling my hair like he was reigning a horse. Still can't move my neck right."

"Adèle!" Christine laughed. She never grew tired of the older woman's frankness.

"Gerard's always so damn grateful I even spread my legs for him – short men tend to be like that – that he'll dine on some oysters, shall we say, until I've had my fun, then I can just lay there and let him enjoy himself while he pumps away."

"Well, I'm glad your evening was fruitful."

"Not as fruitful as yours. I was there long enough to borrow the morning paper." Adèle produced a copy of *Epoque* from the folds of her discarded coat. "You're a sensation."

What Christine felt was curious, like parts of her body had suddenly turned into something hard and shaking. It wasn't quite the same as the fear when she disappointed her teacher, but it was akin to that panic, and she had no idea why.

"Someone wrote about me?"

"Of course! It was an event for everyone in the upper set, all the reporters were there. Society and music. I'm sure you're the topic all over Paris this morning."

"Oh no..." Why did that make Christine feel ill?

"It's good!" Adèle laughed. "Listen to this: 'While we were treated to a few admirable offerings from Signor Fontana and the always agreeable Opera Orchestra under the baton of Maestro Bosarge, the real triumph of this celebratory night was reserved for the hitherto unknown young artist, Mademoiselle Christine Daaé. Mademoiselle Daaé was delightful in the Letters duet with Madame Valerius (who remains criminally under-used at the Palais Garnier)'"

"Does it really say that about you?"

"Shush, keep listening. 'Daaé stepped in at the last moment for La Carlotta, who had taken incomprehensibly and inexcusably ill, and the unplanned nature of her debut makes the utter triumph of it all the more remarkable. Daaé sparkled with Juliette's Waltz, so much so that we hope that this influences the Opera to finally mount a production of Gounod's other great work. But this was nothing compared to the seraphic triumph and superhuman notes that she gave forth in the final trio of *Faust* and a splendid encore with The Jewel Song."

"*Seraphic*?" Christine wanted to bury herself back in her bed and hide from the thousands of unknown eyes she suddenly felt upon her.

"Oh, it gets better," Adèle smiled as she continued to read. "'It is without a doubt that we have discovered a new Marguerite the likes of which the Opera has never seen before, of a splendor, and radiance hitherto unsuspected. But we must ask: Why has so great a treasure been kept from us? Why was it only in Carlotta's absence that this new jewel in Paris's crown was unveiled? Nothing is known of this new Swedish Nightingale, but her northern origins and superhuman genius have led many to speculate that she is indeed a hidden progeny of no less than the greatest voice of the north, Madame Lind herself."

Adèle barely finished the sentence before bursting out into hysterical laughter, which Christine joined. "They think I'm *Jenny Lind's* secret daughter?"

"Well, you see there's only so many Swedes who can sing, my dear, you all must be related," Adèle chuckled, wiping her eyes. "Thank heavens we have some time off."

"What?"

"Oh, that's right, you ran off before the news," Adèle said. "We're dark for two weeks, while they find some new damn managers. Good news for you too I think, since Carlotta would have already had the old ones get rid of you at this point. Not that you wouldn't have your pick of venues with reviews like that."

"I told you, I only want—"

"To sing at *the* Opera, I know," Adèle sighed. "At least with new management you'll have a chance. By the way, why did you leave? Never known you to be spooked by the Ghost."

Christine shivered, remembering her angel's despairing look across that room. "I was just tired."

"Oh yes, well, you left that little Vicomte quite heartbroken."

"What?" Christine had barely thought about Raoul since her angel had given her the sublime gift of his touch. Now the memory made something nervous and furtive twist inside her. She had meant to drive him away, but what if it hadn't worked? Or what if it had? She didn't know which possibility worried her more.

"He spent the whole night looking for you," Adèle replied. "I told you. Antoine is his brother's hanger-on. Philippe finally dragged the boy out around midnight. He looked completely heartbroken. And truly, I'm impressed if whatever lover you say you don't have is worth spurning a Chagny. He must be quite a wonder."

Christine swallowed. "He is."

Her angel had given her everything, even that which she had thought was impossible. And yet, why did she feel like she had committed some sort of crime in the night when she thought of Raoul de Chagny's broken heart?

11. Influence

The carriage ride across the Seine to the livelier districts of Paris from the *Faubourg Saint Germain* was always tedious for Raoul, but today it was damn near maddening. The coachman was being overly cautious with the horses, Raoul knew it. Yes, there were slicks of ice in the street, but the geldings could manage it. Raoul was ready to tell the man as much and remind him how to do his job. But Philippe's sigh as Raoul raised his hand to knock on the side of the carriage stopped him.

"The Opera will still be there in ten minutes, I promise you," Philippe said. "You've waited this long, haven't you?"

"*I* did not choose to wait," Raoul snapped back. It had been two weeks and three days since his world had changed its orbit when he'd seen her on that stage.

He had told himself he was dreaming in the weeks prior, when he saw a face in the chorus that looked so familiar. After all, he'd looked for that same face around every corner for six years, every time he heard a soprano voice or a violin at a country fair. But then at the New Year's gala, there she was: Christine Daaé, more radiant than he remembered and singing with skill and passion that even his untrained ear knew was unequaled in all of Paris.

There had been a moment, he swore it, when her eyes had alit on him as she sang, and his heart had leapt at the recognition. It had emboldened him to seek her out afterwards, certain she would remember. And for a second, he was sure she had. Then it had all gone wrong, and he had been denied the opportunity to remedy it since. Philippe's refusal to escort him to the Opera and Sabine's vocal displeasure had been a sore spot at dinner for days until his brother relented last night. Still, the wait, like this damn carriage ride, had been torture.

"Well, you should have," Philippe said. "I don't see why you're so eager for that little strumpet to humiliate you again."

Raoul slouched into the seat and glowered out the window. Christine's laughter still echoed in his head. It snuck up on him in quiet moments; the cruel, alien sound like a slender knife, stabbing him again and again. But it didn't torment him nearly as much as the memory of the other voice he'd heard: the man in her dressing room who had told her to love him, who had been given her very soul. How Raoul hated the fiend.

"I only wish to speak with her," Raoul muttered. "There's surely been a misunderstanding. I know she wouldn't forget me, nor would she avoid me without some reason."

"I do admire your high opinion of yourself, dear brother, but I must remind you of the dead-end that path leads to."

"The same one you're headed towards with that dancer of yours?"

Philippe rolled his eyes. "Sorelli makes good dinner conversation and when dinner is over, she's limber and amenable. But I will never marry her, nor do I pretend to love her. We both know this because that's the way it's done. And if I thought you just wanted to dip your wick with this songbird of yours, I'd say have at it, but I know you and I know you think you can just take up with this peasant like you're seventeen again."

"We don't call them peasants anymore," Raoul shot back.

"Maybe we should," Philippe said grimly as they rambled past the *Place de la Concorde*. "Less than a hundred years ago our kind were taken to the guillotine right here by those entitled nobodies who thought they could rewrite the world. The same mongrels who think they can make some law now and erase our titles and ignore the way of things."

Raoul squirmed. Philippe would never stop calling himself Comte de Chagny, no matter how meaningless the appellation was in the new world of the Third Republic. Raoul on the other hand had savored his last two years at sea where no one cared he was born a vicomte. He had just been Raoul and it had been enough. Just as he had been to Christine, years ago.

"I know she's not the right class but..."

"She's not even the right *species*, dear brother."

Raoul continued to stare out the window as the rolled down the *Rue Royale* and turned right at the grand Madeleine church, which soured his mood even more. Raoul had always disliked the Madeleine. It was wrong to build a Catholic church to look like a pagan temple, but that decision had been made by men four regimes ago.

"You don't know her," Raoul muttered as they rode up the *Boulevard des Capucines*.

"Neither do you, that's my whole point!"

Raoul couldn't argue. He didn't know Christine, not anymore. But he *had* known her, and loved her, and he knew that she simply could not be the kind of girl who spoke ardently to mysterious men alone in her dressing room without reason. (No matter what Philippe insisted about the moral character of artists or what the papers theorized about her.) The girl he had known had been good and pure, and so too had been Christine as Marguerite on that stage. Her soul had to have remained as pristine as before...despite that she claimed to have given it to another.

The carriage came to a stop at the patron's entrance, the one that had initially been planned as a pavilion for Emperor Napoleon III, who had commissioned a new opera house after that anarchist had tried to throw a bomb at him in the old one. Irony of ironies that the man had been deposed before a single note was ever sung from the stage, but men like Raoul and Philippe still benefitted from his grand monument.

The building was honestly too large, in Raoul's estimation. It looked like a train station on the outside, bright and shining, but within it was dark and labyrinthine. It gave him a thrill to finally be there, closer to her and closer to answers, but there was something else about the place that made his skin crawl.

"Please, try to remain composed," Philippe muttered as they turned a corner and found themselves in an absolute madhouse.

They were in a foyer, respectable and not as ornate as the rest of the Opera. At the end stood a pair of carved double doors, before which a bespectacled mouse of a man stood, attempting to speak over the crowd of at least half a dozen well-dressed men trying to be heard.

"Good heaven, this is chaos," Philippe said. "What on earth is going on?"

"Did you think it would be quiet for these fools on their first day?" The brothers turned to a familiar voice and Philippe let out a laugh as he saw Antoine de Martiniac leaning on a column.

"We didn't think *everyone* would be here," Philippe scoffed. "Surely they're not making patrons wait?" Antoine shrugged in reply, louche and useless as always.

"What are *you* doing here?" Raoul asked, narrowing his eyes at the man.

Antoine was tall and slender, with light blonde hair and piercingly cold blue eyes. He was handsome, older than Raoul but younger than Philippe. His smile always had a cruelty behind it that Raoul had grown to detest in the months he'd known the man. Or perhaps he detested that he had returned home to find a scoundrel with a failing estate had insinuated himself into Philippe's life.

"Adèle encouraged me," Antoine replied. (His tone implied something untoward, Raoul was sure of it.) "She said no one's even seen these two and everyone is getting restless. Hasn't your ballerina said as much?"

"She might have," Philippe answered. "Whenever she starts in on Opera gossip, I must admit, I start to drift off."

"Can't the artists come themselves?" Raoul asked, and Antoine gave a scoff of derision that was almost as offensive as Philippe's condescending sigh.

"This place is for the ones who pull the strings, not the marionettes," Antoine replied. "And pulling they all are."

Raoul's attention followed Antoine's gaze back to the crowd. Upon better inspection, Raoul recognized a few of them from visits and dinners over the past few months, and perhaps even before. They all looked alike in their top hats and dark winter coats, clearly all patrons.

"Please! Gentlemen!" The little man in front cried, his voice straining. "Messieurs Richard and Moncharmin will be happy to take your concerns about the Opera by letter if you would be so kind. But they are quite busy today with new business."

"We all have the same letter," a man in front declared, pulling a paper from his coat as the chatter subsided. "And in it, we demand assurances that La Carlotta be restored to the stage!"

"Oh, so that's it," Antoine said under his breath, understanding something Raoul did not.

"The National Academy of Music is no place for a woman like that Daaé, if that's even her real name," another man piped in, and Philippe immediately grabbed Raoul's arm to hold him back from charging.

"I assure you, sirs, that your support and concerns will be made known! Now if you don't mind, we do have other work," the secretary gestured to the exit and the cadre of patrons sighed as one and began to leave.

"Oh, Philippe, I didn't know you were enlisted," a man whose name Raoul could not be bothered to remember said as he passed.

"It seems I am, against my will, on the other side of this war," Philippe replied with a dark look to Raoul. "Alas."

"Oh, well, good luck then. You'll need it if Carlotta isn't placated," the patron replied with a laugh, tipping his hat before going. At last, it was only the brothers, Antoine, and the secretary left in the office lobby.

"As I said, – Oh! Monsieur de Chagny! I didn't realize—" The man began, but the door bursting open behind him cut him off.

"Rémy, where are those ledgers? I asked for them an hour ago," an older man demanded as he stepped from the office. What hair he had left was white, trimmed neatly around his bald head and styled into sideburns. He looked exhausted and annoyed, especially when he saw that he and Rémy were not alone.

"Yes. We're still looking, Monsieur Richard," Rémy replied, in clear panic.

"And did we not make it clear that you were to send away the claque," Richard said with a glare at the men. Rémy looked green.

"Yes, of course, but this is Philippe de Chagny and—"

"*Comte* Philippe de Chagny," Philippe interjected. "And we're not here on behalf of the Spaniard."

"The Swede then, is it?" Richard shot back. "Or is she a gypsy? Or a Jew? I've heard so many things about the illustrious Mademoiselle Daaé in the last weeks I cannot keep it all straight."

"Christine is a good Christian woman and anyone who would imply otherwise is a villain!" Raoul burst out. Philippe heaved a sigh as Antoine covered a snigger.

"And who are you?" Richard asked, looking Raoul over.

"This is my brother, Raoul," Philippe replied. "The *Vicomte* de Chagny."

"Don't worry about me, I'm not half as rich as him," Antoine added with a smirk. "Though, to hell with it, I prefer Daaé as well. Or at least I have a friend that does."

"Don't we all," Richard growled back, his fist tightening around a letter in his hand.

"Raoul and I both wished to visit in order to commend Mademoiselle Daaé's glorious performance at the gala," Philippe went on, smooth as silk despite Richard's frown. "I don't know music, not really, but it was quite a relief to hear a soprano that didn't make me call for more sherry from the concierge. Indeed, Raoul here wished to enquire if you knew where we might send our regards in person."

"Christ in heaven, I'm not a madam," Richard balked, and Raoul's cheeks began to burn once again.

"Monsieur, that is not at all what I meant!" Raoul yelped.

"I do not care," Richard snapped. "I am concerned only with sorting through the financial mess my predecessor left me and determining if he and Poligny were insane, being swindled, or simply the most incompetent fools to ever set foot in a theater! For now, I bid you good day!"

Richard turned and stormed back into the office, slamming the door behind him, leaving Rémy shaking.

"Why, I've never been so disrespected by a manager, anywhere!" Philippe huffed.

"I am so sorry, Monsieur le Comte, they are getting used to things. There's quite a lot that Debienne and Poligny neglected, and they are also dealing with...well, they think it's a joke now but..." Rémy bit his lips, shaking his head. "I have to go." Without another word, the man rushed away.

"Well, that was interesting," Antoine commented. "Shall we go to the club for an early luncheon?"

"I have to find Christine," Raoul protested. "Especially if people are spreading rumors about her or threatening her!"

"And you think a young patron looking for her high and low will make her *less* talked about?" Philippe asked back.

"I *need* to see her," said Raoul.

"You need no such thing," Philippe retorted.

"I can get a letter to her."

Raoul turned to Antoine in shock to find the man, as usual, smirking like a cat who had just stolen some cream. "What?" Raoul asked.

"Adèle sees her every day. I'm surprised you haven't asked me before." Antoine said it innocently enough, but it still felt like an insult to Raoul. Indeed, he hated that he hadn't thought at all about how Antoine's mistress would obviously know Christine.

"Well, there it is, you can write to her over lunch," Philippe declared and began to herd Antoine and Raoul away.

"I'll warn you now, my friend," Antoine said as they walked. "The odds are high that your Christine has already found a patron to protect her. She wouldn't have come from nowhere the way she did without the backing of someone with influence."

Raoul scowled. He knew for a fact that there was someone else trying to claim Christine's affections, and he would not rest until he could confront the man face to face. That was the whole point.

Erik was not used to headaches. The novelty of the faint pounding in his skull did nothing to abate it, but it matched nicely with the tired, hollow feeling left by the restless nights since his new managers had taken residence in the office above him. He'd been listening for over an hour, and he ached to his bones from maintaining his post in the cold, cramped space under the floor. He wasn't used to spending so much time on administration, which made the headache worse. Nor was he used to being confronted so swiftly with the consequences of his own actions. These ailments were, perhaps, related.

"The directors will be here soon, we should get things in order," Armand Moncharmin said cautiously from above. The man sounded as weary as Erik, another reason the Ghost preferred him to Firmin Richard.

"Meet with them somewhere else, you don't need me," Richard snapped. "I don't see what they need in the first place."

"Well, they're understandably nervous with the delay in the premiere of *Rigoletto* because of the closure," Moncharmin stammered. Erik could imagine him, sweat on his brow beneath his brown curls. Perhaps he was cleaning his spectacles for the twentieth time. "And I think they, like everyone apparently, wish to know who will be singing Marguerite on Friday. Among other things."

Erik straightened. This is what he had been waiting for. To his annoyance, Richard scoffed. "If I could actually get these books in order, I'd know," the elder manager replied.

"What does it have to do with the books?" Moncharmin asked.

"You heard the crowd. Most of the patrons who care about who sings are for Zambelli, but that Comte or Vicomte or whatever and his friend are for Daaé." Erik clenched his fist. Which Vicomte did he mean? "If the books were balanced, I'd just tally how much the two sides were worth and decide that way."

"That's terribly mercenary."

"It's good business."

Erik was filled with a wave of hate for Richard and a foolish longing to have Debienne and Poligny back.

"This should be my decision, I'm the artistic director," Moncharmin argued, however weakly. "I favor Daaé as well. And showcasing her is advantageous. All of Paris is talking about her, no matter what they're saying. *That's* good business."

"Get to your meeting," Richard muttered. "And tell Rémy I want to know where those damn letters were posted from. And to send a message to Debienne and Poligny that their joke has worn thin."

"I don't think it's a joke, Firmin," Moncharmin said. In the dark below, Erik sighed. He had been clear and firm in his communications with his new managers, even given them a grace period for the delivery of his salary for the month. Perhaps such explicit support for Christine before he knew what kind of men he was dealing with had been a mistake. But there was no going back.

"I will not be made a fool, Armand, now go do something useful," Richard growled, and Erik bristled on Moncharmin's behalf. At least both of them could be free of the man for a while now.

The world was full of men like Firmin Richard, Erik thought to himself as he made his way out of his hiding place and into the halls of his opera. It would be a challenge, making this man believe in ghosts. Men like him believed in nothing above money and keeping the machinery of business running. No matter that the engines of such machinery were fueled by the blood and sweat of people Richard would never give a second thought to.

Erik considered following Moncharmin, but he didn't want to be late. Though Christine had, unencouragingly, not been summoned for today's rehearsal, that did not mean she wouldn't be singing. Their lesson was scheduled for the practice room, as he needed to provide her with accompaniment and thus required the piano.

But he was not the first to arrive.

Erik had chosen this room so many months before due to its similarity to the manager's office, specifically the trapdoor in the floor that allowed him to enter and exit without being seen. But today the hidden space beneath the boards afforded him a rare gift:

the sound of Christine playing piano above him. He knew it was her, of course, because it was Mozart. The *Sonata Facile*.

It was easy to forget that Christine had been trained in music her whole life. Indeed, Erik wondered if her father had also taught her the violin or another instrument that she had not yet shared. Her skill at the keyboard was not inconsiderable, though it was nothing compared to her voice. In the stifling darkness, nearly knelt beneath her feet, Erik's heart swelled in his own secret worship of the music and the woman who made it.

They had become even closer in these last few weeks, as the Opera had fallen into silence and then chaos. He had pushed her harder than ever in their lessons, as if it would somehow atone for the boundary he had shattered when he touched her. It hadn't. She had risen to his every challenge and in turn, what choice had he been given but to reward her?

He had pampered her, filing her little refuge with books from his library and sweets stolen from the kitchen. But no gift equaled the gilt music box that played the secret song only she knew. It must have been like magic to her when it a appeared by her bed. How could she know that Erik had stayed awake two nights fashioning it, and a perfect copy for himself? The way the melody had instantly inflamed her when she opened the casket had made every sleepless hour worth it. And so had her ecstasy that night and every night she'd remained in his domain.

He hadn't touched her again, at least he could say that. But he had commanded her, telling her where and how to place her hands, enticing her to imagine they were his once again. It never failed to intoxicate him to see her unravel under his control. As his intransigent managers, a closed opera, and the fickle world had continued to frustrate and challenge him, there was no balm like the power her held to make the most sublime woman shatter with pleasure at his word.

But it was not lust he felt now, it was the comfort of her mere presence, like a true angel above him. It filled him with love and sadness. Perhaps they were the same thing. A lifetime ago, it had been the sound of Mozart in the darkness that had saved his miserable young life. It was fitting that the same composer continually brought his angel back to him.

The allegro resolved to its gentle conclusion and Erik waited, wondering if she could sense him. He had no explanation for her ability to know when he was there. As in so many things, perhaps it was she who was truly magical.

"I used to play that for my father. Especially near the end," Christine spoke aloud, her voice soft and sad. "It was comforting, I think. Or I hope."

"I know it was," Erik replied, listening as the floorboards creaked above him when she moved. He waited several agonizing seconds to be sure she was in her correct spot before he emerged, like shade from a grave, hidden by the piano.

It was always like dawn, seeing her for the first time in a day. And sometimes her beauty was so bright it took him a moment to see the details. But not today. She looked as tired as him, and just as worried.

"It doesn't mean anything, you not being called to the rehearsal," he told her.

"Adèle says the managers have better things to do than fire me, and that if they did, it would—"

"It would spell disaster for them in ways they can't imagine," Erik finished for her, his own ire rising at the thought. "I promise you I will protect you, no matter what. But I am sorry you have to live in this limbo."

"I just hate not knowing what will happen either way," Christine replied, fingering the corner of the score on the music stand before her. "I hate how men I've never met have this power over me."

"To live in the world is to be subject to the power of men and money and all the greed and cruelty that goes with it," Erik muttered.

"You know, some duchess invited me to sing at her house for a charity concert," Christine said with a hollow laugh. "Can you imagine it? Me; performing for some party like a trained bird."

"Indeed I cannot," Erik replied, his thoughts growing still darker as he remembered his own past 'performances' for people like that. Christine gave another deep sigh.

"I said no of course. I think she'll take it as an insult. Sometimes I wish I didn't have to be a part of any of it." Christine looked back up, as if she sensed his alarm at the words. "I don't mean the Opera. I just – I know this is my life and it's always been my dream to have this career but—"

"But?"

"But if there was a way, I could simply just make music, without all of this—" she gestured at the walls. "To just sing for you and be with you always...I think I'd be content."

"Oh."

Erik had chosen, many years ago, not to dream. He did, of course, walk in impossible worlds as he slept, like anyone. In the last weeks, sleep had become a torture of its own as each night he'd found himself tormented by the fantasy of touching her again, and the nightmare of her terror when she broke her bonds and saw him for himself. But while he was awake, he refused to indulge in fantasies of what could be.

It had taken him a while to suppress that human impulse to imagine a different life or the future. That's why he tended to make decisions that an uncharitable sort might call rash. Because for him, there had not been a tomorrow for a very long time. He hadn't even thought much about Christine's future, beyond putting her on his stage and keeping her there. He had always been a man without a future, so there was no point.

But now he did.

He saw her, smiling in the sun, somewhere in the country. He saw green fields and flowers in her loose hair. He saw her laughing, as music played. He saw her happy and free, with him somehow beside her beneath a blue sky. But even imagined sun burned his eyes.

"Alas, we must make do with the world we have," Erik said, the dream fading.

"I guess so," Christine said with a sad smile. "I'll live in joy, right now, because I am with you."

"That is more than a start, my brilliant student."

He hoped he could keep her happy, for her moments with him now. Even if all went well with the new managers, foreboding still weighed on his heart. For their lesson, he carried her through all of Marguerite's most challenging ensembles, and then even a few of Gilda's. He was meticulous and discerning, and by the end of things, he could tell they were both as tired as ever.

"You need to rest now," he told her, even warmed by her pout at the command.

"Please don't tell me I have to go home. It's so hard to sleep there, so far from you," Christine said. "Adèle's going to supper with her patron tonight. I'd rather not be there when they get home."

"I would never deny you refuge here," Erik replied. "Go eat, see the sun if it's out, and then come back to me. I'll be there waiting."

"As it pleases you." Christine's expression darkened temptingly, and an ember of desire flared within him.

He waited for her to leave to sigh. Just because he hadn't touched her in the days since the gala did not mean he wasn't actively fighting the urge to do so again every waking moment. His hands practically burned with the desire to feel her skin once more. And beyond that were other, unthinkable desires. What would it be like to embrace her? To hold her? To truly make love to her? To feel her kiss...

Erik shook off the fantasy, retreating to the dark halls and corridors until he was close to the dressing rooms and stage. He kept to the shadows and watched various singers make their rounds until none other than Armand Moncharmin arrived in the wings, looking harried and glum.

"It wasn't that bad, come on," Robert Rameau called after the manager. Erik cocked his head in interest. Moncharmin apparently had stopped in on the rehearsal from which Christine had been excluded.

"She's worse than you told me she'd be, and you told me she was a terror," Moncharmin sighed as Rameau caught up to him. "The audacity of demanding more money, when we can barely keep track of the money we have!"

"Maybe she's received better offers," Rameau said. "It's possible. Some other director might not have actually heard her."

"She has to be mad to think she can hold us hostage now, when we have a more than suitable replacement literally waiting in the wings."

"Carlotta doesn't believe that," Rameau replied, taking Moncharmin by the elbow and guiding him to a secluded corner. Or one that appeared secluded, given that Erik was hidden near to it. "She's only listening to her toadies. They're parroting all the same absurd rumors she started back to her about how Christine is a miscreant or a novelty or untalented. None of them know or even are willing to acknowledge how good she really is. The truth doesn't matter, just the story."

"I guess you'd know about that," Moncharmin muttered, a slight edge to his voice but also deep familiarity. In fact, Erik remembered now where else he had heard Moncharmin's voice before this: in Rameau's dressing room.

"Don't be petulant, Armand, I'm trying to help you," Rameau replied warmly, confirming Erik's suspicions. "The way Carlotta sees it; you have two options. One, you surrender and pay her more or two, you turn to Christine who will inevitably fail. In that scenario, she'll get her money and Christine's career will be over."

"She can't contemplate someone actually being better than her? I guess she is a soprano," Moncharmin rejoined, thoughtfully.

"And I wouldn't put it past her to make sure Christine fails," Rameau said. "It wouldn't be the first time. And given that she thinks she was poisoned before the gala, I'd say it's likely. She has some stagehands in her pocket who make accidents happen, and then conveniently blame it on the Ghost."

"Doesn't she know that the Ghost is Christine Daaé's most vocal supporter?" Moncharmin grumbled, looking suspiciously over his shoulder, which would have made Erik laugh were he not seething in rage knowing that Carlotta was abusing his reputation.

"Oh, well, that makes sense. She's quite mysterious, that one," Rameau said. "And why didn't you tell me he'd made contact?"

"I've been rather busy you know. And I didn't ever think you were—"

"Telling the truth?" Rameau let out a dry laugh. "I would never lie to you about *him*." In the dark Erik smiled, at last, some respect.

"What is he?" Moncharmin asked, shivering visibly as both men turned their eyes to the dark around them. Did they feel him watching too?

"I have no clue," Rameau said. "But meet for supper at my flat tonight and I'll tell you all my theories."

Moncharmin met Rameau's sparkling eyes with a look of apprehension and desire. "I might be late."

"I'll wait," Rameau smiled, tracing the line of Moncharmin's jaw with his thumb, intimate and tender. "I know you couldn't do this without me."

"I'm in this mess *because* of you," Moncharmin replied without much bite.

"And what a glorious mess it is," Rameau smiled.

Erik watched them walk different directions, a familiar ache in his chest as he did. He could never even share a hidden love like theirs with Christine, not while she loved a lie. He could neither give her blue skies or darkened flats or anything more than music and glory and a fleeting touch in the dark.

And so that was what he would do. If Carlotta needed a push to let Christine perform, so be it, he'd encourage her gambit and protect Christine from any wrath that might follow. There was more than one way of making a diva disappear.

"There we are, lovely," Julianne declared as she stepped away so Christine could see herself in the mirror of the costume workshop. It had been more than kind for her friend to offer to alter the dress for Christine, among many others. Christine had been told by enough people at this point that she had to dress that part of a diva, but she hated the discomfort, expense, and wait at a dressmaker's salon. And so she had made do with cast-offs from Adèle and Nicole Duval, like the one she wore now.

Despite being slightly stolen, the dress was the height of fashion now, thanks to Julianne, and Louise. It was a deep red brocade, with an underskirt and blouse of purple, with matching ruffles along the edges. There was white lace and brass buttons at the wrists, as well as along the modest neckline.

In her time at the Opera, Christine had also learned how to better style her hair beyond a simple chignon, though it tired her arms and she understood why so many women needed maids just to get ready for a day out. Today she'd been moderately successful, and so, much like at the gala, the reflection she saw staring back at her was again a woman she barely recognized.

"Thank you for this," she said after too long of a beat. "It's wonderful."

"So why do you look so sad?"

"I'm not sad, I'm just…" Christine sighed. There was no word for it in her vocabulary. There were still moments every day that she was so happy, when she was near him and singing for him, but more and more she would find her quiet moments filled with foreboding and the strange, sad feeling that even the things she loved most were sliding away like sand on the shore. "Everything about my life has changed and yet it's all the same and I feel so…lost sometimes."

"You'll hear something soon," Julianne assured her. "If not for *Faust* tomorrow, at least for *Rigoletto*. Carlotta's barely even been to rehearsals for it, and she still doesn't have an actual understudy."

"She'll be there today," Christine sighed. "Just like everyone else."

"Don't worry about them," Julianne said with force. She'd had to repeat the admonition to Christine so many times in the last few days as more rumors had swirled around her, reminding her exactly how vulnerable she was and how much people who had never spoken to her were willing to believe the worst of her.

"I know, I know," Christine sighed. "I don't know why I care."

"Because you're human," Julianne replied with a sigh. "And humans are stupid."

"Oh thank you."

"I'm serious, we all want to be welcomed into the wide world," Julianne went on, and Christine suddenly felt foolish and selfish when she saw the wistfulness in her friend's dark features. "People like you at least have a chance at belonging, and so you want to. Even if you talk to ghosts."

"I don't—"

Julianne gave her a look. "I heard a voice the other day when I was coming to your dressing room. And I know you probably can't tell me anything, about your teacher or ghost or angel or whoever he is. But I just want you to be careful."

Christine gulped. She had no idea what to say. At least Julianne believed, but it was terrifying to think that they had been heard. And – not for the first time in the preceding weeks – it made her feel more scared than special that she had such a strange patron. "Don't tell anyone," Christine whispered. Indeed, how much worse would the rumors about her be if people really knew the truth.

"Come on, I'll walk with you, I think everyone is going to be trying to get a look at our new lords," Julianne said, squeezing Christine's hand encouragingly. "Jammes told me Moncharmin came by the *Salon du Danse* yesterday and tried to introduce himself to the wrong person. He thought that painter was in charge since he was paying such close attention."

"Well, Monsieur Degas does look very distinguished when his hands aren't covered in charcoal," Christine muttered as they took the winding path towards the stage. "He's quite nice, if you've never spoken to him and—"

"Shh!" Julianne pulled Christine aside as a man turned a corner into the hall. For a second, given Julianne's reaction, Christine had expected her own ghost to appear, but it was someone else. The man had copper skin, a neatly trimmed black beard, and wore a dark fur cap, brimless and softly folded in such a way that the edges nearly met at the top.

The stranger walked slowly, as if he was looking for something and easily noticed Christine and Julianne staring from down the hall. He said nothing, just nodded politely and turned the other way. Julianne shivered even so.

"Who was that?" Christine whispered as the man disappeared into the dark.

"How have you been here this long and never seen the Persian?" Julianne demanded, tugging Christine with her towards the stage.

"That was him?" she asked and Julianne nodded.

"You know, he talks to the Ghost too," Julianne said. "Jammes told me that Mercier and Gabriel saw the two of them talking in a hall together."

"What?" Christine had heard many rumors about the Ghost. Most she didn't believe for they were so out of character from the angel she knew. The tales of floating heads wreathed in flames or him demanding money from the managers were as absurd as the story that he could talk to the rats. But she'd never given any credence to the rumors of the Persian being in league with the Phantom. She had always assumed he was some employee who was only noted as 'always lurking about the Opera' due to his race.

"You can ask Jammes yourself," Julianne said as they reached the bustling stage where it seemed the entire Opera had assembled ahead of rehearsal. Jammes was with the rest of the rats in a corner, clustered like a bouquet of snowdrops in their white tutus. She made eye contact with Julianne and almost smiled before she noticed Christine and returned to scowling.

"I don't think she'll be interested in telling me," Christine muttered. Jammes had yet to forgive Christine for achieving a sliver of fame, much to Julianne's consternation.

"I guess you could ask Gabriel and Mercier, but they look rather busy," Julianne commented. Indeed, the directors were in the process of filing onto the stage along with Charles LaRoche from the ballet and Bosarge. Behind them were two men who had to be the new managers. Christine and the rest of the Opera took in their new leaders. They both looked incredibly tired for men who had only been on the job a few days.

Bosarge clapped his hands quietly, bringing the assembled company to silence as easily as he did the orchestra. "Thank you all for coming," Bosarge began, looking around the crowd. Christine found herself looking as well. Everyone was there. Everyone *except*

Carlotta. "It is my honor to introduce you to our new managers, Firmin Richard –" the older man gave a bow "and Armand Moncharmin." Moncharmin at least tried to smile. "Messieurs."

Bosarge stepped aside and Richard glared at his younger counterpart, indicating who would be speaking.

"Good day to you all," Moncharmin began, his voice shaking. "We are both truly honored and excited to take on these great responsibilities. We also apologize for the disruptions that this transition has caused. We assure you that things will be sorted out soon. However, and I do hate to do this now but—"

"*Rigoletto* will premiere on the tenth, not the fourth," Richard said flatly, and a murmur went up. "We will also need to delay today's rehearsals until this afternoon. Those of you who are actually needed can reassemble at two o'clock. The rest of you get back to work. Good day."

Richard turned and walked off stage, with the directors and Moncharmin trotting after him in consternation as the company burst into confused murmurs.

"I hear they can't get Carlotta out of her dressing room." Christine and Julianne spun to see Adèle smiling behind them. "She's had to barricade the door since the lock doesn't work. I wonder if she's pouting in her tub."

"Why on earth is she throwing a fit now?" Christine asked.

Adèle shrugged. "I don't think her patrons are making the impression she wanted. Maybe because her rival has such influential patron of her own." Adèle grinned suggestively and Christine's stomach clenched.

"What are you talking about?" Christine asked, her stomach falling.

"You'd know if you hadn't been avoiding me and your own damn home for days," Adèle replied. Christine blushed. She hadn't wanted to leave the protective enclave of the Opera at all lately. Things out in the world were too confusing, and even things here were becoming too much.

"I'm sorry," Christine muttered.

"Don't worry, I'll still give you your present. Or your patron's present, as it were." With a grin, Adèle produced a letter from her pocket and handed it to Christine. "Someone is eager to get your attention."

"What?" Christine grabbed the letter, her hands shaking with anxiety. "I-I should read this alone."

She didn't wait for Adèle or Julianne as she rushed to her dressing room. The letter was a leaden weight in her hand, but she couldn't feel the Angel near her. Not yet. Maybe she had time. She locked her dressing room door behind her and rushed to the vanity, lighting the oil lamp with trembling hands. She held her breath as she read.

My Dearest Christine,

I first must apologize for my untoward behavior the night of the gala. I was overcome with affection when I saw you. Especially after holding your memory so long in my heart. And I have held it, my darling playfellow. I have thought of you all these years apart, as I have no other.

I know you must remember me as well. I saw it in your eyes. Perhaps you were overwhelmed that night, or did not wish a scene, or perhaps there is some other reason you could not speak to me. I admit, the idea that some other fellow may have stolen your heart before I could reclaim it terrifies me. But I will not be deterred. I will be there at your door and in your audience every night until I can laugh with you again as we did in those days in Perros.

I have also made sure the managers – the fools – know that the Chagny patronage is dependent on your success, not that awful Spaniard's. We shall continue to support you, be assured.

Please, write back to me or you shall surely break the heart that has always been yours.

~Raoul

She read it twice, her heart pounding more with each line. She had tried so hard not to think of Raoul in the weeks since the gala. Tried and failed. She'd told herself over and over that it was forbidden, that she couldn't have such distractions. And she knew logically that even if she were free, she could never be his. His family had made that clear long ago. And she didn't want to be a mistress or a kept woman. She didn't know what she wanted, but even so, it was as if something incredible was being offered to her in Raoul's scrawling hand.

Her hands continued to shake as she slipped the letter into the chimney of her oil lamp and watched the flames quickly consume the paper. Even when it was ashes, she couldn't breathe...because now she could feel her angel watching.

"What did he write to you, your little Vicomte?" The Angel's voice was ice. She closed her eyes, the sound sending new tremors through her.

"He says he's supporting me, with the managers, against Carlotta." It wasn't a lie, but she couldn't tell him more.

"You don't need him, that's been taken care of," the voice said, soft and dangerous as if it was just behind her. "Right now, Carlotta is telling Richard and Moncharmin that she's been otherwise engaged for tomorrow night. A duchess made her a very generous offer to sing."

Christine's mind raced, as well as her heart. The air around her thrummed like the moment before a storm, heavy and electric. Her eyes were still closed, but she knew the room had darkened. And she felt him close.

"How..." she whispered.

"There is no miracle I would not work to assure your place on my stage," his voice whispered in her ear. "To hear you sing upon it, for only me."

There was such power in those words and such seduction. The reminder that she was his, entirely *his*, made her ache. Beneath her corset, her breasts grew heavy, her stomach fluttered, and her sex ignited with need. It would be shameful –how easily he could reduce her to a quivering mess of desire and deference – were it not such an exquisite thrill.

"Only you, I swear," she breathed.

"No mere boy could give you anything compared to what I can," the Angel intoned, half a song, and Christine let out a soft whimper.

"I know." She found that she was gripping the edges of her vanity, eyes still screwed shut as she waited for him to act.

Every nerve in her body was alive with anticipation. For weeks she'd dreamed of feeling his touch again, of surrendering to him entirely. Would he finally gift her with that ecstasy again now? Her mind swam with fantasies of what he could do – of what she would *let* him do – each vision more obscene than the last. She saw herself, bent over her vanity with her pretty skirts pulled high around her hips as he finally took her entirely, driving into her with unquestionable force that would make her scream.

Instead, he began to sing, low and soft, their secret song that acted on her like a spell. She moaned, clenching her thighs as tight as she could, her hips squirming as she chased the pleasure coiling in her gut. She could feel him inches from her, and she knew that if she opened her eyes, she would see his shadow looming behind her. But she didn't. She would obey.

He sang to her, intimate and insistent, and the dream filled her mind. She imagined wantonly the feeling of being possessed by him. Filled and fucked. Consumed and claimed. And for a second in the fantasy, he was more than a shadow, more than a ghost in a mask.

He was a man, real and vital, adoring her with his heat. He wore no mask, and his face was handsome and familiar...

"I'm yours," she moaned, guilt filling her as the image shattered, even as the delicious tension in her body grew and grew. "Only yours," she repeated, begging forgiveness for just the thought of another inside her. His song intensified, his power and voice touching her in ways no mortal man ever could, reminding her who she served. Who she loved.

The song rose to its climax as Christine's fingers dug into the vanity, her every muscle tense and ready. Then just a note shy...he stopped. He waited for an excruciating moment.

"Mine," he whispered in her ear, and caressed her cheek with the barest touch.

She came with a guttural cry, her body shaking with pleasure and release as fresh moisture bloomed between her thighs. It cascaded through her, lifting her to that same sublime peak she reached when she sang for him. It was heaven, for a few glorious seconds. It was heaven with an angel beside her.

She opened her eyes slowly, finding that the oil lamp was indeed out, and she was entirely in the dark. But she also knew that he would not be there when she turned. Her breath was ragged as she lit the lamp once again, her hand still unsteady, but now for a completely different reason.

At last, she caught her own reflection in the vanity mirror. Her cheeks were flushed and her eyes dark. Did she look debauched? She didn't know. But she felt more herself than she had all day.

"You're beautiful," her angel whispered from the walls, reading her thoughts. "They're here."

"Who?"

She jumped at the knock on her dressing room door.

"Mademoiselle Daaé?" a male voice asked from the other side, one she had heard for the first time only just recently. Sure enough,

Armand Moncharmin was waiting on the other side of the door, with the directors behind him, as well as Robert Rameau, who was smiling broadly.

"Messieurs?" Christine asked.

"I know this is quite a thing to ask as we are just being introduced but," Moncharmin began, with little confidence. "But things have developed regarding Madame Zambelli and—"

"You're on, my dear," Rameau cut him off. "For rehearsal today and *Faust* tomorrow night."

"You haven't even asked if I know the part," Christine replied, satisfaction filling her. It was indeed just as he had promised. A miracle.

"We have been reliably informed that you do," Gabriel said.

"Well then, we should start preparing, don't you think?" Christine asked with her best smile.

Rameau grinned in response. "My dear, nothing will prepare you for what's in store tomorrow night."

12. Crescendo

Erik often considered his preparations for a performance akin to an artist's. After all, he was putting on a costume, readying himself to play a role. Though if he was honest, he thought with a sigh as he fastened a gold cufflink, that applied to everyone in the audience. They all had parts to play, masks to wear, cues to attend to. His masks were just more obvious.

Tonight, however, he took extra care in his preparations. The last few days (or had it been weeks?) had run him ragged. So much so that he cast a sad look to his bed as he buttoned his crisp white shirt. When was the last time he'd slept there? When was the last time he'd simply *slept* more than an hour? He wasn't sure. But the exhaustion and exertion would all be worth it tonight.

The letters, the money, the lies, and the threats; all of them assured that Carlotta would be far away tonight, dressed up for an engagement that didn't exist. Erik wished he could see the viper's face when she realized she'd been duped. But it was far more important tonight to see Christine's.

He finished with the knot of his white tie and donned his finest silk vest and jacket. Both the audience and the performers had maids and valets to help them dress, something he always found so strange. He hated the thought of another person so close, brushing his shoulders or fastening his buttons; *touching* him. There was one person in all the world he would ever allow so near and even just that dream, an enticing one, made his heart quicken and his skin crawl.

He had been close to her yesterday. So insanely and tantalizingly close. It was the letter that had driven him to the act of madness. The very idea of that boy continuing to pursue Christine had made Erik wild with jealousy. And so, he'd reminded her; he'd brought her to the peak of ecstasy with only his voice and the barest graze of his fingertips. He could almost still feel the heat of her skin, like a brand. He wanted more, even though it was impossible to have it.

He combed his long hair, trying to remember the last time he'd bothered to cut it. His hat and cape were last, along with his black gloves. All told, nearly every inch of him, save his mouth, was covered, an elegant disguise for a monster if he did say so himself.

He gave one last glance to his strange home before leaving, taking in the refuge that had sheltered him for so long. How would his realm of wonders and shadows look to Christine? She'd see he was a magpie just like her and had filled his home with the things they both loved: instruments, books, music, and other wonders. She would like the picture room especially, he thought, so full of forgotten treasures. Surely, she would like the bath...

Again: madness. He was exhausted and not thinking straight. Perhaps at the most tonight he might touch her again, as reward for the triumph in store. He knew in his heart that she expected it; longed for it even. It could be enough. It *had* to be enough because there could never be anything more. Not for them.

And that was alright, he told himself for the hundredth time that week. He did not need more, and he did not want more. His greatest pleasure came from bringing ecstasy to her and the idea of her ever touching him was utterly inconceivable. Not to mention anyone that had ever touched him like that had met a violent end. So many more had touched him with violence and ended up the same. He was a cursed thing, he had to remember that.

But he could bless her. Just her. He had promised her months ago that he would lift her to the highest position a singer could hold, as a diva on his stage. And tonight, that would happen. And she would stay there. A perfect angel above them all, never to be touched by another besides the ghost who had put her there.

The *Grand Foyer* was packed with so many people that the windows had fogged up. Raoul tugged at his collar, jealous of anyone still outside in the chill winter air rather than in this crush of humanity.

"Do try to look like you're enjoying yourself," Philippe remarked from beside him, nodding to yet another pair of society acquaintances as they passed by. The woman had feathers jutting directly up from her coiffure and Raoul dearly hoped the couple were in a box and not seated in front of some poor soul who wanted a clear view.

"Now, now, Philippe, don't you know that looking bored is the best way to get the right kind of attention," Antione scolded, and Raoul shot the man a scowl. "I said bored, dear boy, not sullen and irritated."

"Are you sure your friend gave her the letter?" Raoul snapped in return.

"How is Sabine?" Antoine asked Philippe, turning pointedly away from Raoul, and infuriating him all the more. Antoine's interest in Raoul and Philippe's sister was transparent and unscrupulous, but Philippe didn't seem to care.

"She's well. I tried to get her to come tonight but she's not one for music," Philippe replied. "You'll see her at supper tomorrow, don't worry."

"Perhaps Christine didn't know where to write me back," Raoul said, realizing too late it was aloud. Philippe and Antoine give him twin looks of pity. "It's possible."

"Or perhaps she'd been busy getting ready for her first performance," Philippe offered with what passed for kindness from him.

Raoul sighed. The one useful thing Antoine had done was confirm with every confidence that it would be Christine singing Marguerite tonight and not Carlotta. Raoul cared far less about the performance than about what could happen after.

Raoul cast his eyes about the foyer. Already people were moving towards their boxes, while others sipped champagne and socialized. The women in their glorious gowns were a riot of color in contrast to the men in their identical white shirts and black jackets. Among the crowd of pale faces, however, one darker visage stood out. The man was not only an anomaly because of his race, but in a ghastly breach of protocol, he was wearing a hat indoors, clearly marking himself as foreign. At least he had the decency to keep to the edges of the room, apparently trying to be inconspicuous. Perhaps he was someone's exotic servant.

"Ah, Messieurs, what a delight," Philippe said with a note of disdain. Raoul turned to see who he was addressing. It was the managers, or at least Raoul assumed the man next to Richard was his counterpart.

"Messieurs de Chagny, Monsieur de Martiniac," Moncharmin said with a bow. "It is a pleasure to formally meet you." Richard gave the slightest nod of acknowledgment.

"We could not miss such a thrilling debut," Philippe replied with a glance to Raoul. "Indeed, some of us are beside ourselves in anticipation of Mademoiselle Daaé's return to the stage. We're so glad you came around on that."

"Ah, yes, well," Moncharmin stammered. "Signora Carlotta did help make that decision for us. Or I guess the Duchess of Zurich did by engaging her tonight for her charity concert."

"What are you talking about?" Raoul balked. "That concert isn't for a week, and she wanted Christine for it, not Carlotta. I was the one who suggested Mademoiselle Daaé to her."

Richard's face darkened. "Madame Zambelli made it extremely clear that since we refused to pay a ransom to get her on stage, she was inclined to take a generous offer from the Duchess for a concert tonight. I think she's even taken her little claque with her to cheer her on."

"And why on earth would anyone be paid for a charity concert? That's quite the opposite of the point," Philippe laughed. "I believe your diva has been deceived."

"Who would do that?" Raoul asked.

"My first guess would have been you, Monsieur Le Vicomte," Richard replied sourly. "If I thought you more merciless."

Raoul huffed, taken aback, and looked around to see if anyone else had heard the scandalous accusation, but the only person showing interest was the foreigner in the cap. He averted his eyes when Raoul caught him. "Well, I can't say I'm sad to hear Zambelli has been deceived. Christine will win everyone over tonight, I'm sure of it," Raoul said.

"Whose box will you be joining, might I ask?" Philippe inquired. "We do have room in ours as my sister has declined her invitation for the evening."

"We will be in box five," Richard replied, once again with dire seriousness.

Antoine's guffaw was not expected. "Isn't that supposed to be haunted? No one ever sits there," Antoine said. Richard's face grew so grim at the comment that even Antoine's smile fell.

"That is the rumor my dear partner is determined to disprove," Moncharmin said. His voice was shaking.

"I haven't heard such rumors," Raoul replied, curious. "I knew you theater people were a suspicious sort, but a haunted box seems rather excessive."

"If only the haunted box was the end of it," Philippe remarked, surprising Raoul. What sort of myths were these that even his brother, perhaps the most practical and blasé man in Paris, knew of them?

"If only," Moncharmin sighed as a bell sounded, signaling that curtain was close.

"Good luck with the performance, Messieurs," Philippe said with a nod, which Antoine copied.

"I hope we will see you after, in the *Salon du Danse*, with the other valued patrons," Moncharmin said, even as Richard turned to leave.

"Raoul will be there if Daaé is," Antoine said, and Raoul looked away to hide his embarrassment. Once again, he caught the eyes of the nosy foreigner, but this time the man gave Raoul a polite bow.

It was strange, Raoul thought, as he followed Philippe to their box on the grand tier. Everything was strange, from this mysterious plot to sideline Carlotta, to the haunted box and the foreigner listening to them. And then of course there was the voice in Christine's dressing room. It all confused him, but more than that, it made him terribly afraid that whatever mystery was unfolding at the Opera, his dear Christine was at the center of it.

"I said: you're trembling."

Christine turned to Julianne, blinking. Had she repeated herself? She wasn't sure. Her mind had been racing for two days straight. But she *was* trembling.

"I...I'm so nervous," Christine muttered, looking at herself in the great mirror. Once again, it was a stranger that she saw reflected, but that was the point. The peasant costume was beautiful, with shades of rose and pink, and golden laces for the bodice. Her cheeks and lips were rouged, her eyes lined, and her hair was braided beautifully.

"You look wonderful and you're going to *be* wonderful, I know it," Julianne assured her, taking her hands, and squeezing them. Christine took a shaking breath and nodded.

"Two minutes!" a voice called from outside the dressing room with a quick rap.

"Thank you!" Christine called back and her heart began to make an earnest effort to beat out of her chest.

"Will you be alright? Do you want me to walk with you to the stage?" Julianne asked. Christine knew it was meant as a kindness. Everyone had been kind and helpful in the last day, from the directors to Julianne and Louise mysteriously having a copy of Marguerite's costume ready for her, and even the other singers. (Though, they might just have been happy to be free of Carlotta.) The attention had all been incredible and wonderful, but it had barely left Christine a moment alone with her angel. And that was all she could think of.

"I'm fine, I just need a moment to gather myself," Christine said. Julianne gave her a knowing look and let her hands go. With a glance to the mirror, Julianne finally left her alone and Christine let out the breath she was holding.

She sang through a quick scale, not pushing, since she still had an entire act to wait through before she would even sing a few notes. All she had to do in Act I was appear behind a screen as the devil showed Faust the vision of the beautiful woman he could defile, if he just sold his soul. At least she couldn't get that wrong. She sang the scale again and her voice trembled as much as her body and she stopped, a new wave of terror crashing over her.

She leaned against the mirror, her hand and forehead pressed against the cold glass. What if she failed? What if she opened her mouth and nothing came out? What if Carlotta sent someone to sabotage her? Her angel had been firm with her to not drink or eat anything she didn't see prepared, but what if she forgot? What if she forgot the words or the blocking? What if she fell? What if she faltered and disappointed him? Her father was watching from the other side, she knew it, but what if she failed him again? What if she never heard her angel again...

"Breathe, Christine," the Angel's voice came from all around her.

She gasped like she was breaking the surface of the ocean. He was there, at last. He was with her. She felt like she might weep.

"Again, slower. Just breathe." Christine obeyed and inhaled carefully. "Good. In. And out. Just keep breathing." It helped.

"Do you really believe I'm ready?" she whispered to the glass, wishing with all her heart that somehow her angel could step into the light and hold her.

"I know you are," the Angel whispered, his words wrapping around her instead.

"What if I'm not?" Christine protested, shutting her eyes so she wouldn't cry. "What if I make a mistake and disappoint you? What if—"

"Christine, do you love me?"

"Of course," she answered instantly, her eyes open again, staring at her own reflection.

"Then there is nothing you could do to disappoint me," he said, his voice like love itself made into a sound. "Sing your love to me tonight. That's all you need to do. Don't think of anyone or anything else. If you are frightened, just remember me, and breathe...and know that I will love you more with each breath."

Christine shut her eyes again, this time fighting back tears of love and joy. It was all she needed to hear. "I will," she whispered back, more grateful for the blessing he had given her than words could express.

"And when you are done, perhaps—"

"Places!" came the call from outside her dressing room, accompanied by a sharp knock. Christine jumped, her pulse quickening for another reason now. She didn't need to ask what he was offering or promising. She had been dreaming of it for weeks.

"Go, Christine," the Angel of Music ordered, unquestionable. "Sing for me."

The command echoed in her heart as she left the dressing room and made her way to the stage, all the while feeling as if she was floating. Tonight, she'd sing for him alone and then he would reward her. He'd touch her again, she knew it. Perhaps he'd even give her more than before. However, he chose to bless her, she would treasure it. But first, she would earn it. First, she would give him her soul in song.

She took her place in the wings, listening to the sound of the orchestra tuning, each note blossoming out of another until it was one great wall of sound. The overture began as Christine waited in the darkness, ignoring everyone else around her. She took a deep breath and let it out, loving him.

Erik listened to the overture from inside the walls. Even from there, he could sense the excitement in the audience. They knew tonight would change everything, just as he did. He had no doubt that Christine would amaze them all. Then afterwards, once she was done with the niceties of bowing to the patrons and the managers, she would be his again. Where would be the best place? He wondered, as he ascended a hidden ladder. Her dressing room hid him better but her secret bed in the cellars was softer for her. Perhaps there...

Erik's train of thought stopped abruptly as he entered the hollow column that allowed him entry into his box. There were voices on the other side. Voices he recognized and that filled his heart with fury.

"This is foolish," Moncharmin said. "We don't need to tempt fate this way."

"We are not tempting fate, we are proving that this is all a tiresome joke at our expense," Richard growled back. Erik clenched his fists as he peered through the crack in the column to see their faces. Moncharmin looked terrified and Richard annoyed, as usual.

"Are you so sure?" Moncharmin replied. "You haven't been among the people here. There are too many stories about this ghost for it to all be a joke."

"Spirits do not demand money or interfere with casting," Richard snapped. "Or require boxes. Which is what we are showing right now."

"Are you indeed?" Erik made his voice quiet, using all his skill to make it sound like it was right behind the interlopers. He watched as Moncharmin went entirely pale.

"Who said that?" Richard demanded, springing up to look around.

"Don't be so obtuse, Monsieur, you know exactly who I am," Erik spoke in an unearthly whisper. "And you are sitting in my box."

"We are very sorry—" Moncharmin began, standing and bowing to the empty air before Richard batted his arm in anger.

"Stop that! This is a joke!" Richard said, so loud that someone in another box shushed him. "Where are you?"

"Right here," Erik replied, throwing his voice right to Richard's ear. The manager spun and Erik could not help but laugh. The sound only made Richard angrier. He stalked to the door of the box and wrenched it open.

"Monsieur! I told you he would be upset!" Erik heard Madame Giry exclaim, loyal as always.

"Who came in here? What is going on?" Richard bellowed at the woman. Erik could not see, but he imagined her determined scowl.

"No one, Monsieur! If you hear someone, it is the Ghost! He does not like intruders!"

"I will not tolerate this. You are fired!" Richard declared and Erik's fury spiked.

"You are *not*," Erik spoke through the walls, watching how it made Moncharmin cower. "Though you may retire for the evening, my dear Madame." Erik heard the door slam and footsteps retreat. Once again, someone shushed them from the neighboring box.

"Now, see here," Richard whispered vehemently, coming back into view. On stage, Faust was lamenting his lot. It was time for the devil to appear.

"No, you see here, Monsieur Richard," Erik spoke, every syllable a threat. "I have been more than patient with you until now, but no longer. You serve in *my* opera at *my* pleasure, and I can remove you just as easily as I did your predecessors. Or I can make things for you and this theater much worse. Fatally worse."

"We understand!" Moncharmin said, entirely deferential. "We mean no disrespect!"

"Whoever you are, I will not tolerate such threats," Richard declared through gritted teeth.

"They are not threats, they are promises," Erik intoned. "This will be your last warning."

"We understand," Moncharmin said with force, and grabbed Richard by the arm to drag him from the box. Erik continued to seethe once they were gone. He had one manager at least under his control now, hopefully it would be enough.

He stepped out of the column after a sensible wait, just in time to listen to Méphistophélès make his final offer to Faust. Fontana was in good form tonight, as was Rameau. Erik finally took his seat, hidden from the rest of the audience at the back of the box, considering the stories of the Opera Ghost selling his soul to the devil for a beautiful voice. If only that were so. Faust longed for youth again, but he did not sell his soul until the devil offered something else: the love of a beautiful, innocent woman. Erik could hardly blame the man, especially when the vision the devil presented was of Christine.

She was perfect. Utterly beautiful. And no one knew she was his. He'd already sold his soul to make that so, lied and deceived her in so many ways. And it was worth it.

Erik paid little attention to the rest of act one or the beginning of act two, nor did most of the audience. The soldier's chorus and the devil's blasphemous song to the golden calf were rousing as usual, but everyone was waiting for Carlotta's replacement to prove herself. The muttering grew in volume as Marguerite at last made her entrance.

"*Won't you allow me to offer you my arm, oh beautiful lady?*" Faust sang.

Erik found himself holding his breath.

"*I am neither beautiful, nor a lady, I don't need to take any arm,*" Christine sang perfectly. And in a single line, she had won. Erik relaxed into his seat as Christine exited the stage. He knew she was destined for absolute triumph, all he had to do was watch it play out. The act ended, people milled about and gossiped.

And Erik waited. He wished he could be in two places at once as the next act began. He wished he could be with her in her dressing room, to assure her one more time that she would be perfect. He wished so many things when it came to Christine.

Siébel, Faust, and Méphistophélès came and went and at last Christine was alone on stage. If she was frightened or nervous, Erik could not see it. For a second, she looked towards his box, a whisper of a smile on her face, and then she began to sing.

Erik listened breathlessly as she perfected the Ballad of the King of Thule, spinning out glorious sound as easily as Marguerite spun her thread. But it was the Jewel Song that the audience was waiting for, and it was there that the new Marguerite came into her own. She was even better than at the gala, thanks to the weeks of practice and instruction since then. And perhaps also thanks to the holy fire that ignited in her when she sang. Her runs and exclamations sparkled, and her dreaming phrases soared to the sky. Her final high C still echoed through the auditorium when the usually demure audience exploded in applause.

They were clapping for him, Erik thought, for *his* creation. They were all his at last, just as he'd dreamed. And it didn't move him at all. All that mattered right now was her. The angel on the stage singing her love to him.

In the duet between Marguerite and Faust, Erik's heart raced. Fontana sang better than he had in years. Erik thought of how he had sung this music with Christine so many times, wishing he could take her in his arms as the tenor was doing at that moment.

The chaste maid told Faust to return the next day, but the devil whispered in Faust's ear to listen to Marguerite's true desires. To the dark of the night, Christine sang of her love for a mysterious stranger. And in the darkness Faust returned, to take the maiden's innocence while the devil rejoiced in her corruption. The curtain closed as Fontana embraced Christine, causing Erik another intense stab of jealousy and desire, but the explosion of applause drove the thought from his mind.

The interval began and the whole audience broke into excited chatter. Erik could imagine what they were saying, the praise they were heaping on his student. He stood, drawing back into the shadows to make sure he was not seen. He was not expecting the door of his box to open. He had anticipated the managers. It would have made sense for them to intrude again. The Daroga of Mazenderan was a far more unwelcome sight. As was the look of victory in his eyes as Erik glowered at him from the corner.

"You should be more careful, Erik, anyone could walk in with no box keeper outside," Shaya said, stepping into the box and closing the door behind him. Erik stood frozen, unable to discern the man's intent as he smirked at Erik.

"I didn't think you ever actually attended," Erik replied slowly. "Or that you could afford it."

"I make do," the Daroga replied with a shrug. "I made a point of it tonight. I was simply so curious about what sort of schemes you're up to with these new managers."

"I don't know what you mean."

"Oh, I'm sure you do, old friend," Shaya went on. He looked far too smug for Erik's comfort. "I couldn't figure why you'd get rid of the old guard. I assumed it had something to do with that awful soprano you've been torturing for years. And honestly, I can't really fault you for hating her. But why now? I asked myself. Then I heard a strange rumor. That you've spoken in favor of her replacement. And I realized, this move was not about Carlotta, not fully. All of this chaos has been because of Christine Daaé."

Erik's blood froze and his eyes narrowed. "She's a great talent, can you blame me for clearing the way for her?" he said, trying to keep his voice cool and detached.

"I think there's more to it than that," Shaya countered. "I've been hearing all sorts of stories about how it was her that Joseph Buquet says sicced the Ghost on him. How she came out of nowhere. How she's even seen you."

"You're on dangerous ground, Daroga, I warn you." Erik knew it was a mistake the moment he said it and Shaya smiled. He had just confirmed everything.

"I don't know what this girl knows of you or how she's connected to you, but I do think I shall speak to her."

"She wouldn't listen," Erik hissed.

"Oh, I'm not sure of that," Shaya replied. "As you've told me so many times, men in power here don't listen to the likes of me. But a girl like her? I think she would be incredibly interested to know that the phantom that has supported her career is mortal." Shaya paused, sneering. "Though he is truly a monster."

"Why?" Erik demanded, a hundred catastrophic scenarios playing out in his head. "She doesn't know enough to lead you to me, Daroga. She's innocent."

"That's exactly why. This girl is some sort of treasure to you. A person you cherish. Someone far better than you, that you wish to safeguard from the cruel, callous world." Shaya's eyes darkened in remembrance. "I remember that feeling, of wanting to protect someone. You took him away from me. Don't you think it's right I do the same to you?"

"Shaya, please," Erik whispered. "Don't."

"I'm just going to give her the truth, Erik," Shaya replied with a shrug. "What she does with it will be up to her."

With that Shaya turned. Erik could have killed him then. It would have been easy, even without the lasso. But then he would be the monster Shaya believed him to be. And it wouldn't change anything. He sank against the wall in the shadows of the box, his head spinning and horror churning in his gut.

He had to get to Christine first. He had no choice. He had to keep Shaya away from her until he made a plan. Until...until he could tell her the truth himself. And destroy everything.

Raoul was not a musician, though he had always loved the art. Of course, he'd heard music all his childhood and even been forced into a few piano lessons. But it had been Stellan Daaé and his wondrous daughter who had truly taught Raoul to adore melody and harmony, all those years ago. Since then, he'd never been able to find music that inspired him as much as theirs had. That was, until now.

He had heard *Faust* before, but it had bored him. Now he was rapt, amazed at the power of Gounod's art when Christine was the one bringing it to life. She was fantastic. Inspiring. Captivating. And everyone in the audience knew it. At the interval it had been all anyone could discuss. Well, that and the fact that Carlotta had been completely eclipsed in every way. And grumblings about someone having an argument in one of the other grand tier boxes.

The murmurs continued through the ballet, although Philippe at least paid attention to that, given that his Sorelli was a featured witch among the demonic throng. Raoul didn't care about her. He also didn't care about Faust and Méphistophélès. Like Faust, all anyone could think of was returning to Marguerite. At last, the light rose on the final scene in Marguerite's prison cell. Christine was dressed in a simple white shift and bodice with a scooped neck, which clung flatteringly to her body. Her dark hair was unbound, and the rouge had been wiped from her face. She was once again the unadorned, pure, beautiful girl he had known by the sea so long ago.

Faust called out to Marguerite, and she sang, rejoicing in the sound of her beloved's voice, and oh, the passion in those notes. There was love and hope and something heavenly in every note. It was almost inhuman. Maybe Christine had been blessed by the angel her father had promised. Faust and the devil called to her, but Marguerite resisted. She called to heaven and the choirs of angels proclaimed her salvation. Raoul knew he was not alone in feeling that he too was being lifted to heaven. Christine sang with utter faith, and it was the most beautiful thing Raoul had ever heard. He watched as she truly ascended in those final moments, her voice calling to God and affirming to Raoul that she was the most transcendent, resplendent woman he had ever seen or known.

He had to see her. He had to be with her immediately. He could not let the woman that brought the theater to its feet before the curtain even closed escape him. Not again. She had to remember him, and he had to make her.

He was up and out of the box before the final chords sounded. Philippe had shown him the way backstage weeks ago, and he knew they didn't turn away men like him. Anyway, the attendant was arguing with that blasted foreigner again and didn't give Raoul a second look. He wouldn't wait until the party where she might not be. He wouldn't wait at all.

Christine could not breathe. What she was feeling was like the moments after ecstasy, like she'd reached a new kind of climax that left her as weak and winded as if she had run a mile. She had never given so much to the music. She knew without doubt it was the best she had ever sung. She was in the arms of an angel, or at least a burly bass dressed as an angel, and she almost felt like she was truly in heaven. She wanted to be. God, she wished it was her angel holding her...

In a blink, she was back on the stage and the curtain was rising again. The roar of her own blood in her ears was replaced by deafening applause as someone pushed her to the center of the stage. The lights were bright and blinding as they never had been before, and the noise was incredible.

Christine curtsied coyly, aghast to see the entire audience already on their feet. Her simple movement brought a fresh round of cheers, and she was immediately lost. Thankfully, Fontana and Rameau appeared beside her and took her hands, letting her lead them in another bow. She tried to hold onto them, but they both stepped away, and then bowed again, not to the audience, but to her. It only made the audience go wilder. She still couldn't breathe. She was off-center and cold, her heart pounding and her stomach so unsettled she worried she might be sick.

Christine bowed again, fighting to catch a breath, and turned to leave the stage, but the applause didn't stop. Someone pushed her out again. The clapping and cries of praise simply refused to cease. Christine blushed as tears ran down her face. She was shaking so badly she could barely stand, and the din was absolutely thunderous.

A second time she tried to leave the stage, desperate to escape, and was pushed back on. People were throwing flowers and grooms were pressing huge bouquets into her arms. The scent made her head ache, the grade of the stage made it hard to stand. She couldn't breathe and it was so loud.

She swooned, grabbing the arm of whoever was closest to her. She was falling before she knew what was happening, flowers tumbling from her hands. She was aware of being carried off stage and the sound of clapping slowly beginning to fade. It wasn't until she opened her eyes that she had realized she had closed them. She was almost off the stage, but there were so many people waiting for her on the other side of the curtain. It was hot and loud, and she could not see or breathe, and the arms holding her were gone and people were talking to her, and she could not hear or think. *She could not breathe.*

"Dear God, is she alright?" a voice cried from somewhere far away.

"I just need to...lie down...my dressing room..." Christine whispered, grabbing onto whoever was holding her up. Was she flying? No, she was being carried. In the blink of an eye the familiar curves of her dressing room couch were under her body. Finally, she was home, she thought happily as she opened her eyes.

Christine gasped when she saw the face staring down at her. She had to be dreaming, she told herself as she drew back in confusion, trying to rise and failing. No, it wasn't a dream; Raoul de Chagny was really there, his beautiful face full of worry as he knelt beside her.

"Raoul..." The world was solid again. The noise was gone, and she was safe, with Raoul's warm hands clasped around hers.

"So, you do remember, little Lotte," he whispered, and her heart leapt.

"You're taller now," she breathed back. He grinned as bright as dawn.

"I knew you remembered, I knew it," Raoul beamed just as the door burst open.

"Christine! Are you alright? I have the doctor and—" It was Julianne, and the look she gave Christine and Raoul was scandalized. "Oh. And who is this?"

Just as suddenly as the world had steadied, Christine was in a storm again. This was wrong. Her angel had forbidden this, above all things! And she could sense him watching now. She could feel his rage and it took the breath from her lungs again.

"I-I don't know," Christine stammered, snatching her hands away. "This man helped me in here, but I don't know him."

"Christine? What are you saying?" Raoul asked. "The doctor is here; I think you should let him see you."

"Let me take care of her, Monsieur," Julianne said carefully. "There's quite a queue in the corridor of people that would like to speak to her." The Opera's doctor was standing in the open door, and Christine could hear the crowd now. She was going to be sick or swoon again.

"I'm sure Mademoiselle Daaé would prefer the company of a friend right now, she's obviously very distressed." Raoul countered. "While your help is appreciated, you are dismissed."

"I *am* her friend, you prat," Julianne hissed, and Raoul stood, clearly shocked to be spoken to in such a way. Christine tried to stand as well but found her legs wouldn't hold her. Julianne rushed to her side as she wobbled. "You look awful," Julianne muttered. Christine caught her own reflection and could not disagree. She was pallid as the grave.

"Christine, does your maid always use such a tone?" Raoul demanded and Christine finally found her voice.

"Please leave now," she ordered, digging deep for the last of her strength to stand tall and unsupported at last.

"Mademoiselle, I need to examine you, for your own good," the doctor demanded. Outside the noise increased. Someone was shouting. Christine wanted nothing more than to curl up in the darkest room with a hundred blankets and no sound but her angel's voice. But she had to hear him first. Assure him that her indiscretion had been a mistake.

"I need to be alone," she whispered to Julianne. "Please. Send everyone outside away too. Don't let anyone in. I just..."

"I understand," Julianne said with a grim nod. She turned to Raoul and the doctor. "Both of you! Out!"

"But Christine!" Raoul protested.

"Please go, Monsieur," Christine ordered. No one moved. "Now!" Christine yelled, shocking herself and finally breaking the spell.

Julianne pushed Raoul and the doctor from the room, even as they protested. Christine slammed the door behind them and leaned against the wood, gasping for air. The room was spinning again, and the applause was still echoing in her ear. Or was that her heart?

"Christine..." The Angel's voice was soft, concerned.

"I didn't invite him. I didn't know. I swear," she whispered, tears springing to her eyes. "I'm sorry. I'm so sorry."

"It's alright," he said, drowning out the noise in her head and the fading voices outside. There was only him now. "You were a wonder tonight. A glimpse of heaven on earth."

Now she did weep, letting out a sob of relief. "It was for you. All of it."

"Such a tribute, such a gift...it deserves a reward," his voice was strangely urgent but so enticing. It made her head spin in a different way. She could still barely stand, but she wanted to fly at the same time, filled with hope and joy.

"Please," she whispered, voice shaking. Her whole body was quivering. "I need you."

"Put out the light, my Christine," he ordered.

She felt delirious. Maybe she was. She extinguished the gaslight without hesitation and turned to the mirror, her heart still beating hard and erratic. She braced herself to see her pale reflection, illuminated by the low-burning oil lamp...

But instead she saw *him*. Her phantom. He stood within her mirror, next to her reflection, by some magic. And then her reflection was gone. His voice rose in a fragment of Faust's song to Marguerite, soft and secret, as he held out a hand to her.

"Let your hand forget itself in mine...let me adore your beauty..."

It was like a wave crested, every dream and desire she had nourished for months in the depths of her heart was suddenly real and overwhelming. He was there before her, beckoning her to his kingdom, his fingertips an inch from her as she reached out to him. And the second they touched, the cool tips of his fingers solid and real against hers, the tide overtook her.

The room swam into darkness, spinning around her as she collapsed. But once again, she did not fall to the ground. Once again, strong arms caught her, and she was floating, safe and loved...with him.

"I will take you somewhere safe," she heard him say from miles away. Then there was cold and dark. Movement. Then nothing.

Nothing but his voice.

He was singing to her softly, an old Romani tune. She was no longer in his arms. Somehow, she was on cold ground, solid as stone. But her head was cradled on something soft, and there was cool water against her brow. She could hear the sound of water too, as if they were near a fountain. How strange.

She was not shocked to see him above her when she opened her eyes. He was close, his white mask shining above her in the dark like the moon. His eyes met hers and she smiled as his voice faded. The dizziness and breathlessness were gone, though she was still weak. But at the same time, being close to him at last made her strong.

"Can you stand?" he asked softly. She nodded. She would climb a mountain if she asked her. He rose and helped her up with strong, steady hands. Although they were so cold. What she wouldn't do to have him hold her again though. If only...

The thought disappeared as he began to sing again, in a language both familiar and strange. The song was like nothing she'd ever heard. It reminded her of the folk ballads of her childhood, the ones that seemed to have grown out of the earth itself. But it was more sophisticated than that, like the refined melodies of the Opera. It was strange and beautiful and perfect, like all of her angel's songs. And she knew in her soul that this one was meant only for her. Her ghost held a dim lantern aloft, holding her hand as he guided her into echoing darkness.

Christine could barely see, but she didn't care. The sound of her angel's voice was more beautiful and enthralling than she had ever heard it. It was like a drug, she thought, if it could even be called a thought. She was flying, floating, and his hand was the only thing keeping her tethered to the ground. There was nothing but him: his hand, cold and calloused, but so real; and his shining eyes as they looked back at her, full of love and longing. Yet even those wonders were lost as she drowned in the sound of his voice.

They were descending, down countless darkened steps. Maybe she dreamed it, for she was not sure this wasn't a dream, but she thought she saw distant fires with dark shadows dancing before them. Then they were gone and once again they were going down, into a still, dark world of stone and damp shadows. The meager light of his lantern revealed great arches and pillars as they moved, but she didn't mark them. Not really. All she wanted to see was him. She didn't care if she was being swallowed by the earth or taken to heaven; she was with her angel. Nothing else would ever matter.

They stopped moving, but his song grew more enchanting, banishing every question or fear. Christine gasped as he gently pulled her close to him, his hand letting go of hers and slipping around her waist. She closed her eyes as the sensation of his arms lifting her once again overcame her.

She gripped him tightly, her breath catching in her throat. She was flying, wrapped in his wings, then she was prone once more and he was gone. The world was rocking and moving all around her, and the sound of water mingled with his song. She opened her eyes again and saw him above her, his eyes glittering in the blackness as he pushed a long pole beside him. Was this a boat?

As suddenly as it had begun, the rocking stopped, and he was holding her again. This time she wouldn't let him go; she swore it. Perhaps he sensed her determination because he kept her in his arms as they moved. Where they were, she could not say. Her eyes were half-closed, as he brought her somewhere warmer. It smelled like wax and paper and smoke and there was soft light. It only mattered to Christine because it meant she could truly see his eyes at last.

They were as sad and beautiful as she remembered, golden as the candlelight. But they were also full of love as he continued to sing to her. She gazed into the eyes of her angel and knew she had come home at last even as they moved somewhere darker.

He laid her down carefully onto a soft surface. A bed. It had to be. Her pulse quickened and she caught his hand as it came to her face, tracing her cheek and making her shiver as his song faded at last.

"I'm ready," she whispered, her body igniting at the touch, even as he drew back from her into the shadows. "Please, my angel, show me how I am yours," she begged him as she closed her eyes.

13. Shattered

"You can't stop there."

Raoul tore his eyes away from the door he had watched intently for half an hour and glowered at the man who had spoken. He was uniformed, with a ring of keys at his hip. A fireman. "I'm waiting for someone," Raoul said.

"Then wait somewhere else, you're in the way," the man replied. Raoul scowled and moved to let him pass. He had stationed himself where two halls met, one coming from the stage, the other going who-knows-where. A hundred people had to have passed him by now without complaint. But all he cared about was the still-shut door of Christine's dressing room.

He approached and earned a glare from the mulatto who had stationed herself outside as a guard. The impertinence.

"There he is!" Raoul spun at the sound of Philippe's voice. He was moving up the hall with his raven-haired dancer on his arm and another girl, thin and blonde, probably a dancer as well, in tow. Behind them was Antoine, leading a buxom woman that Raoul barely recognized out of Siébel's breeches.

"I told you he'd be here, sulking like a puppy at her door," Antoine chuckled, and Raoul's face burned.

"And there you are," the blonde said to Christine's maid of all people. "I – we had to take our costumes down all by ourselves. Where have you been?"

"I'm sorry," the maid stammered. "Christine needed me. She asked for privacy."

"Well, she's done with that now," Antoine's partner declared. What had he said her name was? Adèle? "Everyone is waiting to toast her triumph in the salon."

"I don't think she's ready," the maid protested as Adèle swept past her with infuriating ease. "Madame, please! She's feeling ill!"

"I promise to take her right home after," Adèle said and opened the door. "Christine, I hope you're – what is this?"

Raoul rushed after her into the room over the maid's cry of protest. The dressing room was dark. And completely empty.

"Where is she?" Raoul demanded as Adèle turned the light back up. He cast about, as if he could find Christine hiding in the closet or behind a screen.

"Dear Lord, have you lost her again?" Philippe asked from the hall.

Raoul turned to the maid. Her dark face was a tangle of guilt and worry. "Where did she go?" Raoul demanded. "I haven't left since you drove me out. No one came or went. Where did she go!"

"I don't know, sir!" the maid protested.

"This is a new kind of mysterious, even for her," the blonde girl said, bemused.

"Jammes be quiet," the maid snapped, further raising Raoul's suspicion.

"She's right though, Christine has a habit of...finding her own way home," Adèle declared, though Raoul could see worry in her eyes as well. "We should all go. I doubt she'd want us here."

"But—" Raoul was swept up as the women exited the dressing room into the hall.

"Well, if Christine's not bothering with it, I'm not going back to the salon," Sorelli declared. "Shall we go to my flat? I told the staff to have a late supper ready."

"That sounds lovely," Philippe replied. "Raoul, are you coming?"

"In a moment," Raoul called. Philippe and his coterie moved away down the hall, only Adèle looking back.

Raoul looked around, first to the dressing room – the door where he would have seen Christine leave – and then to the maid and her smug friend. "Are you *sure* there's no other way out of that room?" has asked, remembering the man's voice and how that villain had disappeared as well.

"I don't know, Monsieur," the maid replied. "The Opera is a strange place."

"Not so strange that people can just walk through walls," Raoul snapped and to his shock, the girl Jammes laughed.

"You haven't been around here much, have you?" the dancer sniggered, even as the maid glared at her.

"What are you talking about?" Raoul demanded, but the maid was already tugging the blonde away through the hall. "What did you mean by that!" Raoul called, moving to follow them just as a new visitor emerged from the bend in the hall, coming between Raoul and the females. For some reason, Raoul was not at all surprised to see the foreigner from earlier. He looked as worried and flustered as Raoul felt.

"She'll be safe!" the maid called over her shoulder as she disappeared.

"Who will be safe?" The foreigner asked, his perfect French surprising Raoul. "Mademoiselle Daaé?"

"You know Christine?" Raoul demanded. Was this him? The man who had spoken to her before? No, he would recognize that voice.

"No, but I had hoped to speak with her," the man replied.

"Well, you're too late, she's gone," Raoul said. The man's face grew grim in a way that made Raoul shiver. "Do you know where she might have gone to?"

"Nowhere we can reach her," the man muttered. Without another word he turned and walked away, leaving Raoul alone in the empty hall with nothing but questions.

Erik stood frozen, gazing at Christine as she lay in the bed. In *his* bed. He had not planned for this. Since Shaya had left the box, only one thought had driven him: getting her away from them all. From the Daroga and the managers and directors clambering at her door. And more than anything, away from the horrible, handsome boy who had carried her into the dressing room.

And so, Erik had taken her. He'd caught her as she fell and spirited her away into the dark, hypnotizing her with his song and her faith. He had become a strange Orpheus, leading his love into the underworld instead of out of it. The fleeting moments holding her had been maddening and magnificent. He had barely been able to let go. Even now, he wanted to embrace her again, to feel her warmth like the sun.

Her eyes opened, languid and unfocused as she searched for him. She was waiting for him. Waiting for him to reward her, to touch her as he'd promised. He'd told himself on the dark journey home that he would make his confession to her now. But how could he? How could he let her look at him with such trust and love, then break her heart and crush her soul?

"No, close your eyes," he whispered. He didn't want to be seen. Not now. Not as he was. Not as a monstrous man who had lied to her. He wanted to remain her angel. Just for a little while longer.

Her eyes closed and Erik's voice rose in song. The one he knew would inflame her. Their song. She responded immediately, her legs shifting as her hands alit on her bodice. She undid the laces halfway, just enough that she could tug the low collar of her shift to expose her breasts, kneading them as she did.

He followed her lead without thinking, throwing off his hat, cape, and coat; and tearing open the top buttons on of his stifling shirt. He drifted towards her, singing to her in words she did not know, but with meaning she had always understood. *"Close your eyes and forget all the world, in the dark you are mine, my love. From darkness you call me, and to darkness I lead you. But you are light, ever mine as I am yours."*

Her warmth called to him, and he was a moth to a flame, doomed and uncaring as he knelt on his bed and finally touched her. She whimpered as his fingers carefully traced the long curve of her neck, then her bare breasts rising and falling with strangled breaths. Without warning, her hand covered his, pressing his palm determinedly against the searing warmth of her skin.

The thrill was so intense that he shut his eyes. He could feel her heartbeat hammering as hard as his as she guided his hand across her breasts and a sigh escaped her lips. His voice was low and rough, praising her and entreating her with his song, and she pulled him closer still. He straddled her without thinking, suddenly trapping her beneath him as he found her unattended breast with his other hand, rolling her nipple between his fingers so that she sighed in delight.

Christine moved her hips beneath him. Not to escape, no; she was seeking more. But it was enough friction to alert him to his desperately hard cock. At the same moment, her free hand slipped between them to caress the bare skin of his chest, trailing up to his neck. Towards the mask.

He gasped, his song dying in his throat as panic seized him. Her touch *burned*, setting his skin ablaze with fear and memories of a hundred beatings, wounds, and scars. He acted on pure instinct, snatching her hands away from his skin and trapping them above her head in a powerful grasp.

"No," he breathed, and she whimpered in turn, squirming beneath him in a way that sent intoxicating pleasure to war with the fear and panic still screaming in his head.

"Please, don't stop, I need you," Christine begged, her voice distant and desperate. "Bind me, blind me. Anything. Please. Just don't stop."

He knew in that moment that he could take her. In her lust and faith, she would give herself entirely to her angel. He could have her now as he'd always dreamed. Her angel could make love to her this one time in the dark before he fell forever.

Erik held his breath, terrified, and tempted by the thought. He trapped her wrists against the pillow above her with one hand, undoing his belt with the other as he began to sing to her again. The belt slid free just as she sighed, lost in his song. She did not protest at all when he wove the smooth length of leather around her wrists. On the contrary, the restraint seemed to only increase her arousal.

"Please, take me, my angel, I'm yours, please..." she babbled as he rose. A silken kerchief was easy to find, assuring that no matter what, she would not open her eyes now. She was panting when he finished tying it, trailing his thumb over her lips as he drew away. One final touch then. He had placed the music box – a perfect copy of hers – on his bedside a week ago, so he too could have their secret song at his disposal beside him in the dark when he thought of her. And it would serve just as well now.

She turned her head curiously as the music box began to play. But in a second, she was under the spell again, just as he was. She lay on the bed at his mercy, her legs spreading as he freed his aching member from the confines of his trousers. It would be simple to sink into her, Erik thought, in horror and awe. She would open for him and cry out in joy as he filled her. He could imagine it so easily.

And imagining was all he would do, he swore to himself, as he took hold of straining member. It wasn't about his pleasure, not strictly. It was about saving her. But the Christine in his mind as he stroked his cock was different. Yes, in his mind she was just as beautiful, just as enthralled and overcome as she was now, as her body moved beneath his free hand. But she didn't sigh "angel" as she arched to seek him. Instead, he imagined her saying his real name. It would never happen, of course, but in the fog of his passion, he let himself dream it. He imagined what it would be like to be loved for himself, wanted by her. And he came with a shudder, spilling onto the sheets beside her.

The orgasm fogged his mind as much as it cleared it. He found himself above her once again, both hands on her now. He had saved them from the ultimate disaster, perhaps. But he still owed her an angel's reward, didn't he?

He continued touching her, letting go of all thought. The music he had used so many times to captivate her echoed in his own mind, whispering of forbidden delights. And why not listen? Why not give her all she desired and deserved? He pawed at her soft, quivering breasts and made her moan in slavish need. Why not drink of the devil's draught and sell his soul for his Marguerite?

Her whole body arched when his lips found her nipple. He suckled and licked, his hands busying themselves on her thighs and hips. Her legs spread easily and eagerly for him as he took his place between them on the bed. Like a starving man, he turned his attention to her other breast, loving the counterpoint of her sighs with the music that played just for them. He wanted to be slow, methodical, but she responded so beautifully to his attentions, to his lips and hands, that he found himself moving lower sooner than planned. All his plans had gone wrong tonight anyway, why not one more?

He pushed her skirts up to her ribs, caressing her as he did. She was bare underneath, no corset or drawers. She'd sung for him tonight like this, ready for *him*. He felt drunk, mad, and intoxicated as he kissed her belly, soft and smooth beneath his mouth and fingers. And then he moved lower, the scent of her drawing him like a siren. She trembled at the first touch of his finger to her dripping folds, the barest contact causing her hips to rise. He wanted more, wanted to give her more. He let his breath caress her, the music spurring him on.

"Please!" she cried, and he wondered distantly if she even knew what she was begging him for. Either way, he would give it.

It was there, safely hidden between her alabaster thighs that he truly lost all reason, helpless to desire. It would not do to have cold leather against that warm, welcoming skin. So, he removed the mask just as he claimed her. He held her hips steady, fingers digging into her soft flesh, and let himself taste heaven at last as he hid his face in the dark of her desire.

Christine gave a deep wail as his tongue found her and another as he began to explore her thoroughly. She tasted like ambrosia: salt and spice, hot and rich. He licked and sucked, testing her, and thrilling at her responses. Her cries of pleasure were louder than the music now, as something feral awakened in her with each movement of his tongue against her trembling sex. He could make out words at times, exclamations, and entreaties for him.

"More, please, more," she panted. "I need you in me. *More.*"

He could give her that too.

She opened so easily to his fingers, giving a strangled, satisfied gasp as he filled her. He kept up his tongue's ministrations as well, his focus intent on the swollen, hard nub just above where his fingers fucked into her, in rhythm to the music he had composed just for her. There were no more words in her cries now and he loved it. It was so different from the perfect music she had given him just an hour before, as she'd surrendered her soul to his power on Paris's greatest stage. Now, as he devoured her, far below in the dark, that same voice was broken and raw as she screamed out in ecstasy for him alone.

He could feel her climax approaching; her thighs stiffened, and the frantic rhythm of her hips froze, her body arching off the bed. She was suddenly silent, her cunt tight around his fingers, her pleasure cresting at his touch. But she needed one thing more.

"Now." He spoke the word into her flesh and the dam broke. She spasmed and bucked, breathlessly keening as he coaxed her to more. He wouldn't let her stop, not so soon, he wouldn't let her come down from these heights. He licked at her as fresh juices covered his hand and chin, a flood of delight made manifest as she cried out and convulsed again and again.

Too soon however, she collapsed, boneless and panting. He withdrew, his own breath ragged. He fumbled in the dark for his mask, panic rising in the naked moments until he replaced it. Only when it was secure did he unbind her hands, gently caressing her wrists where her restraint had left red marks. He righted their clothes, stealing a few more caresses as he did.

And then to his shock, she entwined her fingers with his.

"Hold me, please," Christine whispered, pulling him to her. He obeyed without question, folding her into his arms so that her head rested above his heart. He could feel her smile against his skin.

The music box had stopped playing, and the silence around them was gentle and soft. So was she, as she relaxed against him, blanketing him in warmth and contentment. There was so much he had to do. There were illusions to break and truths to tell. But it was so easy and perfect here in her arms. And he was so tired. He hadn't even taken off the blindfold around her eyes. He should do that and so many other things.

He hummed a lullaby and kissed her forehead instead, listening to the sound of her breath as she fell asleep in his arms. And he drifted to sleep in hers.

Raoul did not like Sorelli's flat. It was gaudy and overcrowded with trinkets, the exact kind of excess one might expect from someone new to the ability to spend money without care. Her selection of brandy was also miserable. Or maybe he was the one that was miserable, sitting in a corner with a half-empty glass while Philippe and Antoine laughed with their women. Meanwhile, Christine was lost.

"She'll be fine."

Raoul looked up into the face of Adèle Valerius. She had to be older than Antoine, but she was still rather beautiful, especially now, looking rather rumpled from whatever the two of them had been up to while Raoul stewed.

"You don't know that. Christine could be in the hands of some unscrupulous person," Raoul muttered. It sounded absurd to say it aloud.

"No, I don't know it, but I doubt it," Adèle said, joining Raoul on the settee. "Christine is strong and smart, and she always manages to find her way home. You do know she lives with me, don't you?"

Raoul's jaw went slack and then tensed again in anger. "Antoine did not mention that."

Adèle laughed. "He might not know, he doesn't pay attention to much."

"Does Christine have some paramour? You of all people must know."

"I'm not sure." It was not the answer that Raoul had expected and Adèle's face was unreadable. "I think there's someone. And she never denies it fully if I ask. But I've never seen her with anyone either. But, well, you heard her tonight."

"What do you mean?"

Adèle gave him a sympathetic look, like she might give a sweet, stupid child. "The way she sang, my boy. The way she always sings lately: like someone truly in love."

Raoul frowned. He couldn't argue with that. All he could do was hope against all reason that maybe that love was for him, and not this mysterious other. It was a foolish hope, he knew.

"Adèle! The wine!" Antoine yelled from another room and Adèle rolled her eyes.

"What on earth do you see in him?" Raoul asked, resigned.

"Well, he does have a massive...fortune." Raoul blushed to his ears and Adèle let out another husky, musical laugh. "Is that not enough?"

"He doesn't though, you know. Have a fortune," Raoul said without thinking and Adèle raised a dark brow. "He used to, but he's spent it all. Sold half his estates. In a year he'll have nothing if he's not careful. That's why he's hoping to marry my poor sister."

"Does Philippe know this?"

Raoul sighed again. "He does. But our father and Antoine's died on the same day in the same disaster. Philippe thinks that makes them brothers of a sort. As if he doesn't have a brother already with actual morals."

"Perhaps it's your hero's heart that he finds so tiresome," Adèle said, but her face and voice were kind. "Don't worry. I like it. I think Christine might too if she had the chance."

Raoul's heart leapt as she smiled. "Do you think I have a chance?"

"I have no idea, darling, and I do want you to be ready to have that heart of yours broken if she does belong to another."

"I'm willing to risk it."

Adèle sighed, patting her skirts as she stood. "Well, then I think I'll head home now to wait for her. To our flat. At number ten on *Rue Notre Dame des Victoires*," she said pointedly. "Do tell Antoine...something."

"Thank you," Raoul said, his hope surging. "I will call until she sees me."

"And what will you do if she tells you she's taken?"

Raoul set his jaw and his heart in determination. "I will ask who this man is and demand to speak with him, so I can tell him he should treat Christine with respect and honor. She deserves an honest man. A good man. Not someone who hides his face from society or the world."

Adèle looked at Raoul with a final, pitying sigh. "You are right, dear Vicomte, she does. But so few of us get what we deserve."

Christine dreamed of her father, standing by the sea. She could hear the pounding of the waves as she chased after him to the shore, trying to glimpse his face one last time. And then he was gone. It was just her and the endless, roiling ocean and far off, the boy she loved was pulled under the waves.

But it was alright. She wasn't alone. An angel was with her, holding her back from the void. The waves struck the sand in an insistent rhythm, even as the feel of his hands on her skin ignited a new fire within her. She tried to turn to see him, but he disappeared too, even though she could feel his breath against her skin.

"Christine, you have to see." Her father's voice was calling to her, sad and distant. Or was it the angel's? The waves beat harder. Louder. Loud as a heartbeat against her ear. But whose heart could beat beneath the sea? Was she drowning? "You have to *listen*."

Christine startled awake, the sound of a heartbeat still steady near her cheek. She blinked to no effect. Alarmingly, she couldn't see at all, but her head was resting against something warm. No. Some*one*. Because she had asked him to hold her, after.

The memory of the night before flooded back. The stage. The dark. The songs. The ecstasy more exquisite than anything she had ever dreamed. And her angel with her. He had covered her eyes. And now she was in his arms, listening to his heart and his breath;

pounding waves and the rising wind of a storm that was on the cusp of overwhelming her.

Christine's hand shook as she raised herself and pulled the blindfold from her eyes. She turned from him before she did. She couldn't look. Not yet.

The room was strange. The light of a few low-burning candles was swallowed by walls hung with black cloth, like the curtains in the wings and the floor was covered in dark, thick rugs. Amid the curtains were paintings that she could not concentrate on enough to make out. They were in a large four-poster bed like nothing she had ever seen, carved from ebony wood to look like it was still a living tree. The other furniture in the room was old-fashioned and mismatched. But the strangest thing was the complete lack of windows.

She remembered being led down so many stairs the night before and now it made sense. Her angel's home she was underground. But why would an angel need a home with a bed and carpets and candles?

She turned back slowly, her own heart pounding as she looked on her angel at last.

He was still asleep, his dark hair spread around his head in a cloud that nearly matched the black sheets of his bed. The visible skin of his neck and chest was deathly pale and somehow *wrong*. His hands were strange too, long and thin, with the same pallidness and odd texture. Christine shivered to remember how they had undone her the night before. All of him was lithe and angular, and even lying down she could tell he was tall. He was still wearing a mask, of course. He looked utterly vulnerable, lying in that bed in a peaceful slumber. And so completely human.

She could see him breathing. She had heard his heart.

A gasping sob escaped her throat, shattering the silence, and the stranger's eyes flew open. If there had been any doubt in her heart before then, there was none now, because the eyes that met Christine's were the same golden eyes she had seen last night and dreamed of for months before. Eyes that had made her believe in ghosts and angels in the dark.

Now they were full of human fear and heartbreak as they stared at her.

"Christine..." he said, reaching for her and she sprang away from him, off the bed.

It was the voice she knew better than her own. The voice she had thought was so beautiful it could only come from heaven. It was the voice that had told her so many beautiful things, that had saved her soul with so many promises. And every one of them had been a lie.

"Who are you?" she demanded, her voice breaking. He stood from the bed, coming closer and Christine stumbled back and away. He froze. The look in his eyes was one of utter despair. "What are you? Angels don't breathe. Ghosts don't have heartbeats and homes. *What are you!*"

"I am not an angel, or a ghost," he answered, quiet and ashamed, looking away from where Christine stood hunched with grief and rage as he tore her faith to shreds. "I'm just a man, and my name is Erik."

It was too much to hear it from his lips. She felt sick and trapped and more than anything, utterly betrayed. It was as if the world was crumbling under her feet, like this stranger standing before her had taken the one she loved and trusted most and killed him in cold blood.

"How could you?" Christine whispered, the enormity of his deception coming into focus. "How could you do this to me?"

"Christine, please..." the man who was not an angel entreated, stepping toward her with a hand outstretched.

"Don't touch me!" Christine screamed, slapping his hand away. "Don't you *dare* touch me!"

The man drew back, almost cowering. Was he shaking too?

She didn't care. "You *lied* to me."

"I've lied for years, it wasn't meant for just you," he defended himself weakly, refusing to look at her as her fury rose like a storm.

"No! You made me believe in an *angel*! Not a ghost!" she growled. "Why?"

"I wanted to help you." He raised his hands in an entreaty. "I never meant to hurt you."

"But you lied to me!" Christine shouted and the man flinched away again. "Why me? Why take everything I ever wanted and destroy it? Why be an angel?"

"It was what you wanted!" he cried out, turning completely away from her, and retreating. "You asked for an angel, and I gave it to you."

"So why did you take it away!" She screamed the question, the force of her fury shocking even her. He still refused to look at her, leaning against the wall, his shoulders heaving as he panted.

"I had to," he protested with difficulty, as if he was in more pain than her. How dare he play the victim now. "He was going to tell you. I didn't want you to find out from someone else. Please, try to understand—"

"Understand? *Understand*?" Rage propelled her as she raised her fist to strike him. And something unearthly moved him as he spun and caught her wrists in his skeletal hands.

"Christine, please—" he begged.

"I built my life on you!" she shrieked, not even bothering to struggle. "I lived for *you*! And it was all lies! Everything I believed – everything I cared about was a lie. What an idiot I am. Did you laugh when you made me such a fool? I gave you *everything*!" Christine stared at the man who had so easily destroyed her, infuriated by his silence. For months, his words had nourished her just as they had poisoned her. Now he had nothing to say. No explanation, no defense.

"I put my soul in your hands, and you took it all away. Tell me: what must I *understand*?" she continued through clenched teeth. "You took every dream I had and distorted it to lies and for what? Just so you could..." she grew sick at the thought of the night before and so many others. "So that you could make me your toy? Your whore? God, you didn't even tell me! You waited for me to find out until after you'd taken what you wanted!"

"No!" he protested and dropped her wrists like they burned him. "Christine, no, that's not...I never..."

"How could you *use me* like that?" she asked, soft and ashamed. "How could you let me—"

"Because I love you!" he burst out and Christine fell back in shock. "I love you," he confessed again, his voice small as he looked down at the ground.

Christine grimaced in disgust. She had known with joyful certainty that her angel loved her but the idea this terrible man should love her was unthinkable.

"You love me?" Christine whispered. "You *love me*, and still you lied to me?" She stalked towards him fearlessly, rage cresting again. "How can you even dare to say that after what you've done?" She was within inches of him again, her voice rife with righteous venom. He still would not look at her.

"Christine, I'm sorry. I never meant for it to be this way," he whispered as he closed his eyes.

Christine shook her head and contemplated the masked face a breath away from hers. Now that she wasn't looking him in the eyes, the mask itself came to her attention. "Yes, you did. You concealed the truth from me. You used me. You hid from me...and you're still hiding from me, still lying."

His eyes flew open. "Christine, *please*, forgive me."

Christine set her chin grimly and shook her head. "No, my angel, forgive me." Without another thought, she tore the mask from his face.

Christine did not understand what she saw at first, as the mask fell with a dull thud on the floor. It wasn't a face. It couldn't be. It was a tangle of horror, inhuman and unthinkable. The nose was like a skull's: a snubbed, ghastly hole. His eyes were sunken too, deep in a face covered in what might have been skin had it not been so pale and sickly, save for the white and red of terrible scars. She was looking at a corpse with living eyes. The face of death itself. She had been wrong, she thought, as she began to shake, sickened by the hideous sight. This was not a man: this was a monster.

The thing in front of her blinked, watching her in terror as she stared. Then slowly that terrible face distorted as fire kindled in his eyes. Christine spun away. She had to run.

"No!" Instantly, he pounced on her, grabbing her wrists again, but this time his grip was like iron. He turned her back to him and she shut her eyes. "Look at me!"

"No, please!" she yelped as he pulled her closer.

"*Look at me*!" The command was as cold as death, and she obeyed out of pure fear. "You wanted to see, didn't you? Well look! Feast your eyes on my curse!" the monster roared and pushed his distorted visage inches from her. "Glut your goddamned soul!"

Christine heaved a dry sob as she struggled uselessly to get away. "Stop!"

"Do you like it? Or do you think it's another mask you can tear away? Let's try!" He grabbed her hands and forced her nails into the terrible, cold flesh, leaving livid gashes behind that made the sight all the worse.

"No!" she sobbed. "Please! Stop!"

"Why don't you scream, my love?" he snarled and shook her roughly. "People pay good money to see monsters so they can shriek:

it's *our* payment you see. It's my recompense for the crime of this face. Shall I tell you how they locked me in a cage so they could scream? Or how they drove me into the dark? Shall I tell you how I took my revenge? Oh they screamed then!"

"You're hurting me!" she wailed as he tightened his deadly grip on her wrists.

"Then scream, Christine! Show me you're like them! Prove it! I can see it in your face. I can *see* your horror! Please, don't try to be polite and hide it. Scream!" he roared, viciously shaking her. "Scream just like all of them! If you don't, I will have to keep you forever, here in our tomb! Would you like that? No? Then *scream*!"

The scream that tore out of her throat burned and cut, filling the room with the desiccated sound of her terror and complete despair. It went on and on, stealing the last breath from her lungs and blotting out the world. She screamed for him and for all the pain and rage and loss. She screamed and he let go of her at last, stumbling away out of her vision. In the silence, she fell to the floor like a corpse.

Christine lay still on the floor and waited.

She waited for his blows or threats to materialize. She waited for her tears to come, for a sob to move her. Shouldn't she cry now if she was doomed? She hurt, heart and body and soul. And she'd cried since she realized the truth. But she couldn't. She couldn't waste time crying when what she had to do for the next few minutes was survive. Right now, she chose to survive.

She looked up, her eyes clear at last.

The man called Erik was curled in the corner, weeping bitterly, and hiding his face beneath his arms. Christine felt a swell of terror as she looked at him, even without seeing his abhorrent face, but it abated as she watched him rock back and forth. Maybe it was because he seemed so small and scared there in the corner. Or perhaps it was the sound of his weeping that eased her horror...because it wasn't just weeping. It was a song. An old folk tune with words in English.

"*There were three ravens sitting on a tree...with a down, a down, hey down, hey down,*" he sang to himself in a thin, childish voice. But it was still beautiful. So very beautiful and incredibly sad. "*They were as black as black could be...*" he sang in the voice that still sounded like heaven, deep in this hell.

This broken man was all that was left of her angel, of the world she had known until her eyes had opened that morning. And she had destroyed him, perhaps more surely and thoroughly than he had destroyed her. Or maybe he had been broken for a long time and she had simply shattered him again. How could he not be, to live with a face like that? To hide deep in the earth, alone? The pitiful thing she looked at now had to be the saddest sight she had ever seen.

Christine crawled toward him carefully, fighting back waves of fear as she retrieved his mask from where it had fallen on the floor. He flinched as he sensed her movements, the way a child braced for a new beating, cowering more fully into himself.

"*Then one said unto his mate, where shall we our breakfast take...*" he sang louder, as if it were a spell to protect him. Maybe it was because his voice reminded her of what he had been. And looking at this strange, monstrous creature hiding away in the dark, Christine's rage and fear were gone, replaced by pity so deep it broke her heart.

"Here," she said softly, holding up his mask, only for him to flinch again. "I'm sorry I took it."

She did not know if he heard her, he only sang, reminding her with each pitiful note that once, she had loved that voice. "*Down in yonder great green field, with a down, a down, hey down, hey down; there lies a knight slain neath his shield, with a down, hey down...*"

"Erik," she said the name softly and he stopped singing, his breath ragged. From the shelter of his arms, he looked at her at last, hiding his face behind his arms and long hair as much as he could, but not entirely. Christine braced herself for revulsion, but it didn't come. The anger in his gold eyes had faded to pure misery. These were the eyes she had seen in the dark months ago and now she knew why there had been such sadness in the Opera Ghost's gaze.

Her hands shaking, she took a deep breath and held the mask out to him. He watched her without moving and slowly she saw a change in his expression, if any expression could be discerned from the horrific tangle of his dead features. She could hardly bear to look at his face, but his eyes were different. In the ocean of despair and loneliness, there was a flicker of hope.

He reached for the mask, hand trembling, and took it from her. The moment he grasped it, he replaced it with incredible defensive speed. His body relaxed, just a bit, and his breath slowed.

"I'm sorry," Christine breathed after a moment.

"As am I," he replied softly. He sagged back against the wall, watching her. "Now you know...why." He gestured towards his face as if it caused him great pain.

She nodded. It was harder not to be afraid when he was silent, but his eyes helped. She looked around the strange room rather than at him even so, feeling lost. Was there even a door?

"Can I go home?" she asked and knew immediately it was the wrong thing to say. His head tilted and his eyes filled with fresh despair.

"But you are home. The Opera is your home," he said, fearful and entreating.

"We're still in the Opera?" Christine asked back, trying to stem her panic and he nodded absently. "How...where are we?"

He looked at her curiously, again giving her the impression of a fearful child, or even an animal worried it would be beaten again. "I can't tell you."

"But..."

"How can I trust you?" he asked, suddenly urgent. "You could tell them. The managers and the police or the Daroga and that boy. You could send them after me if I tell you the secret. Or if you go."

She could see his mind racing as fast as hers, and perhaps his panic and fear were as great. "I won't..."

He tensed, again like an animal, but this time a cornered one ready to pounce. "I won't let them put me in a cage again, Christine, I *won't*."

"You can't keep me in one either," she said with all the firmness she dared and the coiled tension in his shoulders fell slack. "I won't tell anyone, I swear it," Christine went on, unsure of if she meant it. "Just let me go home."

"No, you can't. You have to stay..." he protested, pathetic and penitent.

"Why would you want me to? Why do you want me here now that I know?" Christine asked. Truly she had no idea what this man wanted from her as a prisoner in this dark place. He looked confused by the question, as if it was so simple.

"I told you, I..." he stopped. He had to know how obscene his words of love were, now that she had seen him. He swallowed and looked at her earnestly. "I would rather stay in your light, whatever you'd give me, than be alone again without you. I can be good for you, I swear, I can still help you. I can still be something to you. If you just—"

"If you want that, I need to trust you. You need to trust me." Erik caught his breath at the sound of the words and Christine's heart fell at the flare of hope in his haunted eyes. "And if you ever want me to trust you again, you have to let me go."

"If I free you...there a chance?" he asked, pathetic and penitent.

Was there? Was there a place in her life for this fallen angel who had once been the very foundation of it?

"Yes," she whispered. She truly did not know if it was a lie, but she knew he believed it. He was desperate to. "If you just let me go. Earn my trust, let me earn yours. Please, Erik."

"Alright," he murmured softly. "But you must come back."

"What?" She looked at him in fresh shock, and his gaze was nearly wild.

"I'll send you back up there, I'll trust you so that you'll trust me, and then you have to come back. If you want to...to know all the answers and be my student and..." His voice faded and Christine tried to steady her breath. Perhaps he wasn't ordering, perhaps he was begging. "Please, Christine. You don't know how dark it is here without you."

She shut her eyes to hide the tears that bloomed there, pity once again overtaking her. There it was. An immense, tragic love laid at her feet, too great for her to bear or comprehend. Slowly, she nodded.

"Come then." He stood swiftly and walked away across the room.

Christine rushed to follow him out the door into another space. The room was even stranger than his bedchamber, packed with books and candles and a piano and...no, she had to be dreaming now, there could not be an entire pipe organ here.

"This way."

She jumped at the sound of his voice close behind her and he flinched away from her as she spun. He had put on a long, hooded cape and looked every inch the Phantom now.

"I'll take you the back way, we won't need to use the boat," he said, as if that made any sense. Without further explanation, he turned and walked to an ornate door that opened to pure darkness. But the smell from the blackness where he disappeared was something like walking by the Seine.

"Did you say boat?" Christine asked, scurrying after him into the dark. Instantly a cold hand caught her wrist, stopping her at the edge of some sort of wooden walkway.

"Be careful, my kingdom is a dangerous place," Erik said, and in the damp, echoing dark his voice was also a ghost's once again. From somewhere he produced a lantern, and Christine was sure she saw the meager light reflected in glassy water.

He moved without a sound as he led her through the oppressive dark. He only stopped a few times, listening at the base of a staircase or a crossroad beneath a stone arch for movement ahead. Otherwise, he seemed to know the labyrinth like he was walking in broad daylight, all the while keeping a steady grip on her wrist. At last, they came to dead end. He turned back to her as he hung the lantern on a rusty hook on the dark stone wall.

"I cannot take you any further," he told her as he released her at last. She rubbed the smarting place his hand had been.

"Where are we?" she asked, shivering from fear and the oppressive chill. She was still wearing her damn costume from the prison scene, and she could feel the cold from the ground through her insubstantial slippers.

"Where I first met you," he answered wistfully, as he pushed the wall open, to reveal a heavy gate at the back of the Opera stables on the *Rue Scribe*. A horse whinnied as if to greet them.

"How..."

"No answers yet," the Ghost cut her off. Christine turned, ready to fix her guide with a look of annoyance, but her ire melted away when she met his eyes. Once again, they were full of sadness, but also hope and, yes, she could see it too, love.

"I can go?" she asked trying to calm her breath as it caught in her throat.

"Do you promise; not to tell them where I am?" His voice was tenuous as he held her gaze. "If you send them for me, people will be hurt. Either them or me."

"I promise," Christine whispered, shuddering at the thought of what the authorities might do to Erik. Or what he would do to them.

"You're cold," he said, and without ceremony he swept his dark cape off and placed it around her shoulders, carefully fastening the clasp. Without it, he was just a man again, one who looked at her with fear and love in equal measure. "And can you promise to come back?" he asked, sad and supplicant.

Christine swallowed as she stared at him. If she said no, he might snatch her right back to the void they had just escaped. But if she said yes...

"I don't want to lie to you," she whispered. "I need time."

"You have...until tomorrow night," Erik answered, his voice unsteady. "Come back here at sunset, and I will be waiting. If you are not here when night falls, I'll know I have lost you and I..."

He shut his eyes tight as if the thought hurt too much to bear, and when those eyes opened again, it was like he transformed, as if donning another mask. His eyes were bright with danger and darkness, unquestionable and undeniable as they fixed on her with devastating need.

Christine gasped as the Phantom before her raised his hand and trailed his cold fingers over her cheek. It was barely a touch, the sort that had set her on fire when she had thought it was an angel caressing her. Somehow it still made her head spin. They both knew he was touching her for what might be the last time. Would he be able to bear it if it was, she wondered? Would she?

"Come back to me," the ghost who was not a ghost whispered, beseeching, and yet an unquestionable command. For the slightest moment he leaned towards her, and Christine was sure he would kiss her. The thought made her whole body shudder with fear *and* desire.

Erik withdrew his hand instantly, backing away from her into the shadows. They swallowed him entirely in a few steps, leaving only his mask visible. He inclined his head in a small nod, telling her without words that she was free. For now.

Christine turned away, gulping for air at last. She walked unsteadily into the stables, pulling his cloak tighter and feeling the last traces of his warmth. He *had* been warm, not cold like a corpse. When she turned back, he was gone.

The morning light, even behind the clouds, hurt her eyes and the carriages along the street were like thunder. Christine walked, forcing herself to move with each step, telling herself she was safe now, she was free. She could keep walking and never return if she was strong enough. She could not even look at the Opera as she skirted the back, to the *Boulevard Haussmann*. Nor did she look up as she made her way east towards home. Was it home? He had been right when he said that the Opera was her home, in her heart; or it had been until an hour ago.

She was as surprised to find herself on the *Rue Faydeau* as Élodie Bonet was to see her when she opened the door of the flat.

"My God, girl, what has happened?" Élodie asked in horror. Christine wondered how she must look, like a madwoman with wild hair and pale skin. She was nothing compared to him though.

"Christine?!" Julianne yelled, rushing to the door, and catching Christine as she collapsed in her arms. "Bloody hell, I thought you were lost! I heard a voice in your room and then you were gone and—"

"Please don't ask me," Christine whispered into Julianne's shoulder as her friend held her tight. "I'm never going back," she said at last and finally the dam broke. Her tears fell, her body shaking with sobs as Julianne guided her inside.

"It's alright, you're safe now," Julianne said. "It's over."

14. Returned

Erik's joints ached from sitting so long on the cold stone in the cellars. He had barely made it a few steps after letting Christine go before collapsing, fresh tears and agony stealing his breath and his very will to move. How could everything have gone so wrong so quickly? How had he ever thought there was a chance it could go right?

It was in moments of self-loathing like this that he saw himself the clearest, unmasked, and undone. He was not some ghostly genius; he was a fool who never thought beyond the next second. From the moment he'd seen her, just yards away from where he wept now, he'd acted on every impulse and desire. For three months he had thought of nothing but her and look where it had led him. He was pathetic, humiliated, broken in every way. All because a lost girl had stumbled into his path. Because he had seen her kindness and pity, and in his heart, hoped it would extend to a monster like him.

That had been his dream all along, hadn't it? To steal the light of her kindness for himself. Had he thought she would love him if she knew he was a man? Maybe. But now the thought made him laugh bitterly into the dark.

He sounded like a madman. Perhaps he was one and always had been. He'd gone mad when she tore off his mask. He'd died when she screamed at last.

Erik shrank, curling into his body and making himself small. Safe. He did not know which had hurt more: her heartbreak at the truth or her horror at his face. But those he had expected. Those made sense. Her rage though...he had not been prepared for that. He wished he could erase the memory of her raised fists and furious accusations. But he had deserved it. He was a villain and a monster.

Around him the shadows swayed, restless and haunted, as the lantern flame danced. And they whispered, as they had since he came here. They wept. It had only been since he met her that he had been able to drown out the sound of their suffering with her voice. There was part of him that could admit it now, that he hated his prison down deep in the dark. This was a place for ghosts, for the monstrous dead. Christine would do well to never return to his world again.

But he wanted her to. He had begged her to. And he had to believe that she might. Erik rose slowly, lifting his lantern to drive the shades away. He would not go back to a world without her light, not now. A seed of hope, planted by the compassion he had seen in her eyes, waited in the dark. And he would hold onto that. There was no other choice if he was going to live through the next few days. So that's what he would cling to in order to fill the hours. He would work and build, for her. He would remember that she was kinder than him.

And if she is not? The ghosts around him asked. *What if she does not return?*

Why then, another shadow deep within him answered, he would have to convince her.

Christine wasn't sure how to move now that she had finished crying. She had cried until she couldn't anymore, rocked in Julianne's arms. Julianne had been the one to summon the carriage and guide Christine home. Adèle had gasped and clucked over her when Julianne had led her in their door, but Christine hadn't spoken. She was numb and frozen, unable even to comprehend the events of the last night and day or how she had survived them.

There were soft voices outside her room.

"What happened to her?" Adèle demanded again in a stage whisper.

"I don't know! She won't say!" Julianne hissed back. "She won't even let me take the thing off her she came home in."

Reflexively, Christine pulled the cloak closer around her shoulders. She didn't know why she was holding onto it. It was from *him*, the one who had lifted her to heaven then cast her back into this hell. But the feel of it wrapped around her was comforting. It reminded her of the angel that had protected her, and not the terrifying man who had lied to her. Or the hideous thing that said he loved her and begged her to return to him.

"Come on, you're going to help me," Adèle ordered and a moment later the door opened.

Christine opened her eyes. She hadn't realized they were closed. The fragment of sky she could see from her bed had faded from gray to gaslit orange. The sun was gone and when it set tomorrow, he would know she was gone too. Forever.

The last time she had felt this way had been after Papa's funeral, when there was nothing left to do after he had been sealed away in the cold ground. Once those tears had ebbed, she had not cried again for months. She'd just been a ghost; listless, lifeless, and empty. And she'd stayed that way, until *him*. Now the angel she had loved was dead too.

"Let's wash you up," Adèle said gently as she and Julianne came close. "You look a mess."

Julianne touched her first, just her shoulder and Christine recoiled, pulling the cloak tighter. "It's alright, we'll give it back," Julianne whispered, finally catching Christine's eyes. She breathed deep, glancing towards Adèle.

"I...Can you get me some food?" Christine asked. She didn't want Adèle to see. Not yet.

"Alright. You take care of her," Adèle replied and left Christine and Julianne alone. Once the door was shut, Christine loosened her grip on the cloak and let Julianne pull it off.

"That's a girl," Julianne said with a smile. "Wait, are you..." She was staring at the costume Christine still wore. "Christine, how?"

Christine swallowed and finally stood on shaky legs. She let Julianne undress her just as if it were after a performance. It was careful, gentle. She put Christine into a nightgown before she could be exposed to the cold air. She was almost safe until Julianne looked at her wrists.

"There are marks here," Julianne said. It wasn't a question. "Christine. You disappeared in your costume. I heard a voice in your dressing room. *His* voice."

"He took me," Christine whispered. If there was one person in the world she could trust, it was Julianne.

"*How?*" Julianne asked and Christine shuddered.

"I don't know. I don't understand any of it," Christine replied, tears threatening again. She didn't know how she had moved from her dressing room to the cellars. She didn't know how a man could pretend to be a ghost and convince everyone. The only one who knew those answers was Erik.

"Did he hurt you?" Julianne demanded. "If he did, whatever he is, I will make him pay."

"No. Please." Christine shook her head, drawing her wrists to her chest and retreating to the bed. "He didn't. I don't think he would do that." She remembered his hands like shackles on her wrists as he forced her to look at him, but the image melted away to the picture of a pathetic, broken man weeping on the floor and cowering away from her.

"If it was *him*, I think he might," Julianna said carefully. "Christine, he's hurt people. Hasn't he? Like Buquet."

"Buquet…" Christine gulped even as she wrapped herself in the cloak again. He'd given it to her in tenderness, to keep her warm. Had the same man thrown Buquet from the flies to the stage? Had he done it for her? Again, more questions with answers she'd never know, unless she went back. "I don't know."

Christine shut her eyes again, as a knock came on the door before Adèle entered with a tray. "Well, you moved. That's a good sign." Adèle said, sitting on the bed and placing the tray between them. "Is she talking?" she asked Julianne.

"A bit," Julianne replied.

"I'm not deaf," Christine snapped, trying to glare. Adèle only gave her a kind smile.

"Good," Adèle said. "Eat. You too," she added to Julianne. They chewed the bread and cheese dutifully, and then Adèle pressed a cup of wine into just Christine's hands. Christine drank it under Adèle's discerning gaze. "Good girl."

"I'm sorry if I scared you," Christine muttered into the cup, taking another swig. It tasted strange and sour, but maybe everything would taste strange now.

"I knew you'd be alright," Adèle said with a glance to Julianne. "That's what I told your Vicomte last night. And today when he called."

"Raoul was here? Why?" Christine asked, her heart jumping.

"He was there last night, he saw your dressing room empty," Julianne explained. Her face was still grim as she sat on the end of the bed with Adèle. "He was as worried. All of us were."

Christine closed her eyes, a new weight on her. She had not even thought of Raoul since the night before when he'd left her room. But Erik had said something about "that boy." He clearly did not want a rival. Did that mean Raoul was in danger?

"I told him you were all right. He'll be back tomorrow I'm sure," Adèle sighed then looked to Julianne. "You can come back tomorrow too if you like."

"I'm not leaving," Julianne snarled. "She needs—"

"She needs rest," Adèle stopped her as she rose and guided Julianne to the door. "I promise I'll take care of her."

"It's alright, Julianne," Christine said. "I'll be fine." That was a lie, but it worked. The other women left her alone as Adèle showed Julianne to the door and Christine nursed the cup of wine. It was better each sip and suddenly it was all gone.

When Adèle returned she handed Christine a fresh cup. "She'll be back. Like everyone else. I'm sure Raoul de Chagny will be interested in your broken heart when he returns."

"My heart isn't..." Christine protested but she couldn't finish the lie.

"Isn't it?" Adèle said as she sat back down. "I heard you sing last night, Christine, and I knew you'd done exactly what I told you not to and fallen in love. And then you disappear into thin air and show up like this. What else am I to think?"

"I..." Christine had no idea how she could explain her woes to Adèle. But she wanted to try. She needed to. "I gave my heart to someone who doesn't exist," she said softly, her heart breaking again as she admitted it. "The one I loved is gone. He was never there."

"Doesn't mean that the love goes away," Adèle murmured, her thumb running over her left ring finger, as if she was remembering a wedding band that used to be there. She shook herself from the remembrance. "So, he lied to you about something important. I hate to be the one to tell you, but all men lie. So do women."

"Not like this." Christine could barely comprehend the magnitude of it herself. "I was so stupid to believe him."

"Did he tell you he was rich, and it turns out he's penniless?" Adèle asked bitterly. "Or did you find out he's married and the life you thought you'd have with him is impossible?"

Christine didn't reply, she had no idea how to. She had been a fool to believe, but the illusion had been so convincing. And then there was his voice and his music. Those had not been illusions, they had come from a real, flesh and blood man. How was such beauty possible from a monster?

"It doesn't matter," Christine muttered. "It's over." It made her sick to say it. It made her remember his eyes, full of suffering, staring at her from the dark.

"That might be unwise."

Christine looked up in confusion and the quick movement made her head spin. "What?"

"This man, the one who hurt you. It's your singing teacher, isn't it? The one you won't talk about."

"How did you know?"

Adèle shrugged. "Because no one could sing like you did without a maestro's guidance, and every studio in Paris wants to know who yours is, even my teacher. And any time I saw you after what you called practice you looked like you'd been doing more than singing."

Christine buried her face in her hands in shame, recalling every wanton display for her angel, now knowing he was just a man. "I...He..." Christine didn't think she had any tears left, but they still sprang to her eyes as she looked back to Adèle, whose face grew grim.

"Christine, did he force you?" Adèle asked, uncharacteristically serious.

"No," Christine declared, shocking herself with her own vehemence. She knew with a burning shame that everything he had done to her she had wanted, begged for even. "We never even...I mean, I'm still a virgin. I think?"

Adèle let out a dark laugh. "Virgin is a word men invented thousands of years ago to get better prices when they sold us. So, he never fucked you?" Christine shook her head slowly. "Hmm. What did he do?"

"He…" Christine didn't know why she was talking, but her tongue was loose, and the past had started to feel strangely distant. "He used his hands on me. And his mouth."

"My my," Adèle cooed. "And what did you give him back?"

Christine blinked slowly. "Nothing. He didn't ever ask for anything…back." Even when she had begged for him the night before, he hadn't taken her, Christine thought foggily. Why hadn't he? Did he not want her? He said he loved her…but all he had ever wanted from her was her voice. What did he want from her now?

"Well, how was it?" Adèle's eyes sparkled, ever the gossip. Christine looked away, slowly. She didn't want to think about it, but how could she not? How could she ever forget the heights he'd taken her to.

"It was the greatest pleasure I've ever known." Her head swam to remember it. She had never experienced a peak so intense or prolonged. Did that pleasure await her again if she returned to him? What would it be like to experience his music and the way it entranced and consumed her, knowing it came from a man? Did he expect her to return to his bed if she came back? Did she want that? "But now I know he's…" she argued with herself out loud.

Now she knew he was hideous and dangerous. That should matter, but her horror didn't rise again at the thought. Why was she not afraid now, as she tried to remember?

"So, on the one hand, he lied," Adèle said, pushing the cup in Christine's hands to her lips and guiding her to another sip. "And on the other, he's a brilliant teacher that does things between your legs most men think themselves above and makes you come. Then there's your career to think about."

"My career?" Christine echoed.

"If you truly end it with him, you won't have anyone to help you make your way. That's what I mean by unwise. I can't do much for you, and with what I'm worried Carlotta has in store, you'll need support."

"I wouldn't have a career without him," Christine said slowly, the gravity of it settling in her stomach like a stone. Did her career even matter?

She couldn't even dream of singing again now, not without her angel and teacher. Erik had offered to keep teaching her, he was all there was left of the angel that had inspired her, but how could they go on? And yet, how could she even expect him to tolerate her in his opera if she rejected him? The choice was between her life as she knew it and nothing. The thought did not fill her with anger or terror, it only made her tired.

"So, the question becomes: Are you going to accept this scoundrel with all his lies? Or are you holding out for Raoul de Chagny?"

Christine shook her head sadly at the suggestion, again feeling sweetly numb at the thought.

"Does he love you?"

"He says he does," Christine whispered, recalling his eyes and his protestations.

"Do you love him?"

"I can't," Christine protested instantly, recalling his lies and his face. How could she ever even consider it? "Not now. Not anymore."

"Good. It's better if they love you more than you love them, easier to keep them in check."

"I can't control him. I..." Christine couldn't find the words. She didn't even know where to look for them.

"Shh, no more worries tonight." Adèle stroked a lock of hair away from Christine's face, brushing her cheek just the way he had.

The memory made her shiver and close her eyes. She found that it was incredibly hard to open them again.

"What else was in that wine?" Christine asked dreamily, glancing at the empty cup in her hand and feeling another wave of exhaustion wash over her.

"Laudanum."

Christine gave a small, tragic laugh as she lay back on the bed. Once again, she'd been led astray.

"You need rest," Adèle commanded. Christine shook her head weakly, pushing away thoughts of his voice in the shadows and falling asleep feeling safe in his arms.

"I can't...It reminds me of him..." Christine protested, suddenly terrified of the dreams that awaited and overcome by the feeling of the warm, dark fabric of his cloak being wrapped around her. It still carried the faint scent of him, of smoke and shadow.

"What does?" Adèle asked from far away, and her voice sounded like darkness.

"Everything," Christine breathed, and the world faded to black.

Erik moved deliberately through the catacombs. These tunnels beneath Paris were not like the labyrinth under the Opera where no one came for fear of a vengeful ghost. Here there was still much to fear, but people and things braved the dark despite the peril, making them all the more dangerous. As a terror of the shadows himself, Erik knew this all too well.

Erik barely made a sound as he swept through the hidden roads beneath the city, through air thick with the scent of earth and decay. His journey out of his corner of the underworld had been successful, or at least a good distraction from the maddening and heartbreaking thought of Christine. She had said there was a chance. She had to come back. Each time he told himself that he thought of a new reason why she would never return, and why she would be wise to do so.

Erik froze in his stride, listening to the darkness as he approached the entry to the Opera cellars. He was accustomed to strange sounds down here, echoes of ghosts who had been in residence far longer than his six and a half years. This sound, though it was angry and eerie, was not otherworldly.

Someone was down in his cellars, and they were yelling. There was only one man in Paris who would be so bold and stupid.

"Come out and face me!" Shaya screamed into the darkness around his lantern's halo of light as Erik approached. "I know you're there, you coward!"

"Then there's no need for such a racket," Erik replied with a sigh.

The Persian spun to face him; his right hand raised to the level of his eye. Smart. He did not move or take another step, careful to keep as much distance between himself and Erik as possible. "Where is she?"

"You'll need to be more specific," Erik drawled back.

"Don't fucking play with me, Erik, where is Christine Daaé?" Shaya demanded, the catacombs around echoing with his ire.

"Well, I am sure I don't know," Erik answered innocently. Ironically, he wasn't actually lying. "Did you not get a chance to speak with her as you hoped? That's too bad."

"She disappeared from her dressing room without a soul seeing where she went!" Shaya pushed and Erik took a deliberate step towards the smaller man.

"I only removed her so that you would not frighten her and ruin things," Erik replied calmly, advancing once more so that Shaya had no choice but to back up against the moist stone of the cellar wall.

"Tell me where you have her then."

"I don't have her anywhere."

Fire in his eyes, Shaya took the risk of lowering his hand from his face, only to pull out his pistol and aim it at Erik. "I shall ask one more time."

"And I will tell give you the same answer," Erik replied, keeping his voice calm even with the pistol aimed at his heart. Maybe he could entice Shaya to fire it and end this misery for all of them. Wouldn't that be nice? "I don't know. I sent her home."

"And why would you do that?" Shaya balked. "You don't give up your toys."

"You do not know me as well as you think then, Daroga," Erik replied, cold and calm. How could he explain that this was the only way to earn her trust and that he had perhaps made the greatest mistake of his life by letting her leave?

"Erik, I swear," Shaya growled and cocked the pistol.

"Go ahead and shoot me then if you don't believe me. If I'm the monster you say, then she'll be trapped in my lair, scared and alone with no way out," Erik intoned, imagining his home as Shaya might, a place of cages and torture, not the warm haven he wanted to make for her. "Shoot me and kill her. Or shoot me and find out that I'm telling the truth; kill me for no reason other than your gutless hate."

Shaya stared at him in the dark for an endless moment, jaw twitching. Erik wondered if this was at last the end of their chess game and wished he had been fool enough to kiss Christine just once before his life met its inevitable bloody end.

Shaya uncocked the gun and dropped his aim.

"If you wish to know more of Christine Daaé's whereabouts last night and now, I suggest you ask her yourself," Erik commanded, the words slow and cold. "She lives on *Notre Dame des Victoires*, near the Basilica I am given to believe."

"I look forward to speaking to her," Shaya replied, eyes dark with consideration. "If she knows what you are, I'm sure she'll be more than happy to betray you."

"Or she might want to save me," Erik retorted, equally grim. The more he thought about it, the more he knew it was impossible. "Others have before," he added, just to twist the knife for them both.

"Let us hope that she does not make that fatal mistake then," Shaya said. "You do not deserve to be protected."

Erik smiled cruelly at the edge of the mask as he gave a small bow and backed away. He did not disagree. He only wanted a stay of execution, at least until he knew she wasn't coming. If she was to betray him, he wanted it to be fast. And Shaya deserved to be the one to bring his doom. "That is for her to decide," Erik said.

"This is not over, Erik," Shaya called, his courage returning as Erik turned away down the tunnel towards the Opera. He knew Shaya valued his life and limbs enough that he would not follow.

"Of course it isn't over, Daroga, we are both still alive," Erik called back without turning around.

It was almost impossible to wake in a world without angels. Christine had done it though. She had somehow found the strength to wash and dress and eat a few bites. But now she was back in her room, lying on her bed, staring at the sky. She had slept through the whole morning, thanks to Adèle's drugged wine. The food and the rest hadn't helped. Her mind was just clearer now and all that meant was she could see that she was lost.

She stared at the dark clouds gathering for a winter storm and listened to her breathing. And then stopped.

What was the use in breathing anyway? She had come to life months ago for an angel made of lies. Without him, there was nothing worth believing in. There was no life, no music, no love; just pain and the dark emptiness she had escaped so briefly in the sound of her angel's voice. Everything her father had ever told her had been a lie. Her love and heart were as dead as he was now, and there was nothing good or strong left in her.

You think part of you died with him. Not just the part of you that was brave, but the part that could feel. And believe.

Christine shut her eyes against the memory of Erik's voice.

But you didn't die, Christine. You survived. And you cannot be dead when you sing.

Against her will she gasped in a breath, cool air filling her lungs and thwarting her foolish attempt to die.

Breathing is life, the conscious action of living. Somewhere deep within when you choose to breathe, you choose to live. Some un-surrendering part of you chooses to continue.

She exhaled and inhaled again, remembering the Angel's gentle words. To her dull surprise, she did not hate them. At least one thing had not been a lie.

So, I know you're brave, Christine, because even after all the pain, you keep breathing.

Christine raised her head slowly, concentrating on each breath and finding her strength.

She did not have many things in her room here, she noted. All but one of her dresses and the one she wore now were at the Opera. Still, she made herself wash and dress, and moving became just a bit easier with each passing minute. At last she dared to look at herself in the mirror hanging on her wall. She was pale in her old gray dress, the one she'd worn when she arrived in Paris months ago. She had forced her hair into a bun, but it looked a mess. She gathered the few francs she had collected and shoved them in her pockets. Enough to buy a ticket out of the city if she really did decide to run. It was a reflex, to put on the dark cloak as well. It would keep her warm, wherever she ended up.

She looked in the mirror one more time. The cloak made her hair appear darker and her sad, resigned eyes greener than usual. He had to hate mirrors, she guessed. How strange that his voice had come from one. Would she ever know how?

"Are you going out?" Adèle asked from beside the fire as Christine stole through the parlor.

"I just need some air," Christine lied. Adèle knew it was a lie too, but she nodded slowly.

"Be careful, it looks like snow," Adèle said, care in her eyes.

"I will be." Christine turned to the door, then looked back. "You don't need to worry about me. I promise. And Adèle...thank you. For everything."

"Like I said, be careful," Adèle replied, her face stony and unwilling to acknowledge Christine's attempted farewell. Perhaps that was better.

Christine took a deep breath when she stepped outside, the frigid air smarting in her lungs. She was still breathing, that meant something didn't it? She looked to her right, to the east and away from the Opera.

She could just start walking and never look back. If she walked long enough and far enough, perhaps she would reach the sea. She could go to Perros-Guirec and weep over a cold grave by the vast ocean. She could scream her fury at the real angels, and they would only answer with silence.

"Mademoiselle Daaé?" the voice from behind startled Christine. She turned to see of all people, the Persian, bowing politely, his head crowned with the dark fur of his Astrakhan cap.

"Monsieur?" Christine looked him over, suspicious. This was the man who was said to know the Ghost. Did he know the truth? "May I help you?"

"Mademoiselle, I know you do not know me—"

"I've seen you. Everyone has." The Persian gave a tired smile, amused at her directness. Perhaps he had been expecting someone sweet and naive. He was to be sorely disappointed. "Do you have a name?"

Again, he smiled. "Most people don't ask. My name is Shaya Motlagh. I am, or I was, a chief of police in the court of Naser al-Din Shah Qajar, the Shah of Iran. Or Persia as your people like to call it."

"What is a policeman from Persia doing in Paris, lurking about the Opera?" Christine asked. "And consorting with ghosts, if the rumors are true," she added carefully, and interest sparked in his dark eyes.

"I do not concern myself with phantoms, my lady," Motlagh replied, just as careful in his words as Christine. "Only men of flesh and blood. Men who pose a great danger to the employees of the Opera. I have been trying to reach you since your performance on Friday, to discuss those dangers."

Christine narrowed her eyes. So, he did know. He believed Erik was a danger and wanted to warn her. And he had tried to, before. *He was going to tell you. I didn't want you to find out from someone else.* One piece fell into place as she remembered Erik's excuse for taking her. So, this man was one of the authors of her current crisis.

"Why would you be so concerned with me, of all people?" Christine asked icily.

"Because if such a dangerous man were to have placed you in his sights, you would be in great peril." The Persian's expression was dire, and Christine suppressed a shiver. The beast she had unmasked yesterday and the dark specter that haunted and tormented the Opera – that character sounded like such a man. But it did not sound like the teacher and confidant she had known for months. And it was miles from the poor, lost soul she had returned the mask to.

"If there is such a danger in the Opera, why not tell the police? Or the managers? Why tell me?" Christine asked at last.

"Because they will not believe a man like me," the Persian replied. "But they might believe a woman like you. Especially if you had information to give. Perhaps, where to find such a man."

Christine tensed as the Persian watched her, his eyes entreating. He was waiting, hoping for her to lead him to his prey. He was exactly the kind of person Erik was afraid she would go to. She heard his voice in her memory. *I won't let them put me in a cage again, Christine.*

"I have no such information, Monsieur. I don't know what you are talking about," she replied, cold and aloof as she could manage. The Persian's face fell.

"Mademoiselle, please, my concern is only for the safety of innocent people," Motlagh said, his words tense and clipped as he leaned in closer to Christine. "If you have seen something – if you know *something*—"

"I know nothing. Good day, Monsieur." Christine turned away, heading west out of pure habit. To her shock, the Persian jumped in front of her.

"Mademoiselle, you must listen!" Motlagh pled as he caught Christine by the shoulder, forcing her to look into his desperate eyes. "*He is a monster.*"

Christine fought the urge to shiver at the terrible certainty in his words and the equally strong urge to tell him that he was wrong. She could not remember the sight of her lost angel weeping in the shadows, or the anguish and loneliness in his eyes, and believe that. Not entirely.

"Please, leave me alone," Christine said, attempting to wrest herself away.

"Mademoiselle—" A pair of hands taking him by the lapels and pulling him away cut the Persian off. Christine was not at all surprised by the identity of her savior.

"The lady clearly does not wish to speak to you, Monsieur," Raoul de Chagny declared, stepping between Christine and the Persian. "I suggest you leave her be."

The Persian looked at Christine over Raoul's shoulder, frustrated, but resigned.

"Very well then," the darker man muttered, stepping back to leave. He caught Christine's eyes one more time. "If you change your mind, I hope it will be in time." Christine's insides grew as cold as the winter air around her.

"Are you alright?" Raoul asked as he turned from watching the Persian's retreat.

Christine shook her head and looked to the face she had been so amazed to see after the performance. He looked nervous, which was perhaps to be expected after how she had treated him. His cheeks were red, either from the cold or from running to her rescue, or perhaps both. He was beautiful.

"Again, you rush in to save me, in my hour of need," Christine murmured, again amazed at the man he had become. "At least you didn't almost drown this time."

"I knew you remembered!" he exclaimed and embraced her without any regard for propriety. Christine smiled for the first time in two days, safe in the warm circle of Raoul's arms. She regretted that he pulled away so quickly, blushing and releasing her politely.

"I could never forget you, old friend," Christine assured him as they smiled shyly at one another, and Raoul grasped her hands. "I am so sorry I had to make you think that was the case."

"But why? You've had me in torment for weeks!" he asked, shaking his head in wonder. Christine dearly wished she could take back that cruel laughter, especially knowing now who had forbidden her to consort with her old friend.

"You must forgive me for that, I was tired, and..." she cast about for a lie. "I didn't want to start people talking, assuming that we were in some sort of tryst, and I was using you to get ahead."

"Of course, I understand," Raoul said, kind and understanding. His smile had not dimmed. "I came by yesterday as well. I've been so worried. After you vanished like that everyone was so anxious."

"I'm fine." Christine withdrew her hands from his. "I was just on my way—"

"To the Opera, I'm sure," Raoul replied with a naive smile. "I can't believe they bring you in on Sundays."

"I just go to practice," Christine lied softly. "It's my choice."

"I have my carriage here if you would like me to take you!" he suggested without a hint of guile, his smile refusing to fade.

"Is that proper?"

"I don't care, as long as I can share your company for a little while. Come." He led her to his handsome black coach and nodded to the driver. "We will be taking Mademoiselle Daaé to the Opera."

"You are far too kind, Raoul," Christine muttered as she took in the fine leather and wood that encased them.

"As I said, I've been waiting for weeks to speak with you; this is the least I can offer." Christine looked down at her hands; gloveless, fiddling with the edge of a cloak an unscrupulous man had placed on her shoulders.

"Why would you waste time on the likes of me?"

"Did you not receive my letter?" Raoul asked back. Christine cheeks grew warm and hoped he would think she was blushing because of him, and not from the memory of what her false angel had done to her after she had read that letter. The memory of Erik's voice and how it had affected her made fear twist in her stomach. If she were to go back, could he do that again? Would she want that? Did she have the strength to refuse?

"I...I'm sorry I didn't write back. I was very busy."

"I meant what I wrote, my darling Christine, my heart has always been yours. It still is."

She looked into his handsome face and sincere eyes. He was the second man in as many days to confess he loved her. And it was just as terrifying as when Erik had said it.

"You can't love me, Raoul," she whispered. "You don't know me. Not who I am now, not really." He would not say such things if he knew sins she had committed at the command of a false angel.

"But I do," Raoul protested, taking her hands again. "I've loved you for years. And when you sing, it's the most beautiful thing in the world. It's magic and it's magnificent. I know it's meant to be a show but, I saw your heart when you were on that stage and I...fell in love again."

She wondered what her face looked like, based on how worried Raoul's expression became. She was sure he had meant it as praise, as a passionate confession to win her at last. But it only reminded her of why she had sung with such heart.

"Would you love me if I couldn't sing?" she asked softly. Perhaps there was a chance. Perhaps this was their escape.

"Christine, you would not be you if you didn't sing," he said, touching her cheek. "Your father must be looking down on you with such pride. Surely the angel of music has blessed you indeed, just like your father promised."

Christine shut her eyes, surprised she had tears left, and fought back a sob.

"Oh, Christine, I'm so sorry, I have upset you!" Raoul exclaimed.

Christine did not fight it when he pulled her into his arms, wrapping her in a brother's embrace as he stroked her hair. "Raoul..." she whispered. "There is no such thing as an angel of music."

Immediately, Raoul pulled back, tilting her chin so he could look into her eyes. "My darling Christine, don't say that."

"But he's not an angel!" Christine sobbed, completely bewildering Raoul. "The reason I can sing! The reason I am anything: he's just a man!" Raoul's face was worried and pale, and perhaps even sad.

"Are you talking about the man who was speaking to you, after the gala?" Raoul asked carefully. "I heard him, in your room. Telling you the angels wept."

"You were listening at my door?" Christine's stomach fell. "Why—"

"He's your teacher, this man?" Raoul pressed on.

"Yes, that was him," Christine stammered. What else had he heard that night?

"And you thought he was...an angel?" Raoul asked slowly, which made it sound even more insane.

"I—" Christine bit her lips, pulling away from Raoul's arms. "No. That would be madness, I know. I just thought that he had been sent by heaven until the other night."

"How do you know he was not?" Raoul asked, guileless and expectant. Christine blinked. "This teacher, he seems to have inspired you and guided you. Is that not what you wanted?"

"It was," Christine answered slowly. There was no question that Erik had done everything she had ever dreamed an angel might, and so much more. "He saved me and taught me. He promised me all of Paris and he delivered it." The sound of applause rang in her ears again, and she remembered the magnificent feeling of singing her soul out to him.

"That sounds like a blessing to me, even if it came in the guise of a man," Raoul offered, looking sheepish. "While I do not approve if this man has made advances and will not reveal himself. Or if he's upset you. But I don't think a human's mistakes should be a reason to lose your faith. God works in strange ways, and great miracles can come in the most unexpected of places. At least that's what I believe."

Christine stared at Raoul, her mind reeling. She thought back to arriving at Opera for the first time, seeking the shelter of the stables. If Erik had not been there at that exact moment, her life would be so different. She might not even have a life. How could such a moment of random chance have changed everything? Unless it was not random.

"You think God sent him to me? Or my father?" Christine asked, something strange taking hold in her heart.

"Who else?" Raoul asked with a lop-sided smile.

Christine heaved a breath, looking out to the Opera as they slowed to a stop at the back entrance where the *Rue Auber* met the *Rue Scribe*. For the first time in two days, she felt something like hope, and yet it made her even more confused than before. A tear escaped down her cheek.

"Christine I'm so sorry, I shouldn't have said anything," Raoul entreated. "I came here to win you, not upset you. Though I am glad to know this *other* is just a teacher. I had worried that he was my rival for your heart."

"You didn't mean to," Christine whispered, steadying her breath. She looked again on the boy she had played with and adored in the summer sun by the sea, under her father's watchful eyes, and wished for nothing more than to go back to those bright, simple days. "And you needn't concern yourself with him now."

"I'm glad to hear that. Can I make my offence up to you anyway?" Raoul offered, desperate as a puppy. "Let me take you to supper! You can tell me all about your adventures at the Opera, and I can tell you about what a great diva you will be, then bore you with tales of a sailor's life."

"I can't – not today," Christine answered, trying to sound demure or coy and not like she was unsure if she would even be in Paris or the land of the living when night fell.

"Tomorrow then?"

Christine caught his eye, and his expression grew considerably more serious, perhaps almost hurt. She shook her head. "I'm sorry. I don't know when I will be free. You shouldn't wait for me."

"Christine, please, don't go away again." Raoul caught her hand as she moved to leave the carriage, pulling her close to him again. He stared into her eyes, desperate and entreating, and Christine caught her breath. And just as Erik had, he leaned close to claim her lips.

What would Erik do to them if Raoul kissed her?

"I can't," Christine exclaimed, pulling away before she could be kissed. "I'm sorry. I can't."

She rushed from the carriage, down the *Rue Auber*, only stopping when she reached the great *Place De L'Opéra*. She turned to look up at the great edifice that stood above the huge crossroads.

Three months ago, she had come here in the rain, and now she stood in the same spot as snow began to fall around her. Three months ago, she had looked for an angel, and a man that lived as a ghost had found her instead. Now, he waited for her in the dark below Charles Garnier's grand façade.

Was it not madness to return? Yet, how could she stay away? Without him, she faced a life devoid of hope, where music would never sound again. She would never learn how he had done such strange and wondrous things. There was so much magic that had been so real, couldn't there be a spark of it left? If she left him, was she turning away from the miracle she had wanted? If she ran away now, what would it do to him?

The image that had come to her again and again all day swam into her mind. Not the horror of a monster's face, but the tragedy of Erik, the man, broken and weeping and singing to himself like a frightened child in the dark. How could she see such suffering and make it worse? But how could she commit her own soul to the darkness and dangers of his kingdom? How could she return to him, knowing what sins and desires would surely await?

She stood at the crossroads of the world and tried to breathe.

Raoul watched the buildings and people roll by as his carriage rambled home, unable to understand what had just transpired. For a few minutes, all his dreams had been realized. Not only had Christine been safe but she had remembered him and cared for him still. Her lover was not a lover at all but a teacher, one who did not seem to be in her good graces at that. He'd held her. Touched her. And then once again, she had left him with more questions than answers.

Raoul looked at the sky and then the few people out and about on the boulevards. They were bundled up for the cold. Christine had looked strange and so very sad. Even when she'd smiled, there had been pain behind it.

"Home so soon?" Philippe called from the parlor when Raoul entered their manor. "Did you find her or give up?"

"I found her," Raoul replied, and Philippe gave him a pitying sigh, reading his face.

"I told you, my brother, she would break your heart."

"I do not think it is her will to do that," Raoul said darkly. There were still too many questions. Her disappearance. That strange foreigner who had been pursuing her, then harassing her in the street. The angelic voice that demanded Christine love him. The one she had told Raoul not to concern himself over. But he was concerned. In fact, the whole conversation about angels and her music had been so strange.

"What do you mean?" Philippe asked.

"I mean that there is something important that she is not telling me, and I intend to discover the secret," Raoul replied. "At any cost."

Erik watched as the bluish twilight faded beyond the gate and his hope ebbed with it. She had to come back, he told himself. He could offer her what no one else could: answers, music, hope. But she had seen his face. She knew how he had betrayed and used her. Why would she want him at all? But she needed him, didn't she? The same way he needed her. He wanted her in his lonely life so desperately that he was prepared to take anything she offered, like a beggar or desperate addict. She had said there was hope. Had he done enough to earn her return?

"Please, come back. Let her come back." He didn't know to whom he prayed, but he meant it with his whole soul. A damned soul had no right to a petition, he knew that, but he made it anyway.

The light grew dimmer, and he remained alone in the dark at the edge of his underworld. He closed his eyes and took a shaking breath. He didn't want to see that last light fade along with the last of his hope.

She wasn't coming. And now he had to decide if he would become a monster and claim her from wherever she had run to, or if it was time to truly join the ghosts. He did not think it would hurt this much, he mused, but he felt like his heart was genuinely shattering in his chest. It was almost impossible to breathe.

The clanging of the gate echoed through the dark and for a second, he was sure it was a dream. His eyes flew open to see *her* silhouetted against the last breath of twilight.

Christine stood at the threshold of the living world, still wearing the cloak he had given her, the hood pulled over her head. He could not make out the expression on her face as she walked through the dark stable towards him but it didn't matter. She was here.

Erik unfurled himself from the shadows and raised his lantern. He watched her eyes widen and her breath catch as she saw him, but her steps did not falter. Soon she stood only a foot from him in the faint circle of light. Her eyes were apprehensive but determined as they stared into his, searching. There were still snowflakes caught her hood, and her cheeks were red from the cold. She was the most beautiful sight he had ever seen.

Without looking away from her, he extended his free hand. "You came back," he whispered in amazement and trepidation.

"Did you think I wouldn't?" she murmured back; her voice mysterious but not afraid as she took his hand.

"I hoped," he replied as he savored her warmth through his gloves. "But I did not know if you would forgive me. Among other things."

"The first thing you ever asked me to do was forgive you," she mused. "When you sang to me and made me believe."

"You have always been kinder than me," Erik sighed, remembering the song that had made him an angel. "I still didn't believe you'd really come back to the dark."

She gave a small, sad smile and glanced at their joined hands. "I didn't either. I was ready to run away. Lose myself again in a world above."

"Why didn't you?" Erik asked just as she looked back up at him. Her eyes were clear and calm, her soul shining as bright as the dawn.

"Because I chose a fallen angel in the dark rather than a world of light with no angels at all," she confessed as the light of the lantern flickered around them and the last traces of daylight faded into dusk.

Erik and Christine's story continues in...

Angel's Kiss.

Coming July 11, 2023.

Don't miss out!

Visit the website below and you can sign up to receive emails whenever Jessica Mason publishes a new book. There's no charge and no obligation.

https://books2read.com/r/B-A-RZHV-PTSBC

BOOKS 2 READ

Connecting independent readers to independent writers.

About the Author

Jessica Mason lives near Portland, Oregon with her wife, daughter, and corgi. She had studied opera, practiced law, and has worked as a fandom journalist and podcaster, among many varied careers. But first and foremost she has always been a storyteller. When she manages to stop writing, she enjoys gardening, travel, music, and witchcraft.

Find her on social media: @ByJessicaMason

About the Publisher

Murmuration Books is an independent publisher bringing readers, steamy, spellbinding, spooky, sensational stories. We are committed to diverse themes, new authors, and creative takes on old ideas.

For more, visit Murmurationbooks.com